蛇警探

THE SHADOW
PAVILION

蛇警探

THE SHADOW PAVILION

A Detective Inspector Chen Novel

Liz Williams

NIGHT SHADE BOOKS
SAN FRANCISCO

First Edition

ISBN: 978-1-59780-122-5 (Trade Hardcover)
ISBN: 978-1-59780-121-8 (Limited Hardcover)

Night Shade Books
Please visit us on the web at
http://www.nightshadebooks.com

To Trevor

With thanks to everyone at Night Shade Books,
and to my agent Shawna McCarthy.

ONE

Pauleng Go ducked as the whisky bottle hurtled toward his head and smashed on the opposite wall. He cried out in anguish.

"Lara! Sweetheart! Darling! That was a twenty-five-year-old malt!"

She knew it, too, the bitch. He'd seen her hand pause over an indifferent bottle of Tokyo Gold, before clamping firmly around the neck of the Lagavulin.

"You can afford it!" Lara shouted, at window-rattling volume. "Take it from the money you've cheated me out of, why don't you?"

"Lara, look. I sorted all this out with Beni, you know I did and I know he told you about the new studio rates. Things are hard, even in Bollywood: you know about the tax thing, Beni *explained*. Don't you remember?"

Of course she didn't. He'd be amazed if she could remember what she'd had for dinner last night.

"Lara... put the Chateau d'Yquem *down,* there's a love."

Sixty dollars a bottle and no doubt that would soon be joining the whisky-sodden wallpaper. It wasn't the money. It was almost a crime against God. To Go's surprise, however, Lara did as he asked her. She set the bottle carefully down on the table, turned on her kitten heel, and left, with a glowering ebony glance over her silken shoulder. Go could hear the deathwatch tapping of those heels all the way down the marble hall. With a sigh of mingled exasperation and relief, he picked up his cellphone and put a call through to Beni.

蛇警探

"The thing is..." Beni was saying, twenty minutes later, for the third time. "The thing is, we can't get rid of her. Audiences love her and you know why, it's all due to her—"

1

"Yes, sure, I know," Go replied. There were some things he didn't want discussed over the phone, even though it was supposed to be a secure connection. "I know, I know all that stuff. But she's seriously nuts, Beni."

A pause. "Yeah. I know all that stuff, too. She's kind of bound to be, man."

"You're saying it's our fault?"

"We got her the gig. And the one before that. And the—"

"—one before that," Go finished for him. "You're right. I suppose now we've just got to deal with the consequences."

That evening, he sat down in front of *The Wild and the Blessed*. The first gig… It had been the first time he and Beni and Lara had worked together, before he'd really understood about Lara. He knew what the deal was, of course: he'd been there from the start. But he hadn't really got his head round all the ramifications. And *Wild* had been, well, wild. How could you not fall in love with Lara Chowdijharee? Stunning girls were as common as beetles in Bollywood, but Lara was… well, Lara was something else.

Being nearly brained by a full bottle of your best malt tended to put the dampeners on starry-eyed romance, however. It wasn't the first time it had happened. The rot had started to set in toward the end of the second movie, *The Wild and the Damned*. Lara had been playing the same character—sweet, selfless Ranee Pur—but somewhere along the line she'd started asking for script changes, and getting them. Character changes, too. Big ones. Go—who had after all been responsible for the initial script—had never really envisaged Ranee as the AK-47-toting kind of girl, somehow. Audiences seemed to have taken it in their stride, however, and Go couldn't deny that it had seemed to speak to the modern Indian woman. There were Ranee car fresheners and fridge magnets, Ranee underwear and mouse mats. Lara was under round-the-clock protection, though whether they were protecting Lara from the crazier fringes of her devoted fans, or the crazier fringes from Lara, Go did not really care to consider too closely. Given how she'd begun to treat her producer and her agent, God alone knew how she'd deal with some poor benighted stalker.

Go had been in the industry too long, however, not to recognize the feeling of being held facedown over a barrel, with legs firmly spread. When the last credits of *The Wild and the Blessed* had rolled over a close-up of Lara's exquisite face, he dialed her private number.

"Darling girl? Beni and I have been having a little talk…"

TWO

Heaven hadn't changed much, Chen thought—at least, not on the surface. As he stepped out of the little skiff sent to him by the Celestial Emperor, all the way across the Sea of Night, onto those by-now-familiar shores, redolent of peach blossom and lined with flowering apricots, he could have been stepping back in time, to when he had come here with a demon by his side. He found himself missing Zhu Irzh, this trip. The demon had been seconded onto a case involving a drug-smuggling ring, one that not-coincidentally concerned Zhu Irzh's fiancée Jhai Tserai. The industrialist was on the right side of the law, for a change, although Chen knew how difficult it was actually to pin anything on Jhai. She had a tendency to prove elusive when it came to the finer points of legality, and given that Singapore Three's laws were themselves somewhat mutable, depending on who was breaking or enforcing them, Chen's sympathies did not always lie to Jhai's disadvantage.

Still, there was a definite sense of something missing, whether it was the moral (or immoral) support provided by Zhu Irzh, or simply the fact that the presence of the demon provided a leavening influence upon the endless propriety and pastel glamours of the Heavenly Realm. The late Emperor—now disembodied—might have gone not-so-quietly mad, but the assumption of his son did not seem to have changed things very much. Sighing, Chen walked toward the carriage, pulled by two golden-skinned lion-dogs, that was to take him to the Celestial Palace.

蛇警探

"It's not been easy," the Celestial Emperor murmured, an hour or so later.

"I can imagine." Chen was genuinely sympathetic. "When one considers that China itself has been constrained by thousands of years of tradition, and we are in the far more changeable human realm... You've got quite a task on your hands, if you're really considering reform."

"I don't have a choice," Mhara said. He turned to Chen. The Emperor had changed little since Chen had first met him: the same fall of dark hair, the same tranquil blue gaze. A tall, young man, now dressed not in the massively ornate robes of the Celestial Emperor, but in a linen tunic and loose trousers. He looked comfortable, cool, and above all, un-stuffy. He did not look as though he belonged in this vast chamber, seemingly floating above the cloud-layer of the Palace, its walls decorated with tapestries depicting events so long ago that China had not yet been born as a nation. This was a personage who, Chen reminded himself, chose to travel by bicycle when on Earth.

"There's always a choice," Chen said. "You could be everything your father was."

"Exactly. How about 'mad'? The invasion of Hell—a stupid plan, misconceived in arrogance and entitlement."

"Kuan Yin had told me that Heaven was planning a strategic withdrawal," Chen said. "Take over Hell and use it and Earth as a kind of depository for souls."

"Yes. Heaven—literally—forbid that any more human souls should come here, cluttering up the place, contaminating it with their still-mortal essence. Father lost sight of what Heaven was *for*."

"I suppose the question that comes most naturally to my mind," Chen remarked, "is how much support your father enjoyed. Quite a lot, one would think."

Mhara nodded, turning back to the window to stare out over the mild airs of the Celestial City. "A lot, yes, but it's hard to know how much of that was coerced. I don't mean by force. Heaven's host was completely conditioned to believe in the rightness of the Emperor's judgment. I only got away from it because I was living on Earth, and besides, those of us in the Imperial family have more freedom of will. That in itself isn't very encouraging."

Chen shrugged. "It's a caste system."

"Quite so. The ultimate caste system, in many respects."

Chen paused. "Emperor. *Mhara*. It is always a pleasure to see you, and an honor to enter Heaven. But why *did* you ask me here today?"

Mhara turned and smiled at him. It was only at moments such as these that Chen was fully aware of Mhara's divine origins: Mhara played down the whole god-thing to such an extent that most of the time, it was possible to see him as nothing more than a mild-mannered young monk, one who wore the faint and modest glow of enlightenment, perhaps, but a human nonetheless. But now, if only for a second, Chen found himself dazzled, standing in the radiance of his friend's gaze.

"Chen. What is your job title?"

Chen, slightly taken aback, replied, "Detective Inspector."

"I know, of course. But what is it that you actually *do?*"

"I investigate crimes. Hopefully, I solve them." *I save the world on an increasing number of occasions.* But he did not want to say that: it sounded too flippant, and it was hardly part of his job, anyway, unless one took a very wide overview of things. Then it struck him. "I am the liaison officer between the worlds."

"Between Earth and Hell and Heaven," Mhara said. "And that's why I asked you to come here today. Because if there's one thing I need, it's a liaison officer."

THREE

It was strange for him to go somewhere alone. Usually, one of the Family went with him: Mistress, or the human. Occasionally, he had accompanied the Hellkind to places, but this was a question of duty, not of preference. He had no issue with being alone, or of working without Family; it was simply that it seemed strange. Especially because he had volunteered.

This was not his own loss. At first, when Mistress had told him of it, he had assumed that this was something she herself had misplaced. Creature of duty that he was, a small, cold planet revolving around the sun of Mistress' presence, it was sometimes hard for him to grasp that the affairs of others, including people he did not know, might also concern her. This particular affair, it seemed, was on behalf of the human, of Husband, and that made it instantly explicable.

The missing thing was small. It hummed, with the human magic, the kind that was unthinking. Husband had referred to it as a "bug," and at first he had thought that this referred to an insect of some sort, for these—to his secret pleasure—had proved as commonplace on Earth as they had been in Hell. But further explanations had revealed that this bug was not a living thing at all, but a little machine.

How boring.

Nonetheless, it had been suggested to him that he might be the ideal person to retrieve it, or at least, attempt to do so. He would not be seen by many humans, and if the person who had taken it was not, in fact, of that ilk, then he could be trusted to deal with it. This pleased him. Since the events of a few months past, things had been quiet. Although not confined, he had kept mainly to the houseboat, accompanying Mistress on her regular forays to the local market, but no further. He did not object to this—Mistress was, after all, safe, and as this goal was the primary focus of his existence, then matters were by definition satisfactory—but all the same, they were a trifle dull. It had been suggested on a number of occasions that he might like to accompany Husband to his workplace, and this was intriguing, but regretfully he had felt obliged to turn the offer down. If he and Husband were both absent, then there would be no one to protect Mistress, and he was certainly not going to leave Mistress in the hands of the Hellkind. The demon named Zhu Irzh had a habit of attracting trouble—a child would have noticed this—and Mistress was prone enough to trouble as it was.

But on this occasion, Husband would be home. And so he had agreed to go to the house on Men Ling Street, and search for this "bug."

Men Ling Street was on the other side of the city from Mistress' house-boat. Zhu Irzh dropped him off at the corner, driving an unmarked and anonymous car.

"There you go," he said, as the badger scrambled down from the backseat. "I'll pick you up—when? Couple of hours?"

"Be waiting," said the badger. Living in eternal animal-present, he had problems with the concept of time, but he thought there might be one of those clock-devices somewhere that would assist him. "I will come."

"Okay," said the demon. "I'll put the car in that lot over there, with the others. No one will notice."

"Good," the badger said. As Zhu Irzh drove away, he slunk into the shadows. This part of the city reminded him of his former home in Hell, of the streets that had surrounded Mistress' family mansion. He did not miss it. Keeping Mistress safe had proved a full-time occupation whenever they stepped out of the front door, and sometimes even before that, given her family's plans to marry her off. The badger had not approved. Husband's rescue of Mistress, however many ramifications had come in its wake, had come as a considerable relief. But Men Ling Street was reminiscent of that part of Hell—indeed, for all the badger knew, it might actually have corresponded to it, given the cor-relation between the worlds. Towering dark houses, which might have been warehouses or private apartments for all that their facades betrayed, lined both sides of the street. The upper stories were hidden by wire cages full of vegetation: usually an attempt by inner-city families to have some manner of garden and grow vegetables. But badger could smell the contents of these cages and their odor was of rank decay. Anything green and growing had long since succumbed to the fetid airs of Men Ling Street.

Badger found all manner of interesting things in the gutter. A lot of chemical paraphernalia: syringes and time-delay patches that made him give a faint, derisive snort. There were cockroaches, which the badger snapped up with a slight and surprising sensation of guilt: he wasn't sure that it was profes-sional to snack on the job. Still, one had to keep up one's strength. And they were certainly tasty.

Rinds and vegetable peelings from an overflowing dumpster. This looked like the detritus from a restaurant and badger peered upward, trying to see which building it had come from, but the facades here were as unidentifiable as ever. Badger was coming to feel that this actually was Hell, or perhaps some weird interface between Earth and the otherworld, neither one thing nor another. It made him uncomfortable, and that was saying much.

Husband had explained which building he was to enter. He had difficulties with numbers, so Husband had given him a description, saying that the building had a side door, leading down into a cellar, and that the door was marked with a small neon light. He found this without problems, halfway along the street. The door was locked, naturally, but badger had his own way of gaining access. He shoved a garbage can beneath a window, clambered on top of it, and pushed at the windowpane with his snout until it gave way. He wondered whether he might be making too much noise but although he did not wish to be discovered, it did not greatly perturb him. One could always bite, after all.

In through the window, he curled himself into a ball and rolled down, landing on a hard, dusty surface. Shaking himself, he looked around him.

A narrow, dark room, although this presented no hindrance to the badger's night-seeing eyes. Many curtains: the walls were draped with thick, heavy hangings in shades of crimson and black. The badger found it hard to judge such things, but it seemed to him that both the room and the curtains were old. Yet something had been here recently. Something magical. He could sense its presence lingering in the air, a sour, enticing perfume. He did not recognize it, but he did not think it was human in origin.

Sniffing, badger made his methodical way around the edges of the room, snuffling beneath the edges of the drapes. The presence, however, was in the center of the room, hanging dankly above the dusty floor. It was a moment before badger remembered that he was supposed to be seeking this bug, not the remnants of something's visit, and he knew a fleeting shame. Husband would not have allowed himself to become so easily distracted. But perhaps the two might be connected…

He nosed aside a drape to see what lay behind: nothing, only a paneled wall, with no carving upon the black wood. As far as he could tell, the other walls were the same. There were no doors apart from the main one onto the street and this struck the badger as very odd; admittedly, he had ways of entering places which were not human ways—tunnels, for instance, struck him as wholly acceptable and yet Husband seemed to dislike them, for some reason—but this was a house in a human city, and it was curious to have no means of access into the rest of the building. Curious, and also unlikely. The badger began to hunt for other means of ingress.

He turned from the drapes, intending to investigate the floor, when he realized that the lingering presence within the room was no longer a memory, but had become animate. Whoever or whatever had left it had returned. Something rushed through the room like a wind off a winter sea: harsh, sudden, and chilling. The badger took a step back, but the thing had gone. He had only an impression of something very sharp, with spines, and transparent.

The badger found this stimulating. He bustled after the thing, which had vanished through the drapes on the opposite wall. Perhaps that was the answer: whoever lived in this building was incorporeal, and thus had no need of doors. The badger pulled the drapes aside all the same, expecting to find the same paneled wall that he had studied a short while ago.

There was no wall there. Beyond the curtain lay an immense vista of industry: engines, smoking stacks, and sudden flickers of queasy flame. *Hell!* thought the badger, with a jolt, but he had no time to consider this hypothesis. Instead, something reached out a spiny hand, picked him up by the scruff of the neck, and bundled him into a sack. The badger, squirming around, sank his teeth into an inhuman hand and was rewarded with a yell, but next moment, his jaws closed on empty air. The sack closed around him, he was slung over and up, and the world went muffled and black.

FOUR

Go was both relieved and dismayed to find Lara waiting for him on set the next morning. This was perhaps only the second occasion that she had turned up on time, let alone early, and Go had a profound distrust of changes in actresses' behavior, particularly if they were *this* actress.

"Paulie," Lara cooed. She undulated upward and wound her hands around Go's neck. "How sweet of you to speak to Beni. You're both *darling*."

"Lara, my dear, you're worth it," Go said, with a heroic effort at sincerity. "We both know that. I think sometimes we don't really *appreciate* you." He tried to look contrite. It wasn't a great performance, but Lara was clearly in the mood to be receptive. She dimpled (How did she *do* that? It was really quite weird.) and gave a small, shy smile. The old cliché about giving one's best performance off set came to Go's mind.

"I've been reading the script," Lara said. "I thought we could revise quite a lot of it, actually."

"Did you?" *There's a surprise.*

"There's much more room for Ranee, you know. I thought she could appear in the scene with the terrorists."

"But Lara—that takes place in Laos, and your character is supposed to be in Delhi in the nick at that point."

There was the faintest suggestion of thunder in Lara's eyes, the hint of stormclouds gathering. "It could be a flashback. Or a dream."

"Perhaps a hallucination?" Go said quickly. "These guys are supposed to be drug dealers, after all."

Just give her what she wants, he thought, as Lara's smothering jasmine perfume once again enveloped him. It was easiest in the long run, no matter how much it took out of you at the time.

10

Filming proceeded fairly swiftly once the revised script—hashed together over a long and liquid lunch by Beni, Go, and one of the freelance writers—had been submitted.

"There's one good thing about having worked in porn," Beni said to Go. "It gives you a good background in quick filmmaking. Quick and dirty." He tried not to look smug at the joke.

"There's lots of good things about porn," Go replied, gloomily. "Apart from the obvious. Have you noticed how much *nicer* everyone is? No airs and graces, no tantrums."

Beni shrugged. "They know they're whores."

Go snorted. "Yeah. But do we?"

"*We* do. Unfortunately, Lara doesn't."

Go cast a nervous glance over his shoulder.

"She can't hear us, man," Beni said. "She's back at the studio."

"Lara seems to know all kinds of shit," Go said. "Don't underestimate her. Sometimes I think she bugs my clothes."

Beni looked at him. "Don't get paranoid. She's not a superhero."

"She thinks she is. Look…" Beni might be right but Go found himself lowering his voice all the same. "You and I were young when we found her, right? We were assholes."

"It was only four years ago," Beni objected.

Go refrained from saying that he felt as though he'd aged several decades since then. "We were young," he repeated. "We thought we knew what we were doing."

Beni was silent and Go knew he'd struck home. "We've got to consider the future," he added. At Beni's anguished expression, Go knew that he'd been understood.

"She's a goldmine, man," Beni said.

"Yeah. But the mine's flooding up fast. We have to make money, and get out."

"What are you saying? We should send her back where she came from?" Once again, Beni spoke too loudly for Go's liking and Go hushed him.

"Let's talk about it another time, Beni. Not right now. We'll go out for a drink, how about that?" Preferably in a lead-lined room. On a different continent.

FIVE

Inari did not want to interrupt her husband. His head was bent over a mountain of paperwork that he'd brought home from the station and she knew, from the gentle perfume that rose from one of the piles of parchment, that some of the documentation had come from Heaven. The precinct was supposed to be working toward a paperless office, but they did not seem to be achieving their goal: perhaps it was this new development regarding the Celestials. Chen had not said very much about that, except to convey Mhara's good wishes and to deliver an exquisite flower from the new Emperor. But Inari knew he was busy, and that was why she hesitated to interrupt him. She had to know, however.

"Chen Wei?" she said, standing in the doorway of the little cubbyhole that served as Chen's office. "Badger hasn't come back yet."

At once, Chen gave her his undivided attention. He swiveled around in his chair and she could see concern in his face. "Hasn't he? What about Zhu Irzh? Has he called? He was supposed to be picking badger up after a couple of hours."

"I've heard nothing," Inari said. "Anyway, I think he'd have rung your cellphone."

"Well, just in case," Chen remarked. He fished amongst the papers and checked the phone. "No, nothing." He dialed a number, presumably the demon's.

"Zhu Irzh?" There was silence for a moment, then Chen said, "It's me, Chen. When you get this, can you call me back? I'm at home."

Then he rung off. "Odd," he said, frowning. "The answering service is on."

"Maybe something's happened," Inari said.

"I don't want to run around after either of them like a nursemaid," Chen

12

said. "They're both reasonably competent. Well, mostly. But I also don't think we can afford to be complacent."

"What are you going to do?"

Chen stood and picked up his jacket. "I'm going to talk to the precinct and then go down there. I'll tell them to standby for back-up if I think I need it, but I don't want to start a panic. What's that Western expression? Cry wolf?"

"Chen Wei," Inari said, impulsively, "take me with you."

Chen opened his mouth and shut it again. She knew that his immediate reaction had been to refuse, and she appreciated the fact that he had, at least, considered it.

"I know it might be dangerous," she said. "But I have a responsibility to badger. He's my family familiar, after all. If it wasn't for me, he would not have gone to look for the bug."

"This is damn frustrating," Chen said. "I wanted to treat him as part of the team, not send him into trouble. And I don't want this to turn into one of those farces where Zhu Irzh goes to look for badger, and we go to look for Zhu Irzh, and everyone ends up missing." He paused.

"What exactly is this bug?" Inari asked.

"I'll tell you on the way," Chen replied.

蛇警探

"Sweatshops," Chen said, once they were in the car and turning left into the maze of streets behind Shaopeng. He had already put through a number of calls to the precinct and this had reassured Inari, somewhat. But Zhu Irzh's phone remained unanswered. "There are plenty of them in Singapore Three, as I'm sure you're aware—some of them are legal and some of them aren't. Over the years, we've seen waves of immigrants come into the city looking for work—from the mainland of China, from Laos, from other places in Asia. But never before from Hell."

Inari stared at him. "Hellkind have come here?"

"Quite a number of them. Zhu Irzh and I busted a sweatshop ring last year which was run on similar principles, but the other way round—impoverished humans seeking work in the sweatshops of Hell. Actually, they were effectively being held prisoner, and that's what seems to be happening now, but in reverse."

"Why are demons coming here?"

"It's the same old story, Inari. Work. Since the war, a lot of Hell's industries just can't afford to support a workforce—even though Hell technically won, the conflict with Heaven drained their resources to such an extent that a lot of demons lost their jobs. Also the industries in the lower levels were badly affected—Hell lost its main nuclear plant, for instance. I haven't been back since, but Zhu Irzh has and he says things aren't good—there are power cuts in the main cities every day now, and it's seriously affecting Hell's infrastructure."

Inari shivered. "I don't know that that's a bad thing."

"Perhaps not, from your point of view—a human point of view." Chen smiled at the irony. "But it does displace people."

"How are the demons getting through?" Inari asked. "It's not that easy to just go to and fro."

"That's the problem. They're being smuggled into the city and we don't know how. Zhu Irzh has done some recon work, but it's been pretty inconclusive. We don't know who's behind the demon-trafficking, whether they're human or Hellkind. We suspect both—there must be some liaison between the two for it to work as smoothly as it has. But it's been very difficult to find informers—even the usual suspects just seem too scared. Every time we follow up on a lead, we find an empty building and just enough evidence to show that Hellkind was there, but nothing we can really hang onto. Certainly not enough to build a case on, and without names, we can't even begin to think about prosecuting."

He slowed to let an elderly couple cross the road, and fell silent. It was even more ironic, Inari thought. From what Chen had told her about his recent visit to the Heavenly Realm, part of Mhara's goal was to bring the three worlds more closely together. And here they were, with workers from Hell coming into Singapore Three. She doubted whether it was quite what Mhara had in mind.

She watched as the city slid by, endless streets, at first brightly lit as they passed along Shaopeng and through the downtown part of the city, but then increasingly dark and silent, with some streets looking almost deserted. Inari did not know this part of the city at all, although it featured fairly regularly in newspaper reports as the scene of various crimes, generally violent ones. She had never had reason to come here before, and even though she and badger both hailed from Hell, she could not help feeling vaguely guilty about sending it into such a place. She had not known... but then, she could have asked; regardless, the badger was hardly helpless.

There had still been no news from Zhu Irzh. Inari knew, without asking, that this worried Chen. It wasn't so much that something might have happened to Zhu Irzh—although that was an increasing possibility now that Zhu Irzh's own mother was married to the new Emperor of Hell—but rather that Zhu Irzh might have done something. Got into trouble, and switched off the cellphone to cover it up. It had happened before. Inari did not want to voice these thoughts, however, as she was pretty sure that Chen shared them.

Looking through the windscreen of the car, she saw that they had come to a bleak district of what appeared to be warehouses. Inari blinked at a sudden bite of *déjà vu:* surely she had been here before, that tall building, black as a heart, had once borne the blood-colored awning of a remedy store… Again, a blink, for this was not Hell. But the feeling remained with her, a small, sharp memory like a pin in the fold of a dress that cannot be found and which pricks you when you least suspect it.

Shortly after they turned a corner into a long row of go-downs, Chen stopped the car and called the precinct.

"Who's that? Ma? Excellent." He listened for a moment. "Thank you, Sergeant." Turning to Inari, he said, "They've found the car that Zhu Irzh was using, but there's no sign of the demon or the badger."

"Now we're here, I'll see if I can contact badger," Inari said. It was a long time since she had used this particular piece of magic, a long time since she'd had to. She pulled a long, stiff whisker out of an inner pocket and breathed on it. The whisker burst into a small, cold flame and Inari closed her eyes. "Be careful," she thought she heard Chen say, but in the next moment she knew that she had heard his mind, not his voice.

Dark streets. A locked room, strangely hushed and still. Curtains hanging like heavy strips of flesh, in some odd manner, almost alive. The scent of badger, coming through the flame of the burning whisker, old and earthy and animal, perhaps unpleasant to anyone who was not used to it.

"Badger?" Inari whispered. There was the faintest breath of a reply, a muffled anger, murderous inhuman rage that blazed as slow and icy as magic. Earth magic, the sorcery of tunnels and below-the-ground. Badger magic—and then it was gone, cut off as neatly and completely as though a door had slammed shut. The flicker of the flame touched her fingers, cold-burning through to the bone, and in a breath of smoke Inari's eyes opened and the whisker was gone.

"He's not on Earth," Inari said, dismayed.

"Then where?" Chen said, aloud, but he did not have to speculate. "Hell. He's been taken to Hell. If you are right."

"I think I am. It felt—familiar."

"Then where is Zhu Irzh?" said Chen through his teeth. He opened the door of the car. "Inari, forgive me, but please—will you stay here?"

"If badger comes back—"

"Then still, stay in the car. Badger can look after himself."

"So can I," Inari said, but she spoke softly and the slam of the car door took the words away.

SIX

The Emperor of Heaven opened the doors of the wardrobe and stared glumly at the contents. The wardrobe was huge: as large as many apartments back on Earth, and filled with thousands of floor-length robes. Crimson, jade, and gold. Dragons and phoenixes, twisting in perpetual embroidered flight. Pearls and garnets and emeralds, fire-flashing in the cascading light of Heaven's noon.

Mhara thought: *T-shirt and jeans.* It would not do, and he knew it. He walked into the wardrobe and rummaged through the stiff folds until he found something at the very back of the room. It was silk, and the color of a very pale twilight. It had no ornamentation. He pulled it on and turned to the mirror. His reflection, something in which he had little interest, came as a surprise. An ethereal monk, barely present against the mirrored walls, despite being reflected to baffling infinity.

She was not impressed. He had not expected her to be.

"Mha—Emperor! Where is the Robe of Ten Thousand Years?"

"I've no idea, Mother. Somewhere in the closet, I expect."

"But what is it doing there? Why aren't you wearing it? Your father, when he was crowned—"

"I," said Mhara, very quietly, "am not my father."

"This is a ridiculous piece of posturing! Such pretence of humility is all very well in front of humankind, but it is hardly appropriate in the Imperial Court."

Mhara turned to face her. The Dowager Empress, until so recently the Empress of Heaven, sat at a small table near a high, arched window. Clouds rolled golden beyond, illuminating the brocade folds of her gown. Her face was as he had always known it: serene, calm, lovely, the dark hair intricately braided down her back. Like a mask, he thought. The bitterness of her speech could almost be seen: coiling out into the air and curdling its sweetness. But none of this showed on her face and that, he thought, was no good thing.

"You have not understood me," Mhara said, and at his tone, the Dowager Empress at last fell silent. "I am not my father. You will not, madam, have need of instructing me. I am neither senile nor insane." *Nor am I weak,* although he did not think he needed to say that.

The Dowager Empress said, "I—"

"It is time for you to take your place, Mother," Mhara said. He glanced at a small silver bell and it rang, just once. Immediately the maids were there, fluttering around the Dowager Empress like butterflies. There was a flash in his mother's eyes that might have been fury, or even hate, and that was honest at least, but the next moment it was gone. And so was she, borne away amid a rustling crowd of maidens.

Mhara thought: *Enough.* There was a problem there, he knew. No one would believe that the Empress of Heaven could sour like a too-old wine, but then again, no one had believed that the Emperor of Heaven could be mad. Old gods, it seemed to him, do not wear well. Look at Senditreya, deranged bovine goddess of dowsing, whose rampage through the city of Singapore Three had caused so much destruction.

Who needs Hell, when you have a Heaven like this one? Yet, gazing out across the Imperial City, it all looked so tranquil: the turrets and pavilions outlined against the gold-and-blue. Changeless, eternal, and that was the root of the problem.

Things are going to have to change.

蛇警探

Below, the Imperial Palace was crammed with beings. On the long walk up the marble hall, echoes flickering like moths, Mhara looked calmly upon dragons and spirits, goddesses and lords. Their faces had become remote, statue-still, yet imbued with supernatural presence. All were there in their primary aspects: one was not permitted to send an avatar to a coronation. Only one smiled at him: Kuan Yin, Lady of Compassion and Mercy, who sat in a column of jade robes as though conjured from the green salt sea. And only one winked: a dragon, green-gold eye twitching. Mhara repressed a smile of his own and walked on.

At the throne, several anxious courtiers awaited him. It struck him that they might have believed that he wouldn't show up, that he would have been found later, perhaps, down on Earth, pottering about the little temple that was all the worship he would permit, putting plants in soil. He had, briefly, considered it. But there was an ancient magic inherent in the coronation itself, the weight of words spoken, answers given. When you become Emperor of

Heaven, or Hell, you write upon the universe itself, a litany that can never be erased, that seeps into the fabric of reality, effecting change. He could not, yet, afford to turn down that kind of power. But he preferred to wear it lightly.

He repeated the conjurations after the whispered prompts of the courtier, until the old man realized that there was no need for coaching. The words came from nowhere, as if murmured by the stars, settling into his head, and he heard his own voice, calm and collected. He glanced once at the Empress and her face was marble-still, but he could see the seethe of thoughts behind it.

A problem. Well, now was not the moment to deal with it.

He uttered the final words of the litany and everything stopped, the world's beating heart pausing for a limitless second. And for that second, Mhara could see everything: the clouds of spawned stars, the specks of dust on the paw of a cat, the beat of blood in his mother's head, the depths of ocean and the grains of desert sand. Despair and beauty and silence and terror and the relentless drive of the world, the ruthlessness of life surging on, bearing everything in its wake.

And then, it began again, and Mhara was Emperor-crowned now.

They sang praises until the long day of Heaven faded into soft dusk and Mhara went alone to his chamber, telling the servants that assistance would not be necessary. Tomorrow, the tasks of true governance would start and he needed to speak to Robin—priestess, beloved, and ghost—about her appearance in Heaven, if she chose. He did not think his mother would like that. Tough.

But for now, he needed peace and silence. There was something he had to think about. It was not the desolate churn of suns in the furthest reaches of space, nor the cries of species becoming extinct in the world below. It was not the manifold woes of humans or the fears of the lords of Hell.

During that moment of coronation, of the universe's validation of its supposedly most august son, Mhara had in that all-seeing, omniscient instant, glimpsed something really disturbing. It had been the clawed paw of a badger, disappearing into a red sack.

SEVEN

Chen approached the car with a considerable degree of caution. There was no sign that he was being watched, but it seemed likely. He hoped Inari would see the sense of remaining in their own vehicle; he refused to give her a direct order, she was not a subordinate, and her sense of responsibility to the badger was legitimate. In addition to this, there had been a number of occasions of late in which Inari actually had stayed home in alleged safety, and had been attacked by demons, demon-hunters, and enforcement lords from Hell. She was probably better off in the car.

He made his way along the back wall of the car park, keeping low. There was no one in either sight or sense, but the latter could be deceptive: goddess knew he'd been wrong before. When he reached Zhu Irzh's vehicle, he crouched down before the bumper of the car next to it, and peered out.

There was no indication that the doors had been forced, and no magic hovered about the car. Looking upward a little, Chen could see that the car was also locked. That suggested that the demon had left the car himself, and had voluntarily gone elsewhere.

Chen took a small phial of powder from an inside pocket. This stuff was notoriously unreliable, but Exorcist Lao had been doing some work on it at the precinct lately and had insisted that Chen give it another try. An improved formula, apparently. Chen had no issue with experimentation, but not really under this kind of circumstance. He spoke the spell anyway, and breathed out. The tiny pinch of powder flew outward, spiraling into the night air like motes of jade dust. Soon, a faint sparkle betrayed the presence of footprints, and to Chen's hopeful eye, at least, they looked like Zhu Irzh's elegant pointed boots. Still keeping against the wall, he followed the footprints around to the edge of the parking lot and out into Men Ling Street.

He must remember to congratulate Lao on the improved formula. The footprints glowed a clear, bright green, which Lao had assured him would have little magical footprint (pun intended) in that their glow would be invisible to anyone who had not personally used this consignment of powder. Chen hoped that this was indeed the case: otherwise he had just broadcast his presence to the entire district. He doubted that Men Ling Street was a particularly forgiving neighborhood.

There was the house, the one to which he had dispatched the badger. There was the doorway, down a narrow side alley, and there was the hulking shadowy form, waiting behind a dumpster. Chen sidled up behind the form.

"Hi."

Before the words were even out of his mouth, he was confronted with a whirling silver blade, the sudden rush of a sword as it descended to point at his throat, the rictus face beyond.

"Ma," said Chen, out of a dry mouth. "It's me."

"Sir!" The sword disappeared. "Sorry, sir. I thought you were a hostile."

"If I had been," Chen remarked, "it wouldn't have been for very long." Sergeant Ma had been put through basic martial arts and weapons training, like everyone else in the precinct, but this was something else. The sheer ferocity in Ma's face was not something Chen had ever associated with his large, mild colleague.

"I've been having lessons," Ma explained in a whisper.

"Lessons? From whom?"

"No Ro Shi. The demon-hunter."

"Oh," Chen said. He had further problems envisaging Ma as the protégé of No Ro Shi, lately of Beijing; a man of such impeccably communist credentials that he made Chairman Mao look like a liberal. And one of the most celebrated hunters of demons ever to come out of China. No Ro Shi disapproved, ideologically, of demons. He considered them subversive. "Well, he's certainly efficient."

Although now that Chen came to remember it, Inari and the badger had dumped No Ro Shi in the harbor. Good job No Ro Shi had never made the connection, even though it was now somewhat moot: Singapore Three had had the supernatural thrust so unmistakably in its collective face over the last couple of years that being married to a woman from Hell seemed almost unworthy of comment.

"Ma, what's going on?"

"I've been keeping the building under surveillance, sir, but no one's come into or out of it. I've got people on all sides. Do you think we should go in?"

Chen thought about this. On the one hand, the situation was exactly the same as it had been on the previous instances of busting—or trying to bust—illegal warehouses: as he had related to Inari, they'd gone in and found nothing. Then again, he'd not had two officers missing. Badger counted as an officer in Chen's mind, at least for the purposes of this discussion.

"We go in," he said.

A ram at the door, two officers—Shao and Pa Chin—sent in with guns, a quick survey, the all-clear, and then Chen and Ma entered into a completely empty room with no doors. Curtains lay in piles of dusty fabric around the edges of the room.

"Oh dear," Ma said, with commendable restraint.

"There's nothing here." Officer Pa Chin looked about her.

"No," Chen agreed. "But there was."

The magic was so strong that he could almost smell it. As an experiment, he said to Ma, "Sergeant? Can you smell anything?"

Ma sniffed, and wrinkled his nose. "Why, yes. Something like—I'm not sure. Incense, perhaps? Or blood?"

If the insensitive Ma could detect it, it must be pungent.

"What is it?" Ma continued.

"Magic," Chen said. "But I don't know what kind."

It smelled of Hell, but next moment, of something else entirely: floral and sickly sweet. *Familiar,* Chen thought, *I've smelled that before,* but he did not know where.

"Sir," Pa Chin said, "did someone get out of this room by magic?"

"Has to be," Chen replied. "Unless there's a secret door."

His own magic could not detect that sort of thing, though it might be able to trace the thin, alien thread that still lingered in the room. Quickly, he and the rest of his team made a search of the walls. There were no secret panels or entrances that anyone could detect: the walls seemed solid through and through.

"Okay," Chen told them at last. "There's no point in wasting any more time."

He motioned them to the sides of the room and, obediently, they complied with his instructions. He could not help reflecting on how things had changed. Less than a handful of years ago, he was a pariah in his own department; shunned by the majority of staff apart from the captain and Exorcist Lao, who was not generally that popular himself. He remembered Ma tiptoeing nervously around him as though he might suddenly burst into flames. Now, Ma barely seemed to notice Zhu Irzh, let alone Chen himself, and the other two officers—admittedly on secondment from Beijing, where supernatural incursions might be somewhat more common due to the city's status and age—appeared to treat this as a normal assignment. Pa Chin blinked slightly as Chen pricked the palm of his hand and let a droplet of blood fall to the floor, whereas Officer Shao's attention was fixed on the opposite wall, watching Chen's back.

Chen let the blood hit the floor and spoke a word. No jade fire this time, but a spiral of neon blue that twirled up in a butterfly dance and streamed out and down.

"It's going back under the floorboards," Pa Chin said, clearly fascinated.

In Chen's own opinion, the origins of the magical trace went far deeper than this, but he'd learned to listen to the prickle of instinct.

"Get the boards up," he said. Shao ran out to their patrol car and returned with a jemmy. Together, he and Pa Chin wrenched the central floorboards loose and Chen peered in.

"There's something there."

An empty space, much wider than the crack revealed by the boards. They pried enough away for Ma and Chen to drop down into the room that lay below.

"Well," Chen said. "There's a door here, anyway."

This cellar room felt ancient, much older than the house that lay above it. Singapore Three was a recent city, but it had incorporated some very old villages and estates, including a couple of palaces, and Men Ling Street had been part of the small port area of one of these hamlets, situated on a harbor which had long since become silted up. The walls of the room were made of stone, rough and mossy and emanating a choking smell of damp.

Chen put his ear to the door. He could hear nothing beyond it, but that meant nothing: the door might be very thick. His rosary was wrapped around his wrist: Kuan Yin might no longer be his patron, but the rosary was still Chen's primary weapon, the focus of his power. Ma's sword was drawn. Chen still couldn't get used to that.

"Right," he mouthed. "*One... two... three...*"

He kicked the door, aiming at the lock, and the old wood was more fragile than it seemed, for the lock splintered and gave way. The door fell open with a crash and Chen and Ma were through.

Looking back, he wondered that the smell had not been worse than it was. Even so, Ma gagged and Chen clapped a hasty hand over his mouth and nose, keeping the rosary hand free. Some of the bodies had been here for some time, but others looked quite fresh, recently butchered. A skinned torso twisted on a chain, boiled eyes gazing vacantly into Chen's own. There were, perhaps, a dozen of them, in various states of dismemberment. The sound of sad spirits wailed briefly in his ears and then were gone.

Chen brushed past the corpses to the end of the room. The floor beneath his feet was sticky with blood. It was a meat locker, nothing more. It ended in yet another blank wall, but looking up, Chen could see a hatch, half-buried in moss. Whoever, or whatever, had stashed the bodies here clearly had little interest in keeping their meat cold or fresh.

"Better ask Shao to bring up the missing persons file on the car computer,"

Chen said. "I should imagine we've got a number of results in here."

Corpses, yes. But no sign of demon or badger.

EIGHT

To Go's relief, he had managed to talk Beni into some sort of agreement.

Sending Lara back was not the best thing to do, but the only thing. Having secured Beni's concurrence, however, Go found himself faced with two further problems: Lara's kindred did not want her back, and Lara herself did not want to go.

Delicate negotiations were therefore called for. And probably a large bribe. It was not an issue that Go had anticipated when they first met Lara: kidnapping, yes, okay. That could be dealt with. He'd foreseen tears, threats, maybe even some kind of Stockholm Syndrome, but not quite the degree of enthusiasm that Lara had actually displayed. The idea of a ransom, which hadn't even been in Go's mind in the first place, was summarily dismissed when Go had had a visit from Lara's sister.

蛇警探

At first, he'd thought it was Lara herself, standing in the window of his hotel room at midnight, and his heart had leaped and stuttered in his chest.

"Lara! I—"

"I'm not Lara." A long tail twitched, rustling the curtains. Yellow eyes glittered in candlelight. And he could see now that she was shorter, her long hair a slightly different shade to Lara's jet black, a little russet.

"Then who—"

"I'm her sister. Askenjuri." At least, that is what he thought she said. The name was a hiss and a sigh. She moved toward him and his knees buckled. The light of the candle illuminated her body against the transparent folds of her loose sari and that was wrong, he thought, the candle was in the wrong place, as though she had stolen the light, but he did not care. She opened her

24

mouth and he saw the points of tiger teeth. The sari fell to the floor and she was striped, night-and-firelight-colored, all along her thighs and then that was gone and her skin was the shade of dark honey. She smiled. Her eyes were brown and gold.

"Am I like her, then? Do you think we look alike? People always think she takes after Mother." Now, the voice was a purr. She was right in front of him and he had not noticed that she had moved. She smelled of musk and jasmine and blood.

"No," he'd said in an instinctive croak. "You're *much* prettier."

Askenjuri's smile widened. The lie must smell, Go thought, rank as a day-old dead goat. But she didn't seem to mind, though the smile was mocking. "Ah, ah, ah… I'm sure you're just being kind." Definitely mocking. But it wasn't just mockery. There was something behind it and he did not know what it was. That made him nervous.

"How did you get *in?*" Think, man. You have to *think*. But the blood was beating in his head like the sea, in out, in out, and his body was heavy and hot, gravity pulling him down and down…

The carpet was surprisingly comfortable. She was standing over him and there was the distant engine of a purr. "Why, through your little fire." She gestured toward the candle. "Did you light it for her? Are you expecting my sister?"

"I think she's screwing her agent tonight," Go managed to say out of a dry mouth, and Askenjuri threw back her head and laughed. Her throat was golden, the stripes only faint.

"Ah, but, my sister screws *everyone*, you see. Has she screwed you, I wonder? She will. We were all so pleased when you took her away, my mother, our sisters, the princesses—everyone."

"Princesses?" He and Beni had aimed at someone—well, *humble*. They thought it might lead to fewer complications.

"We're all royal, you know." Again, the twitch of a tiger tail. "But some of us think we're more royal than most. Like little Lara."

"What are you telling me?" Go said thickly. There didn't seem to be much love lost between them; this didn't seem to be some kind of revenge trip. Thank God. If that was the right thing to think anymore…

"We don't want her back, little man. You can keep her. If she grows tired and wants to go, let her go. But don't send her back where she came from. We've all had *quite* enough."

"Oh," Go said, and that, and variations upon it, were all that he said for the next five minutes or so, because Askenjuri was flicking open the zip of his jeans and licking her lips with a tongue that really wasn't anything like a human being's, and then she sank down on top of him.

In the morning, she was gone. Go woke, feeling as though he'd been beaten with hammers. There was a long lacerated bruise down his chest and stomach—it looked as if an elephant had sat on him—and his head pounded. It was like the flu, but worse.

He did not, naturally, mention Askenjuri's visit either to Lara or Beni. Lara simply did not need to know—it might upset her, like he really cared—and any information that he possessed and Beni didn't was useful information, to Go's scheming mind. At first, he'd been afraid that Askenjuri might have marked him in some way—magically, as with a psychic bruise—but if she had, Lara did not appear to notice. Just as well.

NINE

Seijin moves like water, like wind. Old teachings come back to mind as they glide over the plateau, things learned in the monasteries and palaces of an earlier China. But this is not China, whatever the claims made by Beijing, and not any calendrical time: this is *between*. Seijin, looking up, sees Himalayan heights in the far distance, barely distinguishable from cloud, and the stones shift underfoot, now golden, now gray. Seijin smiles and casts a handful of coins on bare earth.

Resolution. But with changing lines.

Oh. You don't say.

The coins turn to leaves as Seijin watches and a sudden gust of wind carries them away, spinning them out across the plateau to cloud-mountain. Seijin sighs. To think that this had been intended as a rest.

"What do *you* think?" Seijin says out loud. "Stay, or return?"

Female self steps out, long black hair whipping in the wind of *between*. "What does it matter? We can choose our time of return."

"Within limits," male self says, emerging beside her. Seen in a dark place at night, perhaps there wouldn't be all that great a difference between them: the hair, the slanted, opaque gaze, the scaled armor. Female self is of slighter build, and looks young, but in fact female self was always dominant, until the Riders came and she went into hiding for a while, no more than a hundred years or so, but enough to give male self the upper hand. Seijin's smile widens. Interesting times.

"Within limits, true." Female self is earnest, brow furrowing. "But there is still a great deal of time. The Emperor of Heaven has only just been crowned. We could not have acted before that."

"Still, the contract is running now," male self says.

"You are *so* impatient."

"We have wasted time before. You have to make a choice. Stay in *between* forever or act. Which is it to be?"

"I could wish for *between*," female self says, a little wistful. "I get tired of all this running around."

Seijin, hollow on the plateau, laughs. "All right. I've listened. You both have your way. Another night here and then we return to Earth."

Female self is reabsorbed. Male self hesitates, only for a second, but it's enough to make Seijin frown. Obedient as a hound, male self slides back into place and Seijin is once more liminal, but complete.

This time, the palace does not take so long to reach. *Between* shifts and rearranges: it can take days to cross the plateau, or only a few hours, and there's no predicting it. But shortly after the conversation, Seijin comes around an outcrop of granite and there it is: the Shadow Pavilion, towering and gray as the rocks on which it stands. Seijin bows, once, then climbs the long flight of stone steps and knocks, once, at the doors.

"Who comes?"

"Lord Lady Seijin." And bows again.

The doors—ancient, the color of twilight, made of wood so weathered that they more closely resemble stone—creak open. The Gatekeeper stands within, barely visible even to Seijin, but a glance over the shoulder shows that night is not far away and that tends to leech the Gatekeeper of whatever shades it might possess.

"Do you seek entrance, to this your own abode?"

"I do, if it is the Pavilion's wish." A ritual exchange, but one that a person must take care to perform correctly. Not everyone gains access to Shadow Pavilion and with night on the way, that's not a good thing. Even if you are Seijin.

The Gatekeeper says, "Then enter," and stands well back as Seijin glides in. Seijin follows the Gatekeeper upstairs to a room, one of the best suites, although this has not been requested. As the Gatekeeper moves hastily away, Seijin wanders across to the window and looks out across *between*.

Night is coming fast, visible as a shadow gliding over the land. But the mountain peaks are still touched with the fire of the sun, glowing rose-gold, and there is a crescent moon hanging over Himalaya, sharp as a silver tooth in the oceanic sky. Female self pulls hard, wanting to stay.

Time to retire? Seijin muses. It's become a familiar argument in recent years but this latest contract, this is too magnificent to refuse. After this—if one survives it—would be the perfect time to retire, the crowning glory of a long, long life.

How often, after all, is one contracted to kill a god?

TEN

Inari was wrestling with her own conscience—something that, as a demon, she is not even supposed to possess, but which may have come from that human ancestor, the ancestor who had brought such shame on their family, tainting it as she had with mortal blood. Inari had often wondered about that woman, since learning of her existence. She would be long dead, but what had happened to her soul? In Hell, presumably, since she had abandoned the Imperial Court of China and fled the shores of Earth for those of Hell. But if in Hell, then where? Not in Inari's own family home, that was for certain, unless—horrible thought—they had imprisoned her somewhere.

You could keep a soul in a jar, after all. Inari remembered the high ebony jars that had stood on the landing of the mansion, and despite the stuffy, intrusive heat of Men Ling Street, she shivered. Her thoughts returned to the present. She was sorely tempted to get out of the car and go after Chen, but reason prevailed. She would be more hindrance than help if he encountered a problem, and besides, he had asked her to keep a sense out for badger.

There had been no trace of the family familiar, however, and she was growing increasingly anxious and frustrated. It must be like this on most stake-outs, she thought. Long hours of tedium and worry, waiting for something to happen.

And then something did. There was a sudden sharp rattle at the back of the car. Inari turned in her seat, crouching so that her head was below the line of sight, and squinted out the rear window. Nothing was visible. But then the rattle came again—a curious sound, like an instrument, a gourd full of beads. And it was peculiarly compelling.

Inari felt all the worry drain out of her mind, as gently as water trickling through a crack. A moment later, and it was all gone: she felt blank and clear. With detached interest, she watched her hand reach out and flick the lock of the door open. She got out, to stand in the fetid atmosphere of Men Ling Street, which she could now study with no concern at all. *That* was interesting, that small section of dark, shadowed wall behind the trash cans. She thought she ought to go and have a closer look at that.

The rattle came again, playing on her senses and seeming to shake the air around her until it quivered into heat haze. It was hard to see clearly now, but this didn't matter. *Off you go, into the darkness by the wall. See what you can find.* Coaxed, encouraged, Inari walked slowly forward until she was level with the trash cans. Somewhere, there was a terrible smell of rotting fruit. *Ignore that, it's irrelevant. Come along now.*

And so she did, and it was summer: not the humid, stifling heat that descended on the city like a lid, nor the torrential downpours that signaled the beginning of the season, nor yet the firestorms of Hell that scoured the great plains bare of life, but a sweet, calm, mildness of day. There were small green flowers springing up beneath her feet and the stench of rot changed to a balmy perfume. Inari stood entranced. This was not even like Heaven—so pretty and yet just a little sickly with it. This was redolent of growth, of life rather than stagnation, and she breathed it in. The rattle sounded again, a stealthy little clatter right at the edges of her awareness and she did not even turn her head.

Someone was smiling at her. A girl, dressed in ivory.

"Hello," the girl said, and her voice was warm. One of her hands was behind her back. "I've got a present for you."

"Hello," said Inari. The girl reached out her hand and then her head burst like a melon, blood and gray matter erupting in a gushing fountain of blood that covered Inari. It reminded her forcibly of her brother's establishment: he had owned a blood emporium, back in Hell. She was too startled to scream. She simply stood, looking numbly down at the crumpled corpse of the girl, except that it was not a girl, but an armored man—no, a demon. There were claws. She did not recognize the breed but that meant nothing; Hell was filled with all manner of persons. One hand clutched a rattle. Inari bent down and picked it up. It was a hollow sphere, made of stretched skin and from it depended many tiny bones. Someone reached over her shoulder and took it from her hand.

"Better let me have that, miss. Are you all right?"

The voice was sharp with concern. It added, into a handheld radio, "Hostile is down. One victim, probably in shock. I need a medical team."

Inari turned. "It's all right," she said. "My husband—he's not far away. Detective Inspector Chen."

The man—tall, with iron-gray hair and a long, harsh face—said, amazed, "You're *Chen's* wife?" And then, more sharply yet, *"And you're a demon!"*

Oh, thought Inari, Oh *dear*. She'd seen this man before, and moments after that first appraisal, the badger had pitched him off the deck of the houseboat and into the harbor. His name was No Ro Shi, principal demon-hunter of the Beijing government.

ELEVEN

Go and Beni stood at the center of the room, their hands linked by a long red sash. Around them burned candles, crimson and gold, sending tongues of tiger-colored flame up into the smoky air. Beni had thrown a handful of incense on the brazier and it smoldered, filling the room with a pungent, gingery scent.

"We're only going to get one shot at this," Go warned his colleague. "We've got to get it right."

Beni looked uneasy. "I still think she should actually *be* here."

"Yeah, right. That's entirely realistic. Lara, darling, just come and participate in this ritual for us, would you? It'll send you back to Hell and your unloving family and seal you there forever."

"I understand the reasons for it," Beni remarked. "I just think it would stand a much better chance of working. Couldn't you have slipped her something?"

"Like what? I tried that once, when she was being particularly difficult—put enough valium in her tea to knock out an elephant and what happened? She stayed wide awake and chattering on. She's not human."

"Couldn't you have asked a remedy man or something? An expert?"

"And tell him what? 'My friend and I, we conjured up this tiger spirit from Hell in India, and now she's a famous movie star, but she's gone bonkers and we want to get rid of her.'"

"You don't have to tell them the truth," Beni said, exasperated. "Make something up. It's what you do for a living, after all."

"I don't want any openings for blackmail. You know what these people are like. Look, we don't have infinite amounts of time. Are you going to help me or not?"

Beni gave a sullen nod. "Yeah. I suppose."

At the other end of the room, lit by a hundred candles, stood a shrine to Lara. Go had raided the archives for stills and these now adorned a wooden frame: Lara in black and white, posing like Ava Gardner; Lara in Bollywood Technicolor, a fuchsia sari whipping around her; several shots from a *Vogue* shoot and images from her latest movie. The only pictures that Go had failed to come up with had been images of her tiger-self. Lara was cagy about that, too aware of possible consequences, and although Go had surreptitiously tried, he'd never succeeded in capturing a picture of Lara in her true, or at least, non-human form.

"Okay," Go said. "Here we go."

Letting go of the sash for a moment, he cast a handful of banishing incense onto the brazier. It hissed ominously, smoke billowing out in an acrid cloud across the room and making Go's eyes water and sting.

"God, that stuff's strong," Beni said, coughing. "What did you put in it?"

Go did not reply. He was trying to read the scroll that stood before him on a music stand. It was familiar: the same spell that they'd used to bring Lara here, but—a classic touch—in reverse. Nervously, he intoned it.

"Nothing's happening," Beni said.

Go did not reply to this, either. He was not sure that Beni was right: perhaps more sensitive than the agent, or more paranoid, it seemed to him that they had suddenly attracted all sorts of attention to what was going on in the room. He had the sensation of a thousand eyes fixated upon him, a thousand ears listening, and he had no idea who they might have belonged to. He continued with the litany, which had to be recited three times, as the atmosphere in the chamber curdled and congealed like old milk.

"Oh my God," Beni said suddenly.

Go had come to the end of the third recitation and he looked up. There was a mass of movement around the base of the shrine, spreading outward. At first, he thought they were dustballs, but then little red eyes opened and through the incense smoke he glimpsed the skittering ghosts of rats and mice, a thin, transparent snake winding its way through the floorboards. A shape—much larger—stepped out of the air, seemingly made of smoke. It was a child, hair streaming down her back, mouth open in horror, a blood-red necklace around her throat that gaped and spilled.

Go and Beni cried out, but she was gone, taking the vermin-spirits with her.

"What the hell—?" Go whispered.

Beni glanced feverishly about him. "It's the house, man. This is such an old place—must have been full of psychic crap. You just sent it onward."

"No bloody Lara, though." The realization of failure ran cold down his spine, despite the choking warmth of the room.

"Oh *yes,* bloody Lara," a voice said. Go nearly dropped the sash. The child had not been the only thing emerging from the candlelit mouth of the shrine. At first, there was only an outline in the air: tall, slender, tail twitching.

"Shit," he heard Beni's panicked murmur.

At the top of the outline appeared two furious yellow eyes. And then the teeth. A moment later, Lara herself was almost fully visible: naked, with the black slashes of her tiger-striped marking all the way down her body. Her face, however, had changed and instead of the beautiful human mask it was elongated, snarling, the jaw dropping impossibly far to show the razor teeth.

"What are you *doing?*" Lara said, in a voice that was more of a growl.

"Lara—look, babe. Things change."

Beni, Go thought, don't make the mistake of trying to *reason* with her. She's way beyond that point. She's never been *at* that point. Even at her sweetest, logic had never been Lara's strongest feature.

"You know what I'm saying?"

"Beni—" Go said, in warning. *You're not firing a bloody grip or something.* But the warning went unheeded. The agent was too accustomed to talking his way out of a problem. "Things haven't been great for any of us lately—I know you're not *happy*, babe, and there was the whole pay dispute thing, which I fully concede was unfortunate, could have handled it a lot better, and—"

"So you're sending me back to Hell?" Lara said, in that voice that still was not human, at all, and filled with fire. "You brought me here, and now you can't handle it, you can't deal with me because I won't be your simpering demon bimbo, and you're trying to send me *back,* you pathetic little *shit.*"

"Lara—" Go and Beni said together, but it was at Beni that she sprang. Go had a single, appalled image of Lara: her long legs bending backward at the knee, claws ripping on the polished wooden floor, her striped body arcing through the smoking air as she fell upon her agent and tore out his throat.

That was almost all he saw, because Go was off and running, knocking over the guttering candles in his flight for the door. He kicked the door open and fell out into the hallway. The clear, warm air came as a shock, as if he'd been punched. For a despairing moment, he thought Lara had struck him in the back.

Almost, but not quite all. Staggering against the opposite wall, he took one look back and saw, behind the curtain of sudden fire, Lara's head raised and fresh red blood running down her chin into the flames. The gold of the fire was trapped in her eyes and then she leaped upward. He heard the crash and shatter of broken glass as she sprang through the window and then Go himself was stumbling backward, bare feet slipping on the boards of the hallway, and he threw himself out of the front door and into the still and midnight garden as the house caught light and flared up like a firecracker.

TWELVE

It was a relief to reach the temple. Mhara stepped out of the oppressive air of Heaven into a calm, white-plastered room: the little annex that he and Robin used as a portal. Robin—priestess, ghost, but still scientist—had come up with a spell that keyed the annex to her own soul, and Mhara's: nothing that could be stolen or used, but enough to deter anyone following either of them through, either to Heaven, or from it. It was sad, Mhara thought, to have to be so untrusting, but it was the way of things and he supported Robin's installation of the spell. He could see it now, taking the form of a thin gilt lattice, suspended in the air before him. He reached out a hand and the lattice was gone.

"Robin?" There was a lamp burning somewhere in the temple; he could feel its tranquil small presence and that of another, far more complex, being. He followed the sense of those two presences until he came to the main room of the temple, the shrine that lay at the end of the simple living quarters, just inside the main door.

This, too, was plastered white, and the shrine itself bore no image, only a lamp and a niche for a candle. Robin knelt in front of it with her back to him, solid enough in this soft light, although sometimes her form flickered a little, as if seen through clear water.

"Hello," Robin said, without looking round. "How did it go?"

Mhara sighed. "Tedious. I wish you could have been there."

"Well, I could have," she agreed. She had decided against attending the coronation. *I'm not one for big state occasions, and anyway, I don't want to cramp your style.* She'd felt it might be embarrassing for the new Emperor, having his dead human girlfriend showing up on the big day. "I'm sure your mother thought I'd have made a scene. Would you like some tea?" She motioned to a battered iron kettle that set on a table near the door. "I just made some oolong."

Mhara laughed, but he did not feel able to contradict her. "Thanks, I will." He went to the table and poured steaming green liquid into a bowl. "And Mother made a bit of a scene herself. Wanted me to wear the big state robes, and I thought—not my style. She's going to have to get used to that and she's going to have to get used to you, Robin. I've already explained to her that you're here to stay."

"I thought," Robin said, without turning her head, "that you might be up for some sort of political marriage."

"Robin—this isn't the Heaven of thousands of years ago, not anymore."

"Does Heaven know that?"

Mhara sipped tea. "I don't know. It will have to take it on board at some point. I'm up against a tradition like a juggernaut and I'm not going to be the one that gives in."

"No," Robin agreed. "I don't suppose you will." For the first time, she turned her head and looked at him. Robin thought, Mhara knew, that she had a very ordinary face: typical of the region, rather thin, with straight black brows, a long mouth. Mhara did not agree; it was not that he considered her beautiful, as that he did not really care. In Heaven, one was surrounded by the exquisite, a continual parade of glorious beauty that, after a while, became rather boring. He found Robin's neither-plain-nor-pretty features restful, after all that extraordinariness. Moreover death, and a more settled situation, had smoothed out the habitual lines and frowns of worry that she had worn when Mhara first encountered her, down in the laboratories of Jhai Tserai's corporation, and had lent a serenity to her face that made it more restful yet. Mhara enjoyed looking at her and did so now.

"The question of a political marriage will come up," Mhara said. "My mother will make sure of it—I'm certain she has half a dozen candidates in mind from various other Heavens. Angelic powers, devas, houris. It doesn't matter, Robin. Things have changed. Heaven is as subject to the march of time as anywhere else, we're a quarter of the way through the twenty-first century now, and I'm not subject to my mother's rule. This is a terrible thing to say but I don't even have much respect for her—she saw what my father was becoming and she didn't do anything to stop it."

"Well, we'll just have to wait and see what happens," Robin said. "It won't do much good for me to talk to your mother, but I suppose I can try if I have to."

"There is," Mhara remarked, "absolutely no point in winding her up."

Robin patted him on the shoulder. "Sometimes, going out with you is really surprisingly normal. You don't even look very Emperor-esque, if that's any comfort."

"Unfortunately, I am starting to feel some of its burdens." Mhara put the tea bowl down. Talk of his coronation had just reminded him of something. "Have you heard from Chen or Inari lately?"

"I saw them at the weekend. They brought those—" Robin pointed toward a spray of elegant white orchids in a vase "—I forgot to tell you. Coronation present."

"Was Inari's badger with them?"

Robin frowned, remembering. "I think so. Yes, it was. It went for a root in the flowerbed while we were having tea. I know it's sentient but I can't help thinking of it as a sort of dog. Or a teakettle, obviously."

"But you haven't seen or spoken to them since then?"

"No. Why?"

"I think," said Mhara, opening the door, "I'd better have a quick word with the detective inspector."

It was, he discovered, a beautiful evening. For once, the air above the sprawl of Singapore Three was clear, fading down into an intensity of sunset green. There was a brief flash of gold from the horizon, along the line of the sea, and Mhara felt the benediction of the sun as it slipped out of sight. He had a sudden, dizzying vision of it as a distant star, the little zip and flicker of the world as it orbited. Then it was gone and the lights of the city lay before him, peaceful in this liminal time of twilight in spite of the faint roar of traffic.

The temple, until so recently no more than a ruined shell, stood on a slight rise in an outlying suburb, backed by the wall of hills that rose in the north of the city. The view was pleasant from here; there were trees, and occasionally a rainy breath of mountain air. This, more than Heaven, had become home. Mhara was pleased to be back.

There were several ways of contacting Chen, but when on Earth, the new Emperor preferred to work with traditional methods. He clicked open the shell of his cellphone and dialed Chen's number. No reply. Mhara tried the houseboat and got an answerphone message. Well, it was a pleasant evening, not late, and if he recalled correctly, it was a Friday. Maybe Chen and Inari had gone out, and he would not blame them if they had. He left messages on both phones, just in case. The image of a badger's paw, disappearing, was still fresh in his mind, and more than any of the multitudinous horrors of the world glimpsed during his coronation, it filled him with an unaccountable unease.

THIRTEEN

Seijin came back to Earth on a golden day in October, stepping out of the still airs of *between* into a brisk, leaf-whipping wind. A temple stood before him—not Seijin's own, for no one builds temples to half-breeds, or assassins, no matter how elevated their origins might be. This place—a rambling, ornate structure covered with gold leaf and red lacquer—had been erected several hundred years ago to the Emperor of Heaven. *Former* Emperor, female self reminded Seijin reproachfully: it would not do to forget the very purpose of returning here. Seijin considered the temple to be somewhat vulgar and overdone; female self thought that they had always been ahead of their time when it came to internal décor. But that was irrelevant. There was business here.

Seijin skirted the carp pool that lay in front of the temple, mirroring it to perfection when the wind died and the ripples across the water stilled. There were glimpses of the reflected curls of the temple roof in between the sodden yellow leaves—before the Emperor's downfall, these would have been assiduously raked out of the pool every hour by the temple servants, but now that the Emperor was gone, the leaves formed a glossy carpet across the water, with the bright shapes of goldfish and carp flickering beneath them. Seijin raised the hem of the robe and stepped out onto a leaf. Visibility from the temple precinct was good: the staff would by now be aware that they were about to have a visitor. Seijin walked lightly across the path of leaves that covered the pool, scattering shoals of fish. You'd think they'd be used to magic, Seijin thought, but then, the short-term memory of fish is nothing to write home about.

Nor, sometimes, is the memory of gods.

By the time Seijin stepped onto the once glassy surface of the marble steps at the far end of the pool, the temple servants were waiting. Their normally bland faces wore, Seijin was not displeased to see, the same expression as that adopted by the Gatekeeper of the Shadow Pavilion: an agitation overlying fear.

"Honorable Lord Lady Seijin!"

"I need," Seijin said, bending down to the ear of one of the servants, "just to check the date." The genteel dilapidation of the temple might betray its former master's absence, but one never knew: problems had arisen before when moving from *between* and the worlds: betrayals, traps. One must always remain vigilant.

The servant confirmed the date and Seijin gave a gentle smile. "That's good. Thank you. Now. I understand someone is waiting to see me."

Preceded by much bowing and scraping, which Seijin ignored (always such a fuss with these people), the way to the temple's current occupant was shown. The interior of the temple had been cared for rather better than its grounds; Seijin walked past glittering tapestries, on marble floors inlaid with golden flowers, beneath a host of floating candles, to the inner sanctum, a windowless room redolent of jasmine.

Seijin did make a bow, but only a very little one.

"Madam. You wanted to see me?"

"I did." There was no bow in return, of course. She was seated on a throne at the far end of the room, beneath a gleaming canopy. Sky-blue robes, embroidered with clouds, pooled around her feet. She held a peacock feather fan, half-concealing her beautiful face. "I am glad that you came so promptly."

"The gladness is mine," Seijin replied. "*Between* is sometimes… tricky."

"I'm sure. You experienced no difficulties? You were not followed?"

"No." This said with a degree of some confidence: Seijin had experience of many tricks. "Might I confirm that you have not discussed our arrangement with anyone else, however?"

"No one. Not even my most trusted advisers. I find that my son has become inexplicably popular. My husband was on the throne for over a thousand years, you see. Spirits are like children, they crave novelty, and now they have it."

Seijin gave a thin smile. "A honeymoon period, I am sure."

The silence behind him was suddenly very noticeable, with even the hushed and reverent sounds of the temple abruptly cut off. Seijin knew, without needing to look, that turning around would not reveal the door; the chamber had been entirely sealed.

"Indeed. Thank you, Seijin, for your tact." The Dowager Empress' smile was equally thin. "But then again, if you perform correctly the task for which you have been contracted, the honeymoon will not be followed by a marriage."

"Well," Seijin remarked philosophically, "certainly not a happy one."

"When we last spoke, it was of necessity a brief meeting. My son had not yet been crowned, and I was not sure—I felt that this regrettable procedure might be necessary, but I had to make certain." The Dowager Empress spoke earnestly and Seijin granted her the weight of full attention. Difficult not to, in any case: Seijin might be beyond most of the rules which governed the three worlds, but this was, after all, Heaven's own Empress and she commanded a degree of concentration. It was hard to look anywhere other than her lovely face: no wonder she had held so much power for so long, even with an Imperial husband and the sheeplike nature of the inhabitants of Heaven.

"I understand," Seijin murmured. The Empress rose in a rustle of sky-blue and cloud—not simply the color, Seijin saw, but actual fragments of sky and wisps of mist—and came down the steps of the throne to stand beside her latest employee. She put a hand on Seijin's arm and the coolness of her fingers penetrated the armor.

"I have heard a great deal about you, Lord Lady Seijin. A child of Heaven and Hell, born on Earth. Male and female, in one body. Light and darkness. Some people call you an abomination."

"Some people," Seijin said, smiling, "are not wrong."

"They tell me you began your—career—in the Khan's armies. That you were trained by one of the monks he had captured. That you were responsible for massacres at Samarkand."

Seijin said, deprecatingly, "This, too, is true. All except the massacre, although I was involved. But I prefer subtlety. One on one, as they say nowadays."

"They say you have not had a commission for some years. Perhaps, for half a century." The coolness of her hand was deepening into frost; Seijin had to struggle not to pull the arm away.

"Ah," Seijin said. "But did they also tell you that this is because I turned many offers down?"

"No," the Dowager Empress said, considering. "They did not tell me that."

"I had proposals from kings and dictators and presidents. From Führers and gangsters. Nothing interested me sufficiently to accept it. Some foolish folk attempted to coerce me, and were taught the nature of their error. Some attempted to bribe, which is a little more intelligent. But my current place of residence is *between*, you see, and there I have no need of wealth."

"You are sometimes called the Lord Lady of Shadow Pavilion," the Dowager Empress said.

"I have all I need in the Twilight Lands. But that is not to say that I have retired." Here, female self made a small, mute protest, which Seijin ignored. "Your proposition was most interesting. I did not hesitate to sign your contract. To kill the Emperor, your own son?"

The touch on Seijin's arm burned like ice. "Do you *judge* me, Lord Lady

Assassin?"

Seijin turned to her full-on, and said, "I don't judge. I just kill."

FOURTEEN

Badger clawed, fought, struggled, kicked, and bit, but the thick hessian surface of the bag would not give way. Recognizing a temporary defeat, badger lay still, uncomfortably bundled. Doubtless it might be easier to undertake this journey in teakettle form, but in this aspect, the badger's sense of smell was somewhat impaired, although he was still able to see and hear. So he remained in his animal being and let himself be bumped and carried through wherever it was that he was being taken.

He thought it was probably Hell. It smelled like Hell: there was a reeking undercurrent of stale iron that was extremely familiar. Which part of Hell, though?—that was the question. Had they come straight to the upper levels, or were they moving through one of the lower? If the latter case, then badger might himself start changing, although this was by no means inevitable. Into what, remained to be seen.

He could get little sense of who, or what, had snatched him. The person did not seem to smell of anything apart from a faint scent of magic, which to the badger's mind was suspicious. Humans smelled of human, whatever cultural factors might come into play (Westerners had that odd dairy stink, for instance); Heavenkind always had that unwholesome note of peach, and demons smelled of—well, anything and everything, usually noxious. But this person—impossible to tell. That meant that someone had gone to some lengths to disguise their natural odor and probably their appearance as well. Badger gave a growl, just to see what the response would be. None whatsoever. That meant that his captor was not afraid of him.

Annoying.

The journey continued for a while longer. Badger occupied the time by trying to get a sense of his surroundings, and also in attempting to contact Mistress. He thought he could sense her, but only occasionally, and she was very, very far away. Back on Earth, in other words. If he were being carried deep into Hell, then he would soon lose all trace of her. Badger growled again and this time the bag was given a sharp hard thump. Badger subsided. But wait! He had stopped moving, and there were voices.

His captor was speaking, but badger did not understand the language. It wasn't Mandarin or Cantonese, or any of the tongues of Hell. He did not think it was English, although that gabbled lisping language was not one with which he was particularly familiar. He'd heard it on Mistress' television, however, and this just did not sound the same.

Someone was having a bit of an argument, though, unless badger was greatly mistaken. Then the bag was pulled abruptly open and badger's world was flooded with scent.

Cumin. Ginger. Fire. Jasmine. Shit. Frangipani.

The badger blinked, dazzled by the onrush of color that accompanied these odors. Crimson and yellow and gold and a deep rich blue; emerald and purple and ivory. Never mind the lightshow. Badger bit the nearest thing to hand and was rewarded with the taste of blood. Someone yelled and badger received a blow to the head that made the new world ring. Badger was not particularly bothered by this. He snarled. A loop was thrown around his neck and pulled tight.

"We can kill you, little demon," said a voice. "No trouble at all."

Wait, badger counseled himself. *Wait.* He knew there would be an opportunity. There always was. It was easier to see now. He was in a high, red room: crimson walls, brighter than blood, and veined with sequins. A silk hanging covered half the door and on it played multicolored embroidered birds. Somewhere, there was an eldritch parrot screech and the hanging fluttered, as if a wind had passed through the room. Outside, between open columns, the badger saw a sky the color of roses.

"Where is this place?" the badger said.

"Why…" the voice replied. A woman materialized out of the air: oiled hair, yellow eyes. Gold and citrine carried a drenching light. She raised a hand, mailed in metal lace. "You are in Hell, little demon."

The badger stared at her, coldly. "This is not the Hell that I know."

"Who said it was yours?"

蛇警探

She put him on a collar and leash, keeping nimble fingers well out of the way, and the indignity pained him more than anything else. Then, with the silken skirts of her sari whipping around her heels like gilded mist, she led him down indigo corridors and ivory, past a room in which a naked woman and two naked boys lay entwined, past another in which a woman wept alone. The woman had feathers instead of hair, vivid as a parakeet, and her arms were mottled with blood. The badger filed all this away for later: he had seen much before.

Then they were heading down a long hallway, and here badger saw that the wall was decorated with many wooden and metal plaques. Attached to each of these was a head: some human, with eyes like boiled sweets. Several were white-skinned, wearing curious round hats. Some were clearly demonic, but of forms unknown to the badger. None, however, were animal and of this, the badger approved. At the end of the hall, in front of a lacquered ornamental table, lay the skin of something that had been twice the size of a man, black-skinned, with tufts along its spine and a tusked head. It was slightly askew; badger's new captor pushed it back into place with her foot.

Next, he was taken outside under a long colonnade, heat struck him with a spicy rush and fountains played in the gardens below. Something arced and golden hissed up into the shadowed ceiling of the colonnade: a small winged snake. Below, running through ornamental stands of hibiscus, were a herd of black antelope, spotted with red. They were singing as they went, with voices like off-key dulcimers.

Beyond the gardens, he saw mountains, Himalaya-high, but their snow-swept summits were crested with palaces carved of ice. There seemed to be something beyond that, another mountain wall, high and higher yet, but he could not see it clearly. He could smell the wind, though, the snow-breath that carried with it cardamom and sherbet.

"Come along," his captor said, and tugged not-gently at the leash. She pulled him through a door at the end of the colonnade and here, all was darkness.

"I've brought him to you," his captor said, into shadows.

"Oh *good*." Another female voice, silvery as bells, and a lamp flared up.

The badger thought: *I have seen you before. I have smelled you.* Golden-eyed and tiger-striped, she still had her human face, but as it came into the circle of light cast by the lamp, he saw that it was not the same woman.

The last time badger had seen a tiger demon in her Hellish shape, it had been in his own houseboat home, in the arms of Zhu Irzh, in Chen's borrowed bed. Husband had *not* been pleased, when informed of this indiscretion. Jhai Tserai, industrialist, schemer, demon-who-could-not-be, at least under the poorly understood laws of Earth. Jhai had taken suppressants to conceal her tiger stripes, her tiger tail. Now, the badger stared. *Yes. You are the same kind, if not the same woman.*

"Oh, he's *adorable*," this person gushed. "Look at his little paws! And his little nose!" She stretched out a finger.

"I really wouldn't—" his captor began.

Moments later, badger found out what tiger flesh tasted like. Surprisingly *gamey*, but then, they were carnivores.

The tiger demon hissed and swore, clutching the stump of her severed digit. The lamp went out, the room became magic-black. Badger's ears rang with the sudden power of a spell. "That's better." Whole again, she looked down at him, flexing the renewed digit. "Do that again, you stripy piece of shit, and I'll be walking on a badger-skin rug."

FIFTEEN

Go did not know where he ran to. He dimly remembered stumbling through the garden, blundering through shrubs and bushes—his clothing was torn and full of twigs—expecting at any moment the rip and roar at his back. Then out into the street, out of the quiet suburb which had provided, through his own and Beni's folly, no sanctuary at all, and sprinting now down to the main street, not really thinking at all, just needing to get away. Sirens screamed out; he'd seen flashing lights, heading for the blazing house behind him. He remembered the swerve of a car, distant shouts. His hands were skinned; he must have fallen at some point and this, too, was a vague memory, the sudden shock of hitting warm, gritty stone, rising, running on.

Now, he was at the port, end of the line with the sea an oily blackness under the rocking lights. Everything that had been opaque before he stopped was now hyper-real: the lights, the slap and hiss of the sea, the smell of petrol and weed and rot. His heart slammed against the wall of his chest; his lungs burned.

Beni, he thought, *Beni is dead.* Lara killed him, ripped out his throat. They had known the danger of what they had brought to the world, summoned up from Hell, but somehow—despite the final, disastrous ritual and the reasoning that had led up to it—he had failed to take that danger on board. Lara, with her tiger teeth and her terrible temper, had still seemed somehow controllable. *Face it,* he thought. *You underestimated her because she's a chick.* A demon chick, true. But female and therefore not quite the threat that, he now realized, she should have been. And now she was after him. Knowing Lara, she wasn't the type to believe that revenge was best served cold. Piping hot, with a side order of chilies. Maybe poor old Beni was better off dead.

Then it occurred to him that Beni, though dead, was still around; at least, his soul was presumably intact, and where would that be now? Waiting to enter Hell, probably. He mouthed a silent apology, much good that would do Beni. Wherever he might be, his co-conspirator was no longer in a position to be of any help at all. Go was on his own. And that left the question of what the fuck he was going to do now.

He couldn't go back to the studio; Lara might be waiting. The house, with his possessions, would be a charred, flooded ruin by now. He had very little idea of the penalties involved in conjuring, then banishing, demons in this part of the world. Did foreign demons count? If a forensic team investigated the house, they were likely to find the mortal remains of Beni. Would they think Go had killed him? Go was suddenly thinking very coldly and clearly, shock draining out of his numbed brain. Lara was after him. The police might well be, too. What it boiled down to was: Who was he most afraid of?

Well, that was easy. An hour later, Pauleng Go walked into the station house of Harbor Precinct and turned himself in.

蛇警探

The person he needed to speak to, so the desk clerk informed him, was one Detective Inspector Chen.

"But he's not here at the moment," she said. "He's out on a case. I'm afraid you'll have to wait."

"Can you put me in a cell?" Go asked, hating the note of desperation in his voice. The clerk stared at him.

"Whatever for?"

"Someone's after me. Someone really dangerous."

The clerk frowned. "You said this individual is of supernatural origins."

"Yes. Indian supernatural origins. And very, very angry."

"Does he know you've come here?"

"*She,* and I certainly didn't tell her. But she might be able to find me. I've no idea, to be honest. I don't know what her capabilities might be."

"I can put out a call on her. Do you have a name?"

Thank God she was taking him seriously, at least. Somehow, he'd expected ridicule, disbelief. "Yes." He paused. An ensuing conversation unrolled, movielike, in front of his inner eye. There were some advantages to being a scriptwriter, it seemed:

"*Her name's Lara Chowdijharee.*"

"*Your pursuer has the same name as a film star?*"

"*No, my pursuer* is *a film star.*"

"*I thought you said she was a demon.*"

"*She is. We summoned her up from Hell and turned her into a star.*"

The clerk's eyebrows rose so far that they nearly floated off the top of her head. "*Lara Chowdijharee—the movie star—is a demon. And she's after you, you say? Was instrumental in burning down your house? Tore her agent's throat out with her teeth?" Stealthily, under the desk from a different camera angle, Go watched the desk clerk's hand move toward a panic button, the one reserved for visiting lunatics.*

Back in the real world, Go said, "Uh. I mean, no. She said her name was Cherry. But I don't think it was her real one."

The desk clerk nodded. "All right. I understand what you're telling me and we do take this kind of threat very seriously, you know. I won't put you in a cell, because we might need it later on, but what I will do is put you in the interrogation room. It has no windows and the door can be locked from the inside. Would you like some tea?"

With heartfelt gratitude, Go replied that he would.

SIXTEEN

When Chen went back outside to await the arrival of the forensic team, he found Inari sitting on a low wall near the car in the company of No Ro Shi.

"What *happened?*"

No Ro Shi looked at him. "Could I have a word with you in private, Comrade?"

With a sinking heart, Chen told him that he could.

"Your wife's a demon."

"I'd noticed."

"Does Captain Sung know?"

That was a rather more conciliatory statement than he might have expected from the demon-hunter. Perhaps No Ro Shi had mellowed.

"If he does, I haven't told him. Look—"

No Ro Shi sighed. "This makes things very awkward. I respect you, Chen. Your wife, despite her origins, seems to be a decent woman."

He *had* mellowed.

"I'll tell him, unless you plan to. Now, can you tell me why she isn't in the car where I left her? What are you doing here?"

"A while ago, this would have been unthinkable," No Ro Shi said, as if no question had been asked of him. "But now, things have changed, in this city, in China. Your partner isn't human. Where is Zhu Irzh, by the way?"

"That's the problem." Chen explained. No Ro Shi stared at him. "We have two officers—effectively—missing. And both are demonic.

"Both of them can be trusted," Chen added, rather more sharply than he intended. "And both were investigating the same case." He told the demon-hunter what he and Ma had discovered in the basement of the warehouse. "The forensic team is on their way. Meanwhile, I've ordered a search of the area. Now, about Inari."

It was his turn to listen to an explanation.

"There was a demon shaman, with a luring rattle. He was trying to snare her. From the look of things, he was succeeding."

"Even though Inari is, as you helpfully point out, herself demonic?"

"Shamans from Hell wield a great deal of power," No Ro Shi said. "It does not surprise me that he was able to gain a hold over her, especially as she was not expecting it."

Chen sighed. "I have you to thank for saving her, then. I'm afraid this kind of thing is not all that unusual. Inari has—family—in Hell. The marriage was not popular."

"I understand," No Ro Shi said, with more sympathy than Chen might have anticipated. At this point, Ma came panting up, looking troubled.

"What's happening?" Chen said. His gaze kept drifting toward Inari: he wanted to go to her, but duty kept him where he was.

"Three drug dealers, a pimp, and some smuggled goods," Ma informed him. "But no sign of Zhu Irzh or your furry friend."

"All right," Chen said. "Keep looking. I'm going to be occupied with the forensic team for a while anyway. If we don't find any trace of them in a couple of hours, take your officers back to the station."

When Ma had gone, No Ro Shi said, "You mentioned your in-laws. Is there any other reason why a demon might come after you or your wife?"

"Not that I can think of," Chen lied, and felt a twinge of conscience at it. A police inspector might not attract all that much attention, even if he did liaise between the three worlds. But the Emissary of the Celestial Court of Heaven was another matter entirely.

蛇警探

It was close to dawn, with a gray veiled shimmer over the port, by the time that Chen, Inari, and No Ro Shi got back to the precinct. There had been no sign of Zhu Irzh or the badger, and the forensic unit was still investigating the contents of the cellar. Chen thought that they would be there for some time. The captain had not yet arrived for work, so Chen was at least spared the discomfiting task of informing him about Inari; he was not certain how much of an issue this would prove to be. He installed Inari in the waiting room with a cup of tea, which she accepted gratefully. She had not said much since her ordeal at the hands of the shaman, and Chen was not sure why this might be: weariness, the aftermath of a magical attack, shame? He could not tell and this worried him.

"Are you sure you'll be all right here for a bit?" he asked, for the third time.

Inari said, "Yes. I have my tea. Thank you." Her face was very pale, even granted that her complexion was usually that of rice flour. But there was no color at all in her cheeks, and her eyes, behind the dark glasses, looked strained. Chen squeezed her hand.

"I'll try not to be too long."

It had occurred to him to send her home, but they could not spare the personpower at the moment and the badger was missing. She had already been subject to some kind of assault and Chen felt as though his worst fears were being realized: a nagging instinct told him that this whole affair was concerned with Mhara's recent offer, and if hostile forces—who?—were trying to attack Chen, they might well choose to do so through Inari. He left her sitting in the waiting room and his heart felt as heavy as lead.

He had barely reached his desk when a call came through from the duty clerk.

"Detective? There's someone waiting to see you. He came in last night and, well, he's got a problem."

"He and a thousand others," Chen said. "What kind of problem?"

"He says a tiger demon is after him."

"A tiger demon?" Oh gods. Jhai Tserai. If someone wanted to strike at Jhai, an earlier line of reasoning asserted itself, they might well do so through those close to her, too. He was not sure how much of a secret Jhai's nature was at the moment: she had ruthlessly suppressed both nature and information regarding it, but there were a growing number of people who knew. Perhaps this person was one of them?

"His name's Pauleng Go," the clerk said. "He's in the interrogation room."

"Why? Have we booked him? Oh," Chen said, realizing. "Security, of course. I'll have a word with him."

Maybe it wasn't anything to do with Jhai. Chen tapped his rosary, for luck. Maybe this individual was simply nuts. It happened. It would be nice to have an ordinary lunatic to deal with, for a change.

Pauleng Go's lunacy was not, however, obvious, apart from the fact that he was barefoot in winter. Coming into the interrogation room, Chen saw a slight, rather fey young man, the sort whom women would probably find appealing, although it was difficult for him to tell. Go had an alarmed air rather like a nervous horse, a sort of eye-rolling, about-to-bolt quality. But his clothes were clearly designer gear, even to Chen's unsartorial eye.

"Detective Chen?" A reasonably cultured voice.

"That's me. Mr Go, I believe? And you're having problems with a tiger demon."

"Let me start at the beginning," Pauleng Go said.

"Go ahead." He had the feeling that this might take some time.

Pauleng Go certainly knew how to tell a good, concise story, which Chen supposed to be an attribute that came in handy if one were a scriptwriter. His tale was unlikely, and yet to Chen's experienced ear, it had the ring of truth. He had never seen one of Lara Chowdijharee's films, but for a time her face had been plastered over every billboard and hoarding in the city and he thought he remembered seeing her on some late-night chat show or other. A tiger demon? Well, one of the city's premier industrialists was, so why not a movie star? And it even had a warped kind of logic: the movies required glamour, and tiger demons certainly had that. Besides, it would be a simple matter to check Pauleng Go's identity.

"Do you have a background in magic, Mr Go?"

"No. Well, yes. In a manner of speaking. My father was a professional exorcist. I grew up in Kuala Lumpur and then we moved to Delhi when I was in my teens. I saw a lot of shit. But I didn't really have the gift, you know? And I wanted to be a writer, so I told the old man that I wasn't prepared to follow him. We were estranged for a while but he's cool with it now. I picked up enough to be able to do a basic summoning. And my friend—the guy who Lara killed, Beni—he and I had a great idea for a film, but it needed a really great leading lady."

"Surely there are scores of young actresses just waiting for their big break?"

"We needed more than that. Certain qualities, you know?"

Chen was not sure that he did, but Go seemed to have some kind of artistic principle in mind: he was making hand gestures which seemed too abstract to be a representation of the female form. "One night, we'd been drinking, and Beni and I thought it would be a cool idea to summon up a demon. Dad had to do it in Delhi—I saw a tiger demon once, only for a few seconds, but man! Impressive."

"They are," Chen agreed, thinking of Jhai. "And you were successful."

"Yeah, until she started freaking out on us. Making demands, threats…"

"I can imagine," Chen said. Unfortunately, he thought he could.

"So we decided to get rid of her… send her back to hell. We actually summoned her up but something went wrong—I told you, I'm not that experienced. I know it was stupid."

"Also," Chen said quietly, thinking of Inari in the waiting room, cradling her cup of tea in both wan hands, "also somewhat unfair. Demons aren't ciphers. It's not a video game."

Go looked at him and he could see that the young man already knew. "I know. She had every right to be pissed off. I can't blame her for what she did, but I need help now."

"We'll do what we can," Chen said.

Go's head went up and, for a moment, Chen thought that the young man's spirits had revived. Then he saw that the look in Go's eyes was one of fear.

"Shit," Go whispered. There were footsteps coming along the passage. "*Lara.*" The name was a breath. Go's face was ashen. "I can—I can smell her."

"Stay there," Chen commanded, unnecessarily, and rushed for the door, which was unlocked. But he was too late. The door swung open and a woman stepped inside.

"Hello, Detective," said Jhai Tserai.

SEVENTEEN

Seijin left the temple of the Emperor of Heaven shortly before nightfall and decided not to return to Shadow Pavilion. Hospitality at the temple had been offered, of course, but Seijin had declined. The Dowager Empress had already departed for her Celestial home and Seijin did not fancy the prospect of a night in a temple to a dead, failed god, surrounded by nervous servants. But there were temples and temples. Singapore Three was not all that distant; there was certain to be lodging there. Besides, male self had come up with an idea.

Seijin chose to travel swiftly, rather than merely to step between the airs. Standing still, female self brought the world to them, wrapping woodland, folding the small trickle of a river. Seijin stood still while the golden leaves whipped by, tasted water on a breath, watched as the lights of the city burned closer.

There. It was lit by its own light, to Seijin's otherworldly vision, standing on a slight rise before the roar and tumult of the city. Such a small place, humble, unassuming. It was clear why the Dowager Empress held such objections. Seijin, on the other hand, rather admired this approach; it was certainly to be respected. But a contract was a contract, after all, and Seijin permitted only the occasional sensation of personal sentiments.

Shortly before the temple came within stepping distance, female self gave Seijin an anxious nudge and, with a nod, Seijin acquiesced. A woman stepped from the air, middle-aged, hard-faced, and weary. She'd had hopes, once, of an education and children, but prostitution and drugs had taken care of all that long ago. She'd managed to go straight, however, and she had an offering, in thanks: a small bunch of golden leaves. Seijin, all selves, retreated a short way behind her eyes and watched as the temple drew close.

Very modest, in fact, and recently restored. Interesting.

54

A knock on the door—tentative, as if unsure of admission, although there was a lamp burning in the window of what was evidently the main hall. It was a moment before the door opened and Seijin braced a little, reaffirming the disguise. It was to be hoped that this would not be too easy; there was no satisfaction in that.

"Good evening?" Not the new Emperor, of course—but who knew? He seemed the type who might very well answer his own front door. Instead, a young woman stood there, dressed in a monk's gray tunic and loose white trousers.

Why, my dear, Seijin thought. You're dead. Even more interesting.

She was not an obvious ghost; Seijin wondered whether a human would even be able to tell. A slight transparency about the face was the giveaway, but she seemed solid enough in the world, able to open doors, for a start.

"Hello," Seijin stammered, looking down. "I brought a gift—that is to say, I have an offering, I wanted to give thanks—"

"Of course." Very professional, but they must get all sorts here. "Would you like to come in? The temple is open and you can stay as long as you need to. If you would like me to pray with you, please ask."

"Thank you," Seijin whispered. "You're very kind."

Heaven hit as soon as Seijin walked through the door. It had not been like this in the temple of the former Emperor and, somehow, he did not think that place had ever possessed this luminous quality—not the overcontrolled atmosphere of Heaven as it currently was, which made it such an irksome place to be, but a wild, sweet, strong sense, like mountain water.

Well, well, Seijin thought. You really are Emperor, aren't you? A strange sensation, stealing over the mind and the heart, something not felt for many years, that Seijin, stepping into the main hall of the temple with its lit lamp and single spray of orchids, was astounded to recognize as awe.

I have stood in the multitudinous presence of deity, and been merely bored.

And with that, was not a small degree of fear.

But it soon became apparent that fear was neither an appropriate emotion, nor—given Seijin's disguise—a useless one. With female self nervously prompting, Seijin sank to knees on the polished wooden boards before the little shrine, head bowed.

"Please—madam, would you pray with me?"

"Of course," the spectral priestess said. "And call me Robin."

It seemed that Robin was alone in the building, but Seijin felt that the ability to tell for certain had been lost. Confidence had fled on stepping into the temple and that in itself was exciting, if a worry. Impossible to remember how long it had been since a target had appeared who was worth all that training, all that pain. Perhaps, Seijin now reflected behind borrowed eyes, only a god would ever have done.

A stolen glance at Robin revealed the priestess kneeling trustingly beside Seijin, head bowed. Of course, with all that power at her disposal, she would have little reason to fear anything mortal, and besides, she was already dead. She must have been given special dispensation to remain here on Earth and Seijin marveled at the work that had been done; she was so little distance from fully human. It was only when one reached out, listened for breath or the tick of the heart and found absence, that one realized the truth of her nature.

And there was no way of knowing how much, in turn, the dead priestess might be able to detect. Seijin cast concerns deeper, burying them in the inner recesses of the mind, the gaps between male and female self so deep that they could have lain in the caverns underneath Shadow Pavilion, and concentrated upon prayer.

EIGHTEEN

There were eight of them and they were sisters. Badger knew this because they all had the same smell, and he thought they looked similar, but that was always difficult to tell. Apart from Mistress, Husband, and a handful of others, badger found humanoid beings hard to tell apart. They stood in the middle of the echoing hall, the translucent crimson draperies billowing between the columns, drifting on the cardamom wind. Slowly, flames emerged from the air, floating amongst the draperies and burning with a soft, clear fire.

One of the demons threw back her head and gave a snarling cry. The women's garments sank to the floor, melting into pools of the same soft fire, and vanishing. The badger watched, impassive. Slowly, not keeping pace with one another, the women began to change: stripes appearing across thighs and haunches, faces elongating into wide-whiskered muzzles. Only the eyes remained the same, golden and fierce, mirroring fire.

It would not be wise, badger thought, to make a run for it now. He thought of the antelope glimpsed in the garden below: courtiers, or dinner? Wisest to keep silent and still, wisest to wait. And see, something new was happening.

He came out of the air, gradually solidifying just as the flames had done, and at first, the badger thought he was a flame. Scarlet and gold, with a single black thread running through it all, the colors of hibiscus, of roses, of sunset. Then all these colors merged, resolving into a slender man in a fire-colored tunic and trousers, with gilt bells around one ankle, a long column of black hair, and eyes that were also the shade of night, with a golden circlet around each iris, like an eclipse.

He was smiling.

"Girls, girls, there's really *no* need—and who is *this?*" The eclipse-eyes turned to the badger. There was a sudden, crushing weight, as though the sun had fallen. Ah, the badger thought, with chagrin. Not just a demon, then. A little bit more than that.

"Prince Agni, this is one of the things that was taken through. A creature of earth, from China, but not of Earth." The voice, emanating from a tigress' throat, was entirely human, with no trace of a growl. "From their Hell, you see."

"But this is a beast," the tiger prince said. He held out a faintly striped hand and the badger cowered back at the heat that blasted from it. No chance of a quick bite here, then. "I was expecting something in the form of a man." A soft voice, but something in it spoke to the badger of fire and it seemed that the tigresses recognized this also, for there was the shuffling and rustling of discomfited cats.

"That person, also, was taken, do not worry, our hireling did not fail us."

"Ah, I see. My apologies, ladies. I should have made more certain of my facts." But the tigresses said nothing, nor would they have done so, badger realized, even if they had been chastised. There was only one power in this room. "Where is he?"

"In the dungeon, Lord Prince."

"Good. I'll pay him a visit a little later."

Badger's ears remained pricked throughout this conversation: someone else had been taken, then. Who? Zhu Irzh? He had been closest to the location when the badger had been snatched. "As for the animal—keep it leashed. Perhaps we might hunt it a little later; I understand they are carnivores." He turned back to the badger. "What do you say, creature of earth? Can you hunt more than beetles?"

"I have hunted men," the badger replied.

An elegant eyebrow rose. "Have you, now? Then perhaps you will have the chance to do so again." A sharper glance. "This is not your only aspect, is it?"

"No." Badger was what he was, no point in denying it. But it was slightly embarrassing, all the same.

"Perhaps you would like to change for us? Come, ladies, keep our guest company."

Eight tiger-skin rugs decorated the floor and pooled into flame, each with a naked girl arising from it.

"Oh, all right then," the badger growled. Moments later, a battered iron teakettle sat rocking on the marble floor. At least, the badger reflected sullenly, his hearing was not quite so keen in this particular form. It cut down the tinkling laughter and cries of "How *sweet!*" But only by a little.

The thing about old teakettles, even ones with a collar and leash, is that people forget they are there. Badger was carried with some ceremony, and not a little caution, on a cushion into an adjoining room where the tea setting was kept, and placed amongst cups of porcelain and jade. The end of the chain was tied tightly to an iron ring set into the wall.

"There." The tigress who had carried him in bent down to speak to him. "I don't know what you can do in this form. Spit, maybe? We'll have to put you on the stove a little later and see what happens to you then. But for now, this will be your place."

Badger was used to being a teakettle for long periods. It was restful, though he could have done without the collar. The demon went away after that and badger passed into what counted as sleep, but he woke as soon as he heard voices, coming from just outside the kitchen annex. The voices were hushed and conspiratorial, and those sorts of conversations were always worth listening to.

"Does he know where she is?"

"He trusts me to keep him informed."

"And have you?"

"Of course not. Don't be stupid. You know perfectly well what we agreed to do. But there's a problem. She nearly came back."

"*What?* When?" There was real panic in the voice.

"Last night. You were with Agni, otherwise you'd have noticed."

"Yes, it was my turn. At least, I swapped with Urushi because she had a headache and—"

"Aruth, don't go *on,* that doesn't matter. Anyway, we were all in the main hall and suddenly she was almost here, you could see her. Just her outline, but I thought the little bitch was going to manifest completely. Urushi dropped a glass."

"But what does it mean? Has she decided to come home?"

"You really are quite *dim* sometimes, Aruth. You know perfectly well that we took steps to stop that happening and the only person who could have countermanded that is Agni. And Agni doesn't know. No, what it means is that the humans who took her have got tired of her and are trying to send her back. They nearly succeeded, even despite our measures. And that worries me."

"If she *does* come home—"

"She won't be pleased. More to the point, neither will Agni."

"We should never have done it." This voice—younger, more timid (for a tigress)—had a definite prey-on-the-run quality, to badger's ears. "If Agni finds out—"

"Yes. Well. We're just going to have to make sure that doesn't happen." There was a note in *this* voice, badger mused, that did not sound at all like prey, more than a hint of a growl.

Silence, a meditative kind of pause, and then footsteps, retreating. *Interesting,* badger thought. It wasn't the first time he'd been able to use overheard information to his own advantage. And somehow, he did not think it would be the last.

NINETEEN

"Sorry," Go stammered. "I—must have freaked out there for a minute."

Jhai Tserai looked at him curiously. "What's he talking about? Who are you?" Then she smiled. Not many people could resist Jhai's smile, Chen thought, even when they knew she was trying to pull something. That demon-glamour… It didn't hurt that Jhai was beautiful, and (currently) wearing a silk jacket of silver-shot purple that outlined a modest, but appealing, cleavage.

Go was clearly smitten, even after a rough night. Chen wondered whether he would, on reflection, recognize Jhai for what she was: he must be one of the few people in the city to have wittingly encountered a tiger demon before, and Go might be reckless, but he wasn't entirely stupid. "My name's Pauleng Go," the young man said. "I write for the movies."

"Really? Which ones?"

Go named a few.

"Oh, I *loved* the first one. I thought it had a really interesting undercurrent of post-modernism and combined with the background of—"

"Maybe," Chen said mildly, "we could save the film reviews until later? We have a bit of a problem here, Jhai."

"Sorry, Detective. You must be wondering what the hell I'm doing here at this hour of the morning."

"Yes, since you ask."

"I just got back from Beijing; I was going to pick up Zhu Irzh. He said he was coming off shift first thing."

Chen sighed. "Mr Go, would you excuse us for a moment?" He ushered Jhai through the door, then went on, "He would have been, but he's gone missing."

"What?"

Chen explained.

61

"Oh, *great*," Jhai said. "I know this is trivial, but I wanted him to come and look at wedding dresses with me."

Wherever Zhu Irzh might be, Chen thought, he might be considered to have got off lightly.

"Zhu Irzh isn't the only one to go astray. Inari's badger's AWOL as well—the two are almost certainly connected."

"Do you think this is anything to do with me?" Jhai asked.

Jhai's habit of assuming that the world revolved around her was less arrogance than pragmatism: it frequently did. "It's a distinct possibility," Chen said. "Ever since your engagement was announced, Zhu Irzh's public profile has been prominent. Frankly, I wouldn't rule out kidnapping."

At least she wasn't the hysterical type. Jhai's eyes narrowed in an expression that Chen had come to know well, and she caught her bottom lip between her teeth.

"I can't just go home and sit there, after this. Is there anything I can do? Miss Qi's not here, unfortunately—visiting family back in Heaven."

A pity, Chen thought. Jhai's Celestial bodyguard would have come in handy right now.

"I doubt you'd just sit, Jhai. You have a company to run, after all. But put your own security on it—it can't hurt. We're overstretched."

"All right. But I don't want to get under your feet, Chen."

Oddly enough, Chen thought he could trust her not to. He said so. Then he added, "Could you come in here a moment? I don't want—" he gestured toward the interrogation room.

"Sure." Chen led her into one of the other empty rooms.

"That young man in there. I wasn't interrogating him, as such. He's in there to keep him safe. He says there's a tiger demon after him."

He had the pleasure of seeing Jhai look genuinely startled.

"Two shocks in five minutes, Chen. I don't know how you manage to stay so calm."

"Inside, I'm like Munch's *Scream*. Get ready for another one. That film you liked so much? This girl starred in it."

"You're joking. Lara Chowdijharee's a tigress? I *knew* there was a reason I identified with the protagonist."

"The thing is," Chen said, "do you actually know her?"

"The surname's assumed, obviously. But—yeah, I do. Didn't recognize her on film, though—I've only ever met her in her more demonic aspect, and on screen and under make-up… This lot are all my distant cousins, you see. Mother left Hell—our Hell—under a bit of a cloud. Fell in love with someone. A young lady. A very rich young lady, whose father owned a small pharmaceutical corporation, among other things. Had me by artificial means. Grand-dad, if one can call him that, died, and one of the things that got passed over to Mother was the pharmaceutical side of things—that's where Paugeng comes from."

"And of course your mother never returned to Hell."

"No reason to. Besides, our side of the family comes from Kerala—there's a long history of matriarchy in the region. Go-ahead women are nothing new there, but in other bits of India and Hell, things are rather more backward. Mother never really took to Hell. Thinks it's a bit—well, a bit *Bollywood*, I suppose."

"But this demon—Lara—she's a relation?"

"A cousin. She's one of nine sisters who live in a palace called the Hunting Lodge. It's in a region of Hell ruled by my cousin—another cousin—called Agni, who's really more of a demigod than a demon. Father was a fire deity. Great combination genetically, with all that tiger blood. Nice enough bloke, actually. Bit smarmy. He's been up here a couple of times. Can't say the same for Lara, which is probably why she's never looked me up."

"You don't get along?"

"I'm okay with strong women," Jhai said. "Which may surprise you. I respect them. But Lara's just a bitch and she's also really quite thick."

"Oh dear," Chen said, inadequately. "Go thinks she's actually unstable."

"It wouldn't surprise me. But all of them are a bit nuts. Agni's the sanest of them and even he's had his moments. What's Lara *doing* here?"

Jhai wouldn't be winning any Least Psychotic awards any time soon, Chen thought, but he kept that to himself.

"Go summoned her up," he explained. "Thought it was a good idea."

"Jesus."

"He's now realized the error of his ways, I think. Tried to send her back where she came from and it didn't work—he admits he's no expert in magic. She killed his business partner and burned his house down."

"Yeah, that sounds like Lara. What are you going to do about this, Chen? Try and find her, or what?"

"I have rather a lot on my plate," Chen said. "I know this is a substantial favor, but I was wondering if you could take charge of Mr Go? At least keep him safe."

"Don't take this the wrong way," Jhai remarked, "but Paugeng's got quite a number of secure units. He'll be safe enough with us and even if Lara shows up, I might be able to talk her out of doing anything too violent. I wouldn't count on it, though. But you can't keep him here. She comes from the Hunting Lodge, remember? There's a reason for that name. Good sense of smell, that side of the family. And if she shows up here and there's resistance, she's likely to do a lot of collateral damage. Paugeng's safer."

"Thank you," Chen said. "I'll leave it up to you whether or not you divulge the family relationship."

"Hmm," Jhai replied. "Best not. He seems freaked out enough already."

Any questions Chen might have had as to whether Go recognized Jhai for what she was, even subliminally, seemed irrelevant. Go was clearly delighted to be in Jhai's company, pathetically grateful for such a powerful champion, and offered as much help as he could to Chen in tracking Lara down.

"We're going to have to find her," Chen said in an undertone to Jhai as she led Go out of the building. "I can't guarantee she'll survive it."

"I should have more family loyalty," Jhai said, "but I won't blame you if you have to put her down."

"It'll be a SWAT unit, not a vet!"

"You know what I mean. Try and trank her—I'll send you some stuff, if you want. It's a difficult one, Chen. If we catch her and send her back dead, she'll be really pissed off. But so will the family. I know dead isn't really dead in our case, but it's the principal of the thing. Whereas if she's sent back alive, at least they can't get all uppity on that score."

"We'll do our best," Chen said. "But we'll have to make sure she stays where she's supposed to be."

"There are extradition agreements for that sort of thing." Jhai looked doubtful. "Don't always work, though."

And on that less than reassuring note, Chen had to be content.

TWENTY

Next morning, with much giggling, they made tea with the badger. He endured this, sensing that to complain would generate even more entertainment. Besides, it was a function of his non-animate aspect and he'd learned to get used to it over the years. Eventually, however, tea was poured and badger immediately reverted to his animal aspect. He took care to shake himself vigorously, ensuring that drops of boiling water flew over the tiger demons. There were squeals.

"Ow!"

"My *dress!*"

Badger showed teeth and was hauled across the room by his leash and chained to the wall.

"Hunting day today," one of the women said. Badger thought it was one of the girls who had been engaged in so interesting a conversation the day before. "You'll like that."

Badger merely grunted, but then curiosity won.

"What is to be hunted?"

The tigresses looked smug. "You'll see, you'll see," they chanted in unison.

"We ought to get ready," one of the women said. "It's nearly time to go down."

They left badger alone in a flurry of silks, only to reappear a short time later wearing leather harnesses and not a great deal else. No weapons, but then, of course, they would not need them, any more than badger needed more than his own sharp teeth. Their mood, a barely controlled, feral viciousness, was infectious: badger grew restless on the end of the lead and was glad when he was unchained and taken downstairs. The tigresses took him back through the long gallery, chattering as they went, but when they reached the end of the colonnade that looked out across the gardens, they took a long flight of steps, leading down.

Soon, badger was standing on earth once more, even if it was not the soil of his own home. He snuffled it: it was of a strange texture, more like spice than earth, and strongly smelling. It was a rich cinnamon brown. This part of the garden was heavily manicured: planted with rhododendron and azalea, erupting into a profusion of scentless blossom in a variety of reds and golds. Overhead, the sunless sky burned blue and the heat struck the badger like a blow, even accustomed as he was to the climate of his own Hell and the city besides.

The women took a narrow path between the bushes that led onto a wide sward of grass. Here, were more people: demons with curling moustaches and hot scarlet eyes beneath intricate turbans; a bevy of girls with blue skins and small, polished tusks tipped with gold; a glowering woman the color of polished bronze, wearing a quiver of glittering arrows between her quadruple shoulder-blades.

Toward the back of the crowd, the badger spotted Prince Agni, dressed all in gold and mounted on an animal that badger initially took to be a horse, but which was covered in little black scales. It had clawed feet and an arrowed tail and reminded badger of some of the beasts he had seen in stables back home. Maybe they'd imported it, or perhaps these things were commonplace. As badger watched, it champed at its bit, displaying impressive teeth.

"Guests!" Agni called, his voice carrying easily through the throng. Everyone immediately fell silent, although the four-armed woman scowled even harder. "Thank you all for honoring us today with your presence. We have many delights for you before the main hunt; I invite you all to gather at the end of the terrace, where we have a number of spectacles for you."

The crowd drifted to a marble expanse, dotted with urns. As badger was pulled past, a small muffled groan came out of one of the urns, intriguing badger. Was someone in there? But he had no time to investigate. Everyone was lining up for the first entertainment.

This turned out to be the four-armed woman. She held two bows, one in each set of hands. A flock of bright birds, red as blood, was released from a cage by a distant servant. The birds rocketed up into the sky and were brought down, twitching, by a storm of arrows. Everyone applauded, politely, and the four-armed woman gave a stiff bow. Then the performance was repeated, with the archer's back toward the flock. Maybe she had four eyes as well, badger thought. This sort of thing did not greatly interest him, although the birds might be worth trying. They looked plump.

After this, the tigress who held the badger's lead gave him a nudge with her toe. "It's your turn."

"What?"

"And now," Agni said, "a demon from a neighboring Hell, all the way from China, to be pitted against our dogs!"

Badger had automatically assumed that he was to be the hunter. It did not appear that this was to be the case.

He was shoved down the steps and his lead jerked away. Badger turned, snarling, but the tigress was already bounding back up the steps. Behind him, came a blood-curdling yell.

Four dogs, if one could call them that, were leaping across the grass. They were huge, scaled like the horse-beast, with curling teeth and glowing eyes. Their sides were pitted with scars, presumably from earlier encounters. Above their growls, badger heard a sound, a very small, swiftly muted sound, from the terrace above. He turned his head a fraction, just to see. Above him on the terrace, wearing a black linen shirt and trousers, his wrists bound in front of him and shackles on his bare ankles, stood Zhu Irzh.

TWENTY-ONE

There was a moment of silence, then an uproar, just as Mhara had expected there to be. Inwardly, he sighed. His father had held all the prerogatives of Celestial Emperor, and one of these was the Command of Belief: the power assumed on coronation which meant that if the Emperor believed something to be right, then every other denizen of Heaven believed it also, with the exception of the Emperor's own immediate bloodline.

It was a power that Mhara had declined to assume. He did not think that Heaven had quite accepted this as yet.

One would think they'd be grateful to have been released from this epistemic shackle. But Mhara knew, only too well, that people don't necessarily want freedom of thought. What they wanted was certainty, and maybe this had been one of the delights of Heaven: you knew what to think, you did not have to worry or fret, you could bask in the unreflective surety that the Emperor conveyed upon you. But now, freed by an unprecedented degree of humility on the part of the new ruler, you were prey to all the worries and difficulties of an independent mind.

One could almost feel sorry for them. Almost. But it wasn't a luxury Mhara was prepared to grant. Thinking about this that morning, as he stood gazing out over the Celestial City, Mhara gave a small, ironic smile. By imposing an intellectual democracy on Heaven, it might very well be that his views were as dictatorial as any that had been held by his father.

Then, still wearing that irony draped about him like a cloak, Mhara had gone into the Great Hall of the Imperial Palace and informed his subjects that they could now think as they pleased. He'd been right: they didn't like it. The outcry had lasted for several minutes, while Mhara waited. When he did not respond, the courtiers fell silent, one by one.

"This is not the way things were done," Mhara said, speaking mildly. "My father ruled Heaven as his ancestors did before him; he followed a tradition which has held sway here for millennia, since even the very early days when we were nothing more than a small collection of tribal gods. But things change. Things move on."

"Emperor, may I speak?" That was one of the most senior courtiers, a man named Po Shu. In an ordinary environment, Mhara would have termed him close to the previous Emperor: with the thought-control issue, that relationship was in reality impossible to assess.

"Of course. And please say what you think." He did not hold out any great hopes of directness. With the thought-ban gone, other controls might simply emerge to take its place: self-censorship, on the basis of currying favor and an eagerness to please.

Po Shu said, "With the utmost respect for your august views—" This kind of remark went on for a little time and Mhara waited patiently. It would not be possible to rush them. Finally, Po Shu got to the point. "You are indeed correct when you say, with such perceptiveness, that things are subject to change. But this is Heaven, where matters remain eternal."

"I bow to your wisdom," Mhara said. "But I might remind you that things have in fact changed, over the decades. Slowly, perhaps, and in a manner that is pleasing to all—the designing of a new pagoda, maybe, or an ornamental garden. And I have already mentioned our origins as tribal gods and lordlings: we ourselves—our nature and our relationship to humankind—have changed a great deal since then. You will also be aware that my father, who may have seemed so conservative in comparison to myself, was on the point of introducing a huge change to Heaven: sealing it away from Earth. Moreover, he took you to war and that can hardly be regarded as maintaining the status quo. I'm afraid that the changes to which I am referring will be as radical, but hopefully less destructive."

"Radical, Emperor?" Poor Po Shu looked like a man who had accidentally swallowed a beetle.

"Radical," Mhara repeated, and let the distasteful concept sink in for a moment before continuing: "You will doubtless all be wondering what form such proposed changes will take."

They looked quite terrified. Mhara went on, "What is the essence of our relationship to the human world?"

"Compassion?" someone ventured after a moment.

"Sanctuary, after the spirit's travails upon Earth?"

"Love?"

Just as he'd thought, they had forgotten.

"More than all those things," Mhara said, "it is service. And it is the role of service that I plan to reintroduce."

Still raw terror, but some of them were also looking intrigued and Mhara felt a small surge of hope. They had been left in the comfort of unreflectiveness for too long, these benign spirits, these small gods. His father had done them no favors, but now, with good fortune, they might remember who they were and what they were for. "Some of you," Mhara explained, "will be going to Earth, to assist in environmental programs and disaster relief. Our jurisdiction is not beyond China, but you may yet accomplish a great deal. *And* you will meet with opposition. Hell will always interfere: they bear us no small degree of justifiable resentment over our part in my father's war. You will encounter resistance from humans, too. People have agendas and vested interests and they will prove reluctant to give those up, even if it is pointed out to them that a reward will be waiting in the afterlife. It will not be easy."

He studied them, noting who looked shocked, who appeared angry, and who might be resentful. It was not only humans who had vested interests. Only a few—but still a disappointing number, in fact, given what Heaven was supposed to be. But there were also those who looked excited, rising to an unanticipated challenge. There was even one, a local water spirit from the look of her, who said, "We should have been doing this before, shouldn't we?"

"Yes, you should. But you were not encouraged and my father's rule was dictatorial."

"I should like to go to Earth," the water spirit said. "My river has gone; it disappeared when they dammed the Yangtze. I should like to see what I could do about flooding, rather than sitting up here watching carp frolic in ponds."

"Very good," Mhara said. He did not think she had said this simply to please him. "All of you, please begin to think about what you might achieve, how you might help." He rose from the throne. "I look forward to your responses. We will reconvene tomorrow at the same hour."

He waved away offers to escort him to the upper rooms and left by a side door. As he stepped through the door, however, there was a sudden rustle of movement. But when he entered the passage, there was no one there. Frowning, Mhara walked quickly and quietly to the end of the passage and listened. Someone was walking away, almost at a run; he could hear the hissing of fabric against the floor. Someone wearing a robe—or skirts? He inhaled cautiously. Peach blossom, the ubiquitous scent of Heaven, but stronger and more pungent than the usual faint odor, with subtle undernotes of bergamot and jasmine. He recognized the perfume; it had been made specially. It belonged to the Dowager Empress.

TWENTY-TWO

Life was weird, reflected Pauleng Go. One moment your house had been reduced to a smoldering ruin and you'd been forced to run for your life, pursued by a hysterical demon bent on revenge, and the next, you were reclining on a chair overlooking the harbor, with an iced tea, and a beautiful woman pottering about in the next room. He still found it difficult to believe that Jhai Tserai had taken him on board. He knew who she was, naturally—it was a real blast to find out she was a fan—and he'd heard some pretty odd stories about her, including one that she was herself engaged to a demon. She'd mentioned that in the car, sitting in the back with him while the chauffeur steered the Mercedes expertly through the city traffic.

"Yes, my fiancé's from Hell." Her dark eyes had dared him to make any cracks about that and Go, mindful of his position and his gratitude, had refrained. "He's a nice guy, though. He's a vice cop here in Singapore Three."

"How do you meet someone like that?" Go had ventured to ask.

"Oh," Jhai had said vaguely. "Through work."

Go preferred not to take that line of enquiry any further—vice cop, eh?—but then Jhai said, "He's not around at the moment. He's off on a case."

"So when's the wedding?"

"Next spring. You can imagine what my schedule's like."

"It would make a great movie," Go remarked before he could stop himself. "Top industrialist meets demon, falls in love."

Jhai looked a little startled, then she laughed. "Yeah, I suppose it would. The course of true love hasn't exactly run smooth, either. Lots of adventures on the way. I'm not sure I'd be prepared for you to film it, though. I don't know who I'd want to play me."

"Ever acted?" Go asked.

A sidelong glance. "All the time."

They'd reached Paugeng shortly after that and Jhai had installed Go at the very top of the building.

"It's the apartment we use for visitors. We encounter a lot of problems with industrial espionage—everyone in the pharmaceutical industry's the same, it's such big bucks—so security here is very, very tight. If anyone does come after you, they'll be intercepted long before they get to the second floor, let alone all the way up here. Unless your demon can fly?" She grinned.

"Not without a hang-glider," Go replied. He was not quite convinced. He'd somehow got himself into that state of extreme paranoia where everything seemed possible: What if Lara somehow materialized out of the air, just as she had during the banishing ritual? As if she had read his mind, Jhai said, "By the way, when I mentioned security—it isn't just armed guards and computer systems. There are magical wards on this building—*feng shui* guards and some customized stuff, too. We're set up for all eventualities."

"Impressive," Go said. But if her boyfriend was a demon, who knew what she'd had to contend with? It made him feel easier, however.

"I need to do some work," Jhai said. "There are servants; ring the bell if you want anything. You look like you need some sleep, though."

"Thanks," Go said. "I really appreciate it. Can I just ask—I mean, why are you doing all this for me?"

Jhai's face was inexpressive. She said, "I've had problems with Hell before now. Not just the Hell attached to China. Let's say there's some mutual feeling involved, shall we, and leave it at that? Besides, I owe Chen a few favors. He's a decent man."

"Can he really help me, do you think?"

"I don't know," Jhai said. "But I do know how hard he'll try."

TWENTY-THREE

He had fought dogs before, on the streets of Hell, and he knew that location was everything. Rather than fight these hounds on the palace steps, badger turned and bolted, heading for the cover of the bushes. As he wheeled around, he saw the palace for the first time in its entirety: a sprawling crimson building, lacquer gleaming like blood, the white marble pillars standing out like stripped bone.

There was a stand of hibiscus at the far end of the grass. The badger made for it, as fast as his short legs would carry him. He felt a hot breath on his hind paws, just as he reached the shelter of the bushes. These plants had spines. Badger was used to that, but he did not think the dogs were. A wailing yell from behind him confirmed this opinion. Badger pushed through the undergrowth, which became increasingly dense, snuffling and snorting, sounding out the ground beneath. Somewhere, there was a hollowness, and this could only be a good thing. But the hounds were not far away; he could hear them whining, running parallel to his own course, presumably on the far side of the bushes. Soon, there would be a place at which they would break through.

And sure enough, it came, just as the badger stumbled out into a small clearing. There was a hole!—badger's spirit soared, but it also meant that the ground was uneven, the hibiscus less dense, and a black scaled head was even now bursting through the scarlet blossoms. It was too close; badger could not risk a leap for the hole and so he turned, growling.

The dog snapped, a teasing play.

"There are four of us, little demon. And only one of you. So we will take it in turns, before we rip you apart."

"I have something to tell you," badger replied. The dog put its great head on one side, the clever, fierce eyes glittering.

"And what might that be?"

"This," the badger said, and sprang. His jaws closed around the dog's nose, biting through the thin scales and rewarded with a scalding spray of blood. The dog screamed. Badger curled up, bringing heavy hind paws under the dog's chin, and tore out its throat. The dog crashed to the ground, just as the others charged through the bushes. Teeth grazed the badger's shoulder, he spun around, snapped, missed, snapped again, and locked molars onto an ear. The dog jerked, frantically.

"Stay *still*, stupid bitch!" a canine voice instructed. Again, the badger felt the graze of teeth and used the momentum of the dog's own movements to whip to and fro. Up and over, landing on the dog's back and biting through her spine. A dreadful howling filled the clearing, and badger, finally, was in reach of the hole. He jumped, turned, and backed down it, hoping with some desperation that it was deep enough. His last view before the spice of unfamiliar earth swallowed him was of two snarling heads, with the whining ghosts of the slain hounds close behind. But they were too big to fit down the hole. Badger slithered further, wriggling and scraping, turned a bend, and they were out of sight.

蛇警探

Earth. It was not the soil in which he had been born. That had been black and crumbling, a nourishing loam which had brought badger forth, forming him out of its own substance, reaching deep within itself to draw up metals, forging him in the furnace roar, only dim now but still a tumult of light and fire in memory, making him dual-aspected, teakettle and badger. Earth had told him secrets of itself: where it was hollow, where dense, the long, slow stories of stone, the hard, bright tales of metal. Badger, having learned, had then been ejected: spat out onto an immense slope of hillside. Looking up, he had seen the volcanic cone rising behind him: a mountain, a deity, its world-filling presence still recognizing the small spirit of a badger demon, reaching out and down while badger cowered against the ground, wishing earth would swallow him and take him back. The presence, Fujiyama, sweeping over and out and gone and leaving the cone—far larger than its counterpart in the human realm—shining snow-pale against a rosy sky.

He had wandered after that, exploring this new world of over-ground, encountering others, *kappa* and *miko,* things that tried to bind him and things that tried to kill him, to dispatch him to the lower levels of this particular Hell. And finally, one had succeeded: badger swept up in a net, a shout of triumph, a sorcerer with bones rattling from his hat who cut badger down and shackled his feet, then took him Elsewhere, fleeing between the worlds to a mansion in China-Below. Several spells later, there was badger: indentured to an august family. He minded, at first, but there was a baby to protect and badger discovered that he did, after all, have a sense of purpose and duty, if not much of a heart.

Mistress. Unprotected, somewhere far away. This would not do. Resolute, badger scrambled around into the narrowing passage. But he could sense that the tunnel went on. Badger started digging.

Distance was easy, time was not. He had traveled some way: a few hundred yards before the tunnel opened out again. There was even a crack of daylight in the ground above, a slot widening into over-ground. Badger was very cautious. These gardens had been made, it was not wild ground, and that meant there was an even greater chance of them being fully known and mapped. He did not want to burst back into the above to find the dogs waiting. He proceeded with great care, smelling, listening, waiting. But he could not scent the dogs and he knew them by now: a rank, musky odor like a long-buried bone, and it occurred to him that this was what they were: summoned up, flesh magicked onto old ivory.

Over-ground was a surprise, when he eventually poked his nose into it. The gardens were gone, or seemed to have done. This was forest: wild, a high canopy filled with chattering, sharp-toothed creatures and flashing birds.

Interesting, thought badger. In his own Hell, distance did not mean very much: it was fluid, mutable, unlike the fixed spans of the human realm. You could turn a corner and find that you had come five hundred miles. From badger's admittedly limited experience, most Hells seemed to be similar. So perhaps he had already come a great distance from the gardens of the tigresses' palace. And perhaps not. Better be careful.

Badger listened, but the only sounds around him were those of this unnatural realm. It was hard to know what to do, other than to begin walking and hope that there would be a portal to somewhere else. All worlds were linked, but only at certain points unless one was particularly gifted in traveling between them: the gods, for instance, were better at this than most people, but one would expect that. Badger, not even a small god, had no such talents. He snorted, and trundled on.

TWENTY-FOUR

Inari sat bolt upright. Beside her, Chen lay in peaceful slumber: a tidy sleeper, his hands rested together on a gently rising chest. Clearly, he had made no sudden movement that might have startled her into wakefulness. Yet she was awake, with no idea as to what time it might be, nerves jangling, her head filled with a black pressing presence.

What is the matter with me? Inari thought. A glance at the clock revealed that it was close to midnight. She lay back, but calmness would not come and sleep was out of the question. She reviewed the events of the previous day—the same day? The last few hours blurred and merged in her mind, running like water. They had eventually left the police station—Inari had managed to sleep in a chair in a side office, but Chen had been working throughout—and come home to no badger, no demon, and a subdued supper. Chen had also been compelled to explain to his captain that he'd illegally married a demon from Hell.

"He took it very well, considering. Said that since my second-in-command was demonic and we'd managed to save the city a couple of times, the climate had changed somewhat. Besides, he *sent* me to Hell a few months ago on that ridiculous equal ops thing, so he didn't have much ground for complaint. Suggested we go to dinner with him and Mrs Sung. When things calm down a bit."

So that secret, which they had guarded so long and with such care, had fizzled out on revelation like a damp firecracker. Just as well. Inari had had enough drama.

Things might have gone relatively well at the precinct, but there was the whole shameful issue of the shaman to consider. No Ro Shi had really been very nice to her, but she didn't deserve it. What a stupid thing to have done—well, allowed to happen. She should have known better. Hadn't she grown up in Hell, surrounded by magic? Hadn't she traveled through the lower levels, visited Heaven? She was a woman of the worlds now, no longer the fragile young girl whom Chen had been obliged to rescue—and yet some… *magician*… had snapped his fingers and off she'd trotted, like an obedient ghost.

Weakness. Her mother would have blamed that human blood, that taint, but Inari thought of the humans she knew, who had fought dark magic so bravely, and she could not fall back on prejudice. She would not make excuses for herself. She would not sleep, either. Quietly, so as not to disturb the slumbering Chen, Inari got out of bed and padded into the main cabin to make tea.

It was very quiet. Outside, a gentle tide slapped against the sides of the houseboat, making it rock. Inari took a cup down from its secure place behind the little rail and set it on its stand on the table, before putting the kettle on. That reminded her of badger and she clenched her fists against the tabletop: demons find it hard to cry. Badger had been by her side all her life, the family familiar; she was not even sure where he had come from. Her mother had been vague on the subject. He was not a Chinese demon, but a spirit from across the water, and once, on coming to Earth, Inari had offered to set him free from bondage.

Demons find it hard to smile, too. Badger had refused. *I could break this spell at my own choosing, Mistress. It is duty that keeps me by your side.* She understood what he meant by that and she had been more grateful than she could say.

She looked at the teakettle; a small antique one that had belonged to Chen's late mother. It was boiling now, steam whistling through its spout, and she reached out to turn off the burner. As her finger flicked the switch, the kettle subsided, but steam continued to pour out of its spout, billowing out around Inari as though she had stepped into a cloud, its soft heat filming her skin beneath her silk night-robe. Inari stood very still, her hand still reaching toward the stove. A world was coming toward her and she did not want to disturb it. Somewhere far within, a despairing voice cried: *weakness*—but it was swallowed in the drifts of mist, as the shadow-world came closer yet, and gently drew her in.

蛇警探

She could see again; the mists were lifting, surging up into the heights of the rocks. Inari stood in a monochrome landscape: sharp black rocks, white sand, gray shadows. A bleak place, not without its own stark beauty. Ahead, at the end of this enclosed valley, the gap in the rocks opened up like a missing tooth, revealing a distant pass. Just before that, she saw a pagoda, an elegant structure, somehow difficult to see. It was easier to glimpse it out of the corner of one's eye, coming into sharper focus then, its curls and angles decorated with the crescent moon.

Wind lifted white sand and sent it skittering across the valley floor. Inari knew that this was not Hell, but if not there, then where? It certainly wasn't anywhere on Earth—the pagoda was proof of that—but it was too austere for Heaven, unless it was some kind of Zen minimalist version.

Not far away, something rattled.

Inari whipped round. Her whole body felt as though it had been struck with a hammer. For a moment, the world, too, rang: the blank sky above her spun, the dust whisked up. Then all was once more calm. The rattle came again.

"Who's there?" Inari demanded and her voice sounded very shrill in this silent land. And besides, she thought she already knew.

He stepped out from behind the rocks and Inari, filled with horror, knew that she had last seen him in Men Ling Street, a dark shape amongst the garbage cans.

"It's you," she whispered. "They said you were a shaman."

The shaman grinned. Not a big demon, but hunched and shuffling, wrapped in a motley arrangement of skins and tattered scraps of fur, some still with flesh attached. His face was blue, although it was difficult to tell how much of this was the original skin tone and how much might be tattooed: spirals and dots of blue extended beyond one makeshift sleeve to creep along the hand that clutched a rattle, from which hung many small bones. His eyes were like black seeds. Small tusks protruded from the sides of his mouth.

"And so I am. You can call me Bonerattle. I will call you Humanwife."

"I am not human," Inari said, a fluttering attempt at defiance that made the tusked mouth grin wider. "I am a demon."

"Oh, so!" the shaman said, mocking. "And yet you are the wife of a man, Humanwife." He frowned. "It used to be more common."

"My husband will find me," Inari said. "He is a hunter of demons."

"Is that so? I thought he was a worker with demons. Yourself, the striped beast, the tall one. I've been watching you."

"Why am I here? Where are we?"

"This is *between*," Bonerattle said. "One of the rift-valleys, the cracks in what people so stupidly consider to be real."

"I see," Inari said slowly. "I thought *between* was a myth."

This appeared to delight the shaman. He swung the rattle and the bones clattered and hissed. "If even demons think this is not real—consider the power of it! One can do anything." He gestured, making the rattle shake further. "Over there, is Shadow Pavilion, home of one who plans a great wrong."

"A great wrong?" Inari asked. "Who lives there, then?"

"That is the home of Lord Lady Seijin, one of the greatest assassins who has ever lived. One who plots to slay the Emperor of Heaven?"

"Mhara?" Inari said, blankly. "But—he's a god."

"Don't say his name! And you know that gods can die."

"Yes, but—why are you telling me this?"

"Why," the shaman said patiently, "so that you can prevent it."

"But you're a demon," Inari said.

"A technicality. I am of demon blood, true. But I am not from Hell. I am one of the guards of *between,* and if the Lord Lady succeeds, then all will be lost. Heaven will crack asunder, Hell's gates will open forth, and *between* will fall through and be lost."

"So that is what you care about?" Inari asked. "This place?"

"There you have it. We keep ourselves to ourselves here. There are rare things that cannot enter Heaven and yet are too pure for Hell. Things that humans have driven out. You may see this place as a kind of conservation effort. I am charged with their preservation, it is my duty, in expiation of an ancient wrong which is really too dull to go into at the moment. Usually, the actions of Hell and Heaven do not concern us. Let them get on with it, we say. But the Lord Lady has taken hold of this final ambition and does not realize the consequences."

"Couldn't you speak to this assassin and explain things? After all, if they live here…"

"If Seijin succeeds, then it will not matter to the Lord Lady whether *between* disappears. Seijin will be able to live anywhere."

"But why come to me?" Inari asked.

The shaman's beady eyes dimmed. "You were the only one who listened."

"No Ro Shi—the one who vanquished you—seemed to think you were a wicked thing," Inari said.

"There are those who would say the same of you."

She was unable to answer that, recognizing its truth.

"I walk in the bone worlds," Bonerattle said. "Among blood and whispers. Humans don't tend to like that."

"All right," Inari said. "I know Mh—" A finger like a tendon was placed swiftly across her mouth.

"Don't say the name," the shaman said. He nodded toward Shadow Pavilion. "Names carry on the wind."

"I know the person concerned. I'll talk to him if I can." *He might even listen,* Inari thought, and realized, *Why, I might be able to help, after all. If any of this is true.*

Bonerattle's tusked head jerked up and Inari turned to see what he was looking at. Mist was boiling down the mountainside, licking out like smoke and touching the sides of Shadow Pavilion. A moment later, the pagoda was enveloped in cloud, shot with stormlight. The air was filled with the metal of oncoming rain and a distant crack and flash came from beyond the pass.

"The Lord Lady is coming home," Bonerattle said. "We need to get you back." He raised the rattle and shook it like thunder. Inari blinked, suddenly doused in a chilly wetness. Then she was standing in her own kitchen, with her mother-in-law's kettle clutched firmly in her hand and the lights of the boats rocking in the harbor beyond.

TWENTY-FIVE

This is how it begins. You start with the highest intentions, driven by the purest motives. You will not, you tell yourself, stoop from these elevated goals, because you can't afford to. You have to set an example, to yourself as much as to others. Once you let that go, it's a long downward slope, rocks gathering speed until you're caught up in the avalanche, falling, falling, with the lights of Hell speeding up below you.

And gods have the furthest to fall.

Mhara knew all this—how could he not, given what he was, he thought? Yet it still seemed a damn good idea to spy on the Dowager Empress, try and find out what his mother was up to. She'd been spying on him, after all. But Mhara knew that this didn't justify anything. The spying itself would be a relatively simple matter, although he would have to undertake it himself. He did not trust the Court, any more than—so it seemed—the Court trusted him. Some of them might rise to the challenge that he had set, but they'd still be a bit wary. Of necessity, Mhara was too much, too soon, for a world that was used to deliberating for decades before decisions were reached. To the Court, Mhara must seem to have all the attention span and sense of responsibility of a three-year-old human child.

In order to spy, there was no need for devices or magic. There was, so he believed, very little chance of being found out, and in any case, this was his palace and he was entitled to know what went on in it, especially if that proved to be against his best interests. All Mhara would have to do would be to sit here in solitary peace and meditate; send his awareness forth on the flicker of the Celestial wind and listen to what his mother was saying. But staring out of the window, the marble below suddenly seemed a long way down; how much further, then, was Hell?

It was not honorable, and he was Heaven's Emperor. Principles warred briefly with expediency, and even Mhara was slightly surprised to find that principles won. The ground was close: he could see every waterdrop on a rose petal. But Hell had become very far. So, that was how it worked. He wondered how his father had managed to circumvent a constraining set of ethics. Maybe madness helped. Or maybe madness was the result.

The gardens were particularly beautiful at this time of the day. A walk in them would be just the thing to clear the head. Mhara went downstairs and out toward the gardens, heading for sunshine.

The gardens attached to the Celestial Palace were very old. Legend had it that they had been the first part of Heaven to be reclaimed from the void, fueled by human worship, landscaped by devotion and hope. Mhara walked past ancient groves of acacia, rustling in the breeze, past roses that, in a different culture, would form the Platonic essence of rose. It was not long before he found himself down by the lake, a long stretch of silver water, crossed by a little bridge at its narrow end and starred with shining lilies. In the center, another bridge arched out to an island, on which sat a small temple. A nice place to sit, and look back at the Palace, or inward toward one's own thoughts. Mhara crossed the bridge, followed by the great shoals of carp that lived in the lake. He should have brought some breadcrumbs. Once he stepped onto the island, however, the fish flicked up out of the water and changed into birds, silver and gold, with haunting voices that murmured through the trees. Mhara, smiling, headed for the temple. No one was about. He imagined that the Palace, now only just visible through the leaves, was humming with agitation like a hive; himself, veiled, had lifted the lid and given it a good shake. Here, on the island, Mhara permitted himself the luxury of doubt: it was too easy to think that you were doing the right thing. Look at the human ruler Mao: forcing the country on its Great Leap Forward, the future shining like a beacon. And look how it had ended, in a mire of stultifying bureaucracy and corruption, taking murder and fanaticism in along the way. Perhaps the old Emperor had thought he was doing the right thing, too. A horror of self-righteousness had to be preserved, without locking one into an inability to act.

Beset by such thoughts, Mhara sat gazing out over the lake, only half seeing the play of light on silver water, the little boat that had set out from the dock on the far side. In it, sat a woman, trailing a long sleeve in the water. Her robes were the color of rose petals and her long hair was piled up on her head and skewered with silver pins; one of the many court-dwellers who liked to come to the lake of an afternoon. Mhara thought of letting her know that he was on the island—one of the birds could be dispatched—but even though he might be Emperor now, that did not, to his mind, give him an automatic right to disrupt other people. So he sat still and watched as the boat glided across the water toward the temple. Soon, it disappeared behind the trees. It might make the woman uncomfortable, to find him here; she might feel that she had intruded. And it was time to return to the Palace, anyway, he'd had his moment of quiet and there was a mountain of paperwork to get through. Mhara stood, glimpsed a white curling feather on the floor, and on a whim, stooped to pick it up.

Something whirred through the air, burying itself in the plaster where, a second before, Mhara's head had been. Mhara looked up at a quivering hairpin, embedded in the temple wall. Realization came in its wake. A courtier of Heaven might not have understood, but Mhara's real home was on Earth and not such a nice neighborhood at that. He snatched the pin from the wall, avoiding the sharp tip just in case of poison, and ducked behind one of the pillars of the entrance.

He could not see anyone out there. Mhara closed his eyes and called on Ubiquity: it would enable him to see, but not, perhaps, to act. There were limits to even a Celestial Emperor's power: natural breakwaters, set there by the universe itself, to prevent gods from going to war. It hadn't always worked.

Nothing. Ubiquity enabled him to stand on the dock and stare down at the empty boat. There were no footprints, only a slight disturbance in the long grass to show that someone had passed this way. Mhara, still outside his own body, followed them up the curve of the island toward the temple. He was aware of his physical self, just a small flutter of fabric behind the pillar, and in actuality he reached down and tucked it away. But there was no sign of the woman who had come in the boat—except, he had not remembered that rose tree, those pink-and-candy blossoms. If he looked very carefully, the outline of a human figure was just visible. She was standing very still, merging into the background like the myth of chameleons.

Mhara was more intrigued than afraid. Whoever she was, she had gained entry to Heaven, had been able to borrow a boat and get close to its Emperor, all without any alarms being raised. Unless—well, how far could he trust the Court, after all? That was a related issue, but it would wait. For now, he had this puzzle to deal with. This woman was highly skilled in magic; he could feel it gliding over her in great, calm waves. There was no sense of anger, none of the simmering rage that might drive a person to kill. Instead, all he was able to feel from her was that magic, something unfamiliar to him—was she foreign?—and an intense degree of focus.

The wind stirred roses. A great sweet rush of perfume filled the garden; petals fluttered and a hand was raised to her head as she reached fluidly up and plucked a second pin from her hair. Behind the pillar, Mhara stepped out and threw.

Even from his dual vantage point, the next few minutes were confused. Mhara saw several things at once: the silver pin flickering through the air like an arrow, thrown with the force of his own Celestial magic, the woman turning, startled to a degree that surprised him, a glimpse of a beautiful, remote face with eyes that were drowning wide, and then the pin striking, shattering the woman into fragments. Then there was nothing left but the pin amid a shower of rose petals, gliding down to rest on the calm green grass of Heaven.

TWENTY-SIX

Badger had no idea how long he had been traveling, but he thought he had gone no more than a mile or so. It was hard to tell, through the dense undergrowth that covered most of the forest floor. He had met some interesting things: a giant wasp, fortunately uninterested in badger spirits; a woman who had stepped out of a tree, opened wings, and soared up into the canopy; and a lizard who had looked at the badger with an old, wise eye and spoken to him in a language that he did not understand. This might not be his own Hell, but it had the same sorts of things in it.

There was also a river. It was slow and green, running sluggishly between banks of mangrove, and badger had the distinct impression that there were a number of things in it, all best avoided. He followed the river nonetheless, traveling downstream, on the principle that it must come out somewhere. He disliked this aimlessness, feeling that he functioned best with some order to his day, but there was no helping it. And then, at a bend of the river, he heard something. It was growling.

Badger's hackles were immediately up. He recognized that growl: tiger! He slid down the bank to the water's edge and coiled himself under the mangrove roots. A voice spoke.

"Where is he?"

The badger thought dark thoughts. He recognized the voice, too—one of the tigresses, though he could not have named her. He thought it was the one who had proved timid during the conversation overheard in the kitchen. Then the reply came, "I don't know. He was here a moment ago. You keep searching along the stream."

The sound of large, padding feet and a crashing through the undergrowth. The tigresses were not being particularly subtle about their hunt, but then again, why should they be? This was their preserve. Badger could hear a great deal of rooting about and then the voice—and this one was definitely the one from the kitchen, the one who seemed to be planning something—said to herself: "Hah!"

She was coming closer. Badger scrunched into the root hole, wondering whether it would be safer, on balance, to slide under the water. He was a reasonably strong swimmer, but then, so are tigers. He could smell her now, a rank feline odor, growing stronger by the minute. Next moment, she was down the bank in a rush and the badger was confronted by the unwelcome sight of an enormous golden eye.

"There you are, little demon!" the tigress said, and reached in a gigantic paw. Badger flattened himself against the wall, hissing, but suddenly the tigress was gone, upward. There was a gurgling yell and the green waters of the river were spattered with drops of dark blood. Someone jumped lightly down to stand on the roots; badger looked up into a familiar face.

"Hello, badger," said Zhu Irzh.

蛇警探

The badger stared up to where the striped body hung, still swinging over green water. The fur was blackened with blood, the golden eyes were filmed.

"Impressive," the badger said, rather grudgingly. Zhu Irzh shrugged.

"Not my doing. The trap was already there." He pointed to a thin band of wire hiding under the roots of the tree. "Someone's been busy. I saw it when I came through here—doubled back and let her catch up, then tripped it. It's an effective snare, to collar something like that."

"Whose doing?"

"I've no idea. I imagine some of their prey must have got away from them, just by the law of averages. Maybe there are people living out here."

"And what has become of her?" Badger nosed the air in the direction of the tigress' body.

"Same answer—don't know. Presumably this Hell functions like other Hells; there might be lower levels. Hope she's got a nasty shock, anyway."

"There are more," badger said. "Seven at least."

"Yeah, I know. I met all of them, before I was dumped on the lawn and told to make a run for it." Zhu Irzh drew the badger back behind a thick trunk of mangrove. "We ought to get moving. You know what? This lot are nearly my in-laws. If I'd known getting married was going to prove such a hassle, I'd have made sure I stayed a bachelor."

蛇警探

Night fell fast and red, the sky above the canopy deepening to a starless crimson.

"Tigers are supposed to be nocturnal," Zhu Irzh said, uneasily. "Does this bunch ever sleep, do you know?"

"I do not. I have had little to do with them. Thankfully. I expect they captured us at the same time?"

"Yeah, I went in after you. Time was up and I waited for a bit, but I didn't hear from you and I got worried. Walked through the door and that was it—I don't remember what happened. Everything went dark. I don't think I was hit on the head." He put a hand to his cranium. "No sign of it, must have been magical. And they must have been *good*, to take me with such little difficulty."

"I was bundled into a bag," the badger said, sourly.

"Bad luck. Come to think of it, they must have been pretty good to get *you*."

"Thank you." The badger was grateful at this attempt to save his face. Zhu Irzh wasn't such a bad sort, really. "You said these demons are your family?"

"Family-to-be. They have some kind of relationship to Jhai. You know her mother's from Kerala? These are Keralan demons. A very old clan. They used to live wild in the jungles of Hell—one of them was kind enough to explain it to me, just so I knew why I was about to be killed. But in the nineteenth century, when the British came to India and set up the Raj, they hunted tigers. Wasn't popular."

"I have sympathy with that," badger said.

"Well, yeah. So that palace came into being—Hell grew it, apparently. Brought a demigod down—that would be the prince—and gave him a harem. Their role was to hunt the souls of British big-game hunters, soldiers, that sort of thing."

"But if they are your woman's family," badger said, "why are they trying to kill you?" It was not that he was unfamiliar with the concept: Mistress' relatives were continually endeavoring to poison one another, for instance. But badger liked things to be clear.

"I don't know," Zhu Irzh said, rather wildly. "Maybe they just don't like me." His expression, as far as badger could interpret it, was one of incredulity. "But it's more than that, isn't it? They must know how to *really* get rid of demons. Let's say a tigress jumps out of that tree right now, tears you and me to pieces. What happens to us?"

The badger thought about this. "We go to the lower levels? Or return to our own Hell?"

"Must be the lower levels here, because otherwise we'd just be transported home, and could return to Earth. They must have a way of making sure that we can't get back. They're not just hunting for sport; they're hunting for keeps."

And away in the darkness, something snarled.

TWENTY-SEVEN

"Murdering the Celestial Emperor?" Chen said. "That's ambitious."

Inari, still very pale, sat twisting her hands together on the couch in the main cabin of the houseboat. There was no question that Chen did not believe her, but he wondered whether this shaman-between-worlds had simply been lying. It seemed an odd, elaborate deception, however. He did not like, at all, the thought that his wife could be spirited so easily away; that this individual had some kind of hold on her. He intended to give No Ro Shi a call very soon: the demon-hunter seemed to have a grip on this sort of thing.

"Have you ever heard of this person? Lord Lady Seijin?"

Chen shook his head. "No, but that doesn't mean anything. The depths of my personal ignorance are as yet unplumbed—there's so much out there, Inari. I'm hoping No Ro Shi might be able to shed some light on the subject."

"Are you going to speak to him?" Inari said. Evidently their thoughts had been running along similar lines. Chen looked at the clock. It was now just after 2:00 A.M.

"I'll call him now, leave a message on his answerphone."

But he was in luck. The demon-hunter was up.

"Citizen Chen?"

"We've got a further problem," Chen said. "I'm reluctant to discuss it on the phone. I don't want to disturb you, but—"

"I work best at night," No Ro Shi told him. "Give me twenty minutes."

蛇警探

"I have heard of this person," the demon-hunter said, a little later. He folded his long body into an armchair, looking as though he entertained ideological

89

objections to personal comfort. "A very old individual, almost legendary. Born in the time of Genghis, and rode with the hordes. A murderer, a barbarian, who changed with the times and yet remained the same."

"This 'Lord Lady' business…" Chen began.

"A walker between worlds. Seijin is both male and female, born of a demon father and a Celestial mother, or perhaps the other way around. But, whichever the case, born on Earth and thus able to move between all worlds at will."

"And now resides in a place called *between*."

"I don't know a great deal about *between*," No Ro Shi said. "I have always thought that it was itself a myth. It is supposed to be the birthplace of possibilities, falling as it does between the cracks in the worlds."

"If the shaman was telling the truth," Inari said, timidly, "I've been there. And it didn't feel like anywhere else I've ever been."

No Ro Shi regarded her with something approaching kindness. "It must have been alarming."

"What are we going to do?" Inari said. "Warn Mhara?"

"As soon as possible," Chen said. "In fact, if you have a vehicle with you, No Ro Shi, I suggest we go to the temple as soon as we can. It's the best way to get in touch. I don't have any other method at the moment, although that was due to change." He had the sense that things were once more moving too quickly, time sweeping him along in its tide. Not a comfortable sensation.

They all went. Chen wanted Mhara to hear Inari's story in her own words, and he was highly reluctant to leave her on her own after what had been happening. He had the suspicion that this was somehow all connected: Zhu Irzh's disappearance and that of the badger, this tale of assassinating Mhara. But there was no instinct accompanying it: no gut feeling. He was not sure how much store to place in that.

Though it might be close to dawn, the streets were still filled with people along the central area of the city, spilling out of the clubs and demon lounges and bars. Many of the lounges had been newly legalized, under revised trade agreements with Hell; how things had changed, Chen mused, as No Ro Shi's four-by-four spun past the glaring neon signs. Next thing he knew, there would be blood emporiums opening up alongside the delicatessens. Hard to ignore Hell these days; difficult to maintain a rationalist agnosticism, but there were still plenty of folk who managed it, unable to see the visitants from other realms. Chen was not sure whether this would be a comfort or otherwise. On the one hand, you'd miss a great many disturbing things; on the other, it must appear as though the rest of the world had taken leave of its senses. But then, the Chinese were used to that.

Chen's reverie was disrupted as No Ro Shi swore and the vehicle veered sharply to the left.

"What the—"

"Hostile on the far side of the road," the demon-hunter snapped. Chen turned in his seat and saw a cloudy presence. At first, he thought it was a swirl of mist, but it was solidifying. Then, abruptly, it was gone. No Ro Shi slammed on the brakes, pitching Chen forward in his seat.

"Sorry!"

Something was standing in front of the car, a swathe of fog. As the vehicle skidded, then stopped, Chen looked into the heart of the mist and saw a tall, slender figure. It held a blood-red sword in both hands, not ready to swing, but balanced across them as if presenting the sword to a student. Dark hair fell back from a high brow. Its eyes were golden, like a demon's, and it was smiling. Impossible to tell whether the tranquil face belonged to a man or a woman. It raised the sword, a clear salute, and smiled. Then the mist was torn away, as though a sea wind had blown across the street and dispelled it, taking the figure with it.

"I think," Chen said to the gaping No Ro Shi, "that we might have met Lord Lady Seijin."

It was almost dawn when they reached the little temple of the Emperor of Heaven, a white glow to the east signaling the rise of the sun. Chen felt he would be glad when the night was over; gods knew that enough things had befallen him in broad daylight, but it was easier to think, somehow. Night-time was the ghost time, the time of the spirit world, not meant for those who walked in the light. Or who tried to, anyway. A relief to step out under the lightening sky, a greater one to walk up to the temple door and have it swing open to welcome you into a calm, lamplit space.

"I heard the car," Robin said.

Mhara was not there: from necessity, he was resident in Heaven for most of the time these days. If Robin was lonely, she did not say so, and Chen would never cause her to lose face by asking such a personal question. "I don't sleep much," she said. "Being dead seems to have cured me of being tired, anyway." She looked at No Ro Shi and smiled. "I've seen your picture in the papers."

No Ro Shi bowed. "You know my convictions. I honor you nonetheless."

"Thanks," Robin said. "I don't imagine it's easy, being a communist in the face of everything that's been going on. Doesn't really make it easy for the State, does it? Having the supernatural continually interfering."

The demon-hunter returned her smile with a thin grimace of his own. "I manage. At least you are on the side of goodness."

"Well, I try."

Inari had gone to kneel in front of the little shrine, reaching out to light one of the small candles.

"You don't have to do that, Inari," Robin told her. "Mhara's a friend."

Inari said, "That's why I'm lighting the candle."

"Been rather a rough night," Chen said, and explained why.

"Ah," Robin said, after his concise account had ended. "That would explain that."

"I'm sorry?"

"Someone tried to kill Mhara this afternoon." She raised a hand and the walls of the room glowed with a faint blue light, a mesh extending from floor to ceiling. "Just checking. After today, I made sure we were as secure as possible."

"Then we were too late," Inari said in a small voice. She looked stricken. She felt, Chen knew, responsible, no matter how irrational this might be.

"I said 'tried,' not 'succeeded,' " Robin said. "Besides, I'm not even sure if he can be killed. Maybe the attempt was of something else entirely—some kind of binding, for instance."

Chen frowned. "I don't know what the parameters are here. If he's killed, wouldn't he just end up back in Heaven?"

"His father was disenspirited," Robin reminded him. "Thrown off the Wheel of Life and Death. It *is* possible."

"What happened?" Chen asked.

"He was at the lake and a woman threw a hairpin at him."

Chen's eyebrows rose. "That doesn't sound all that serious an attempt, to be honest."

"I know," Robin replied. "She didn't succeed in hitting him, either. I don't know what would have happened if she had."

"He's sure it was a woman, is he?"

"I don't know," Robin said. "From what you've just told me, this Seijin can pass as either. It seems to fit."

"And you haven't noticed anything strange here?"

"No. The only person who's come to the temple in the last day or so was a supplicant, just a street person, to pray."

"There was nothing strange about her?"

"Not that I could tell. She prayed, lit a candle, then she went away." Robin's head snapped toward the door. "Hang on."

"What is it?"

Robin smiled. "It's Mhara." A moment later the Celestial Emperor, wearing linen trousers and a loose jacket, stepped through the door into the main hall. He carried something small wrapped in silk.

"Hello," he said to Chen and the others. He did not seem surprised; Chen did not yet know the extent of Mhara's abilities. Was the Emperor omniscient? No time like the present; he asked as much.

"It's selective omniscience," Mhara said. "I can—if I choose—know more or less everything that happens in Heaven and a lot of what occurs on Earth, although that's more opaque. Events in Hell come in snatches—otherwise my father might have succeeded in his attempt to conquer it."

"And *between?*" Inari asked. Mhara's face became somber.

"I can't see *between* at all."

"Hmm," Chen said. "It seems that *between* can see you. Inari?"

And once again she told her story.

"It could easily have been Seijin," Mhara said, when she had finished. "I thought it was a woman, but I didn't get a very close look at her." He held out his hand and the silk fell away, revealing a long, slender pin. "This was the weapon."

Chen leaned forward and studied the object. It was an ordinary old-fashioned hairpin, made out of silver, the kind that women used to skewer an elaborate hair-do. Without even touching it, however, he could tell that the tip had been sharpened to a razor-fine point; the silk had a tiny slit in it, where the point had gone through the wrapping.

But despite its conventional appearance, the hairpin reeked of magic: a nebulous grayness surrounded it, blurring its edges against the silk whenever Chen looked at it from the corners of his eyes.

"Yes," Mhara said, softly. "It's enchanted, and I don't recognize the spell. It's very old. That's all I can say."

"If the Emperor of Heaven does not know it," Chen said, "then a humble police inspector doesn't have much of a chance."

But Inari said, "Bonerattle might know."

TWENTY-EIGHT

Pauleng Go slept for a long time, well past the break of day. When he finally struggled awake, from uneasy dreams in which teeth and fire figured large, and reached for the clock, he found that it was close to noon. Rubbing his eyes, Go hauled himself out of bed and went to find the shower.

When he had finished showering, there was a knock on the door. Go opened it, to find one of Jhai's flunkies on the other side: a young man with impeccable manners who informed him, with just the right amount of regret, that Jhai had been obliged to go to Shanghai on business, but would be back later that night. Meanwhile, he was to make himself at home and if he wanted anything, to let the staff know.

Go ordered coffee and went outside to sit on the balcony, a long curve of metal that overlooked the bay, and tried to concentrate on a script. But it was impossible for him to believe that his normal life would ever be resumed: How could he go back to the ordinary round of writing and networking, knowing that out there lurked a beast bent on vengeance? Something would have to be done about Lara and he was hoping that Jhai might have some ideas. Besides which, he needed another agent.

Abandoning the script, he went inside to the room's PC and logged onto the net, where he spent the next hour or so obsessively hunting down reports of the incident. All he could find was an account in the local paper of the fire, and mention that a body had been discovered in the ruins. But things like this happened in Singapore Three every day: the report was embedded in a column that mentioned two other fatal fires. There was nothing to be gained by studying the past. He'd be better off looking for a decent exorcist.

Having effectively confined himself to the guest apartment made Go restless. He certainly had no plans to go into the city, but he found himself curious about Paugeng. Jhai's corporate headquarters was the last word in

94

modern architecture, a curving structure that he'd seen featured in numerous newspaper and magazine articles before he'd even set eyes on it in person. He knew a little of its history: the original building had been destroyed in one of the series of earthquakes that had shaken the city some years before, and Jhai had seized the opportunity to completely rebuild, though Go thought he remembered hearing somewhere that the laboratories which lay beneath the site had remained intact and were still unchanged.

Go did not expect to be allowed the run of the whole building and he did not want to piss Jhai off. He summoned the young man and asked if there were any areas of the building that were off limits.

"They will be immediately obvious," the young man said, smiling. "We have very good security systems."

"It's nice to know."

"We do have a gym and bar area. Would you like me to take you down there?"

Go, not usually fanatical about exercise, surprised himself with the enthusiasm with which he agreed. "Bar" sounded good, anyway. He followed the young man to a set of elevators and was taken to the seventh floor, where a pleasant atrium led onto the bar area, commanding a slightly different view from the one he had seen from the guest apartment; the curve allowed him to see right out across the harbor to the hump of islands. The gym itself was well equipped, including a sauna and a pool, and beyond it, glass doors led out onto an enclosed garden, enfolded by the curve of the building. The young man disappeared unobtrusively, leaving Go to enjoy the facilities.

Having no money was embarrassing, but it appeared that, as a guest, Go was not expected to pay. He ordered a beer and sipped it on the terrace, wondering whether to go into the pool or explore the gardens. This was the kind of choice one didn't mind having. In the end he did both, borrowing shorts and a towel from the desk, then wandering out into the gardens as he dried himself off. It was late afternoon now, and still hot. Go felt himself steaming gently and he sat down on a nearby bench to resume the beer.

How pleasant. It must be nice to be filthy rich, Go thought, not for the first time. He'd been doing all right—Beni had made sure of that—from the movies' income, but unless you really scored as a scriptwriter, the money wasn't that great. You were still at the bottom of the feeding heap. If he kept it up, he might not do too badly.

If he lived.

Amid the ornamental shrubs that encircled a kind of Zen garden of bark chips, something rustled. Go turned, frowning. Something flickered past his vision, too fast to see properly. A bird? It had seemed to shoot up the curved wall, vanishing at the summit. Go's skin grew cold, he felt as though he were the subject of a thousand eyes.

The building was very secure, Jhai had said. Go put the beer down on the bench, repeating Jhai's words under his breath like a mantra, and stood. The garden was empty—but just as he told himself this, the bushes rustled again in an invisible wind and this time there came the unmistakable flash of stripes past Go's appalled vision. Then nothing. It was like watching a wildlife documentary: *And here we glimpse the rarely seen tiger demon.* Go did not wait. He sprinted across the garden and slammed the glass doors shut—much good that would do, but it gave the illusion of safety, if only for a moment. The bar, get to the bar and tell the barman that there was a problem; he could summon security. But the barman was not there. Go searched the bar for any sign of a telephone. Nothing.

"Hey! Anyone there?" he called out.

Outside on the terrace—a growl. Go stumbled against the bar and knocked a glass off its perch. The growl had come from the front of the building but the garden was on the other side—his head whipped from one to the other but the sound did not come again. Go relaxed, but only for a second: out on the terrace, a shadow passed across the glass, something large and sinuous.

Go nearly shouted, then thought it might draw attention to himself. Run, fight, or hide: these were his options. His breath had started to catch, like an engine stuttering before running down. *Get to the elevators,* he thought frantically—but he took the wrong door, into the gym. Behind him, glass shattered as something leaped easily through.

Go had never thought of himself as a warrior, except in odd fantasy moments watching fight scenes on television. He did not expect to fight now, but desperation and fright gave him a kind of out-of-body experience, in which he saw himself bending, reaching, wrenching a set of weights off the press and turning to face whatever the hell had just banged through the door behind him. Just beyond the bench press, a tiger prowled.

"Oh god." Go, suddenly, was shouting and running forward, swinging the weight in a lunatic explosion of anger and fear. If he had been sufficiently conscious to think about it, he would have expected the casual swat of a giant clawed paw, the rending heat and fire of his own flesh as Lara tore him apart. Instead, the tiger stood up on its hind legs. The tail shrank, the muzzle collapsed in upon itself. Claws and teeth retracted, the tiger's ruff became a smooth cascade of hair, and in a billow of red and scarlet the beast changed down to a woman, who grabbed Go's weight-bearing arm in a grip like an iron vice and forced it away. Go stared into yellow eyes as she shoved him onto his knees, unable to look anywhere else, locked by the gaze of the tiger demon.

A tiger demon, yes. But not Lara.

TWENTY-NINE

Seijin was unaccustomed to nursing wounds and found the sensation was not uninvigorating. Female self was resigned to the situation, but male self had been giving Seijin no small degree of grief.

"This is shameful! The loss of face has been—" Male self stammered for an appropriate adjective. "Insupportable!"

"Face has been lost before," female self reminded him gently. Seijin was once more in the upper story of the Shadow Pavilion, looking out across the shifting, gray landscape of *between*. The crowds that had heralded the arrival were now dispelling on the upper slopes, but the light was low, sending golden streaks across the gray plain below. Seijin watched as a small herd of ghostly deer emerged from behind the rocks and made their way out onto the plain; then something must have startled them, for their white tails went up and they skittered away, finally fragmenting into mist.

"Face has not been lost for many years!" male self protested. "This is a great dishonor."

"My defeat was by the Celestial Emperor," Seijin reminded himself. "There is little dishonor in that."

"All the same—"

"And now we have a notion of his mettle," Seijin went on. In fact, the Emperor's abilities had come as a surprise. It just went to show that one should not underestimate an opponent, no matter how much inside information one thought one had possessed.

"His time on Earth has weakened him," the Dowager Empress had informed Seijin. "His liaison with this—this human *ghost*—has shown a deplorable degree of self-indulgence. He will not submit to duty, he shows no reverence for the past."

From the words of the Emperor's mother, Seijin had formed certain opinions of Mhara: someone young, in Celestial terms, probably willful and petulant. There would be power there, yes, but little guile. Yet the Emperor had not only seen Seijin coming, but had gained enough knowledge of the assassin's movements to outsmart Seijin and seize a weapon.

That, if Seijin had been the anxious sort, was the really worrying thing. Female self, herself shadowy against the shifting tapestries on the Pavilion's wall, sank onto a seat and wrapped her hands together. "He has taken a pin! He can follow us here, if he chooses."

"I am not so concerned about his pursuit," Seijin said, reflecting. "After all, his powers will be greatly diminished here in *between*. But what it does afford him is the opportunity to spy."

"What if he sends someone else?" female self asked.

"Who? A necromancer? You forget who we are."

"I remember what we were," female self faltered. And of course, Seijin remembered, too.

蛇警探

A river, at twilight, the water flowing oily and slow between the high banks, crashing with the blocks of ice that snowmelt had brought down from the heights. Seijin stood in a cold wind, looking out across the steppe. From the slight rise beyond the river, the plains stretched gray and endless, the grass shifting and whispering in this last wind of winter, spring on the way. Its taste came fresh on the air and Seijin reached out hands, welcoming this change of season when power came most easily. These liminal points, the change of the season, the hour. Power ran strong under the land, beneath the black, still-frozen earth, arcing in webs from the mountain summits, all the way across the plains to the distant birch-haunted tundra.

Seijin had been up in the mountains for the past week, hunting the spirits of a wolf pack that had threatened a tribe's meager herds. Sometimes, things did not know they had died, living so close to the otherworld that their recognition of their own death was no more than the sense of a cold wind blowing. Running the wolf pack down among the icy rocks, the black glitter of a ghost's eye in the darkness, drawing on the power of the waning moon to rip the beast apart, send it screaming down to Hell. Now, years later, Seijin wondered how many of those ghosts had ended up in *between*, racing the shadow plains. All the wolves had gone, the last cub spirit shrieking out into the winter air, disappearing. Then Seijin had come down from the heights, bearing spirit-scalps on a long thread, casting it down before the tribe's sha-man as the warriors had stared in awe and horror. It had amused Seijin to allow female self the dominance, seeing the desire in their eyes as she shyly smiled, need chased by fear as they saw the scalps wither into a bloody smoke and blow away.

One of them had come after her. One of them had died.

Pleasant memories. Seijin, standing, curled hands against the windowsill, feeling the muscles ache. Not a familiar feeling. Memory brought the river back, standing on that rise and watching the ghost lords ride the steppes, the Golden Horde on their fast, sleek ponies, sweeping from the east as they had once done, to sack and plunder the rich cities. But that was over a hundred years gone, Samarkand rebuilt into a glory of blue tile and golden dome, a city of sun and sky. If the horde reached it now, Seijin knew, watching the warriors ride by, they would sweep through the walls unseen. Perhaps they might make a child cry, give a seeress bad dreams. Nothing more than that. And as if he had heard, the man who rode in their midst turned his head and looked toward Seijin. Under the domed helm, his face was contorted into a familiar snarl, the eyes flat, black, mad.

"Hey, cousin!" Seijin cried to the Khan. "Guess what? I'm still here. Who'd have thought that, eh?" Then turned to the river and spat. In an instant, the ghost horde was gone, the grass hissing in the night wind. Seijin looked up and saw the Hunter of the Greeks striding across the late winter sky with the blue star at his heels.

"Enough," Seijin said aloud, raised a hand and slit the air.

蛇警探

And now, back at Shadow Pavilion, the only home Seijin had for a handful of hundred years. Returning again, as so often. The servants were staying out of the way, although there was no real need. Seijin had grown tired of torture, some while back. But then again, that had been during the tedium of invincibility, and that, it seemed, was no longer an issue.

THIRTY

Zhu Irzh and the badger sat high in a tree, looking out across the rustle of the jungle. The badger had eaten some beetles, which had disagreed with him.

"You want to be careful, you know," the demon told him, swinging a booted foot. "Eating things in other people's Hells can be dodgy."

"I needed food," the badger said, stoically. "I will cope." He spat out a fragment of glittering wing and they watched it float down to the ground. There had been no further sighting of the tigers, despite occasional distant growling.

"They've probably gone back to the palace," Zhu Irzh said. "Can't see them hunting too late into the night. I imagine a party is in order." He looked at the badger. "How d'you fancy going back?"

"To the palace?" The badger thought about this. It had a certain appeal. "We could kill more things."

"Not *quite* what I had in mind," Zhu Irzh said patiently. "There are rather too many of them. I was thinking about the portal. There's got to be some way of moving between the worlds—I don't think I was unconscious for all that long and it seems reasonable that we were brought directly to the palace. Which way did they bring you in? Did you see?"

The badger told him.

"Same here," the demon mused. "A corridor, with hunting trophies. Seems like a clue to me."

"Well?" the badger asked him. "Should we go back?"

"What do you think?"

"I don't like skulking about."

"No," Zhu Irzh said thoughtfully. "I didn't think you would."

"Do you know the way?"

"Not really. I think if we follow the river, we've got a good chance of making it back to the grounds of the palace. There were a lot of streams and ornamental fountains beyond the hunting lawns and that suggests a water supply, even in a place like this."

They were careful, following the river back, keeping eyes and ears open for anything that might be lying in wait. When they skirted the place at which Zhu Irzh had trapped the tiger, the badger saw that the water was bubbling and there was a strong smell of blood: something had dragged the tigress' body down into the river and was still engaged in the process of tearing it apart. Alligator demons? Well, why not? Apart from this, the jungle was humming with life. Something the size of a man, with green-glowing eyes, swung down out of the branches and stared at them.

"Good evening," Zhu Irzh said, but it hissed and was gone, back up into the canopy. "I don't like meeting so many people," the demon complained. "All it takes is for someone to report back…"

"Perhaps the tigers are not popular," the badger suggested. Zhu Irzh conceded that this made sense.

After a time, the jungle began to open out, with clearings and glades that did not seem natural to the badger. Then Zhu Irzh put out a hand, trapping the badger's nose.

"Hang on."

"What is it?"

"There's something there. Looks like a building."

The badger snorted. He did not entirely approve of buildings. Keeping close to Zhu Irzh—it would be unfortunate if they became separated, as he was not convinced of the demon's ability to manage without him—the badger inched forward. Through the roots of a dense stand of mangroves, he could see a small, domed structure.

"It is ruined."

"Hmm," Zhu Irzh said. "Actually, I'm not so sure."

The badger was unconvinced. The building did not look inhabited; it was of marble, but the creepers and vines had grown up it in coiling profusion and the walls were stained with what smelled like mold, a dank, green odor that filled the clearing. In amongst the vines were carvings of humans engaged in sexual congress, a feature that passed the badger's understanding.

"I think it's a temple," Zhu Irzh whispered.

"Why?"

"I don't know. I've seen pictures of buildings like this, in magazine articles. Also, it feels like a temple."

"Who is it dedicated to?"

"I don't know. Think we should find out?" The demon's teeth flashed in the darkness. Before the badger could advise caution, Zhu Irzh stepped over the mangrove roots into the clearing and strolled over to the temple. The badger followed, scenting the air.

Inside, up a small flight of steps, the temple was clearly in poor condition. Some of the vines had broken through the roof and curled down the central pillars. The floor was slippery with fallen leaves. A small green snake, like molten jade, hissed at the badger without malice as it glided by. The badger murmured a greeting in return and went in pursuit of Zhu Irzh. This was not hard, for the temple was composed of only one room. He found the demon behind a pillar, staring at a statue.

"You asked who this place was dedicated to," Zhu Irzh said. "There's your answer." He gestured toward the statue. It was of a young woman, round-faced and smiling. She stood on one clawed foot, and was depicted in the act of playing a long flute, raised to her lips by taloned fingers. A tail curled around her ankles. But like the rest of the temple, the statue was spotted with mold, although it had not become corroded.

"Who is she?" the badger asked. "Do you know?"

"No idea. Some minor demon, perhaps." Zhu Irzh glanced around. "Looks like a central theme of lust, anyway." In a moment of whimsy that was lost on the badger, he kissed his fingertips and touched them to the woman's smiling lips. There was a blinding flash of light, dazzling the badger and forcing a growl out of him.

"Oh dear," Zhu Irzh said. The young woman stepped down from her pedestal, dark eyes glittering, mouth twisting with fury, and punched Zhu Irzh in the face.

"Where is he?" she shouted.

"Who?" The demon spat black blood. "I'll say this for you, madam, being turned to stone doesn't seem to have done you a whole lot of harm."

"Did he send you? Has he decided that, suddenly, I'm to be brought back to court? As a little 'entertainment,' perhaps?"

Her naked limbs were still dappled with rot, the badger noticed, almost masking her musky odor. She smelled of amber and spice, a smell that even the badger recognized as strongly sexual.

"We're… not local, let me put it that way."

"Oh." The girl stepped back and surveyed Zhu Irzh. "No, you're not from here, are you? Did he capture you?"

"By 'he,' do you mean the prince?"

"Prince?" The dark gaze flashed sparks, which showered to the floor and hissed out among the fallen leaves. "He told me I would be a queen! Queen Sefira, that's what he promised me!"

"Let me guess," the demon said. "You're a forest spirit. A deva? You probably started out as a tribal fertility totem and as things got a bit more sophisticated, you changed accordingly. This is your temple, in which fertility rites of various forms of intensity were carried out. The prince shows up. He says he's a god. This is actually true. He offers you marriage, screws you for a couple of months, gets bored, tries to persuade you to go back to the sticks. You refuse, throw a scene, get turned to stone to shut you up."

The deva stared at him. "How did you know?"

"My dear," the demon said. "It's the oldest of old stories. Happens all over the place. Especially to little country spirits like you."

"What a bastard," the deva said. "I really thought he loved me, you know? I can't believe I was so stupid. Who's he got up there now?"

"A coven of tiger spirits," Zhu Irzh said.

"*What?* Those bitches? In my forest?"

"These are hunting grounds now. Sorry."

The deva wrapped her arms around herself, as if cold. The badger watched Zhu Irzh's eyes travel across the deva's cleavage, and gave a mental sigh. Human-type people were all the same. It was not something with which he had any sympathy. He poked Zhu Irzh with a claw.

"We are looking for something. Ask her."

"Oh!" the deva said, looking down. Insultingly, it seemed she had only just realized that the badger was there. "Isn't it sweet?"

"Fine," the badger said, and teakettled. A muffled iron voice said, "*You* can carry me, then."

THIRTY-ONE

Chen was clearly unhappy with the idea of Inari traveling to *between,* but it was equally unacceptable to risk Mhara.

"Besides," Inari said resolutely, "I'm the only one who knows Bonerattle. He might not speak to anyone else."

"I accept that," Chen said. "It's just the thought of you heading off into what amounts to this assassin's lands. I don't like it."

"Neither do I," Inari said. The prospect of returning to *between* made her quail, but she had not shrunk from other, equally unpleasant challenges, and she did not intend to shrink from this one, either. "But I'm still going to do it."

Mhara said, "You shouldn't do this. Not for me. I'll go myself."

"You won't!" Inari said, and blushed. She was unused to telling Celestial Emperors what to do. But Mhara saved her face by not smiling.

"We can't risk you," Robin said to Mhara. "If something happens to you, who is your heir?"

"Obviously, I have no child."

"Exactly. So if you… disappear, who would take the throne?"

"My mother." Mhara gave a grim nod.

"Then all the worlds are at risk," Chen pointed out. "Given what you've told me about your mother's convictions, she'd waste no time in re-establishing the old order of Heaven and setting your father's wishes in motion. Heaven severed from Earth, and Hell let loose."

"I may be a demon," Inari said to Mhara, "but you know what I'd think about *that.*"

Mhara sighed. "Then, let's commence."

No Ro Shi said, "We might be able to offer her some protection, at least. A ring of necromancy, for instance, written in blood."

"I'll gladly contribute," Chen said.

The demon-hunter agreed. "It might be necessary. I also will give blood. Then, it should be fired. Inari's protection will last as long as the blood is alight."

"I should give blood also," Mhara said. "I may not have much authority in *between,* but the blood of the Celestial Emperor should count for something."

Robin gave a wry grimace. "I'd offer, but I don't think it would do much good. Ghosts aren't endowed with blood."

Chen gestured in reluctant agreement. "Then let's make a start."

Inari knelt in the middle of the temple hall, eyes closed, hands firmly clasped around the strip of silk that contained the hatpin. Her brother might have worked in a blood emporium back in Hell, but she did not want to watch her husband and friends undergo injury on her behalf. Then it struck her that if they were prepared to give it, she should at least have the courage to watch, to take some of their pain on board. But there was no expression on Chen's face as he held out his hand and sliced open a palm that was crisscrossed with old scars, the workings of spells and conjurations, the necessary price paid for a magical life. Red drops fell into a bronze bowl, making it sing like rain. No Ro Shi was next, and then Mhara. The blood of the Celestial Emperor was a vivid neon blue. Robin's spectral eyebrows rose as the blood sang electricity into the bowl.

"I don't remember it looking like that."

Mhara said, apologetically, "It changes, on coronation. My blood is the blood of Heaven itself."

The blue fluid struck the walls of the bowl, sizzling like lightning. Quickly, Chen seized the bowl and sprinkled its contents around Inari's kneeling form. Then No Ro Shi spoke a word that rang throughout the rafters of the little temple, harsh and summoning. He drew his sword in a sweeping arc and touched the tip to the ring of blood. Inari saw the word run down the sword, a flickering spark, and ignite the blood around her. She heard the raised voices of Chen and No Ro Shi, with Mhara's quieter murmur running beneath. Then everything was blotted out by a wall of red fire.

蛇醫探

Between.

Above her, perched on a rock, Bonerattle said, "You took your time."

He looked like an old vulture, Inari thought: the sharp, black face, the bitter-sloe eyes. The shaman was hunched in his skin and bones as if against a cold wind.

"I came as soon as I could," Inari said.

The shaman leaned forward, all eagerness. "Have you seen him? Have you spoken?"

"Yes. Just now, at his temple on Earth. I've told him what you told me."

"Ah!" The word was a caw.

"But Bonerattle, listen—" She almost spoke the name out loud, then remembered in time. She thought the shaman had heard it anyway. "The person we spoke about has already been attacked."

Bonerattle's head shot forward on a neck that was too long.

"Already?"

"Yes, in Heaven."

"But the Lord Lady Seijin was not successful."

"No. This is how it happened." And Inari told him Mhara's tale.

"This weapon. Let me see it." Bonerattle's black gaze was sharp. With great care, Inari unwrapped the silk and held it out.

"This is a *ru-lun*," Bonerattle said, in awe. He sat back.

"I don't know what that is."

"An ancient metal, forged from the heart of a star. Something that fell to Earth millions of years ago, but did not reach the planet's surface. Fell instead into *between,* became a legend. The smith took pieces of it."

"The smith?"

"Every story starts with something forged," the shaman said. "Find the smith, you find a spell."

"And spells can be reversed?" Inari asked.

"Exactly."

She did not know how much time she had. She explained this to the shaman, who laughed. "The blood of the Celestial Emperor will surely burn long and long. But we should be swift, anyway. I know where the smith is to be found, if the land will let us in."

Inari followed Bonerattle up amongst the rocks, the shaman skipping and dancing like a mad child. It seemed to her that she could feel the protective ring of blazing blood, a warmth upon her skin. But the thought of Seijin was enough to make her grow cold—the audacity of it, someone who would try to slay a god. The Lord Lady was assuming monstrous proportions in Inari's mind; she told herself not to be so fearful. But it was a fear more for others than for herself, of what would befall them all if Seijin succeeded.

And how had the assassin entered Heaven, anyway? Had someone let Seijin in?

Inari's thoughts soon turned to the badger and Zhu Irzh; there were more people to worry about than simply herself. Her world was quickly reduced to simple things, the necessity of watching where she was going, for they were up above the mist line now, the fog swirling about Inari's face and filming her skin and hair, and the rocks underfoot were smooth and treacherous. It seemed to her that she could glimpse shapes and forms in the mist, gliding presences with ragged wings and eyes that were like holes into shadow. When the shaman paused, Inari touched his arm.

"What are those things?"

The shaman said, "I don't know. Shadows of the worlds beyond, perhaps. They're always here. They never harm."

"Are you sure?" Inari faltered. She had met shadows in Hell, sad souls, lost to memory and almost to sentience, that creaked and croaked in the darkness of corners. These things still carried power, like a dust in their filament wings.

"I have never known them to do harm," the shaman said, less than reassuringly. "Do not worry, humanwife. Can't you hear the forge?"

And as soon as he spoke, Inari realized that she could indeed hear it: a distant roar, counterpointed by a harsh tap-tapping. It was coming from the rocks up ahead, the summit of the stone-strewn slope. It was growing hotter, too, and then she noticed that the mist that streamed past them was not fog after all, but smoke. There was an acrid tang on the wind, the scent of fire. The tapping grew louder, more insistent, as if someone were beating a small drum.

Inari followed the shaman behind a rock and saw that they were standing above a small valley. It glowed: the rocks beneath were hot coals, the earth sizzling and blackened, the valley walls stained with soot. Occasionally, spires of flame gouted out from cracks in the earth. At the end of the valley stood something too bright to see, but Inari, glancing at it from the corners of her eyes, thought that it was a little building, three-walled, with a sloping roof.

The scene might have been fearsome, but Inari was used to the fires of Hell, the forests of flame that lay far beyond the city limits, and besides, after the monochrome shadow and gray of *between,* the valley was almost welcoming.

"Tread where I tread," the shaman commanded, and Inari did so, placing her feet carefully upon the rocks on which Bonerattle walked. It was like a game, children following one another across an old and ritual pattern. Only once did she slip, her ankle turning slightly on a loose boulder, and the hem of her skirt touched the coals and flared briefly into light. Inari beat it out, while the shaman waited impatiently, some little distance ahead.

Now that they had drawn closer, the forge had become easier to see. Behind the falls of fire, it was a modest structure, assembled out of what Inari at first took to be plaster and stone. But then, following Bonerattle across the final bridge of coals, she saw that the sides of the forge were made of bones: the enormous femurs of something long dead and legendary, the roof of the forge formed by the upper part of a skull. The eyeholes would easily have encompassed a man; the twin tusks reached almost to the ground and twisting horns extended back, balancing the forge against the fiery ground. Inari felt a pang of pity for it, but as they approached, the skull spoke.

"A shaman and a demon?"

"I need to speak to your master," Bonerattle informed it. "Is he within?"

"He is. I know you. You have been here before. But the demon has not."

"Your perceptiveness knows no bounds," the shaman said, waspish.

"It's not easy, without eyes. Master is here, and will see you. Go inside."

Inari stepped over a steaming lintel, into the heart of the forge. Within, the bone structure was even more apparent, the pitted ivory of the walls scorched and cracked. In the center of the room stood the forge itself: a massive anvil, made of something harder and heavier than iron, with a presence almost as great as the skull that surrounded it. The bellows breathed out and fire licked the walls of the forge.

"It's alive," Inari said.

"Oh yes. Most things are, in *between*."

Inari's eyes were adjusting to the intense brightness, but as she watched, the anvil hissed and the roar of the forge subsided to a dull red glow. Inari blinked. Someone was sitting at the back of the forge, a man as wiry and thin as a skeleton, bones and sinews clearly visible through a translucent covering of skin, blackened by fire. Sharp teeth showed in a grin. His eyes were white, as if filmed by cataracts.

"Bonerattle. You again. At least your guest is prettier."

"Are you a demon, too?" Inari asked.

The smith laughed. "No, just very old. I've been here a long time. And other places. We used to get around more. You might say I'm semi-retired."

"We've brought you something," the shaman said. "A piece of your own work, if I'm not wrong." He held out the silk-wrapped hairpin.

"Aha," the smith said. "I was wondering when use would finally be made of that."

"You remember it, then?" Inari said, and cursed herself for stupidity: of course he would remember, he was an artist, and she felt deep within that nothing that ever passed his anvil would be forgotten.

The smith's grin widened. "Naturally. This is an old piece, made when I was younger and more foolish. Now—even I would think twice. This is a substance that can cut the wind: forged star-stone, in the days before metal was known to men. I made it for a demon. Her name was Ti-tao and she was a consort to both the Emperors of Heaven and Hell. She had hair that was thirty feet in length and she needed a pin with which to bind it. This was that pin and it has a twin sister."

"You made it for Ti-tao," the shaman said, "but now it has become a weapon."

"Ah, it's had a long history. Ti-tao came to a sad end, these people usually do. Her consorts both accused her of treachery and she was said to be imprisoned here in *between,* beneath a river of molten iron. She is almost certainly disembodied. After that, one pin was given to Heaven and the other to Hell, in remembrance."

"So this pin must have come from either?"

"Presumably Hell," Inari said, "if it was used to try to kill the Emperor of Heaven."

The smith's white eyes were expressionless as he said, "So, that is why you're here? Do you wish to assault Heaven, little demon?"

"No!" Inari said indignantly. "The Emperor of Heaven is my friend."

The smith's eyebrows had been singed away long since, but his eyes widened nonetheless. "Is that so? Unusual. But then, you have a precedence in Ti-tao of the glorious hair and I'm sure you must be almost as beautiful."

"We're not lovers," Inari said, blushing at the thought. "I owe him some allegiance."

"Besides," Bonerattle explained. "There have been many interesting things happening in the three worlds lately. Wars, invasions, goddesses gone mad."

"I don't get out much," the smith remarked. "And I absented myself from the affairs of the Realms a long time ago. But that doesn't mean that news is not welcome. Moreover, it's always of interest to see what has become of one's work."

"We need to know," Bonerattle said, "about the spells that are attached to this pin."

The smith frowned. "I know that both pins were cursed. Ti-tao's hair was what made so many fall in love with her, and so it was her hair that was the focus of her consorts' anger. They had it cut off, before she was imprisoned, and I don't know what became of it. The pins were cursed, as I have told you, and separated: they were held to be more powerful if they were together. I wove only one spell into them when I made them, and that was a spell of beauty which called upon the power of the star from which they were forged."

"Maybe that's it," the shaman mused. "Something from outside the orbit of the solar system, something from the deep universe, away from the spheres of the three worlds."

"Maybe only something like that can kill a god," Inari suggested.

"The sister pin," the smith said. "Do you know what became of that?"

"The assassin might still have it," Inari said.

"If you could put these pins together," the smith told her, "then perhaps you might have a weapon which could strike at even such a liminal being as this assassin. It's not hard, by the way, to know who you are talking about."

Inari was about to reply when the forge roared, so loudly that she stepped back in alarm. Then she realized that the sound had not come from the anvil or the fire, but from the building itself, the skull from which the forge was formed.

Bonerattle seized Inari by the arm. *"Run."*

Inari had become used to obeying instructions like that. She did so, and the moment she stepped out of the forge, she found herself in a very different landscape. The valley was cold and dead, all fires extinguished and the coals no more than crumbling lumps of rock. A mist was swirling down from the heights, filling the valley with a wintery breath. The shaman and Inari stumbled up the slope, slipping on ash. In the sudden chill, Inari realized something: the protective warmth of the circle of blood had gone. Back in Mhara's earthly temple, the fire must have gone out, leaving her exposed. She glanced back and saw that the forge was prudently folding itself up, the jaw hinging down, the femurs folding until a small white box stood on the smoldering ground and was then swallowed by it. Smith and dragon, making a swift exit. She could not blame them.

Just ahead of her, the mist curdled and congealed, forming a solid white cloud, and out of it stepped someone, smiling.

A woman, Inari thought at first, but then she saw that beneath the armored tunic, the shoulders were a little broad, and there was a telltale swelling in the throat. But the long black hair, swept back in a queue, and the delicacy of feature might easily have told a different story. The dark eyes held a genuine warmth, almost compassion, as the figure reached out a hand in which rested a small bow. The glittering tooth of an arrow was aimed directly at Inari. She heard a crack and a whistle as the bolt was released, looked down in horror to see it hurtling toward her, and heard herself cry out, "Chen! Help me!"—then she was kneeling on the floor of Mhara's temple, her husband by her side, clasping her by the shoulders and saying, "Inari! It's all right. You're safe. You're home."

Inari opened her hand. The pin lay within it, wrapped in silk, as safe as she was.

THIRTY-TWO

Go felt himself grow cold, then hot, then icy. The demon reached forward and put her hand to his cheek; heat burned out of her palm, as if he had been touched by the sun.

"You're afraid," she said.

"Of course I'm fucking afraid!" He wasn't even certain that he had spoken aloud.

"You smell of my sister."

"Oh god!"

The demon frowned. "Don't be scared. My name is Savitra. I came because my sister almost returned home. We can't let that happen."

"We can't? How did you get *in* here?"

Savitra looked puzzled. "I followed a scent. There was a hunt last night, but then when my sisters and I returned to the Hunting Lodge, we thought that someone should come to Earth, to find her."

"Find her and do what?"

"Why, bind her, of course. You obviously don't want her here. We don't want her at home." Savitra's beautiful face screwed itself into an expression of deep distaste. "Such a bitch." She looked around her, and Go had the distinct impression that she was scenting the air. "There's someone else here."

"Well, yeah. This is a big corporation—there's lots of people in it."

"I don't mean humans. I mean one of my kind. What is this place called?"

"The name of the company is Paugeng."

Savitra's face cleared. "Why, I know of this organization. It belongs to my cousin. To Jhai."

"What?" Go had the feeling that you get during the course of a nightmare, when you think you're free and suddenly it all comes boiling back again.

"Your *cousin?* But Jhai's human."

Savitra gave a growling snort. "Oh no she's not. She's one of us. She just lives here, and passes."

"Passes? Jhai's a big shot."

"Don't use that horrible expression!"

"Sorry. Anyway, she isn't here." Thank God for that. Go didn't think he could cope with two of them right now. "She's away on a business trip."

But by the time he said this, Go swiftly discovered, it was already history. The doors banged open as Jhai, with a face like thunder, came in at a run, surrounded by security personnel.

"Meeting wrapped early. This showed up as a security breach, just as I'd got back—Savitra, what the *hell* are *you* doing here?"

Savitra bridled. "I might ask you the same thing."

Jhai turned to the security detail. "Okay, guys, nothing to worry about. Just my mad cousin. Probably thought she'd surprise me."

"I seem to have succeeded," Savitra said.

"Out." Jhai motioned to security. Without the presence of a large quantity of men in body armor and guns, Go's natural inhibitions vanished. He said, "Ms Tserai? Jhai? What the fuck? You didn't tell me Lara was your fucking cousin! What was the plan? Have me over for feeding time?" He was aware that his voice was rising. "You didn't tell me!" It was a child's plaintive whine.

Jhai sighed. "Mr Go. Savitra. The bar is *this* way." With that, she swept back through the doors of the gym.

" 'The bar is *this* way,' " Savitra mimicked, mincing cruelly. "Nice to see you, Savitra, been such a long time. *Bitch.*"

Or rather, Go thought, cat.

He felt a bit better nursing a large scotch. At least Jhai's whisky selection was upfront and honest. And, if not ashamed (he doubted that Jhai Tserai had much acquaintance with that particular emotion), his hostess did at least seem to feel that some kind of explanation was called for.

"Look. Mr Go. I probably should have told you, but what could I say? Yeah, the demon who killed your friend and burned down your house? She's my cousin. But don't worry about it."

"Who knows?" Go asked. "Here in Singapore Three, I mean."

"Gods only know, to be honest. It used to be a very closely guarded secret, for obvious reasons. Demonkind weren't allowed to have property or holdings on Earth." Jhai made a face. "At least, not unless they were Chinese demons. The establishment here is riddled with corruption—I'm sure half the bloody government hail from Hell."

"It would explain a lot," Go said.

"But in the last couple of years, all sorts of shit has been happening, goddesses running riot through the city, great rifts between the worlds… Demons live and work here, like my fiancé, wherever *he's* got to."

"Is he missing?" Savitra said, and it was impossible for Go to mistake the note in her voice. That, Go thought, would be satisfaction.

"He's gone AWOL, yes. I'm looking into it." *None of your business*, said Jhai's own tone. "Anyway, my point is that things are changing. At first, no one knew about me except my mum. My fiancé obviously knows about me, and so does Chen, and his wife, and his wife's familiar."

"His wife's what?" Go was aware of a familiar feeling of confusion.

"Never mind, it isn't important. All those people are as discreet as they come, but the thing is, once a handful of people know, it acts as a kind of conduit. Information is like water. Once there's a little hole in the dam, it starts to trickle out."

"I know what you mean," Go said. "The film industry's like a sodding sieve."

"And now you know," Jhai said. For a horrible moment, Go thought she'd intended some kind of subtext: *And now we'll have to kill you.* But it seemed that no such sinister intention was present, for Jhai went on, "That's not a problem, under the circumstances. Frankly, I felt you needed help, given that Lara's my cousin."

"To be fair," Go said, "it's my fault she's here in the first place." He took a reassuringly large swig of scotch and looked out across the city. It was twilight now, with the lights of shipping starring the distant curve of sea. A burning hand rested lightly on his own.

"No, no," Savitra said. "We are really very grateful."

"But now we've got to find her," Jhai told him. "Find and bind."

"How do you propose to do that?" Go asked. "With magic?"

"Not exactly," Jhai said. She looked at him and he saw, not quite for the first time, the ruthlessness in her dark eyes. "With bait."

蛇警探

He couldn't believe she'd talked him into this, but on reflection, he'd had remarkably little choice, faced with two tiger demons. They seemed to be multiplying, although Jhai had reassured him that Savitra had now returned home, confident that Lara wouldn't be coming back any time soon.

"I can't cope with her," Jhai complained. "Never stops bloody talking. I told her to go back and stay there—we'll deal with this."

At the time, Go had wondered at the advisability of finishing that very large glass of Laphroaig, but now, as its peaty warmth formed a barrier between himself and an unwelcome reality, he was glad that he'd been so irresponsible.

He stood in a grove of trees, in one of Singapore Three's rather unsuccessful parks. Originally, Lotus Park had been intended, as most parks are, as both a green lung in the city's heart and a place for respectable citizens to stroll whilst enjoying the beauties of nature. The city had grown up to incorporate patches of woodland, and some of this still remained amidst the lily-fringed pools, the ornamental bridges, the skating rink, and the rosebushes.

Not to mention the discarded syringes, the phials of the more experimental narcotics, and the small sad balloons of used condoms that littered the leaf-strewn concrete on which Go was standing. At least the latter was evidence of *some* degree of responsibility.

He felt like a tethered goat. The tethers might be invisible ones, but they still seemed as binding as shackles. Directly into his ear, a voice said softly, "Here, kitty, kitty."

Go jumped and found himself staring into Jhai's face. She was wearing a black jumpsuit, the Dolce & Gabbana version of a ninja outfit, and the effect made the oval of her face appear disembodied among the trees. Above, a chewed moon floated in rags of cloud.

"Don't do that!"

"Sorry. How're you doing, Go?"

"Is there any sign of her?" Go asked nervously. In her earlier dismissal of the use of magic, Jhai had, it seemed, been not entirely open. They had deployed it already, back among the trees, taking a hypodermic of Go's blood and scattering it into a conjured wind. The blood, black in the faint gleam of the moon, had swirled up like a string of broken beads, hurtling out into the trees and then the city. Go's skin was still prickling; he felt unpleasantly linked to the city itself, everywhere at once, catching fragments and snatches whenever he turned his head. And Jhai… he was not unfamiliar with the powers of necromancy, but whereas his father had possessed a thin current of it, Jhai had dragged it out of the ground as though hauling an express train behind her. Once again, Go lamented his stupidity in having anything at all to do with this shit. Find a therapist. Blame his parents.

"Don't worry," Jhai said now. "Won't be long."

"Great," Go said, weakly.

"No, seriously. This is a good thing. She'll show up, she'll follow your blood, assume you've been hurt. Lara's never been what you might call a rocket scientist."

"To be honest, I did have her down as a bit of a bimbo."

"None of them are all that bright. The brains seem to have gone to my side of the family." Jhai tried, and failed, not to look smug. "Anyway. She'll show, she'll try to kill you, we'll rescue you—there's about twenty of my people in the trees, you just can't see them, and they're magically hidden—and then we'll go back to the bar."

"Sounds fantastic."

"It'll *work*." She gave him a pat on the shoulder. "Hang in there, man." She melted back among the trees, leaving Go alone in the humid darkness. The air was filled with the pungent smell of a stagnant pond, of distant cigarette smoke, of fried food and his own sweat. A group of young women strolled along the side of the pond, some way from where Go stood. They were laughing and chattering; one of them had a bag of some kind of takeout food and they were all dipping into it. He envied them. When this was all over, he was going to have a normal social life.

He looked up at the moon, swimming out from cloud. *Just you and me now, moon.* And then the tiger roared.

THIRTY-THREE

Back in the Shadow Pavilion, Seijin twisted a long strand of black hair between fingers that were a little cold, despite the fire. A pity the smith had evaded capture, but that could be rectified at leisure, later on. If this was the chosen path. Male self, as ever mindful of face, insisted that it should be, but Seijin was not convinced. Revenge, generally considered as a waste of time and energy, had never been a huge feature of the assassin's psychology. Pride was all very well, but pride was frequently expensive. It was, however, important not to repress male self's views: Seijin sometimes thought that he was the earliest, most primitive aspect of the Lord Lady Assassin, and one should not lose touch with one's roots.

With this in mind, Seijin took one of the longbows down from the wall and accessorized it with a quiver of arrows, made of the gray wood of *between* and tipped with congealed moonlight. Then the Lord Lady swept a cloak of misty gauze over one shoulder and stepped lightly down the stairs of the Shadow Pavilion. At the last step, the word of cloud-conjuring was spoken and Seijin's form was hidden by the mists that lay *between* and the world of men.

On Earth, the city was oppressively hot. Seijin was grateful for the cloak, providing a cloudy layer between the Lord Lady and the polluted air. Earth had been a fresh world, once, but the camps of the steppe nomads had always been filthy with discarded debris and Seijin had seen long ago that things did not change much; they merely became more complicated.

And some things did not.

It was too demeaning to prey upon the weak, like asking a leopard to chase mice. There was a curious thread of spilled blood running through the city air, reeking of a predator's magic, and the assassin was tempted to follow it, purely from curiosity. But it was clearly someone else's hunt and it would be ill mannered, to say the least, to interfere: Seijin placed great store on courtesy.

It was too often all one had left.

After some thought, Seijin selected the target based on location: the man was coming out of a dojo in the Bharulay District of the city, a rough area. Seijin, with some satisfaction, saw that the man moved like a killer, and there was the ghost of blood upon him, a psychic stain. It would not have mattered if the man had been entirely innocent of life-shed; it was only important that he be some kind of warrior. Seijin decided to test a theory. Summoning female self to the fore, the Lord Lady stepped out of the shadows and cast the cloak of mist away, to seep into the shadows of the street and disappear.

Easy to see through the target's eyes for a moment, easy to take in the slight, slender girl with the dark hair, the lost look, the fearful expression. Easy to hear through the target's ears the faltering voice, "Excuse me? Do you know the way to Shaopeng from here? I thought…"

"C'mere."

And Seijin, tottering a little as if on too-high heels, did so. A brief exhilaration, an indulgence really, of hands closing around the throat, a whispered hate-filled voice, and then the hammer of a human body against the wall as Seijin flung him aside.

Seijin said, softly, "You may fight if you choose."

The prey ran forward, screaming, any discipline acquired at the dojo long since lost. Seijin did not bother to remember the details of the encounter. The assassin played with the man for a while, before growing bored. The next time the prey turned, battered now, staggering, but still upright, Seijin notched a silver-tipped arrow to the bow with slow ease and shot him through the heart.

That night, in the Shadow Pavilion, the Lord Lady dined on human flesh, lightly steamed. The liver and heart went to the Gatekeeper; Seijin did not particularly care for offal. Still, it helped to keep one's strength up and the man's savage essence was gratifying after the relative defeats of the day. And there was still time for an early night.

THIRTY-FOUR

As it happened, Zhu Irzh did not have to carry the badger-teakettle very far.

"Between worlds?" Sefira the deva said. "You want to get back to Earth? This temple was a gateway, once."

"Finally, something goes right!" the badger heard Zhu Irzh say. "Come on then, badger. Back we go."

"Wait," the deva murmured. "It's not as simple as that. There are different keys to every gateway."

The badger wanted to hear this, unimpeded by an iron skin. He turned back into his animal form.

"Well," Zhu Irzh said, a trifle impatiently. "Can you tell me the key to this one?"

"Look around you," the deva said. She moved a little closer to the demon. Zhu Irzh and the badger did as she instructed. The interior of the temple was as dank and uninviting as before.

"What?" Zhu Irzh asked.

The deva gave an exaggerated sigh. "Then look outside, if you cannot see."

Zhu Irzh and the badger stepped cautiously out of the temple, into a clearing that was still empty, still quiet. The temple, with its entwined erotic carvings, seemed to merge into the tangled vines, a phosphorescent white-green.

"I can't see anything that looks like an—oh," the demon said.

The badger glanced up at him. "I still do not understand."

"No, I don't suppose you would. This is a humanoid thing."

The deva was purring. "Come," she said. "This is not for beasts. This is a temple of love."

"Rather you than me," said the badger. "Call me if something needs biting."

An hour or so later, the badger and a somewhat disheveled Zhu Irzh once more stood in front of the temple. The deva was still within.

"Well," the demon said. "It could have been worse."

The badger had a brief, but uninteresting series of memories of the last hour: the deva's gleaming limbs, now as white as the marble of the temple, now as dark as the surrounding vines, twining with the body of Zhu Irzh, eyes glinting in the shadows as the carvings of the temple wall crept out, one by one, still dappled with mold and damp. The curve of the deva's breasts as she arched her back, her cries soft as moths…

The badger had spent his time rooting for beetles, a much more rewarding pastime.

"This is taking longer than I thought," Zhu Irzh said. "What's she doing in there?"

"I don't know. Moreover—" The badger, unused and uninterested in the mating rituals of two-legged things, was tentative about this next suggestion, but went ahead anyway, "I know that, should Husband-of-my-Mistress look at another female, Mistress would not be happy, although I believe she would understand."

"In other words—" Zhu Irzh was not slow on the uptake "—how am I going to explain this to Jhai?"

"Just so."

"Do you think I'm a total fool? She'd have me disembodied. This was dictated by necessity and thus I have no intention of telling her."

"That would seem to be wise."

"I trust you'll be equally discreet?"

"It is of no consequence to me," the badger said, with perfect truth, although he filed the information away, just in case it was ever needed.

"Glad to hear it. What *is* she doing in there?"

The demon's question was soon answered. The deva appeared in the doorway of the temple, flushed and distressed.

"The gateway has not opened!"

"Oh damn," Zhu Irzh said. "Maybe we need to try again?"

"No, that won't work," the deva replied. "Although—should you wish to return at any point, I will not be unamenable." She looked more cheerful, the badger thought. "Perhaps I should go on holiday, to China."

"You'd be welcome," Zhu Irzh said, which the badger considered to be unlikely, given what had just happened. "However, that presupposes that any of us can leave here. Which, you're telling me, suddenly isn't possible."

"But it has always worked before," the deva said. "Tantric magic is very powerful, it opens many possibilities. In ancient times, it was used as a transgression, a breaking of natural law in order to split the worlds apart and travel between them. There is nothing to say that this has changed, although in recent days, the transgression has lessened because of changing morals."

"So you think that might have caused the gateway to become inactive?"

"Maybe. Unless the prince closed it down when he turned me to stone."

"Whatever the reason," the badger said, "the gateway is not working and we are wasting time."

"I wouldn't call it wasting—" Zhu Irzh began, but a glance at the badger caused him to fall silent. "You're right, of course. Well, if this gateway does not work, we need to find one that does."

"There was one in the palace," the deva said.

The demon sighed. "Back to Plan A. Can you get us into the palace? Do you know a way?"

"I used to. There was a passage not far from here, in the ruins that form the old part of the palace. As people lost faith, the place fell into disrepair. I don't know if the passage is still passable."

"We have to try," said Zhu Irzh.

The deva was, at least, correct: the ruins of the old palace were not far away. They made their way through the skeins of vines, pushing aside huge leaves. Trumpet-shaped flowers rose out of the shadows, whispering allurements that were lost on the badger, if perhaps not Zhu Irzh. But the jungle seemed to have changed, even to the badger's animal instincts: the scents becoming headier and more sensuous, the air perfumed with musk. He put this down to the deva's restored presence, but wondered with unease whether the changes might not alert someone at the Hunting Lodge to the fact that a possibly unwelcome alteration had occurred. *Let's hope that they are all sleeping. Let's hope.*

The jungle was thinning out now, and badger's hackles prickled. Moments later, they were looking out across the lawns of the Hunting Lodge. The palace itself seemed quiet, though torches burned and flared along the terrace; badger could smell smoke above the increasingly narcotic scent of jasmine. High in the palace, in one of the tall, crenellated turrets that stood at either end of the long building, a lamp was burning. The deva nudged Zhu Irzh.

"That's the prince's chambers."

"So he's still up," the demon said. "Oh, great."

The deva shook her head, as if in denial of the entire circumstance. "You don't understand. He very rarely sleeps."

Zhu Irzh looked at her. "It's not unknown for rulers in my own Hell to have a personal connection with their premises. The king is the land, that sort of thing. How closely *is* Agni linked to this realm?

"I don't know." The deva looked blank. "We didn't discuss that sort of thing. Actually, we didn't discuss much at all."

"I don't suppose you did."

"Will he know if we set foot in the palace?"

The deva did not answer. But the badger said, "Things go on in this palace of which Agni is unaware."

Zhu Irzh, interested, said, "Oh? What sort of things? And how do you know?"

As concisely as possible, the badger related the conversation that he had overheard in the kitchen.

"The women plot things behind Agni's back."

Zhu Irzh gave a snort. "*There's* a surprise. I bet he thinks he's got them all well under control."

"Actually," the deva said, "he does not trust them. He believed them to be continually scheming against him."

"So you did discuss a few things, it seems?"

"This is what I overheard. People talk, especially servants. The sisters are Agni's harem and they plot, as all harems do." She sighed. "This place reflects the ancient world, not the modern one. I understand that on Earth, women can have direct power these days. But when I was created, from the lap of the world, women could only use what they had, their bodies and their circumstances."

"I don't think one needs to go into too much feminist outrage on their behalf," Zhu Irzh murmured. "They are tigers, after all."

"Yes, but Agni is a demigod. Who do you think has the most authority, if all are called before Vishnu and asked to account for their actions?"

"This may be of historical interest," the badger reminded, "but it is not getting us into the palace. When does dawn come?"

"I don't know," the deva said. "You lose track of time, being a rock."

"It feels like midnight or more," Zhu Irzh said. "We don't have all that long."

The deva led them around the side of the lawn, out of sight in the shadows of the walls.

"What about guards?" Zhu Irzh whispered.

"Agni used to have them. The arrangements might have changed, I don't know."

For the moment, there was no one in sight. They crept along the balustraded wall that separated the upper level of the terraces from the lower, then beneath an arch that took them into a courtyard. The deva thrust Zhu Irzh back just in time and he trod heavily on the badger's paw; the badger stifled a snarl.

"Who's that?" A dog-visaged person, with tusks and armor, came into view.

The deva gave a bell-like laugh. "Why, I've come from the forest. It's lonely out there, you know."

The badger did not pretend to understand humanoid beings, but he did grasp that most male servants of a vaguely relevant species, when confronted with a naked, perfumed woman and time on their hands, will respond in a positive manner. The deva made shooing motions with a hand, as the dog demon drew her inside the guardhouse. Zhu Irzh and the badger wasted no time in slipping by.

"Where now, do you think?" Zhu Irzh hissed. And the badger discovered a fact of remarkably pertinent interest: he was able to smell himself. The trace was very faint, but nonetheless unmistakable. The badger nudged Zhu Irzh and told him so.

"You can smell you?" The demon looked at him blankly.

"Yes. From when I was brought here. We smell strongly, you understand."

"I had noticed, didn't want to say anything, seemed a bit rude."

"Why should it be rude?" the badger asked, puzzled. "It is a fact. My scent is rather stale, but I can still follow it."

"Do you think you can find where they brought you in?" Zhu Irzh asked, with a nervous glance toward the guardhouse. Yelping cries were emanating from it.

"I will have to," the badger remarked. "She cannot keep him entertained forever."

"She's having a damn good try."

The only problem with pursuing the fragile scent was in determining whether it led back to the point of entry, or forward into the palace. After some casting around, the badger thought he might be coming close to the point at which he had been released from the bag, and sure enough, they could see through a window that they had reached the hall. The cries from the guardhouse were diminishing; they did not have long.

"This way," the badger told Zhu Irzh. They ran along the wall, the badger tracking the scent. Unfortunately, this had been the time during which he had been within the bag and the smell was less pungent than it would otherwise have been. But it was possible to locate the scent, nonetheless. With the demon close behind, he ran up a flight of steps, under an ornate jasmine-fringed arch, and into a further courtyard.

There was a block of black stone in the center of the courtyard, a rough, unfinished archway, leading to nothing. The stone should have gleamed in the light of the torches, but instead it seemed to swallow any illumination. The badger felt an instinctive repulsion; this was not a healthy place.

"Shit!" Zhu Irzh's whisper cut the air.

"What?"

The demon was staring upward. The badger followed his gaze and found that they were directly underneath the room in which the lamp was burning.

Now, all the lights went on, blazing out across the courtyard and casting the shadows of demon and badger into sharp relief. Above, silhouetted against the sudden glare, Prince Agni's figure stood, still and impassive, staring down at them. Behind, the torchlit night erupted into a frenzied baying. Prince Agni had let loose his hounds.

THIRTY-FIVE

This time, it really was Lara. Go could hear her padding around in the darkness, but she smelled like the woman he had known: the strong musky perfume she favored was very distinct. He held his breath, fumbled for a cigarette, trying to look as though he'd just stopped for a moment in some endless flight through the city.

Surely she wouldn't fall for this? How mad was she, really? As if in answer, there came a growl. *Don't look up, don't breathe.* Would she wonder why he wasn't reacting to her presence? Did she truly think he might not have noticed? Then there was a sound that seemed to split the world and Go did look up at that, just in time to see the fire of yellow eyes as Lara leaped.

She hit him full on and Go, screaming, went down. The cigarette flew out of his hand and, weirdly, he watched the full arc of its trajectory as it hurtled into the pond and hissed out. Lara's stinking-meat breath made him gasp and retch, as though she had somehow sucked all the oxygen out of the immediate atmosphere. She had knocked the breath out of his lungs, his ribs ached with the shock of impact, but when she reared back Go still managed to find the strength to stagger to his feet and try to run, as if his body had been subject to sudden possession by a desperate spirit. Somewhere, someone else was shouting, but Go was past the point where he was able to distinguish words. Then he tripped over a tree root and fell full length. There was a curious noise like a puff of wind, then a shriek and a thump that shook the world. Go stayed where he was, facedown in loose earth, unable to move.

A moment later, however, someone was hauling him to his feet. "Come on, Go. You did it. She's down." Jhai's voice sounded exultant. Go was, for the moment, unashamed to lean his full weight on her; she bore it easily.

He had to drag his head up to look at Lara. The tigress' body lay twitching in spasms, a little distance away beneath the trees. Go's breath deserted him once more; she was surely twice as large as an ordinary, earthly tiger. What had he and Beni been *thinking,* to conjure up a monster such as this? Go looked back on his only-slightly-younger self with a feeling of wonder, as one who considers a madman.

"Yeah," Jhai said, following his gaze. "That's Lara, all right. Typically unreasonable."

"Is she—dead? *Can* she be dead?"

"No, we just tranked her. She'd just be shot straight back to Hell if we killed her here, and given what Savitra's told me, they'd make sure she came back again. Twice as angry. Which, I'm assuming, you'd prefer she didn't?"

"Too right," Go quavered. "What about a binding spell, then?"

Jhai made a get-moving gesture to the figures in the shadows. "On its way."

Go watched as the tigress' inert form was loaded onto a stretcher. It took half a dozen security personnel even to lift her. Jhai, watching also, shook her head. "I'm going to have her snapped permanently back to her human form once we've got her under lock and key. Much more manageable."

"Couldn't you do that here?"

"Look around you." Go did so, and saw that quite a few bystanders had congregated.

"If we did, and someone recognized her, called the media—you can see it, can't you? 'Movie Star in Stun Gun Shock.' Much better that they just see a dangerous wild animal of whom yours truly has just rid the city."

Admiringly, Go shook his head. "You seem to have everything covered." But he'd thought that last time, and turned to meet a tiger's eyes.

"Not quite everything," Jhai said. "I've got a fiancé to find. And you look like you need a drink."

No exaggeration there, Go thought. He'd nearly needed new trousers.

蛇警探

Go drank rather a lot, back at Paugeng, but it didn't seem to have much effect. Like most writers, he'd always been able to hold his booze, but this was unnatural: he'd already had three triple scotches and they might as well have been Perrier. Perhaps this was some aftereffect of industrial-level fear, or maybe—a disconcerting thought—it was the aftereffect of magic itself. He was still strangely aware of his blood roaming around the city. The sensation was fading, but still present. Since he wasn't getting any benefit from it, Go decided to stop drinking. He put his empty glass down on the bar, just as Jhai came through the door.

"How're you doing, Go?"

"Freaked out," Go told her, with truth.

"Okay. We've got Lara human, stable, securely contained, and semiconscious. Want to come and have a look at her?"

"Not particularly," Go said, but he rose anyway and followed Jhai to the elevator.

Paugeng's levels descended a long way. Go had heard that the new building had been built upon the foundations of the old, but he hadn't realized that the underground complex was so extensive. Jhai could be doing anything under here, he thought: missile silos, gladiatorial arenas… Not a comforting thought. He also hadn't realized that Paugeng's cells were quite as developed as they were, either: thick plexiglass walls and a lot of equipment that Go eyed askance. He didn't think Jhai was torturing things, exactly, but some of the individuals in the cells did not look entirely human.

Lara, however, did. Go had never seen her bedraggled before—even in the movies, when she'd been bloodied and beaten, the make-up department had made sure that her lip gloss remained intact and her mascara had not run. But now she seemed small, hunched into herself, head drooping. Go, however, was not fooled and when she looked up at their entrance, he knew that he had been right. Lara's eyes blazed like captive suns. When she saw Go on the other side of the plexiglass, she gave a silent snarl. She did not try to launch herself at the cell glass, but for a moment, Go thought she might. Then she saw the bodyguard at Jhai's shoulder and subsided.

"I'll need to question her," Jhai said. "But not until Chen gets here."

"You called him?" Go asked.

"Yes, but it's late now and the poor man ought to have some kind of a break. He's been having a difficult day, I gather."

"He's not the only one. Any sign of your fiancé?" Go chanced a look at Lara's face and wished he hadn't; her eyes were fixed on him and him alone. The expression in them was not encouraging.

"No." Beneath her cheerfully ruthless exterior, Jhai was genuinely worried, Go realized. He had no idea what kind of things befell demon consorts, but based on his own experience he doubted that it was anything good. "Anyway," Jhai said. "You've seen her now, you can see how securely we've got her, and Chen will be coming here in the morning to have her questioned. So you might be able to sleep tonight."

"Thank you," Go said. He doubted whether sleep would be on the agenda, given how wired he still felt, but it was comforting to see just how closely Lara was confined. And—stupidly—until Jhai had reminded him about Chen, Go had forgotten that Lara was the prime suspect in a murder case. He and Beni might have broken the law in summoning her up in the first place, but she had actually killed someone, a human, on Earth. This thought cheered him up more than anything else. Back in Paugeng's guest apartment, he found himself finally able to sleep, after all.

And yet, there were dreams.

蛇警探

He was following someone, but he was very small, almost infinitesimal, and nearly disembodied. Nearly, for he could feel some kind of form around him, enclosing him within itself like a pearl. He floated, at the level of a human hip, drifting through a kitchen. It was dirty, the floor and counter stained with what looked like blood, or red mold. As he floated by, a hand brought a cleaver down and with a dull *thunk*. Go smelled fresh meat and the odor was oddly alluring, drawing himself within its orbit like a captured star. But he did not like the look of the cleaver, so with an effort, he pulled away and sailed out through a grille into the street.

Fresher air, but not by much. He could tell that the city was humid, that it had just rained—and at the safe summit of Paugeng, Go's corporeal form stirred slightly in sleep, roused by the sudden monsoon hammer of drops against the windows. He wandered along the street, seeing distorted dark houses and then the flare of a neon sign. Above, he found that he could feel the stars, but not see them in the light pollution cast by the city: small distant spirits, faintly singing. Then, something seized him, an effortless snatch, and he was pulled down an alleyway as if sucked along by some airy riptide.

There was blood. A great deal of it, spilling in glorious profusion over the rainy concrete, mingling with water and running slowly down the gutter. Human blood, fresh, but there was no sign of a body. He cast about, seeking its source, found nothing. Yet he could feel someone there all the same, the dull glow of a fading spirit, and then a presence which slammed him back against the nearest wall, splitting, fragmenting, cohering once more to discover that this was the shadow of a presence only. It was nothing like Lara, but it frightened him more. A strong, calm sensation, with something so raw beneath it that the bubble of blood which contained a small portion of Go's own spirit fled shrieking into the comparative safety of the city beyond.

This was not all that Go dreamed. There were other things as well, other deaths. A woman slain, messily, alongside a stretch of black water. A child, head striking the wall, a sudden silence. Two dogs in a pit, a throat torn out. Go dreamed them all, lying restless in his bed, until the first light of the sun drew the magic from his dispersed blood like morning mist and Go was once more in one place, if a little diminished, waking with apprehension to the new day and whatever it might bring.

THIRTY-SIX

They must have simply opened all the kennels. The courtyard was filled with a flood of dogs, the same scaled beasts that had nearly torn the badger apart so short a time before.

"Go, go!" Zhu Irzh shouted, and the badger did not need bidding; he threw himself at the ominous mouth of the gateway on the demon's heels. A dog snapped and caught the hem of Zhu Irzh's long black coat. There was the sound of tearing silk; the badger thought he heard Zhu Irzh cry, "Oh bloody hell! Not again!" The demon took hold of a handful of coat and wrenched it free of the hound's mouth. The badger, feeling the sheer of teeth, teakettled. The dog howled, receiving a mouthful of iron, and the badger bowled himself forward, nearly knocking Zhu Irzh flat.

But the gateway was opening. Zhu Irzh and the badger hurtled through. The badger found himself in a sudden, muffled world, as confining as the bag. It was as though the walls around them had stolen sound; he could still hear the baying of the dogs, but it was stifled, heard through some barrier. As badger again, he cannoned into Zhu Irzh.

They stood at the mouth of a long tunnel and, even under these desperate circumstances, the badger felt a great reluctance to enter it. There was something wrong with it, even to one born in an ancient Hell. Zhu Irzh seemed to feel the same way, for he hesitated, only for a moment, but long enough for someone to coalesce into the air ahead of them.

"Go, then." Agni appeared amused, the gold-rimmed eyes gleaming in the shadows. "See how far you get. Remember, the hunt goes on."

A dog howled, startlingly close, and galvanized Zhu Irzh into movement. He pushed forward, through the insubstantial form of the tiger prince, and into the tunnel. The badger, once more, followed. He glanced back once to see Agni staring after them, smiling gently.

Long and long, and far away. The badger had a short memory for things that did not matter, and even hurt faded, given time. But he found later that this journey back to the world of men remained with him, unfading, as bright and fresh as the first time, emerging in his animal dreams.

A circle of fire, flames rushing and gushing in glittering waterfalls, horned faces grimacing between them. Zhu Irzh ducked as a thick red person raced toward him, swinging a scimitar like a grin. The badger stepped back as Zhu Irzh hurled himself down and up, bouncing on the balls of his feet, but the red person was nowhere to be seen, swallowed into light and fire. Then heat reached out and licked them with a long golden tongue and both the badger and Zhu Irzh cried out, only to find that they were unharmed, although the badger smelled slightly singed.

蛇警探

Somewhere else: another jungle, a temple like a pyramid, its steps covered with monkeys that had the wise, sad eyes of old men. They all stopped their quiet conversation when the badger and the demon stepped into the clearing, staring. At the temple's summit, the badger glimpsed someone very ancient, half-ape, half-man, with a golden gaze. He raised a ringed hand and the green leaves whirled up and through them, carrying them away.

蛇警探

Another forest, different, fresher. Above the treeline, the badger saw a spire of mountain, the glassy shimmer of a glacier wall, and for a moment, was consumed by an unfamiliar longing that in a human might have been called homesickness. Zhu Irzh was frowning. "This is like the Himalayas, or something."

"Have you been to the Himalayas?"

"No. I've seen them on TV."

The sky was as clear as the mountain stream that bubbled up through the rocks on their left. The badger, taking chances, went over to it and drank. It, in turn, was like drinking light. Zhu Irzh eyed him askance.

"Careful."

"I am thirsty. It is very pure."

The demon was still frowning. "I'm not sure this is a Hell, you know. I think perhaps we've been ascending."

"Do you think we deserve that?"

"God knows," the demon said, with a trace of irony. "Does this look like Hell to you?"

It did not. The trees, dark evergreens interspersed with splashes of rhododendron, filled the air with a resinous scent. The earth was russet, crumbling and fertile. Cyclamen pushed its way through the long grass, aconite and aster. Overhead, a faint crown of stars could be seen, even though it was still bright day. The badger agreed.

"But still, it is not where we wish to be."

"No. Although it's a lot nicer than our own Heaven. Not so managed, don't you think?"

"It *is* wilder," the badger concurred. Somewhere from deep in the woods came laughter and the sound of running feet. A small deer burst out from beneath the fronded branches, a dappled thing, golden-horned and golden-hooved, with knowing brown eyes. The appealing effect was slightly mitigated by a pair of sharp little fangs.

"Oh," it said. "I'm sorry. I didn't know anyone was here."

"We're—visiting," Zhu Irzh said. "Actually, we're also lost."

"Why, how can you be lost? This is the Forest of the Shepherd. All is known here." The deer took a closer look. "Ah, but you are foreigners, aren't you?"

"If we're trespassing, I can only apologize," Zhu Irzh said. The badger hoped that the demon was not about to divulge to this being that they were actually on the run. Heaven it may be, but they could be wrong, and in the badger's experience, not even Celestial creatures were wholly to be trusted.

"No, no, all are welcome. But where are you headed?"

"Earth?"

The deer raised a gilded hoof and delicately pawed the ground, in what the badger thought might have been a gesture of astonishment. "The world of men? A long way from here. How did you get here?"

"A long story for a long way," the demon said.

"The Shepherd loves stories," the deer said. It raised its head and whistled, a curious, birdlike sound. Moments later, a whistle came back, faint on the wind. "I'm to bring you to him."

The sinking sensation the badger experienced was, he knew, shared by Zhu Irzh; he could see it on the demon's face. But Zhu Irzh had been correct: they were lost, they needed help, and better from this seemingly inoffensive being than some of the other individuals they'd encountered lately.

Zhu Irzh appeared to be thinking along similar lines. He said, "Okay."

The deer led them along the stream until it widened, the little mountain brook becoming something closer to a torrent. The deer sprang nimbly across a series of rocks, evidently placed to form a bridge.

"If you don't mind—" Zhu Irzh said, and scooped the badger up. The badger bore this indignity as best he could: his legs were too short to hop from stone to stone as the demon was now doing. Looking down, he saw that the rushing water was full of silver fish, swimming upstream as fast as lightning. On the other side, however, the deer was gazing upward.

"There is rain on the way." And the badger could smell it on the wind, see the clouds gathering. A wilder Heaven indeed. "Never mind, we will soon be at the temple."

This lay a short distance through the trees. There was more laughter, accompanied by singing, and then a single thread of flute music that drifted through the pine branches and silenced all other sound. Beside the badger, a grove of rhododendron released its flowers and the huge white blooms floated through the air, glowing as if candlelit, to light their way. The demon looked impressed.

The temple, when it appeared, was an immediate improvement on the deva's neglected place of worship. This was no ruin, rising in ivory marble from the forest floor and linked with trees that grew up through the stonework as if cultivated, forming a pattern of shadows across the walls and floor. A pool, lily-filled, lay before the temple, reflecting it back. Each one of the blossoms floated in through a small trellised window, disappearing. The flute music went on.

The deer led the badger and Zhu Irzh up the temple steps. Inside, a group of women sat on sequined cushions. They wore saris in every shade of blue and green and silver, shimmering like starlight. Not all of them were young; two of the women were gray-haired, with serene, lined faces. A bronze bowl, filled with water and a single lily, stood in front of the flute player, who sat surrounded by flowers.

The badger nearly ran. Beside him, he saw Zhu Irzh falter, as if unsure whether or not to bow, and then the demon did.

"My Lord."

The flute player was slender and blue-skinned, the color of early morning frost, with eyes as golden as the horns of the little deer, who now curled at the flute player's feet. Curling black hair fell to his shoulders; he wore a sun-colored sarong.

"I am the Shepherd," the flute player said.

"I think," the demon remarked, very politely, "that I might have come across you as Lord Krishna."

"That is one of my names, yes." No invitation to call him by it; the badger knew how much it took to be on first-name terms with gods. It seemed "My Lord" would do.

"We're lost," the demon said. "I'm terribly sorry about all this. We didn't mean to trespass."

"How did you get here?"

"Well, I don't really know. It wasn't our choice. My companion here and I were taken captive on Earth and ended up in one of your lower levels, at a place called the Hunting Lodge."

Here, the deer raised its sharp-toothed head and gave a most surprising hiss. The women's faces became somber and sad, and Krishna himself flushed to the shade of a stormcloud.

"Ah," Krishna said, putting down the flute. "I know of it, of course. Agni's kingdom."

"They came here," the deer said. "With dogs."

Zhu Irzh's eyebrows rose. "That's a bit ambitious, isn't it, for a lord of Hell?"

"Agni has always been ambitious," Krishna said, "and with his tigress harem spurring him on, that ambition has been honed."

"What happened?" Zhu Irzh asked.

"They were sent away. We drove them out. No creature of this land wants their kind here; all live in harmony. There are tigers here, too, who lie down with the deer at night, with the small creatures. This is a place of peace.

"This is a heaven for beasts," Krishna explained. "And that is not popular among Agni's tiger tribe."

"You'd think, wouldn't you…" the demon began, and Krishna smiled.

"Yes, you would indeed. But they say: the spirits of dead animals, often cruelly slaughtered, are kept here as if it were a game reserve, a wildlife park. They do not leave, because they do not wish to, but Agni's tigers cannot understand that, wishing to have full range across the worlds, to make every realm of Heaven and Hell their personal hunting ground."

"Was this why we were captured?" Zhu Irzh enquired. "As a bit of big-game hunting?"

"I am afraid, my dear demon," the Lord Krishna said, "that you are rather too small a game for Agni."

"Oh."

"And yet you were captured nonetheless… Curious. I've heard nothing of Agni's activities of late; it is though he is biding his time. Though one of his harem has gone to live among men."

"She has?"

"In China. She became an actress, in the movies." Krishna pronounced the word carefully, as if not entirely familiar with it. "Her name is Lara Chowdijharee."

"Lara C's a tiger demon?" Zhu Irzh's mouth fell open.

"I have not heard of this person," the badger said.

"You're not really much of a cinemagoer, are you?"

"I see no point in it. The people are too large and they live in dark houses."

"Just think of him as a critic," the demon said to Krishna. He went on: "I know of her. I've no connection with her."

"And yet your lover is her cousin."

"How do you know about Jhai?"

"We are all family," the god said. "Even if some of us live in Hell and others do not, even if some of us choose to inhabit Earth. I know who you are, Seneschal Zhu Irzh. I know what a role you have played, in the saving of your world. I think that if you had not done so, you would not be standing here now; Heaven would have spat you out."

"My Lord," the demon said, "you are a god and you know what gods know. Do you have an opinion on why I was taken to the Hunting Lodge?"

"Yes," said Krishna. "As a matter of fact, I do."

THIRTY-SEVEN

Seijin had meditated upon the matter and was ready to try again. But in the meantime, he found himself confronted with an angry client, and that was something that very rarely happened. Male self would take some time to get over this.

In fact, the client interrupted the meditation session. Seijin had begun by absorbing the warrior's spirit, after feasting upon his flesh. The man had been shadowed, as though maroon veins of anger and spite had run between sinews and muscles, but Seijin did not mind that. It lent piquancy to a vital essence, chili-pepper hot. The Lord Lady took these aspects and set them in their correct place, within Seijin's own spirit, where they burned for a little time, like candles. Then, the assassin settled down to watch within. Coming so close to Mhara had provided an insight into the Celestial Emperor's movements: the images were imprecise, seen through a dark glass, but substantial enough for Seijin to be able to tell where Mhara had been and was going. Female self dutifully noted Mhara's descent to the realm of Earth, to the little temple where Seijin had been so short a while ago, and having been there, the Lord Lady was able to reconstruct the image within the memory of the building.

There was Robin, so grounded, so certain of her place even though she understood its precariousness. Seijin had not objected to the little human ghost. A toughness there, a certain fibrous quality which could be respected. And that could be felt in these other folk: one male, one female. One human, and one demon. Seijin felt a faint twinge of regret: these could almost be the Lord Lady's own parents. Children of such unions were rare, but obviously they did exist, otherwise Seijin would not be sitting here now. Perhaps—and here the Lord Lady allowed a small measure of daydreaming—perhaps a child might one day result from these two, born on Earth like Seijin had been, and perhaps it might be stolen, brought here to the Shadow Pavilion, raised as a successor.

Happy thoughts. But these were enemies, male self was quick to remind Seijin. Any child of an enemy is one's own foe.

Times change, Seijin reminded male self.

But not by much, male self reminded back.

Anyway, these were thoughts for another day. There was work to be done, and with this in mind, Seijin watched as Mhara entered a discourse with the demon and the human and the ghost. It lacked clarity and it was impossible to hear what was being said even though Seijin had cast a small and hopefully undetectable spell within the room. It seemed that this was not working and this, almost more than anything else, gave the Lord Lady an insight into the intrinsic power of the Celestial Emperor.

And then the Gatekeeper came in.

Seijin was unaccustomed to being interrupted, but the reaction was immediate. A raised hand, a flick of the long sleeve, and the Gatekeeper was sent flying against the wall.

"Lord Lady! Forgive me, forgive me, I did not mean to intrude—"

"Then why did you?" Seijin spoke mildly.

"There is someone here to see you. The Dowager Empress, she—"

Seijin rose and gave a low bow. "It is I who should be asking for your forgiveness, Gatekeeper. You were right to disturb me, for such an august visitor. Please show her in."

"Here?" the Gatekeeper asked.

Seijin glanced at the remains of the night's meal, the shattered ribcage, the remnants of organs. "Perhaps not. In the guest parlor? I think that would be appropriate, don't you?"

"Eminently so, Lord Lady," the Gatekeeper quavered. "Shall I show Her Highness there now?"

"Yes," Seijin replied. "I shall see her shortly."

The Dowager Empress was livid, and this disturbed the calm airs of the Shadow Pavilion to a distressing degree. Seijin could feel them all the way down the stairs, coiling around like serpents. Female self said she would be glad when they'd done with this bitch. Male self agreed, more vehemently. Seijin reminded them that this was a client, and as such, must be tolerated. A contract had been agreed upon and must be honored with propriety until it was complete. Both selves subsided, muttering, as Seijin walked with a smile into the visitor's hall.

The Dowager Empress rose in a rustle and hiss of robes. Her face was, as always, serene, as masklike as before, but as soon as she set eyes on the Lord Lady, she spat, "You failed!"

"Madam." Seijin gave a deep bow, so that hair brushed the floor. "It was not that I failed, only that I have not yet succeeded. This was a skirmish, nothing more."

"A skirmish! My son is alive and well and stalking the ways of Heaven and Earth as if nothing more had befallen him than an unexpected shower of rain!"

"Madam, I would remind you that you are not a warrior. The mettle of an opponent must first be tested." *Better not tell her about the missing hairpin,* female self counseled, and Seijin agreed. "I have now undergone that test and I know what awaits me, what I must do to defeat your son and carry out your wishes."

"What if he finds out?" Ah, this, then, was the crux of the problem: the Empress feared being found out; she had been indiscreet. Seijin gave an inward sigh. Clients always managed to screw things up for themselves, and he supposed that this might be especially true of Celestials. Guilt at wrongdoing undermined them, no matter how ruthless they believed themselves to have become.

And then they blamed you, of course. Seijin gave another bow. "Madam?" Spoken with great sympathy, an invitation to confession.

"He knows I'm up to something."

Seijin feigned concern, leaning forward with furrowed brow. "Are you sure?"

"Of course I'm sure!" the Dowager Empress snapped. Seijin wished that her facial expression would alter, even a little, to reflect her feelings. "He followed me."

"What had you done, Madam, that your son felt it necessary to follow you?"

"I was obliged to eavesdrop upon him," the Dowager Empress said. Was there a hint of discomfiture behind that bland countenance? Perhaps, but only perhaps. "He was proposing all manner of absurd plans to the Court, suggesting—no, insisting!—that some of them should put themselves through hardship and trauma, travel to Earth, if you please, and assist the so-called helpless."

"You do not feel that folk are in need of Celestial assistance?" Seijin spoke mildly, aware of a slight surge of the newly consumed spirit within, the protest of one who believed himself to be a victim.

"These people choose their own paths," the Dowager Empress said, looking amazed that this should even be open to question. "It is their karma, for wrong-doing carried out in a previous life. Or perhaps they choose their earthly lives, in order that they might experience suffering and pain, discomfort and woe."

"Do people make such choices?" Seijin asked, genuinely puzzled. The Dowager Empress gave him a narrow look.

"I should have thought that you might have remembered."

Seijin gave a gentle shake of the head. "Why no. I have only lived one life, Madam. I have no karmic history." By virtue of an otherwise dubious heritage: there were some advantages to being of such mixed blood, at least, though this had not been so evident in youth.

"Maybe you are accumulating karma to come," the Dowager Empress said, beadily.

"Maybe." Seijin's voice remained placid. A hundreds-year-old assassin, slayer of Celestials and demons and men, had surely accumulated plenty of karma, most of it murky. But Seijin had already taken steps, dwelling on these briefly, and in the deepest part of the mind, swiftly borne away and hidden by female self. Seijin was not sure how much the Dowager Empress could read of other people's minds. The Lord Lady had no intention of coming back as anything, of coming back at all.

The Dowager Empress seemed to be waiting for more information and she appeared a little put out when this was not forthcoming. "The fact remains," she said, "that my son must be stopped in this ludicrous reform effort—reform! Revolution, more like, and most unwelcome. Some of my husband's oldest courtiers have come to me, expressing their grave concern—poor things, they do not know what to think! The Emperor guided them in their every notion. How long do you think they would survive in the maelstrom of Earth?"

Seijin knew what she wanted to hear, even if it was insincere. "Surely not so long," the Lord Lady murmured.

"Exactly! And what, might I enquire, do you intend to do about it?"

"I intend," Seijin said softly, "to make a killing."

蛇警探

It took time and energy to get the Dowager Empress out of the Shadow Pavilion, and Seijin begrudged the effort. It might even be necessary to swallow the life of another warrior, in order to keep up one's strength. Seijin hoped not, as the hunting of such took up more energy… and there you were, locked in a kind of spiral. Yet it could not be denied that the Dowager Empress had a point: time was passing, during which Mhara was already, or so it seemed, in the process of making sweeping changes within the infrastructure of the Celestial Realm, and the longer this dragged on, the angrier and more frustrated the Dowager Empress would become. Seijin was not concerned about the matter of personal reputation—this would hold, so male self was firmly told, in the face of some protest—but experience informed the Lord Lady that clients tended to panic, to try to take matters into their own inexperienced hands, and thereby create no end of a mess. The Dowager Empress might be a scheming old bitch, but Seijin doubted whether Her Celestial Highness had ever actually had anyone killed before. Although one never knew. She seemed the classic example of a soul gone quietly hollow, rotting in its ancient shell. And so she was panicking, insisting on action which might not be entirely appropriate. Seijin decided to sleep upon it, and duly went to the uppermost chamber, to take uncertain refuge in dreams.

Morning rolled slowly over the lands of *between,* appearing first as a distant fire in the sky, all around the horizon. Seijin was awake before this happened, standing at the window and watching the ghosts of the night-hunters flit between the rocks. Something with great shadowy wings and a forlorn cry drifted overheard, brushing the window with its pinions, leaving the smell of blood and cold air in its wake. Then the sky crimsoned and Seijin watched the spirits stop in their tracks, freeze, and fade. Today would be the day of the second attempt.

Seijin opened the window and dismissed the view. That would return soon, but for the moment, the air parted like water, as though Seijin had cast a stone into a pool, revealing a glimpse of a different world. The Lord Lady looked down onto Earth, to the small temple that was Mhara's place of worship in the human realm. Like infrared, the temple gleamed white, then glowed a patchy blue to reveal the divine presence within, and other shapes, more shadowy. His Celestial Highness had company, then. Seijin looked out at dim stars: it would be the middle of the night in the city beyond. One of those shapes, the one closest to the Emperor, must be the ghost, Robin; the others—one tasted familiar, but the wards were too strong and Seijin could not see beyond them. Interesting. But the truth of the matter would be discerned soon enough, and it didn't really matter if someone got in the Lord Lady's way.

As dawn touched the sky, Seijin lifted a hand and spat a single silver sphere into the waiting palm. This was the distilled essence of the human warrior, a necessary sacrifice. Seijin breathed upon the sphere until it became too hot to hold, smoking in the hollow of the hand. Gritting teeth, Seijin carried it to the box containing the single remaining pin and bound the glowing, molten thing into the shaft. The spirit, bound, shrieked as it was further tied, and Seijin gave a small smile of satisfaction. Then the pin itself was taken and strapped in to make the point of a long arrow, formed of a demon's thigh bone. Like the Lord Lady, indeed: human, demon, shifting, all manner of wrong.

Seijin held the arrow. One shot, one chance. That really lifted the stakes and the spirit with it; these days had been missed, with so great a chance of failure. The ruination of the previous attempt had been invigorating, and Seijin wanted to capitalize on that, strike while the fire was still hot. A curious metaphor under the circumstances: for *between* was even colder now, the flames of the smith's forge had still not returned and Seijin did not intend to suffer that immortal presence in *between* again. No betrayal—the smith owed Seijin nothing except a grudging tolerance—but all the same, chinks in the armor must be closed.

And speaking of armor… Seijin dressed with even greater care, summoning mist and curdling it into silver gray, hard as iron yet not as brittle, conjuring cloud from the wreaths above the mountain peaks and casting it over a shoulder. Holding the bone arrow, and a long curved bow, won in Genghis' horde so many years ago, accompanied by a scimitar in its sheath, Seijin once more set foot upon the world of Earth.

THIRTY-EIGHT

"You see," the blue god said, as they walked through the forest, "Agni has always had ambitions. It was why the Lords of All gave him the Hunting Lodge in the first place, to keep him occupied. And so far, this has worked."

"But now," Zhu Irzh remarked, "Agni wants—what?"

"Lands," Krishna said. "Territory. Perhaps he always planned this, to keep quietly to the bounds imposed upon him until the time was right, then make his move."

"But what does this have to do with me?" Zhu Irzh asked.

"You are engaged to be wed, are you not?"

"Yes, you knew that already, My Lord. To Jhai Tserai."

The badger thought he had an idea where this was going, but he waited nonetheless. It was neither politic nor polite to interrupt a god, and besides, these were matters of the humanoid world. There was also enough to take note of around him: the plants with their ever-shifting colors, the drift of the wind through the trees. A pleasant place, if foreign.

"Indeed," Krishna said. "To the lovely Jhai. I met her mother once, you know, when she was young and lovely herself, one of the jewels in the crown of the Keralan court. But she fell in love and ran away, years long now. As for Jhai herself, I have seen her only in dreams." Here, Krishna gave Zhu Irzh a sidelong glance, which the demon seemed not to notice, or pretended that he did not.

"She's a great girl," Zhu Irzh said, although the badger did not think that he sounded completely convinced.

"And a rich one, too."

"She's certainly wealthy, yeah. Given how much Paugeng actually *owns*. I mean, I'm sure it's not so much in your terms, My Lord. Gods have much greater resources than the human world, naturally. But in earthly terms, it's not bad."

"And in demonic terms?"

"Well, yes, not bad at all. One can be quite impoverished in Hell, you know."

"But presumably this state does not apply to you? If I may be so impertinent."

Zhu Irzh laughed. "You can be as impertinent as you like. You're a god, after all. My family was always well off but then my parents got divorced and now my mother is, well, on course for being Empress of Hell. She's marrying one of the Ministers. I suppose you heard about the recent unpleasantness?"

"Yes, I heard. You are a prince of Hell now."

"I always think of myself as just a seneschal," Zhu Irzh said, clearly uncomfortable. "I've never had political ambitions—load of hassle and grief, if you ask me."

"Yet, whether you wish it or no, you are a prince of Hell, marrying a wealthy and powerful woman of demon heritage, on Earth. A woman who, even if she chooses not to make much of it, is Agni's cousin."

Zhu Irzh was silent. A golden bird, fire-feathered, flew across their path and a single blazing pinion fluttered down, to land at the demon's feet. After a glance from Krishna, Zhu Irzh picked it up; it had become quite hard, the badger noticed, a gilded jewel. "I can't say I'd actually put this into words," the demon said at last. "Haven't had time. But it had crossed my mind."

"The question we should ask is not: Why you?" the blue god said. "But: Why now, and what is the aim of it?"

"Well, being a detective," Zhu Irzh said ruefully, "I'd say either my murder or my kidnapping is the likeliest."

"And which of these options do you consider to be the most probable?"

The demon gave a wry smile. "You'd make a good police officer, you know… Given that I was put in a hunt, I'd have said murder. But the issue of what would happen once I actually died presents problems."

"Presumably Agni would have some way of trapping your spirit. Couldn't have you simply reappearing in your own Hell. There are ways of doing that, but you have quite a lot of innate power, now, you know. Not because of what you do, or have, but because of what you are. One attains powers, as one's roles change."

"I've a certain amount of magical ability," Zhu Irzh said, with a doubtful glance. "Not much more than that, though."

"That you know of. As I say, your abilities will be changing. But Agni might also have simply been amusing himself prior to your actual murder and any subsequent binding. And kidnapping is indeed an option."

Zhu Irzh said, "If you think my mother would shell out a ransom payment…! The mean old cow would probably pay to leave me there."

"How did she react, when you told her that you were marrying Jhai? Was she angry?"

"Mum? Gods, no. Actually *Jhai* told her that we were getting married."

"Without, as I remember," the badger said, "asking you first."

The demon gave him an icy stare. "There is *possibly* an element of truth in that."

The god was good enough not to smile. "So she was not angered?"

"She was delighted! Started planning the floral arrangements within minutes of being told. All right, Jhai's a foreigner. But she's rich. And she lives on Earth. Mother's been looking for ways to expand her power base all her life. She could have given Machiavelli lessons. For all I know, she *did*."

"And there," Krishna said, standing still and turning to face the demon, "is your key. Your mother approved of Jhai because of what she is. Agni will have had similar thoughts. If he is the one to wed Jhai, he gains access to the human realm, by honor of marriage."

The badger could see that Zhu Irzh was thinking about this. "So why didn't he ask her before?"

"Maybe he did not think she would wed another. She had girlfriends before you, did she not?"

"She's… adventurous, yes."

"Perhaps Agni did not think that there was anything to be gained by approaching her. And then you appear, a bridegroom-to-be. That must have changed Agni's views."

"So, say Agni wants to wed Jhai…" The demon absently broke off a flower from a cascade of azalea. It gave a small scream. "Sorry! What was I thinking?" He dropped the blossom, which became a butterfly on the way to the ground and fluttered erratically away. "But I'm in the way. So he sends someone to get me, someone who captures the badger as well—we were both in the same place, the badger was effectively bait. He sends me out to be hunted, which is taking a chance that I might escape—but I think Agni's the sort of bloke who likes taking chances."

"Quite so," Krishna agreed. "Also, he might consider it sporting."

"In a warped kind of way… I think they underestimated the badger here, too."

"People," the badger spat, "think I am sweet."

"I do not think you are sweet, creature of earth," the blue god murmured. The badger stared at him with great suspicion, but could discern no hint of irony on Krishna's indigo countenance.

"Anyway, yeah, he's not sweet and he's not just a cuddly animal, either. I don't suppose they thought he'd be able to escape on his own. And if one or more of the harem got hold of me, I'd probably be in a pretty bad way even if I wasn't actually killed. Too debilitated to think about trying to find a way back, certainly."

"That may well have been the idea. With sport along the way. They would not have done this had they planned a ransom demand, I think, and besides, there would be terrible ramifications if an Indian Prince of Fire kidnapped a Chinese Prince of Hell. You've no idea—sorry, you probably do—just how difficult these political situations can be. Once Vishnu found out, that would be it for Agni: confined to a jar or something, I expect. No one here wants trouble with the Chinese; we keep ourselves to ourselves, for the main part."

"This is making more sense," the demon admitted. "So they snatch me, take me down to Hell, make sure the only potential witness is off the scene, and bind me in some manner. No one knows where I've gone. I'm sure Chen—that's my partner—will be thinking in terms of some underworld scenario. With my home Hell, I mean. Who'd think that I'd been snatched by the *Indians?*"

"And you would in any case be hidden in the realm of the Hunting Lodge. It's vast, you know; I don't expect you saw more than a fraction of it. But those jungles go on for lands and lands."

"Then, with me off the scene, Jhai's own cousin, whom she hasn't seen for years, shows up to do his familial duty, comfort the grieving girlfriend. Or the furious girlfriend, more likely. Jhai'd probably think I'd run out on her. What could be more natural than the cousin offering her his protection?"

"And marry her. And gain all those things that such a marriage would bring."

"What a scheming bastard," Zhu Irzh breathed, eliciting little gasps of horror from the ladies of the court following behind. "Sorry. I'm really not suited to Heavens, you know."

Krishna shrugged. "It doesn't matter to me. But not to worry, Zhu Irzh. You have some answers, now. And I will do my best to send you home."

"You said that when we left the temple," the demon remarked. "Where *are* we heading, by the way?"

"To the pillar."

"Ah." It was clear to the badger that Zhu Irzh did not know what this was, but the blue god had spoken with a serene confidence. He strode ahead, now the color of a summer sky, and flowers sprang in his path to welcome him. Zhu Irzh and the badger followed, with the soft laughter of the court women behind, and no one saw the thick black shape that slid through the trees in their wake.

THIRTY-NINE

Inari woke early at the temple. They had stayed the night, for it had been late when their final conversation had wound to a close. It was still dark outside, with that heavy pre-dawn expectancy, and rather than wake Chen, she wrapped herself in a borrowed robe and went into the little kitchen of the temple to make tea.

The simple act of placing the kettle on the stove reminded her painfully of badger. They had rarely been separated, and perhaps never for so long. Although the badger had traveled through Hell and back, possessing a solid, silent reliability, Inari still worried about him: she knew he would have come back if he could, and that he had not done so hinted at dire possibilities. She had not thought, either, that she would have come to worry so much about Zhu Irzh. When she and the demon had first met, his intentions had clearly tended toward the amorous. Inari sighed at the memory, an old exasperation coming to the fore. It would be so much easier to be plain. But she had inherited all the beauty of that long-ago courtesan grandmother, a human snatched down to Hell. Inari knew she resembled this woman, with a demon glamour besides, and look at all the trouble it had led to. But if it had not been for her appearance, perhaps Chen Wei might not have rescued her. Then again, had it not been for her looks, he would not have had to…

Since those early days, and the arrival of Jhai, Zhu Irzh had treated Inari like a little sister—affection, respect, combined with some teasing—and she was surprised, now, to discover how much this meant to her. Her own brothers had thought of her as no more than a tool to be used where it would benefit the family most, even if this had meant marrying Inari off to a scion of the Ministry of Epidemics.

And Jhai—who had never shown any jealousy of Inari, who had always treated her with courtesy—must be worried sick.

144

The kettle was boiling. Inari took it from the stove and made a pot of tea, which could be reheated if anyone else woke up and wanted some. The sky was lightening a little, but it was still night, and Inari took her tea into the main hall of the temple, sitting on a small bench to drink it. She took one of the limited selection of sacred texts ("People generally don't bother with those," Robin had remarked. "I certainly don't.") from the wall cabinet and read it, or tried to. Such flowery fulsomeness! Praise to the late Emperor cascaded from the page, in a prose so extreme it formed an almost tangible perfume. No wonder Robin didn't bother with this kind of thing. It made a marked contrast to the simple approach taken by Mhara, to the calm serenity of the temple's interior. Looking around, Inari saw that although the big bowl on the altar was filled with prayer slips that people had left, there were no icons, no gilded statues. The braziers glowed, embers only, and there was not even a lighted candle.

So if there was no candle, where was that smoke coming from?

Inari, frowning, went to investigate, still clutching her cup of tea. The thin thread of smoke was twisting its way through the room. It appeared to be coming from the annex, which led, in turn, into the little courtyard that stood just beyond the annex door. Within the courtyard, on a plinth, set a large bowl of sand. And in front of the plinth was a box containing the thick crimson sticks of incense, of varying sizes and prices, that Robin kept topped up for the faithful to light, that their prayers may be carried up to Heaven with the smoke. In fact, this was not strictly necessary, since Mhara heard most things anyway, but it gave people hope and empowerment, Robin had explained, and it was a tradition with which folk connected.

Inari's frown lifted: how stupid of her! Of course, someone must have lit an incense stick, either late last night, or on their way to work this morning. But the smoke was trickling beneath the door—shouldn't it just dissipate outside, to be borne away on the early morning wind?

Inari felt the need to check. Cautiously, she opened the door to the courtyard—and relaxed. There, indeed, was the stick of incense, smoldering in the bowl of sand, its tip still glowing orange against the shadowed wall.

But surely there was too much smoke, from a single incense stick, and it was pooling about the base of the plinth like seafoam—then Inari knew where she had previously felt this chill across her skin, where the terror that now gripped her had last been experienced.

The assassin Seijin, the Lord Lady of Shadow Pavilion, stepped forth from the cloud, congealing and condensing, smiling gently all the while, and before Inari could turn and run, Seijin drew the scimitar in one sweeping, cloud-dispelling curve and struck off her head.

FORTY

Go and Jhai stared in silence at the hole in the plexiglass wall. The cell in which Lara had so recently been confined was now empty. Go did not want to look at what lay behind them, at what had once been a man. Go's own voice sounded very loud in the ringing quiet of the room.

"I thought you said this was secure?"

"No one's ever got out of here before. Well, apart from one. Zhu Irzh, in fact. He'd been given a drug, he wasn't himself."

"So it's not as secure as you thought." Hard not to sound accusatory and Go didn't see why he should be too bothered about Jhai's feelings right now.

"No," Jhai said shortly. "It isn't."

"There's no point in getting Chen over here, now."

"No. There isn't. But he'd better know. We'll need help in tracking her down." Jhai frowned. "I wonder if she's headed for Hell."

"She'll have it in for you, now," Go said, trying to keep too obvious a satisfaction from his voice. From the look that Jhai shot him, he thought he probably hadn't succeeded.

"Yeah, she will. This won't help family relations, that's for sure. I ought to get in touch with Agni, too, tell him what happened."

Go looked at her curiously. "How easy is that?"

"He's on the phone, Go."

But before she could contact her cousin, and bring him up-to-date, someone called Jhai herself. It was Chen.

FORTY-ONE

Seijin resheathed his sword and stepped over the demon's body. Her head had flown across to the other side of the annex, not far from her shattered teacup. The Lord Lady picked up the head and studied it. The huge red eyes were wide with surprise, the small mouth a little "o".

"Well, well, madam," Seijin said. "I thought I recognized you."

Last seen near the forge of *between,* in the company of that disreputable shaman. *Who are you?* Seijin wondered. Some local necromancer, probably, although it was strange to find such a demon outside Hell. Women like this often used their looks to their own advantage, however; this one had no doubt gulled and glamoured some credulous local into taking up company with her. Seijin had probably done the man a favor. Placing the head gently on the floor once more, Seijin sent a tendril of shadow into the main temple and encountered resistance. The wards outside had been hard to avoid, hence the use of the incense stick, evaporation, and reincorporation. In here, the magic of the Celestial Emperor was even stronger; Seijin had to struggle against it.

The main room was empty. Seijin headed further into the temple, sensing a solitary presence in a small room on the far side. No need to disturb this person, Seijin thought. Male self reminded, with a laugh, that the person would be disturbed enough once he woke up and discovered the carnage. A low jest, female self thought, in reproof.

But here was the target, still sleeping. Seijin was now struggling more than male self wanted to admit, the clear magic of the Emperor beginning to tangle up, to snarl the Lord Lady in its infinitely intricate web. Seijin thought of spiders, not a happy metaphor. Not long now. Here was the door—reach out, careful, careful, through the congealing threads of the magical weave, gliding soft as smoke. Open it, step through, still with care, notch the arrow, with the faint and gratifying sense of that spirit bound to the ancient power of the pin, liminal substances all, made by a liminal warrior. Raise the bow, take aim at the sleeping figure, outlined with sky-blue magic, make certain of the aim, and in that final moment of distraction, become aware that someone has stepped up behind with silent rage and plunged a knife in between the seventh and eighth vertebrae of one's spine.

Seijin kept hold of the bow, but the arrow flew wide across the room, burying itself with a shriek in the wall.

"No!" male self cried, sensing the loss of the second pin. Seijin spun around, just in time to see the figure on the bed shimmer and disappear, not real at all, no more than illusion. Turning, the Lord Lady saw the man who had stabbed him, stepping back, humming with a cold and dangerous magic that was entirely human and wholly unfamiliar.

"I believe," this person said, very quietly, "that you're the one who just killed my wife."

Seijin tried to draw the scimitar but it would not come free. Numbly, the Lord Lady looked down and saw that the sheath had become entangled in the weave of blue, with a dark, sinuous red running through it, securing the sword.

"I do not make apologies," Seijin said. "Nor excuses."

"Just as well." The Celestial Emperor of Heaven stepped between the human and Seijin, holding the captured pin. "Let's see what happens." He thrust the pin forward, striking Seijin in the eye. Female self, blinded, screamed in agony and confusion. The Lord Lady, consumed in pain, began involuntarily to disperse and this was what saved Seijin from capture. Diffusing, dispersing into mist and smoke and cloud shadow, seeping everywhere at first, to a shout of "Keep it in one place!"

Too late. For the heat of the braziers, rising, was carrying Seijin's essence upward, into the rafters and through the cracks, out into the skies of the dawning Earth.

蛇警探

Seijin fled through the dim upper air of Earth, barely noticing when the world changed and the Lord Lady was seeping through the clouds of *between*. Was this what people meant when they spoke of coming home, this half-blind flight from power and pain? It had been a long time since Seijin had suffered serious injury, so long, in fact, that it was barely remembered. You can have too much luck, for too long. It makes you weak, this forgetting.

I will take on more pain, Seijin promised. Now, I have to. It was not an easy admission to make and it made female self spit and wail. Too late for her: if the injury could not be healed, she would have to look out upon the world through the eye of male self, if permitted. Seijin recognized, but only distantly, that she might not be.

Back in the Shadow Pavilion, flying past the astounded Gatekeeper, Seijin sat before a cloudy mirror, looking within. The pin had penetrated to the very back of the eye, causing a thin trickle of blood to crawl down Seijin's cheek. It looked like decoration on a mask. The eye itself was filled with a scarlet pool and nothing Seijin could do, no magic that the wounded female self could conjure up, was able to heal it. Perhaps with time? But Seijin knew, deep inside, that this wound was permanent.

The degree of pain was quite remarkable. Learn from this, Seijin instructed the various selves, but male self was no longer listening. He raged, splitting apart from Seijin and leaving the wounded assassin to sit before the mirror like a languishing courtesan, while he stormed up and down the chamber.

"At least the demon is dead!"

"It makes no difference," Seijin said wearily. "The demon is no compensation, surely you must see that. It was only that she got in the way."

"Something has been slain!" male self exulted, slamming a spectral fist against the window frame with such force that the window burst open, letting in a cloud-drift of air. And that was the moment when Seijin realized that the plastered-over fractures of the last few decades could no longer be sustained, that the splits between the selves had gone too deep for healing.

FORTY-TWO

"I'm so sorry," Jhai said, for what must have been the tenth time. Go lingered by her side, staring down at the demon's body. Not a tigress, not this time, yet how he wished it had been. But this demon had been beautiful, too, and Chen's wife. Jhai had insisted on coming over as soon as she got Chen's message, and Go wasn't leaving her side; he felt, however irrationally, that Jhai was still the only one capable of protecting him. Some kind of tiger-to-tiger thing, perhaps.

Chen spoke with a calm that, Go realized, was in itself a response to shock. "Thank you, Jhai." He'd thanked her the other nine times, too. "What we really need to do now is to work out where Inari is now."

Jhai took Chen to one side, though Go could still hear her. He stayed where he was, at the side of the "deceased" demon. She had been laid on a table in the middle of the temple, her head placed neatly above the severed neck. From this angle, she looked merely as though she wore a thin red necklace. Her body would undergo no decay or mortification, Chen had explained, still with that unnatural calm. Mhara had enspelled it, and besides, demons' bodies behaved differently when they were killed on another plain. The spell sparkled blue around the demon's corpse: Go took care not to get too close.

He heard Jhai say, "Can't Mhara just restore her?"

"Apparently it doesn't work that way. He's not omnipotent."

"Honestly, what use *are* these deities?" Jhai sounded as though she were about to sack an incompetent employee. "Emperor of Heaven and can't even restore the spirit of a minor demon."

"She's not under his jurisdiction," Chen said. "We'd need the Emperor of Hell for that."

"Yeah, Chen—the Emperor of Hell, who owes you one. Big-time."

"That's true, but it takes time for messages to get to Hell's Emperor these

150

days. If Zhu Irzh was here, he could just call his mother and explain, but I'm not sure she'd listen to me."

"She might listen to me," Jhai said. "I'm about to be her daughter-in-law, after all."

"Then please try," Chen said. The man sounded exhausted and Go could hardly blame him. "I have tried to put a call through, but I can't reach her."

"I'll try," Jhai said. "If you're sure there's nothing Mhara can do. Who did this, anyway?"

"An assassin. Listen, Jhai—" and here Chen drew Jhai away into an annex, leaving Go alone with the demon's corpse. Evidently there was something that Go was not meant to hear. Fair enough.

He tore his gaze away from the body and wandered around the room, looking at the sparse furnishings. A serene place, despite what had so recently happened here. Go had never been a religious man, but something in him responded to this Zen simplicity. As he was standing there, someone came out of a side annex, a young woman. She looked tired, but there was also something else about her, something not quite right—it reminded Go of the spirits his father used to raise, as though the girl was already dead. How odd. Not unattractive, though.

"I'm just waiting for Jhai," Go explained.

"I know," the young woman said. "She's still with Chen. My name's Robin; I'm a priestess." She gave him a rather direct look. "I suppose you know your tiger lady's in the news?"

"Lara?" Go's heart felt as though it had dropped through his ribs and hit the floor.

"Yes. I've just been listening to the radio, trying to take my mind off things. Inari—" she gestured toward the corpse "—was a friend, you know? Still is, wherever she's gone." She sighed and Go felt a breath of icy air run across his skin. "I caught the news. Lara went through the early morning market like a dose of salts. One man dead, several people injured."

"This is all my fault," Go said. Things had gone from bad to worse, and all because he wanted to be a Svengali to the movie actress from Hell.

"Well, yes," Robin said. She did not sound accusing. "It is. But these things—I've not led a perfect life myself."

"But you're a nun," Go said, before he could stop himself.

Robin laughed. "I wouldn't say that, exactly. I need to let Jhai know about Lara as soon as she comes out."

"Is the news still on?" Go asked. Some stations were devoted to nothing but the news, recycling it endlessly. He might as well hear this for himself, depressing though it might be.

"I think so. Do you want to listen? I can probably find a station."

"You're being very kind," Go said.

Robin gave a sad shrug. "All I can do at the moment."

Go said hesitantly, "Your—deity. Jhai explained a couple of things to me in the car. Is he here?" *Can he help me?* But Go did not want to ask that. Odd: a few months ago, he'd have been entirely happy to make what use he could of the situation. Now, he felt a definite reluctance to ask for such aid; he was beginning to feel that this would have to be worked through, no matter the consequences. And he had an awful feeling he knew what those consequences might be.

But the news surprised him. Lara had indeed been on the rampage through the port market, but there were other sightings filtering through now, along Shaopeng and in Bharulay. Robin frowned as she listened to the reports.

"Lara's moved fast, hasn't she?" Go said in a whisper.

"I don't think these can *all* be Lara," Robin said. "These places are miles apart and you heard what they just said: these sightings are within the last few minutes."

"Is she using magic?" Go wondered aloud.

"Or there's more than one tiger," Robin said.

FORTY-THREE

Zhu Irzh and the badger stared up into the branches of the pillar. A vast column ascended into the cerulean skies, branching out toward its summit, stone changing to tree.

"I didn't even know this existed," the demon said, awed.

"It sometimes does not," the god replied. Krishna raised the flute to his lips and played a single, fragile phrase. Behind them, the women of the blue god's court whispered and murmured, and the deer gave a whistling cry. All these sounds floated up into the branches of the tree: glistening ebony black, as if containing captive stars, rustling with huge green leaves like curls of jade. High among these leaves, these sounds crystallized, forming a transparent lotus flower, which changed into a bird and flew down.

"This is your guide," Krishna said. The badger looked hard at the bird, which remained transparent and expressionless, a thing of light.

"Fair enough," Zhu Irzh replied. "What do you want us to do? Climb after it? I'm game, but I'm not sure about my friend here."

"I will manage!" the badger snapped.

"You need climb only a little way," Krishna told him. "Then, as you will see, things will become quite different."

The badger's head whipped around. Something on the wind, something rank and distinctly un-Celestial.

"Are you all right?" Zhu Irzh asked, but the little deer said, "I can smell it, too."

"What is it?" Krishna's voice was as soft and musical as ever, but something about it made the badger's hackles start to rise in sympathy.

"It smells like one of Agni's hounds," the badger growled.

Krishna turned to the demon. "You should start climbing."

"Hey, I'm all for getting ahead," Zhu Irzh protested. "But I'm not going to leave you to face that thing; you've been so kind, and—"

"Zhu Irzh." Still soft, but with force. "Go."

It had the impact of divine command, a wateriness of the joints with which the badger was entirely unfamiliar. The demon, however, bowed his head in fleeting acquiescence and put a hand on the pillar. His expression changed.

"This is weird!"

As he spoke, a racing, snarling shape burst out of the bushes. Agni's hound indeed: this must be one of the largest dogs, scaled like a dragon, flickers of fire emerging from its nostrils.

"Do the teakettle thing!" the demon commanded, and with great reluctance, the badger did as he was told. Zhu Irzh slung the iron pot over his shoulder and placed a foot on the pillar, the sole flat. From his limited perspective, the badger could see that they were suddenly on a long, snaking road. He looked back, and there was Krishna with the women, each throwing out a long silk scarf. With the final scarf caught in the deer's antlers, they began to spin, faster and faster until there was a whirling coil of color a little way behind.

"Go!" Krishna cried again, and Zhu Irzh started running. The badger heard growls and howls, saw the scarves whirl faster, a dark shape sucked within. Then the landscape changed and he and Zhu Irzh were picked up by the path on which they stood and taken upward.

蛇警探

Then the world was blue, the sky filled with sapphire light, and he walked on indigo earth. Women walked by, chattering and laughing, balancing jars upon their heads, their saris made out of water and crystal and speckled with diamond light. The demon had stopped walking and stared in open admiration.

"This can't be Hell," he said. And the badger looked up and saw a huge face bending down from the heavens, made out of sky, the dark eyes filled with a vast amusement. The horned moon rested upon his brow; in one hand, he held a trident that was mountain high. He said, in a voice of soft thunder, "You are in the *wrong place.*"

"I won't argue with that," stammered Zhu Irzh. It was one of the few times that the badger had seen him discomposed.

"Then let me send you to the right place," the vast blue being said. His hand came down. Moments later, they were standing on the palm, fingers rising like blue columns, being raised up through streaming clouds.

"Go," the blue god said, and gently blew. The realm darkened into storm-light. Zhu Irzh and the badger floated downward, as lightly as leaves, into the humid air of Singapore Three.

FORTY-FOUR

Inari put a faltering hand to her head. Still there, and that was strange enough in itself: she remembered the shock of the assassin's sword as it struck her, remembered her body, fountaining blood, toppling sideways like a felled tree. There had been no pain, and surprisingly little sensation. The memory that was most clear was, curiously, a moment of anxiety over the broken cup of tea, flying through the air and shattering as it hit the floor. Her eyes had watched, for a few seconds, the streams of tea and blood, mingling like little rivers on the stone floor. Then everything had gone dark, in more traditional fashion, and now she was here, lying facedown on ashy earth with the cloudy hillside rising above her.

Inari's initial sensation, once shock and dismay had made their presence felt, was one of relief. She did not know where she was, but she suspected that she was back in *between,* where at least she had a kind of ally. Bonerattle might help her, or he might not, now that she was of no further use to him, but even a doubtful ally was better than an uncaring family. She was not home in Hell and that was a great blessing, even under the circumstances. And, she could be assured that Chen would do everything in his power to get her back, reanimate her, and Inari had great faith in her husband's abilities. Chen, a modest man, never claimed to be a particularly inspired thinker, but he was persistent, calm, and above all, constant. She could trust him, and so she would.

Also, being decapitated was oddly liberating. Inari had never been slain before, although she knew plenty of people to whom it had happened, and who better than a denizen of Hell to know that this was no kind of end at all, just an interruption in the continuity of being. Seijin, that smiling serenity of a killer, had done his or her utmost, and this was the result.

Could be worse, Inari thought. *Could be a lot worse.* Aloud, she said, "Is that the best you can do, O assassin?" And laughed, because it made her feel better.

But that was all very well and good. She couldn't just lie here, eating ash. The presence of the light, fluffy grayness that covered the ground made her wonder if she was near the place where the forge had been: Had it really disappeared for good, or did it move from place to place? While Chen was working out how to rescue her, Inari knew she must take steps to rescue herself. With this in mind, she clambered to her feet—she might be a spirit now, but she had a very real sore throat, all the same—and started walking, hampered by her long skirts. When she had died, she had been wearing a bed-robe and a nightdress; somehow, these had metamorphosed into a full set of funeral robes, the red of a dying sun, embroidered with black. Long sleeves trailed down past her wrists, and her midriff was supported by a stiff, folded sash. She had the feeling that, if she'd had a mirror in which to look, she would find that her face was fully painted: she put a tentative finger to her lips and rubbed. The fingertip came away reddened, so yes, this was indeed the case, and her hair had also been piled up and pinned. She must look like a geisha doll. Was this what she now looked like on Earth? Had her funeral already taken place? No use wondering about that.

After some time, the landscape had changed very little, although it was true that Inari was making slow progress. The rocks that protruded through the ashy surface were sharp, and she did not want to slow herself down any further by injuring a foot or an ankle. There was no sign of the forge, or of Bonerattle—although when she reached a patch of more open ground, where the mist was less oppressive, she risked calling out. She did not use his name, hoping that he might recognize her voice. But nothing emerged from the cloud and so Inari walked on, reminding herself that she had been in worse places than this: the lower levels of Hell, for example, in which one's very form might change, become more bestial. She did not seem to be changing now. And there was no sign of the brooding pagoda that Bonerattle had called the Shadow Pavilion. Inari was just thinking that, if forced to enter this strange limbo, she had at least ended up in a relatively innocuous bit of it, when she stepped around a rock and before her rose the pagoda.

It seemed even larger than she had remembered from that last turbulent visit, towering on its rock, so high that it almost appeared to lean out across the valley. At least she knew where to avoid… And then found she could not.

The Shadow Pavilion was like a magnet. Inari's suddenly faltering footsteps dragged her down the valley: she tried to resist, to pull away, but was unable to do so. The Pavilion had her now and it wasn't just the tug it exerted on her feet, but a compulsion that made her incapable of looking anywhere else. Inari, a sudden puppet, was dragged toward the pagoda.

The compulsion lasted until she had climbed the steps. She stood looking up at the ancient wooden doors, carved with symbols so old that they had long since lost any meaning, at least any that was known to Inari. Now that she had reached the pagoda, the protective calm that had enfolded her on the slopes had dissipated as completely as mist; she was afraid, of Seijin, of further vengeance. Sometimes even a spirit could be killed—such a fate had befallen Mhara's own father, the late and corrupt Celestial Emperor. The assassin struck her as someone who would not flinch at full measures.

Then someone said, "Ah. You must be the person we are expecting."

Inari stumbled against the doorframe. The person who had addressed her was slight and ghostly, the same gray as the wood of the doors.

"I am the Gatekeeper. I'm afraid we weren't given your name...?"

Inari had no intention of telling him this, for names had power and she did not know what authority the laws of *between* might give him over her. But then the words were dragged out of her mouth as efficiently as she herself had been hauled to the doors of the pagoda. The Gatekeeper fished in a sleeve and consulted a list.

"Ah, yes. I see I was correct. And you came here on your own two feet? Impressive."

"I didn't have much choice!"

The Gatekeeper said, "Usually, Seijin brings them here in a bag."

"I think I am too small a fry for the assassin," Inari said.

"How charmingly modest. And yet, the Lord Lady slew you. That is a very great honor, normally reserved for elite warriors."

"I suppose I should be grateful," Inari said, not without sarcasm.

"Well," the Gatekeeper remarked, unhappily, "you *are* still dead. Let me open the doors for you, so that you may see your new home."

"New home?"

"Why yes," the Gatekeeper explained. "Once you are here, you won't be leaving us again."

But Inari, as she stepped through the old wooden doorway into the Shadow Pavilion, thought, *We'll see about that.*

蛇警探

As she wandered through the Pavilion's labyrinth of chambers, Inari unaccountably felt her spirits rise. Seijin was not here, and who, in truth, might say whether the Lord Lady would even return at all? The assassin had gone after Mhara once before, and been defeated. Inari hoped against hope that the Celestial Emperor would once more be successful. Perhaps Seijin would even be slain!

And end up back here again, two raging ghosts, confined in this echoing prison.

The more she saw of the Pavilion, the greater her awareness of other presences grew. She could not see these beings directly, but if she stood in the corner of a room, or by a windowsill, and glanced out of the corners of her eyes, figures appeared: a woman with streaming hair, ringing her hands in the stiff folds of her old-fashioned robes. A tall, armored man, snarling in fury, clasping a shattered sword. A child, weeping, but when it turned, Inari saw that it had gaping holes where its eyes had once been, and a mouth full of teeth like pins.

None of them tried to speak to her and she wondered whether she seemed the same to them, a half-glimpsed ghost lost in her own pain.

But I don't feel dead, particularly. And whereas the other spirits mourned or raged, Inari planned to push her own woes aside, and find out more.

This was not a simple matter. When she tried to count the number of stories possessed by the Pavilion, running lightly up and down the many stairs and taking note of landings, Inari found that she could not get a grip on it. At first she counted four, and then nine, and then only three. At each ascent and descent, the Pavilion looked the same: the musty, paneled walls; the moth-eaten hangings, decked with spiders' webs; the thick, hand-stitched carpets. A luxurious place, once, a palace. Had the Pavilion ever been somewhere real, the home of some Chinese emperor, the summerhouse of a spoiled princess? Inari had known of buildings being stolen before, and the Shadow Pavilion held resonances. At some time, someone had been happy here; she could feel it, a summer current running through the dust. But those sensations were very faint, long overlain by rage and pain.

Inari had no way of knowing when she had arrived, and she began to lose track of time. She did not think that *between* followed the same time zone as Singapore Three; there was no reason to expect it to do so. But when she next looked through a window, out across the long lands, she saw that the light was fading and a blue twilight was falling. Shapes moved with purpose through the dusk and Inari, however foolishly, felt glad that she was inside.

She turned to find the Gatekeeper standing at her elbow.

"I thought you would want to know," the old spirit said. "The Lord Lady is coming home."

FORTY-FIVE

Zhu Irzh and the badger fell out of the air, from some height, and hit a grimy stretch of ground in a parking lot. Winded, it took some time for the badger to say, "Are we back?" He smelled the air. "Yes, I see that we are."

Zhu Irzh clambered to his feet, dusting off his coat. "That was quite a drop. I should have asked if we could have been put down gently. Are you all right? Nothing broken?"

"I am intact," the badger admitted. He was surprised at how relieved he was to be home: all his animal senses had come alive again at this reversion to his own territory. He had not realized just how firmly he had become attached to this bit of the human realm, but that was the element of earth for you: it claimed and clung. "And you?"

"Also fine, I think. Badger, before we're sucked into yet another maelstrom, I just wanted to say that it has been—well, okay, not a pleasure, but I have valued your presence recently. You are a resourceful creature."

"Thank you," the badger said. It would have been wrong to say that he was touched, but as they left the parking lot, he was aware that the demon had become slightly more incorporated into the list of those he was obliged to protect: not of the same status as Mistress or Husband, obviously, but *still*. At the thought of seeing Mistress once more, he was filled with a distinct satisfaction. He and Zhu Irzh had survived and things were returning to the way they should be.

"I need to find a phone," the demon said. "I lost my cell somewhere along the way—I think one of those bitches took it. I'll have to reverse the charges. I haven't got any money, either. I wonder where we are?" He squinted into the smog. It felt like early morning, and the sea was not far away.

"I recognize this place," the badger said. "Look, there is Men Ling Street. Lord Krishna has returned us almost to the point at which we left."

"You're right," Zhu Irzh said. His footsteps quickened. "Hey, the crime scene people are there. I can see Lao and Ma."

Exorcist Lao's jaw dropped when he saw Zhu Irzh and the badger coming toward him. Ma, on the other hand, greeted the demon like a long-lost brother. Zhu Irzh appeared faintly surprised.

"Ma? What's happening?"

"We've been investigating a series of murders," Ma explained. "Chen and I found bodies here, lots of them, under that house we sent you to. Where did you go?"

"Bodies," the demon echoed, without answering Ma's question. "What sort of bodies?"

"Human ones. It looked like a sort of meat locker. And where have you *been?*"

"Did it, now?"

"What happened, Seneschal?" That was Lao, rather more demanding.

"We got snatched into a dimension of Indian Hell and hunted by tigress demons."

Lao appeared impressed. "Seriously?"

"Well, yeah. What do you think I've been doing? Taking the badger on a bar crawl? What's the date?"

"The twenty-third. You've been missing for three days."

Ma snorted. "Been an interesting three days."

"Where's Chen?"

"At home, I presume. Hasn't come on shift yet. I got a message from him last night to say that he and Inari were visiting the temple—you know, the one belonging to the Celestial Emperor." Ma spoke as casually as someone referring to a bar owned by a friend. "I'd better call him, let him know you're back. He'll be so relieved."

Lao was looking narrowly into the middle distance. "Tigress demons, eh?"

"Several of them. And a demigod prince. It's a whole other world down there, Lao—they've got a lodge, hunting grounds, everything. It's like a fucking safari park. Only the other way round."

"What's the prey? You?"

"Yes, and the badger. But it's a whole setup—they had *guests.* I don't imagine the party was laid on just for us. I got the impression it was a regular thing."

"I'm wondering about this," Lao said, gesturing to the crime scene behind him. His long, gray face twitched.

"What, you think the bodies are connected?"

"Did you go directly to this hunting ground?"

"More or less. As far as I could tell, anyway. There was a bit of a journey."

"But you didn't stop off anywhere?"

"No. You said: *meat locker.*"

"I wonder how long this hunting ground has been in operation?" Lao mused. "Whether they started off on human spirits, the kind of people who wouldn't be missed?"

"But why here?" Zhu Irzh said, although given Krishna's theorizing, the badger thought he already knew. "This isn't a Chinese Hell. There's plenty in India who wouldn't be missed."

But the badger was watching Ma. The big sergeant was staring into his phone as though it had just bitten him, and when his attention turned back to his companions, it was not Lao or Zhu Irzh to whom he said, "Oh god. I'm so sorry."

蛇警探

"Don't worry," the demon kept saying, all the way through the city. "Don't worry. We'll get her back, we'll find a way. This is a temporary thing."

Why did humans—or their cousins—always feel the need to *talk* so incessantly, when something terrible had happened? Why did they babble on? Pain was to be endured, not discussed. The badger ignored Zhu Irzh's attempts at reassurance and stared out of the window of Ma's police car, watching the morning world pass by. Useless to wish that they were once more waking up on the houseboat, with Husband about to go to work, the badger, teakettled, humming on the stove, Mistress padding about, alive.

Mistress, alive. Alive. Not anymore. And in that case, *Where was she?*

Ma said, over his shoulder, "You know, I heard what you were saying to Lao. There have been reports coming in all night about tigers on the loose."

"Oh, shit," Zhu Irzh said.

"One has to assume that it's connected."

"You'd think so, wouldn't you? There can't be two lots. Has anyone been hurt?"

"Rather a large number of people."

"Great. You can run, but you can't hide. They probably followed us up—or maybe they didn't bother, just decided to extend the hunting grounds. Kri—someone we met suggested that might be the case."

The demon continued to discuss the situation with Ma, but the badger had stopped listening. It was as though the last few days had been nothing more than an unpleasant dream; to be vaguely recalled, but no importance attached to it. Now, his focus had narrowed down, condensing all of reality into a single sharp fact. *Mistress, gone.*

It was a relief to reach the temple and see Husband standing on the steps, talking into his phone. When he saw Zhu Irzh and the badger getting out of the car, he ran down the steps to the vehicle. He clapped Zhu Irzh briefly on the shoulder. "Glad you're back, Seneschal."

"Glad to be back," the demon said. "You can't imagine how much."

The badger spoke for the first time. "Where is she?"

"We think she's in *between*." Husband spoke calmly, but the badger could sense how greatly this had affected him: a crimson jangling around the man's spirit, and the badger felt a great affinity with him. Husband was the only person who knew how the badger felt and this was an unexpected comfort.

"Where is that?"

"It's a kind of—land of gaps, neither Heaven nor Hell, where things go if they are neither one thing nor the other."

"But Mistress is Hellkind."

"The person who killed her is not, however. Half-Celestial and half-demon, born on Earth." Husband sat down on the little step of the temple, to address the badger more directly. "I've called Inari's brother, in Hell. The one who works in the Blood Emporium. I didn't tell him why I was phoning—let him think we've had a row or something. Anyway, she might feasibly be down in Hell but she didn't go straight home."

"That is a blessing," the badger said.

"Yes, it is. I don't fancy trying to get further information from Inari's family."

"Could the brother have been lying?" Zhu Irzh asked.

"He could, but on this occasion, I don't think so. He's got no particular reason to lie unless the rest of the family are leaning on him, and—would probably take some delight in going behind their backs, given the indignities that he's undergone over the years. Anyway, I also checked with the Night Harbor and she didn't pass through there. She won't be in Heaven—they don't let demons in, at least, not under those circumstances. That leaves the possibility that her spirit is wandering around Earth somewhere, but why should she leave the temple, in that case?"

"People can get very confused when they die," the demon pointed out.

"True, but I don't think Inari is one of them. She's a demon, after all, not a human new to the Wheel. I think, from what Mhara and I have put together, that she has gone to *between*. It's Seijin's—the assassin's—home."

Zhu Irzh said, "The Lord Lady killed her?" He looked astounded.

"You know about this person?"

"When I was a little boy, I was obsessed with warriors. Like most kids, I suppose. I did a lot of reading about them and sometimes my tutors indulged me. One of them told me about Seijin, where he/she comes from. Impressive individual. Eats people's souls. When I grew up a bit I discovered that becoming a warrior meant discipline, austerity, not drinking, that kind of thing. So I joined the vice squad instead."

Husband did not seem too interested in Zhu Irzh's career choices. "Do you know anything about Seijin? Any weak points?"

"Hasn't got any. At least, unless one counts the whole package. Can't be too stable, being male and female, mixed-species like that."

"There are those," Husband remarked, "who would say that this provided an ideal balance."

"Seijin kills people for fun. How balanced does that sound to you?"

Husband sighed. "You may have a point. Seijin's after Mhara. Inari got in the Lord Lady's way."

"I want to see her," the badger said. Husband looked at him.

"All right."

She did not look dead, but then, the death of demonkind was not like the death of things that had truly lived. The badger said as much.

"I know," Husband murmured. "And she's under a spell, remember. It'll preserve her until we can get her back."

To the badger, the matter was simple. "Then we will go to *between*, you and I, and we will bring her home."

FORTY-SIX

"Look," Jhai Tserai said. "Can't we discuss this some other time? I've got a lot on my mind right now." She turned to Zhu Irzh. "At least *you've* finally shown up."

The demon looked wounded by this. "You make it sound as though it's all my fault."

Pauleng Go was having a hard time with all this. Knowing that Lara had come from Hell was one thing, but now he was surrounded by demons, what with Zhu Irzh and Jhai herself. And Zhu Irzh—from the admittedly brief time that Go had spent in his company—seemed like such a normal bloke, bumming Go's cigarettes and commiserating over his recent circumstances.

"Having survived the setup they've got down there—man, you don't want anything to do with that. I mean, really. The badger and I barely escaped by the skin of our teeth."

Go found his perception shifting to an unnerving degree: one moment he saw the two demons as normal people, and the next, as Hellkind. It was almost like a kind of racial awareness: he'd had a couple of German friends, once, and at first you noticed all the time that they were white, but then it wore off and you stopped noticing. Dealing with demons was similar; it had been like that with Lara. Until they turned into beasts and started killing people, that is.

"I didn't mean that. You know what I mean." Jhai was impatient. To Go, she said, "I really don't think this is a good idea."

"I don't either." Zhu Irzh dropped the stub of his cigarette on the temple step and scoured it out with the sole of his boot. Then, apparently struck by some pang of conscience, he bent down and picked it up. "As I said, I've seen the Hunting Lodge. Freaked *me* out and you can imagine what I'm used to."

Go nodded. He thought he could.

"Trust me, Go. I don't know you, but you seem like a nice enough guy. You made a mistake, well, that happens. We all do that." Zhu Irzh gave a slight frown, as if suddenly uncomfortable in this role of spiritual counselor. "Theologically, it probably is enough to get you sent to Hell." The demon paused, possibly entertaining the thought that the conversation was veering into an unfortunate direction. "That is, I mean…"

"Darling," Jhai said, "you're digging a hole." To Go, she remarked, "It's all very well being noble. It's also all very well thinking that noble might get you killed. But that's not what it's about, as you ought to have realized by now. It's what happens after death that matters."

"Yeah," Zhu Irzh agreed. "As I said, I've seen it."

"Zhu Irzh is trying to avoid telling you this, but I will. Given your actions, and the fact that you're Indian, the chance that karma will send you straight down to the Hunting Lodge is kind of high."

"Maybe that's what's supposed to happen," Go said, stubbornly. Somewhere at the back of his mind, an astonished voice protested: that would be Go's usual self, flabbergasted at this sudden shift to responsibility, facing the consequences of one's actions, all that kind of thing. "I brought her here. It's me she wants."

Beni was one thing. He'd been Go's co-conspirator and there was probably a school of thought that said that they both deserved what was happening to them. It hadn't been until Lara had started killing other people—completely unrelated people—that Go had experienced this uncharacteristic change of heart, and it had taken him by surprise. Maybe his parents had managed to instill some values into their son after all; maybe this was what people meant by a midlife crisis.

Or an end-of-life crisis, as seemed more likely.

"Anyway," Jhai said now, "from what my fiancé's just told me, this isn't necessarily all about you. Lara's sisters don't seem to want her back, but they do seem to want to increase their sphere of operations. That's got nothing to do with you or anything you've done."

"It would probably have happened anyway," Zhu Irzh said. "It's more about me than it is about you. Agni—that's the guy in charge of the Hunting Lodge—wants Jhai."

"Agni," Jhai said, "has proved to be a tosser. But this isn't your problem, Go."

"I called up Lara," Go said. "I ought to be the one who deals with her."

At this point Chen appeared on the temple steps and asked for a word with Zhu Irzh. Jhai went with him, leaving Go alone. Jhai was taking her role as protector seriously, Go thought; she'd done a lot for him already, but she was right: she had problems of her own. And he could not shake himself of the conviction that he ought now to face up to what he'd done. With the stiletto of conscience pricking at him, Go went quickly and quietly down to the roadway and got on the next tram to the port.

蛇警探

He had expected to find the port deserted, shutters barred, police everywhere. But although some shops had been barricaded up, most were still open for business and there were a surprising number of people on the streets. Go kept his ears open but he only heard one conversation, between two elderly women, pertaining to recent events.

"Well, there's always something," one old lady said. "If it's not mad gods, it's tigers."

"I don't take any notice." The second woman snorted. "Can't let it get to you, can you?"

"No, you can't. Too much else to worry about."

Go sidled up to the two women and said, "About these tigers. Have you heard anything?"

"Oh, there was a *terrible* fuss last night. Sirens screaming, policemen with guns. All over the place!"

"Did they shoot them?" Go asked, hoping against hope. Maybe there had been something on the news that he'd missed; things happened so fast in this city.

"Oooh, no, dear. All the tigers got away—I don't know what these policemen were thinking. Very inefficient. But the tigers went away, anyway. This morning's been ever so peaceful."

"Let's hope it stays that way," Go said, with perfect truth. Thanking the women, he wandered away down the street, feeling slightly deflated. Typical: you made up your mind to see things right, even at great personal cost, and it turned out to be a complete anticlimax. But something in him told him that Lara would not be far behind, all the same. He could almost feel hot breath on his neck.

His initial assessment of the number of people around had probably been flawed. It was bustling, certainly, but he remembered coming down here one day in the late summer and it had been nearly impossible to move, such were the crowds around the market. Now, though crowded, Go was able to make his way unimpeded by the flow of humanity.

If humanity was the right word.

This street led along the harbor itself, culminating at the market building: a huge, hangar-shaped structure with a metal roof. Go had heard somewhere that it had been erected early in the city's short history, intended as a temporary shopping center before the installation of a swish new mall. But the contractors for the mall had run off with the money and the makeshift market had stayed. Periodically, there were discussions in the media about tearing it down and putting up something nicer, but nothing had come of this. It was ironic, Go thought: during last year's earth tremors, some of the new, ergonomic high-rises had collapsed like decks of cards, while the rickety market had merely flexed on its pilings over the water and settled back, like an old toad. Having approached the doors—still at this point of anticlimax—Go meandered in.

This was the hardware section of the market: brooms, mops, cleaning equipment, all jumbled together in the stalls. Go made his way between bargaining shoppers, avoided the pleas of stall owners to purchase revolutionary washing powders, and generally let himself be calmed by the outstanding normality of it all.

Normality, however, did not last.

Go was halfway to the vegetable stalls when he first became aware of the uproar. Someone was screaming. There was a kind of ripple in the crowd, a butterfly effect that ran down the row of stalls, causing shoppers to scatter and reform and scatter once more. Go was instantly alert, senses ringing as though his spirit had been struck like a bell. He knew immediately what this was, even before he heard the roar.

Just do it. Don't give yourself time to change your mind.

"Lara!" he bellowed, causing people to look at him askance.

"It's me you want, you bitch! Here I am, then! Come and get me." Folk would think he was mad but that didn't matter anymore; he was going to die anyway and personal reputation had ceased to be of much significance. Go felt as though he had stepped through a door and entered a strange alternative realm: he now could do nothing other than the course on which he had embarked. The removal of choice was oddly soothing. He began to push his way through the now-panicking mass of shoppers, moving salmonlike against the flow, toward his death.

FORTY-SEVEN

Inari, wandering through halls... Silence and lamplight, the soft fall of shadows, the sudden footstep rush.

Seijin was back. The Gatekeeper had told her but she already knew what was on the way, she could feel it in the air, the change. She shrank back among the cobwebs, merging into tapestry, as the old wooden doors of the Shadow Pavilion blasted open and its ruler came home.

Seijin left a wake, which whistled as it swept through the passages of the Shadow Pavilion. Inari felt it glide over skin that was no longer there, stirring non-existent blood, whispering on. The Lord Lady was long gone by the time she stepped timidly out from behind the tapestry, whirling up into the high air of the upper chambers, and Inari, despite her wishes, was drawn into the assassin's path. Moving fast, feet as still as if she'd stepped onto an elevator, magnet-pulled to the presence of the Lord Lady.

Corridors fled by and the tapestries came alive as she passed, coal-bright eyes glancing out, fingers reaching. A small prancing presence, a sad-faced lion-dog, flickered across her path and away. Inari rushed on, unable to stop, locked into someone else's dream; at the entrance to an upper chamber a man in a leather jacket, face full of hate, stepped out of the air, but Inari went right through him. The door banged behind her. She was still at last, standing in a room empty except for the moth-light of a single candle, and the Lord Lady Seijin.

The assassin turned and Inari gasped. The serene presence that she had last glimpsed in the moment before her death was gone. Seijin's face was a blood-stained mask in the candlelight, one eye gone, only a black hollow left where it had been. A thin thread of smoke misted from the eye socket, as if Seijin was burning up from within. Seijin's lips drew back from pointed teeth; each one gleamed red. The Lord Lady hissed like an adder.

"I left you dead!"

Now that the assassin's unnatural calm had dissipated like the smoke coiling out from the empty eye, Inari found that the tables had suddenly turned. She drew herself a little taller.

"But now I am here," she said, and smiled.

Seijin stepped back, Inari moved forward.

"You killed me, here I am. Forever and a day, Lord Lady." The smile was widening into a grin. Inari spread her arms open so that her long sleeves trailed out like a butterfly's wings. As she did so, she felt her feet drifting up from the floor, so that she was hovering. Without knowing how she did so, Inari shot forward, gliding through the Lord Lady with a cold rush like prickling ice.

Seijin cried out, a terrible wail of woe, and Inari knew a moment of pure triumph. Then she was through the wall to the outside, hovering beyond the Shadow Pavilion. The sky was a sparkling sea-green, the shade that lasts only for a few minutes just before the fall of night, and the bulk of the Pavilion stretched below, a vertiginous series of angles, blocks of shadow that made the building look like part of the mountain. At the window of the room she had left, Inari saw Seijin's anguished face looking out, a wan oval, fleetingly overlain by a snarling warrior and a woman's sad countenance. Then they were all gone and the little light went out.

Inari felt slightly foolish, floating here like a blown leaf. Being dead was odd, however: she knew how to do certain things without even thinking about it. She crossed her arms over her breast, pointed her toes, and sank down through the darkening air to the ground. Interesting, to see the Pavilion like this, though ominous. From the outside, there seemed to be much more going on than had been obvious from within. Inari sailed past an entire dinner party and paused to peer through the window, seeing a lavish spread, a table with blazing lamps and glittering silver, but the faces of the guests were somber and their food looked as though it was made of metal. And in another chamber, a woman wept alone, watched by the grave spirit of a child. This was a house-sized Hell, a microcosmic mansion of the slain.

Inari thought: *I am better off than these people.* Her faith that Chen would find her was still strong and the fact that she had managed to disconcert—perhaps even hurt—Seijin was hugely empowering. Then Inari's toes touched the ground, a leaf-light landing, and she was once more dragged to the Pavilion steps.

In, she had to get *in.* Once on the ground, that ferocious compulsion had seized her: she was thrust against the doors as if pressed by an immense wind, with such force that she slid down the unyielding door and lay slumped on the stone.

Someone said: "Is that you, Inari?" What had once been her heart echo-

thumped against her ribs—*Chen!* But it was not Chen; it was Bonerattle.

Inari turned her head with an effort. "I have to get in," she whispered. All the confidence with which she had faced Seijin had now ebbed away, consumed by need.

"Seijin killed you!" the shaman exclaimed. He scuttled out of the darkness, glancing from right to left; Inari wondered what else was out there, remembering the shapes she had seen.

"Yes, it killed me. It came to the Emperor's temple, I was in the way."

"I am so sorry," the shaman said. He put a blackened hand on Inari's shoulder; it was some small comfort.

"It wasn't your fault," Inari said.

"I brought you here, first of all."

"If you hadn't," Inari told him, "I would still have been at the temple and I would still have been in the way and I would still be dead. Tell me, shaman—has anyone ever come here, someone Seijin has killed, and left again?"

"I would like to tell you they have," Bonerattle said. "But the truth of it is, I do not know. The Pavilion is as crammed with spirits as a bottle filled with sand, and I can't enter it."

"But now," Inari said, "I can." She told him what had just happened with Seijin, and the shaman listened intently. The compulsion to get back into the building was still strong, but talking to Bonerattle permitted her to ignore it, up to a point. But it was also fueled by fear of what else might be waiting among the rocks: there were things that ate spirits, Inari knew.

"So," the shaman said, when she had finished. "You are in an interesting position. You are a haunt."

"So it seems," Inari said, with a hoarse little laugh. "What am I to do, then?"

"Go back in," Bonerattle said, "and do your work."

FORTY-EIGHT

Heaven was on the move. Mhara stood in front of the throne, watching as hundreds of people massed outside the Imperial Palace. These were the folk who had agreed to travel to Earth, there to take up roles in Singapore Three, to begin with, to see how they might best assist that city's benighted populace.

He'd left it up to them in the end, no exhortations, no enforced control. And this was what they'd chosen, restoring their Emperor's tattered faith, at least to some degree.

But there was another school of thought. Mhara could sense it, running through the Palace like a thin black wind. Discontent, dismay, a wind that could easily be fanned into flames and burning. He knew who was holding the fan, too. If he closed his eyes, he gained a small, incomplete vision of his mother, standing on the back steps of the Palace, whispering. During his time on Earth, she had managed to close him off to a considerable degree and he shivered to think of what kind of price she had paid to withstand Imperial magic.

Oh, my mother, what have you become? But he already knew the answer to that; it had lain in the whistle of a poisoned pin and the beheading flash of a sword. Mhara's lips tightened. Chen had insisted—with utmost politeness—that the Emperor return to Heaven, that he and Zhu Irzh would handle things from then on. There was too much at stake for Mhara to enter into purely personal engagements, Chen had said, and with reluctance Mhara had agreed.

So he was back here, after the second assassination attempt, to find his mother still plotting. She must be furious, to learn that Seijin had once more failed. Furious, and also desperate, for she must know, too, that her son would now be forced to take steps.

House arrest at the very least, but Mhara did not want to disrupt things still further on the verge of the Celestial exodus to Earth. See them safely off, and then act. With that in mind, he'd better get on with it. The presence of the Dowager Empress was like a poisoned thorn, reaching the very heart of the Palace.

Motioning to the courtiers, Mhara walked down the long hall, so quickly that the courtiers were obliged to scurry in order to keep up. The courtyard of the Imperial Palace was an ocean of upturned faces and Mhara experienced more than a twinge of doubt. He had no wish to be Heaven's Mao, sending them off on their Long March to Earth… Their faith in him, so hard won at first, had kindled to a blaze—and what if he simply let them down? So many longed for angels; he had spoken about it with Kuan Yin, she of Compassion and Mercy, not so long ago.

"They all cry out," the goddess had said. "They all read books about angelic powers—their own culture, other people's. They haunt the churches and temples, hoping for revelation. They see it on the television."

"And what would happen if you gave them angels?" Mhara had asked, unease rat-gnawing within.

"They'd be horrified," the goddess said. This, in essence, was what he was doing now, and would they be grateful? Probably not, but he had to try.

He raised his voice to address them and the murmurs immediately stilled. They were rapt, waiting.

"You are about to begin your journey," the Emperor said. *Don't call it a march, too many memories, even all the way up here. In Heaven's terms, all that was a moment ago.* "Be warned! Earth may not welcome you. There are those who want things made worse, not better, so that they can scavenge on the remnants. Remember what you know already: the human world is filled with predators. But you have to try. Do your best and if you ask, if you have need, then Heaven will take you back and there will be no blame." He held up a hand. "You have my blessing." And it rolled out from his outspread fingers, a blue wave, sparkling through the air, settling over their heads.

A horn sounded. Kylin danced at the head of the procession, the crowd now forming into a neater queue. The manes of the kylin were golden; their protruding eyes gleamed with a ferocious wisdom. They grinned, displaying gilded teeth. Mhara had forbidden them from entering Earth itself, mindful of recent deific incursions: the mad goddess Senditreya's rampage through the city, in her oxen-drawn chariot, was still unpleasantly fresh in human minds. But they would see the Celestials safely through Heaven and across the Sea of Night. Difficult to say when they would arrive: these things took their own time and not even the Emperor could rearrange temporal space, not for so large a gathering. They would get there when they were meant to.

The horn sounded again and the kylin wheeled, herding stray Celestials into line. Mhara watched, hand still upraised, as they set off, a joyful procession, singing, playing flutes, and banging drums. He hoped they'd still be happy in a week or so's time. And it would mean more work for Robin: he envisaged a stream of dislocated Celestial personnel showing up at the temple door, all needing urgent advice about dealing with the human realm. Robin would cope, she always did. But that still didn't mean it was fair.

He watched until, some time later, the last members of the procession threaded their way through the groves of flowering trees and out of direct sight, and the final capering notes of the flutes faded into birdsong. Enough, they were gone, and he would watch over them all the way as far as he could. But now, it was time to deal with the Dowager Empress.

蛇警探

He did not find his mother immediately. He went methodically through the Palace, searching room by room, always half-expecting the strike of a pin between his shoulder blades. He couldn't sense Seijin but that hadn't stopped the assassin last time, had it? He thought of Inari and regret made him shiver. Standing in the middle of an ornate room, one of the guest banqueting halls for visiting dignitaries, causing the silken drapes to billow from the walls, checking for someone hiding. Finally he reached the last chamber of all and she was not there. She had not been on the back steps of the Palace for some time.

Enough and enough. Mhara stood still once more, and summoned her.

The Dowager Empress arrived with a shriek. It was, her son thought, the only time he'd seen her anything approaching disheveled. Her robes still streamed behind her, as if caught in a stormwind, and her hair was coming down. She tried to glare at her son, but the decades of habit held her face in its masklike expression.

"How dare you." Her voice was low and cold.

Mhara said, equally icy, "On the contrary, madam. Since you've been trying to have me killed, I think I've demonstrated admirable restraint."

The Dowager Empress grew very still. "Killed?" she echoed.

"You're a terrible liar, Mother." Mhara circled her, wolflike, and the Dowager Empress tried to turn with him, but was hampered by her skirts. "The Lord Lady Seijin. The assassin. Tried twice and failed twice; I imagine there'll be a third attempt soon. You won't be there to see it."

The Dowager Empress' countenance grew even paler, becoming glassy and translucent. Maybe she'd simply disappear, Mhara thought: that would be helpful.

"Are you threatening me?" the Dowager Empress whispered.

"With what? Death? Treason, a trial? Oh no. I'm going to do far worse than that. I'm going to issue you with a home all of your own. Comfort, luxury, all you could ever need. What son could do more for a mother?" Distantly, Mhara wondered where he'd dredged up this aspect of cruelty: probably no need to work out where he'd got it from, given who was standing in front of him. Now the eyes of the Dowager Empress were distinctly fearful as well as angry, but Mhara meant what he'd said. He'd even had the place made ready, arranged before the Celestials were dispatched to Earth.

"Try not to see it as house arrest—more as a holiday. I'm sure that, given time to reflect on matters, you'll reach a more balanced perspective. Healing. Inner peace."

The Dowager Empress looked as though he had offered her a bowlful of scorpions. "I—" she began, but Mhara hissed, *"Enough."* Blue light surrounded the Dowager Empress, darkening to indigo, muffling her sudden scream. The light lapped around her feet like water, pooling, rippling, then rising to first one wave crest, then another. There was a strong wind blowing, out of nowhere. Mhara looked up and saw stars all around, reflected in the depths, an untethered moon sailed by, its sharp crescent cutting through the waves. Beneath his feet, the bare boards were encrusted with something white and grainy: if this had been an ocean of Earth, it might have been salt. The ship rocked and plunged, causing the Dowager Empress to stagger, and grip the nearest mast.

"Where are we?"

"Why, Mother, I thought you'd know. You can see it from the Palace windows, after all. This is the Sea of Night." Mhara pointed to a bright and distant line. "Look—you can even see Heaven from here. You won't be able to sail to it, unfortunately. In fact, you won't be able to sail anywhere, as this boat is anchored. Permanently." He pointed to the chain, gleaming blue, which ran over the deck and down into the sea.

The Dowager Empress gave him a look that was filled with hate.

"Nor will you be able to leave; the boat's warded. I'm sure you'll get used to a gentle retirement. There's a state room, it's all very elegant. And now, I really have to leave. I'll visit you, from time to time. When things quiet down."

He wondered, as he left, where his mother had picked up some of the curses she was currently employing. Certainly not from the parlors of Heaven. He looked back, once, and saw her standing there on the rearing ship, tiny against the vast expanse of the Sea of Night. Her face was upturned, and she had made some progress, at least, for the mask was finally gone: her expression was one of pure rage.

"Goodbye, Mother," Mhara murmured, as Heaven's shore grew closer and the darkness fell behind.

FORTY-NINE

Go was nearly flattened in the rush, as shoppers pushed and shoved their way out of the market, away from the roar. He struggled toward it nonetheless, dodging around stalls, trying and failing not to knock over stands of peppers, strings of chilies and ginger, baskets of millet. Treading on a slick of grain, he fell, going down under the flying feet of escapees. Cursing at his wrenched ankle, Go clambered to his feet, looked up, saw Lara.

"You!" the tigress said. She was bigger than Go remembered, or perhaps it was the enhanced perspective lent by fear.

"Yeah, it's me," Go said. That fear had already started to ebb, replaced by simple weariness. Suddenly, all he wanted was for this to be over and done with, knowing all the same that it never would. A transition, that was all, stepping from one room into another, into even deeper shit. "Go on then, Lara. I guess I deserve it. I won't even ask you to make it quick. Just get it over with."

"All right," the tigress said. Burning bright, indeed: she looked like a bonfire, all flame and soot, making the spilled colors of the fruit and vegetables pallid in comparison. "All right then, I will." And leaped.

But as she leaped, Go smelled something pungent, a blast of spice, heard a harsh male voice crying out something in a language that was familiar, and not Cantonese. Lara knocked him flat again: Go was suddenly struggling underneath a mass of silken draperies and warm flesh.

"What the fuck?" Lara, no longer tiger, shouted.

"Get off me!" He was sure she'd broken a rib. Go was prepared to meet his death in feline jaws, not to be flattened by a felled actress. This might be the dream of some of Lara's fans; Go, at this point, would rather have been buried in centipedes. Moments later, his command was enforced by a tall man, gloriously dressed in orange and gold, who hauled Lara back by the

175

arms and smacked her across the face when she resisted.

"Agni!" Lara's face was working.

"*You've* been having quite a time." Black eyes, golden ringed, a voice like a purr.

"Who the hell are you?" Go asked, then remembered. The tiger prince, no less. Agni's gaze was predator-cold.

"I might ask the same of you. Are you the man who stole my Lara?"

"I didn't see her protesting much."

"Agni, this is my career we're talking about!"

The prince gaped at her. "What career? You're a tiger spirit. You don't need a career."

"*Jhai* has a career." Lara began furiously tucking stray hair back behind her ears. "This is the trouble with you, Agni. These are modern times and you think all women want to do is kill things and fuck."

"Everyone else seems perfectly happy with that!"

"Oh, that's what you think, is it? My sisters spend half their time plotting against you, Agni."

The prince laughed. "Is that supposed to worry me? Of course they do. They need their little hobbies. They never manage to do any real harm, do they?" He gestured toward Go. "Anyway, if a career is really what you want, you can have one. I don't hold grudges, Lara"—*and I'll believe that when I see it,* Go thought—"and I'll give you a role in the hunting party. Come on, it'll be fun." His teeth glittered. "Like old times."

"I don't think so," Lara spat, and she turned and ran. Go had never been so pleased to see anyone leave.

Agni, smiling, swung around to watch her go, and that was when Go also took to his heels, barely able to believe that he had cheated death once more. But as he ran he heard laughter, soft as a cat's feet, and the voice of Agni saying, "Well, you'd better go after them, hadn't you?"

All Go's courage had evaporated like water through a sieve. He ran desperately, glancing up at the rudimentary exit signs to find his way, banging into stalls and stumbling on the spilled produce. Maybe by now, someone would have alerted the authorities to the fact that there was another tiger incursion within the market; maybe police marksmen would be waiting—but then Go reached the side exit of the market and it was locked. He rattled the metal door, kicked out, but the door opened inward and he ended up hammering on it with useless fists. The authorities—or someone—had indeed responded. They'd locked everyone in.

Behind Go, somebody screamed. Go swiveled around and saw Lara, still in human guise, backing toward him. He wasn't sure if she'd even realized he was there. The tigress in front of them, however, almost certainly had. Lara's form rippled as Go stared, hazing with stripes, a phantom tail switching briefly before disappearing into the air. She was trying to change, he realized, and could not. Ahead of her, the tigress came ever on. Lara's fists bunched with magical effort; her body contorted, and still nothing was happening. The tigress licked whiskery lips.

Go turned back to the wall and started kicking it, more out of panic than anything else. But the old market building responded. A panel of corrugated iron collapsed, letting in a square of daylight. Go threw himself into it, scraping hands against the sharp edges of the ruptured metal and not caring, because he was finally free. He rolled out into steamy heat and found himself in an alleyway, buildings on one side, the market wall on the other, and at the end of it, the port.

Can tiger demons swim? *Who cares?* Go thought. He sprinted for the line of sea, hearing, behind, something battering its way through the hole in the metal wall. Someone else was shrieking, an indication of agony that—even though it was probably produced by Lara and was therefore a good thing— made an arctic sweat break out across Go's brow and dissipate the heat of the day. It spurred him on; he reached the edge of the harbor and hurled himself off the edge.

Down and down, a surprisingly long way to fall, into the sudden green shadow cast by the harbor wall. Go hit greasy water with a splash and a gasp, went under, kicked out, and came up again. He supposed he should try to rid himself of his shoes, but they were only sneakers, and instead he struck out, swimming in a confused mélange of styles that just about avoided taking him in a huge circle. He glanced back, once. A striped head was peering over the harbor wall, teeth gleaming in the sun, eyes full of fire. The sister who had visited him, or someone else? Go did not care. He hoped the lot of them were hunted down and killed; he would have no more to do with magic after this, no more spells, even if it meant starving in a garret....

He was free. He continued swimming strongly, heading for the middle of the harbor, planning to find a boat and haul himself aboard. But that was before something grabbed him by the ankle and hauled him down.

Go swallowed filthy water and choked. The thought struck him, even in these extreme circumstances, that if he didn't drown or wasn't eaten, he'd probably die from some vile disease communicated by the revolting waters of the harbor. A lot went into the port; it was closer to soup than sea. He kicked downward, trying to dislodge whatever it was that had hold of his ankle, and squinted through the murk. He was in the shadow of a ship, now, but the kick propelled him and his assailant out into a shaft of sunlight. Go, half-drowned, found himself staring down into the fierce face of Savitra.

Tiger demons aren't always tigers. As a woman, Lara's sister evidently possessed Olympic-standard diving skills. Her grip on his ankle was unbreakable, a steel fetter, she dragged him down. Go sank through green shadows, dimly aware that the boat above him was receding, to be replaced by winding, curling shapes. *Snakes,* he thought. *Snakes, and I am dying.* It didn't seem to matter anymore, wherever he ended up. The water around him was brilliant, green and gold and shining, radiant as the sun, and instead of the oily warmth of the city harbor, it tasted of mud and weed.

Go's vision swam and pressure laid a huge, heavy hand upon him. And then, just as forcefully, Savitra was dragging him up again. Go broke through the surface with a spluttering shout. He gasped for air, wheezing, trying to keep afloat.

Everything had gone. The boats, the city skyline beyond, had disappeared. Go was looking up into dappled emerald shade, elephant-ear leaves fringing down over a mass of roots into the water. Everything was hyper-real, etched and edged in gold and flashing darkness. At first, Go thought that it was just his vision, affected by a near-death experience, or an actual death experience, whichever it had been. He felt very much alive, if the burning in his lungs was anything to go by. His ears were ringing, and that gradually resolved into the screeching of birds and something else. Monkeys. Which Singapore Three did not have, unless one counted the zoo.

"This is India," Go said, wondering, aloud, and someone behind him answered. "Not quite."

FIFTY

"You're *not* coming," Chen said, for perhaps the eleventh time.

"C'mon. You need me, you know you do. I'm invaluable."

"It's not that I don't appreciate it. And yes, you are very useful, Zhu Irzh. But this isn't Hell. This is *between*."

"How different can it be?"

"And besides, you've just got back from someone else's limbo."

"That's not the same. Anyway, so has the badger."

"It's the badger's job to go with me. If it was just Jhai who needed you here, Zhu Irzh, I'd say—then come with me. But it isn't, it's the police department. Agni's harem is roaming the city—the market manager at the port had to seal off the building earlier and who knows what's happened over the last hour or so. You and Jhai are the closest we've got to experts. And Mr Go, except that he seems to have had an attack of nobility and disappeared."

Zhu Irzh sighed in frustration. "I suppose you're right. All the same—"

Chen clapped the demon on the shoulder. "I know. I'm not trying to get rid of you—I wish you were coming. But someone has to deal with this in my absence and I'd rather it were you and Ma and Jhai. The badger and I will be fine."

Husband understood things, the badger thought. During the course of this swiftly conceived plan to go to *between*, Husband had not, at any point, tried to dissuade the badger from accompanying him. Nor had Husband's superior, on learning of what had happened, tried to prevent him from going. The badger, as a magical creature, knew when the flow of events was carrying people along with it; he could feel the snap and sing of it, and there was nothing now to do except to be taken by its wake. Humankind often did not seem to understand these things, however, and it was refreshing to note that Husband had such a good grasp of affairs.

"When do we leave?" badger said now. Husband turned to him.

"As soon as Lao's ready."

"I'm not sure I'm up to this," the departmental exorcist said from across the room. Lao was squatting on his heels, meticulously delineating a circle in red powder around him. "This is a bit more than I usually have to cope with. Talking of which, where's your Celestial friend?"

"In Heaven, as far as I know. He's got a lot to sort out. An assassin, for a start."

Lao grimaced. "If you run into this character—how are you going to handle it?"

"I have no idea."

"Chen, that's not reassuring."

"Look, Lao, Seijin is a legend. He—she—is one of the great assassins of all time and, moreover, killed my wife. I don't know what I'll do but whatever it is, it won't be the wrong thing to do." Chen held up the pin. "Mhara has one of these. I have the other. Mhara has already injured Seijin. The assassin can be killed, I'm sure of it."

The badger gave a quiet grunt of assent. Husband understood things, for certain.

"When will you be ready?" Chen said now.

"Give me a few minutes." Lao straightened up, groaning. "I need to make an appointment with an acupuncturist. Back's killing me." He handed over a small pouch. "I'm using an adapted spell—it's an old one, for traveling between the worlds, and the only reason I'm doing that is because it's one of the few spells that mentions *between*. But you have to remember: it's untested. I don't know of anyone who's used this. This—" he pointed to the circle on the floor "—is the stuff from the pouch. It's your path back here. If you run into trouble, and need to get back, or if—" he amended this hastily at the sight of Chen's expression "—*when* you find Inari, you activate it with your own blood and it'll get you back. I'll need a blood sample now."

The badger watched as Husband held out his hand and submitted it to Lao's needle. A drop of blood oozed out and dripped to the floor. The red powder hissed, flaring with a light that made the badger turn his head away. Lao had cleared a small gap, through which he invited Chen and the badger to step, so that they were encased within the circle. Then Lao sprinkled more powder into the gap, closing the circle.

"Remember what I said. Your blood."

"I'll remember," Chen said. He turned to the badger. "Are you ready?"

"I have always been ready," the badger replied.

"All right, then," the exorcist said. "We're good to go?"

A spell scroll fell to his feet as he began the incantation, a quick, sibilant thing that lodged in the badger's skull like a swarm of wasps. The badger reflexively shook his head, but the swarm was growing, shutting out the distant sounds of the city, blurring the sight of the temple beyond the rising red wall of the circle. Then the earth shuddered and shook beneath the badger's paws; he knew enough of earth magic to realize that this was not the world itself that was moving, but Husband and himself, starting to shift as Lao's incantation brought *between* closer and closer yet.

It was not like journeying to Hell, nor did it bear much similarity to the journey down to the Hunting Lodge. In essence, the badger understood, they were not moving: rather, *between* was coming to them, a thin finger of another realm drawn down by Lao's antique magic, gradually enveloping them in a bubble of elsewhere. In the shimmering red air, Husband turned to the badger, who gave a quick bob of the head: *I am all right.* Then they were snatched and away and moving fast, ripping up through all the realms that were: the badger glimpsed the bright shore of Heaven and even thought he saw the towering white cone of the mountain from which he had been born, but perhaps that was wish only and nothing that was real.

Husband said something, or so badger thought, but his words were swallowed by the vast interstellar wind. A thousandfold stars spun by and the badger heard something huge and lost crying out. Then the familiar glitter-black of the Sea of Night fell away below and they were tumbling in a red-tinged mist down a stony hillside.

"Well," Chen said, a breathless moment later. "We're here."

蛇警探

An hour or so later, the badger was certain that they were being followed. He said as much.

"You could easily be right," Chen said, casting an uneasy glance over his shoulder. "We've no idea what lives here, after all. Apart from the ones we're looking for."

The badger looked back along the stretch of hillside down which they had recently come. The red thread stretched behind them, thin and almost invisible, but if the badger turned his head at a particular angle, he could see it: a shine of magic, binding them to Earth. He would have found that reassuring, if he had been able to place any faith in Lao's spells, especially, since the exorcist himself did not seem confident about this arcane piece of conjuring.

"Where do you think this thing is that's following us?" Chen asked now. "Did you actually see it, or smell it, or…?"

The badger gave a frustrated hiss. "I did not. I only sensed it, but I am sure it is there. It keeps moving, in between the rocks, now here, now there."

"This place must be full of spirits," Chen murmured. "Let me know if you notice it again. I can't tell what's here, it's as though someone's thrown a blanket over my head."

"I know the feeling," the badger said. But he had advantages that Husband did not—and the reverse, no doubt—and the strongest of these was his sense of smell. It had stood him in good stead down in the world of the Hunting Lodge, and he intended it to stand him in good stead now. He kept casting about, searching for any traces of Mistress, confident that he would pick them up no matter how slight they might be. She might be dead, but to the badger, this had become a minor inconvenience.

"Anything?" Chen asked. Husband knew what he was doing and had put up no argument with it, letting the badger get on with his job.

"Not yet," the badger said, but a minute later, he had the lie to that. It wasn't the scent of Mistress herself, the smell of her skin or hair, but the perfume that she wore: the odor of flowers, frangipani and ylang-ylang. The ghost of her scent, just as she herself had become a shade in this gray-mist land. The badger raised his head.

"I have her, Chen." It was the first time he had called Husband by his proper name; it had seemed disrespectful before now.

"All right," Chen spoke with a concentrated ferocity that surprised the badger not at all. "Then follow."

It was good to be focused again, good not to be dithering about. The end was closer in sight now and when he looked back, the red thread seemed to have grown stronger, more secure. This all gave the badger hope and he scurried on, skirting the larger boulders down into a narrow valley.

"It would make a certain amount of sense," Chen said, "if we'd come in at the same point as Inari, even if it was by different means. We left Earth at the same place, after all."

The badger thought about this and cautiously agreed, although he knew how unstable these connections could be.

"No footprints," Chen went on, "but then, one would not invariably expect them. Under the circumstances." He spoke tightly and the badger did not reply, deeming it unnecessary. Badger scented on, searching for further traces, but the line was narrowing now, as if Mistress had wandered about for a time and then suddenly made up her mind where to go. He headed after it, with Chen close behind. It led between the stones and boulders and then out into a long valley. At the end of it, stood a building.

"She is there." The badger spoke with absolute conviction.

"That is the Shadow Pavilion," Chen said. They stood still, staring. To the badger, the Pavilion hummed with spirits, as busy as a hive. He could see their dim forms, wheeling around the tottering summit of the pagoda. They were not like birds, their forms ragged and changing from moment to moment, and occasionally fragments separated and drifted down to the ground like pieces of a torn veil.

Chen was peering at the Pavilion. "There's something around it."

"Yes," the badger said, and told him.

"I can't see them very well," Chen said. "They look like shadows. Perhaps that's how it got its name."

But the badger disagreed. "No," he said. "The thing is made of shadows. Can you not see it? To me, it is clear." To the badger, it looked as though bits and pieces of long-ago structures had been welded together: the ghosts of imperial pagodas, fragments of lost palaces, whispers of ancient fortresses that were now lost beneath the sands of Western China. And Chen said, "Yes. Now you tell me this, I can see it. Seijin has raided the world for the spirits of buildings, ransacked and taken."

"Perhaps it was not Seijin," the badger amended. "Sometimes, so I have heard, these things grow."

Chen smiled. "Like mushrooms."

"Just so," the badger agreed, not seeing anything amusing in the remark.

"You still have Inari's scent?"

"I do." It went in a straight line from where they stood, to the Pavilion itself, as far as the badger could see. He checked back. The red thread was still there, but very faint.

"We need to think about this," Chen said. He squatted down on his heels and looked toward the pagoda. "We can't just walk up to it. And unless I'm greatly mistaken, it's not long before dark."

Studying the sky, the badger saw that Chen was right. The light was fading in the smoky heavens and he could smell twilight, an odd, sour odor.

"We'll need to find somewhere safe before then," Chen went on. "What about that presence you sensed?"

"It's following us," the badger informed him. "Do you wish to challenge it?" He was hopeful.

"I think," Chen said, "that perhaps it's time we did."

FIFTY-ONE

Inari crouched in the corner of the room, watching Seijin. Her world had narrowed down to this single focus; at the back of her mind, she understood that this was what it was to be a haunt—to become an obsession. Something within her still cried out for Chen and her home, she knew she had to return to Earth, but revenge had become a greater compulsion now. And both she and Seijin knew it. The assassin, sitting at a small table, turned and looked at her out of that single undamaged eye and Inari grinned back, curling her fingers into claws.

"What are you, that you can haunt me like this?" Seijin whispered, and Inari whispered back, *"I am your madness."* She uncurled herself from the corner and went to stand by the assassin's shoulder. She was pleased to see that Seijin flinched.

"What?" Inari asked, all mocking. "Afraid of me? Oh, surely that cannot be. You are the great assassin Lord Lady Seijin, are you not? The slayer of gods and men? Killer of little demons who get in your way? Surely I can't be disconcerting you?"

"Be quiet," Seijin said, but it was a whisper. The empty socket glared, but something moved within it and Inari, baring her teeth, moved closer. There should have been no reflection inside the socket and yet—there it was, a procession of little figures, as if seen in a tiny mirror.

"Why," Inari murmured. "What can that be?" She had never been so spiteful before, the little voice reminded her, but then again, she'd never before had to live alongside her murderer. "I believe—yes! Aren't those all the people you've killed?" Now that the eye was missing, she realized, Seijin could paradoxically see what previously had been hidden. "If I poked out your other eye, I wonder what you'd see with that? Your own death, maybe? Do you think so?"

"Enough!" Seijin cried, and lashed out. The assassin's arm passed straight through Inari and she laughed. Seijin, muttering wild curses, leaped up and ran from the room. "What's the matter, Lord Lady?" Inari shouted. "Afraid of what you can see, like a child in the dark?" But where the assassin went she, too, was forced to go. She hastened after Seijin, up the stairs, all the way to the topmost chamber. And there, Seijin had paused in the entrance to stand, staring.

Inari peered over the assassin's shoulder. Someone was already in the room. It was a woman, or at least, part of one. Like Inari, she was spectral, wearing robes of immense richness and complexity. But her long skirts seemed sodden, drenched with some dark substance like ink, or perhaps blood. No—Inari looked more closely, it was not blood after all, but certainly something wet. Her face was beautiful, yet it did not look real: she was as white as a doll and her eyes were wells of blackness. Moreover, she was patchy: Inari could see glimpses of the opposite wall through the wet robes.

At first she thought this was another haunt, someone else whom Seijin had slain, come back to exact the penalty, and she felt herself start to smile, but then the woman said, "I am not truly here."

"Madam," the assassin said, and Seijin's voice was shaken. "I can tell that."

"He has imprisoned me."

"What?" Seijin sounded genuinely surprised. "Where are you now?"

"In a boat. On the Sea of Night. Forever." The woman's mouth twisted and it was through this gesture, which broke through the mask of her face, that Inari finally recognized her. She had seen this visage before, but then it had been male and belonging to someone else. The woman looked like Mhara, but whereas the new Emperor's face was filled with a genuine tranquility, this woman looked as if she had been feigning it for decades. And it seemed she had.

"You have one last chance," the woman said. "Without payment, now. He knows."

At this Seijin laughed, a sound of genuine merriment. "Look around you. This is my kingdom, the only home I have or need, the only one I will ever be permitted. I could have had any fortune I wanted. I'll kill your son whether you can pay me or not."

Inari heard herself say, "You'll have to reach him first. You haven't done so well up till now, have you?"

The Lord Lady swung around. Inari saw Seijin's mouth work, but the assassin said nothing.

"Who is that?" Mhara's mother said, very sharply.

"A spirit, nothing more."

"A friend of your son," Inari said, coming forward. She brushed through Seijin and the assassin felt unpleasantly hot, burning up with furnace fire.

Was Seijin ill? Let's hope so. "I was there when your hired help failed, Lady. He killed me instead."

"I don't know who you are," the Emperor's mother said, eyeing her askance. "I wished no one else any harm." But then her gaze narrowed and she said, "You are a demon. I knew he consorted with such. Are you one of his women, then?"

Inari spat and a glowing coal shot out of her mouth and singed the floorboards. "I have a husband. Your son is my friend, nothing more, and you insult both of us."

"She makes a bold ghost," the Dowager Empress said, sneering. "Will she be so bold when she is dispersed, or confined?"

"I cannot disperse her," Seijin said sourly. "I have tried."

News to Inari, but then the Dowager Empress said, "Then fetch a jar. Bottle her up. I know a spell, if you do not."

The Lord Lady crossed to a cupboard on the wall and took down a small brass jar. "Let's see," Seijin said. "I'd welcome some peace."

Inari expected to feel the stirrings of apprehension, but did not. She waited, quite calmly, as Seijin opened the jar and began an incantation. The words hissed and echoed through the upper chamber, whistling around the eaves like bats, but Inari stayed where she was. It was an old spell, she could tell: recited in the ancient demon-speech before the languages of Hell had changed to mirror the tongues of men, but it had no more effect than a handful of dust.

"And you are supposed to be a magician," the Dowager Empress said, with scorn.

"Madam, perhaps you should try." Seijin was still polite, but Inari could hear the thin thread of rebellion beneath the assassin's words: with the Dowager Empress confined, would Seijin still feel the need to carry out what was obviously a contract? Inari thought that Seijin would, as a matter of professional pride.

"I will," the Dowager Empress said. She, too, began to speak and now Inari felt a pressure growing upon her, as though she was an inflating balloon. But it was nothing more than that and after a moment, it diminished. The Dowager Empress cursed.

"As you said," Inari remarked, "you're not really here."

The Dowager Empress' mouth opened and she shrieked, but the scream was only a thin thread of sound. It was a long way to the Sea of Night, Inari thought. The Empress was fading, too, her robes pulling her down into the floor like a drowning woman. Inari watched, impassively. The attempted spell must have exhausted the energies she'd used to project herself here. Seijin's face was unreadable. With a final faint breath, the Dowager Empress cried, "My son is in Heaven now!"

Then she was gone, melting through the floorboards like spilled ink.

"Well," Seijin said softly. "So back to Heaven we must go."

For a moment, Inari thought that the assassin was talking to her. Then she saw that one of Seijin's other selves, the male, had drifted out and was circling the Lord Lady, a captured star. Easy to see Seijin's warrior origins in this one: the trailing moustache and pointed helmet adorned with a horsehair tail, the heavily ornamented leather armor. He looked at Inari with congealing hate.

"I must make preparations," the assassin said. Male self was absorbed back into Seijin's form and the Lord Lady strode from the room, followed by Inari. Seijin summoned the old Gatekeeper with a single clap of the hands; the Gatekeeper studiously did not look at Inari and it occurred to Inari that perhaps the master of Shadow Pavilion had access to his thoughts, that the Gatekeeper did not want to give anything away.

"Prepare for my departure," Seijin said. Inari watched as the Gatekeeper, moving with the confidence of long practice, cast powder in a circle: a rusty substance, like dried blood. Seijin stepped within. "I will be back soon," the assassin said, speaking directly to Inari.

"I wish you success," the Gatekeeper murmured.

"Oh, this time it will be." Seijin snapped a hand through the air and a sword was whistling down. It touched the edge of the circle and ignited. Seijin's form grew very small, rushing away at unimaginable speed, but Inari was pulled with it, crossing the circle with a blast of heat that made her shout out, feeling as though it had withered her, a leaf in a flame. Bound to Seijin, the assassin had pulled her along. She saw Seijin's figure up ahead, spinning on its own axis: the Lord Lady did not look real, but like a doll dropped down a well. Worlds spun by and they were crossing the Sea of Night, with Heaven's bright shore rising up. Then over the peach blossom lands, the lakes and pools, calm under the Celestial sky that was so light and yet spangled with stars. Inari saw Seijin's figure hurtling toward the spires of the Imperial City and she wanted to cry out, to warn Mhara, but speed tore her voice away.

A blink, and she was somewhere dark and perfumed. She had caught up with Seijin: she could hear the assassin moving about, muttering.

"I am here, Seijin!" she called, and was rewarded with the assassin's curse. Inari felt elated: With her tagging along, warning everyone she saw, how could the Lord Lady ever hope to achieve their objective? But Seijin laughed.

"Who will believe you? The ghost of a demon? The Celestials have jurisdiction here. As soon as they set eyes on you they will snap you into a bottle."

"Mhara will not," Inari said. "And how do you know that he hasn't told everyone what has happened?"

Seijin was silent at that, and once again, Inari felt triumphant. Despite the position in which she had been placed, she had—in this limited sphere—more power than when she had been alive. A curious circumstance and one which she intended to make the most of.

The Lord Lady, moving with caution, opened a door and light flooded in. They stepped out into a lavishly decorated room: the lacquered walls hung with pale blue and rose silk, a thick carpet covering the floor, antique furniture dating from one of the more elegant historical periods. Paintings hung in gilt frames, their colors glowing. But somehow, Inari thought, it was all a bit much: too perfect, too refined, the pastel shades reminiscent of a sickly American cartoon. She followed the Lord Lady through several rooms, all decorated in the same style, until they came to a door that hummed and sang with magic. Seijin put out a hand and the wards snapped electric-blue. So someone had decided to seal these overwrought rooms away. An interior decorator? But Inari's sardonic thought was soon superseded by understanding: these must have been the rooms of the Dowager Empress, and now that she had been removed to her exile, Mhara had closed them off. Perhaps, as her hireling Seijin appeared to do, the Dowager Empress might otherwise enjoy special access to the Palace through what had been her own chambers.

Thoughtfully, Seijin walked to the window and looked out. Inari noticed that the assassin's male self seemed to be becoming more apparent: the ghost of a helmet now framed Seijin's features, and the assassin's figure was encased in that tribal armor. Inari wondered if this change could be used in some way: Seijin's power stemmed from the Lord Lady's liminal being, after all, and if that was negated by the increasing absence of the female self… It was worth considering, though she did not yet know how it might be taken advantage of.

Seijin was unlucky. The windows were also warded, with the same blue fire. But the assassin did not seem unduly perturbed, and that worried Inari. She tried to move through the wall herself, but an unpleasant shock ran through her incorporeal being, like being snapped by an electric fence. Seijin turned to her with a feral grin.

"See? Heaven's magic doesn't like you, either."

Inari said nothing. She'd choose her moments of engagement, she thought. She watched as Seijin took out a long cord, of what looked like twisted black horsehair. The assassin murmured a spell, a whispering incantation that fell from Seijin's lips in a thin stream and sank into the cord itself. The cord started to glow and Inari had the uncanny sensation that there was someone else in the room, someone familiar. A moment later she recognized it as the presence of the Dowager Empress: not horsehair at all, but the Empress' own tresses, bound into this talisman. The whispering spell went on and the hair began to change, turning to a silkier texture, a lighter shade of black. Like Mhara's, Inari thought, and understood what Seijin was doing: old magic, transformation through the mother-line, and as such, underpinned by genetic science. She was helpless and could only watch as Seijin took the altered tresses and attached them to the horsehair plume on the warrior's helmet. Then Seijin's eyes closed and the troubled face began to melt away in the pale light of magic streaming down from the coil of hair. Bones shifted, muscles glided into place beneath the changing clothes, and within a few minutes it was not the Lord Lady Seijin who stood in the Dowager Empress' apartments, but Mhara himself.

Seijin turned to Inari and smiled.

"Now, let's test, shall we?" Teeth bared, all arrogance now, which sat oddly on Mhara's serene face; distressing to Inari, like a violation.

"I will speak out," she warned, and Seijin hissed, "Yes, but who will believe you, little dead demon, when the Celestial Emperor himself gives the lie to your words?"

Inari did not reply, because Seijin would have heard the weakness in it and she did not want to give the assassin the satisfaction. Seijin turned back to the door. The assassin raised a hand and the wards sizzled out into shadow, fading and then gone. Seijin stalked through, with Inari close behind. If Seijin had been hoping that she would be trapped in the chamber, the assassin would be disappointed: resembling Mhara perhaps, but Inari was still tugged along by the magnet.

FIFTY-TWO

As if he had taken root like waterweed, Go stared, mesmerized, at his captor as she rose from the river. From the neck down, she was a woman, and naked: sleek fawn skin, striped with jet. But her head was the round-eared, sun-eyed head of a tigress and she opened her mouth and roared.

The knife of sound snapped Go into movement. He sprang out of the water, scrabbling and scrambling for the bank, gripping the slimy roots of the mangroves to pull himself upright. He hauled himself clear of the river, expecting at any moment to feel the hot close of jaws on his ankle. The tigress roared again, a pleased, lazy noise. Go could not run, for the undergrowth was too dense, and there was no point in climbing: tigers can climb, too. His chest felt like a furnace, burning up in the pain of almost drowning, he tottered along like an old man, falling over the exposed roots and trailing creepers. He looked behind once, inadvertently. The tigress stood there in the water, unmoving. Waiting for her sisters, Go thought. He didn't even know whether he was still alive. If this was dead, it didn't feel much different. Unfortunately.

Night fell swiftly after that, a dense velvet shawl descending over the forest. Go had no idea where he was, or where he was going. Oddly, neither hunger nor thirst appeared to be entering into the equation, in spite of the sultry, stifling heat. The humidity was intense, even at night, reminding Go of his childhood. He breathed in experimentally: at least he seemed to be able to inhale and exhale still. But that he wasn't even sweating would seem to lend weight to the possibility that he was in fact dead. Go had, however, almost ceased to care.

At least, before the thing dropped on him out of a tree. There was no warning at all and Go had thought he'd been paying attention, paranoid as he was about the tigers. But suddenly he was facedown in the soft spicy earth, the breath knocked out of him and a vast darkness filling his vision. Go struggled and kicked, but it was hopeless. Then, as abruptly, he was released. He raised himself up on his elbows, gasping, and was seized under the arms and hauled up at terrible speed into a tree.

"What the fuck?" Go cried. "Let me go!" It wasn't a tigress: he had a confused impression of long black limbs, much too spidery to be human, and a whipping tail. Something cackled into his ear and its breath was foul, like rotting vegetation. The cackling went on: he thought the creature might be speaking, because the sound had an odd kind of cadence, but it was no language that he knew.

Then it dropped him. Go yelled, seeing the dim forest floor swing up. The thing caught him by the ankles with a jarring jolt and threw him across a branch. The impact winded him again; he croaked for breath. When he finally regained consciousness, he found that his wrists and ankles had been trussed, so that he was strung out between two of the manifold trunks of a large tree, with the initial branch under his ribs. He squinted round and saw the creature looking at him. It was black, with short fur. It had a head shaped like a coconut, with little coal-like eyes. Its jaw dropped down when it saw him watching, revealing a huge expanse fringed with long teeth, reminding Go unpleasantly of an angler fish. It had four arms, ending in a mass of arachnid fingers, and long, jointed legs, folded beneath it.

"Who are you?" Go demanded. The thing chattered away, but whatever it was saying remained incomprehensible. It spoke with some animation and enthusiasm, however. "I'm sure this is fascinating," Go said. "Please let me go." It was the teeth that had done it. Had it not been for that glimpse of jaw, Go might have felt safer with this thing, whatever it was, than down on the ground with tigers prowling.

The animal spat at him, a glutinous skein of saliva that struck the back of his head and trickled down. It smelled of shit. If he really was dead, Go thought, gritting his teeth, all this would just go on and on. Was it possible to die more than once, to keep on doing so until one was just a faded shadow? In which case, everyone might finally leave you alone. Go shut his eyes, and waited for further demise.

The creature continued to spit, until Go was firmly welded to the tree. He endured this, closing his eyes to avoid the spittle and trying to breathe through his mouth. At some point, he told himself, an end would come. He told himself this so often that it turned into a mantra and Go passed into a sort of yogic state of which, later, he was rather proud. When he came round again, the sky had softened to a haze that was neither day nor night, and there was no sign of the animal, for which Go—who had remained a resolute agnostic almost as an act of defiance—was nonetheless devoutly grateful. He was still stuck to the tree, however. He tugged, cautiously, as it was a long way to the ground and there was not a great deal between Go and it. But the bonds remained. He was sure that he'd seen something that behaved like this (nothing Go had ever seen looked like it) on a nature channel, during one of those animal documentaries that you watch when you're stoned. It hadn't made a lot of sense then, either, and he couldn't even remember what kind of thing it had been. Nor could he remember how the prey had extricated itself from its predicament. He had a nasty feeling that it simply hadn't.

It was fairly clear—both from Zhu Irzh's comments and his own observation—that this was indeed Hell, or a realm of it. Go's father had been a firm believer in reincarnation, maintaining that if one had not lived a good life, then one would, in time, be reborn as something unwholesome, probably a beetle. Go wondered whether this was happening now: whether the black being was some kind of middleman, dispatching souls between the realms. Maybe the web in which Go was partially encased would act as some kind of cocoon, dissolving him into a soul-soup before his regurgitation back into the world of Earth.

These theological ruminations were disturbed by a whisper.

"Who are you?" someone said.

Go turned his head and was confronted with someone a lot more appealing than the black entity. Also female, also naked, but with—yes!—no betraying sign of feline ancestry. Yet.

"My name's—" Go hesitated. There were all sorts of reasons, both magical and practical, for not telling her. Besides, he'd only got into this situation through an uncharacteristic bout of honesty. Then again, what had he got to lose? Trapped in a tree, possibly dead, certainly screwed. "My name is Pauleng Go," he said.

The girl bobbed her head in greeting and placed both palms together. "Namasté."

"Hi. And who are you?"

"My name is Sefira."

"You look human," Go said. *And how.*

The girl burst out laughing. "How funny! Of course I am not human. I am a deva."

"I see." Go ransacked his memory for information on devas. Not goddesses, not demons. Created by Vishnu as handmaidens of Heaven. They had always been one of the more appealing aspects of Hindu mythology, to Go's way of thinking.

"If you're a deva," he said, "what are you doing here?"

"I fell in love," the deva said. She looked down, interlacing her fingers in her lap; Go tried and failed not to stare. "With Prince Agni, and he had me brought to the palace. Then he turned me into stone and a demon rescued me. A Chinese demon."

"Aha," Go said. Things were beginning to fit together. "His name wouldn't have been Zhu Irzh, would it?"

The deva's eyes widened. "You know him? There was a spirit with him, a beast."

"Yes, I do know him," Go said. "You might call him a friend." Risky, but if Zhu Irzh had rescued this girl, she was presumably grateful. Go had almost given up making assumptions, however.

"Then you are a friend, too," the deva said. *Right decision!* Go thought. For once. Maybe his luck was changing.

"Look," he said to the deva. "You can see I'm stuck here. Can you help me? A black being imprisoned me up here."

"Oh yes," the deva answered. "They do that. They suck out your essence, later." She pointed to the surrounding trees. "Can you see? There are the husks of the others. Their spirits are still here, but the essence is gone." Now that it was light, Go could see that, indeed, there were faint shapes dangling from the branches, fragile as shadows.

"You know, I'd rather that didn't happen," Go said. "Can you cut me free?"

"I'll try," the deva said. She moved closer, enveloping Go in a cloud of musky perfume. Even under the current duress, his head swam. She began tugging at the webbing with surprisingly sharp fingernails. Soon, Go's hands were freed enough for him to be able to help her; then he was able to swing himself up onto the branch.

"I need to get down," he said. "Do you know a way out of here? Out of this realm of Hell, I mean? If you helped Zhu Irzh—"

"Yes," the deva said. "I do. But only if you'll take me with you. Zhu Irzh couldn't, and now Agni knows I was involved, I think. There are things after me." Her face crumpled. "I don't want to be a statue again and there are worse things he can do. If I help you, will you take me to Earth?"

It was at this point that Go decided, once and for all, to give up self-sacrificing, noble behavior. Look where it had got him. It was time for a personal agenda to reassert itself. "Baby," Go said. "If you help me get back to Earth, I'll not only take you with me. I'll make you a star."

FIFTY-THREE

It was less a challenge, more a summoning. Chen held out a hand, palm upraised. "If you're there, then show yourself." His voice held the sudden ring of magic and the badger was hopeful: human powers altered in both Heaven and Hell, and there was no way of predicting how they would behave in *between.* "Show yourself *now.*" They would just have to hope that the presence sensed by the badger was not the Lord Lady Seijin, but it did not seem Seijin's style, somehow, to skulk around boulders in what was, after all, the assassin's own realm.

But then the person who had been following them stepped out, shuffling, the bones attached to its clothing shivering in the wind.

"You're Bonerattle," Chen said.

A sharp, beady glance, sideways, like an animal. "So I am," the spirit shaman said. "You've come after her."

"So we have. She *is* here, then?"

The shaman's glance shifted to the badger. "A familiar," the shaman said.

"Where is she?" The badger saw no point in small talk.

The shaman pointed toward the pagoda. "There. But Seijin has gone, I don't know where, and it's likely that Inari has gone, too."

"You've seen her, haven't you?" Chen said. "What kind of state is she in?" He spoke as calmly as ever, but the badger could hear the anxiety beneath the words and so, too, could the shaman, for he flinched.

"She is dead, but here in spirit. A strong spirit, too. She's bound to her killer but I don't think Seijin has had an easy time from her."

"Oh good. You said the Lord Lady has gone?"

"Last night, in a terrible hurry."

"How do you know this? Did you see them go?"

"I have been watching the Shadow Pavilion," the shaman said. "Trying to look after Inari, but in truth, there's little help I can give her."

"What about the Pavilion itself? Is there anyone there who might know where Seijin has gone?"

"The Gatekeeper," the shaman said. "I could not speak to him last night, the Pavilion was locked."

"And now?"

"Perhaps."

"If you can take us there, then please do so," Chen said.

"You can see for yourselves where it is. But I will go with you." The shaman peered over Chen's shoulder. "That's your lifeline?"

"A blood line."

"It'll get you back to Earth," the shaman said, "as long as it isn't cut. The Lord Lady has swords that can cut through anything."

"I have seen the Lord Lady wounded," Chen said. "As long as Seijin isn't invincible, we will cope."

"I believe you might," Bonerattle replied, looking at Chen more closely. "You have the mark of gods on you."

Chen laughed. "I'm no god. I just know a couple."

The badger, impatient, was already heading across the stony ground, skirting the rocks. Mistress' perfume was stronger now, but only a little. It was, however, enough to know that she had been here, in some form. Now, they would find her and restore her: to the badger's way of thinking, matters continued to be simple.

"How do you know Seijin hasn't come back?" Chen asked, some time later. They were standing close to the steps that led up to the pagoda, keeping out of sight of the main entrance.

"The presence of the Lord Lady is like a star in the heavens," the shaman said. "I can feel it."

The badger looked up at the Shadow Pavilion. From this brief distance, the origins of the building were even more marked: he could see bits of it fading out of sight even as others regained prominence. Spectral balconies manifested and grew translucent again; a flight of steps appeared, leading down to empty air, and were gone. The ghosts that soared around it were more ragged than they had seemed from further up the valley, and although one might have thought that they would have been woeful, desolate, they had merely the sense of emptiness; of shells of spirits, flocking to the pagoda from long and weary habit. A dreary place, the badger thought, and he was accustomed to bleak.

"This does not look very stable to me," Chen remarked.

"And yet it is," the shaman said. "It is a place of spirit and everything here has nowhere else to go. You will see when we enter."

"Ah," said Chen, "So you *can* get us in."

"As I said, I will try."

But he did not have to try very hard. As they went up the steps, the doors swung open without warning and an old spirit tottered out.

"Shaman, you have come! And with company." He barely spared Chen and the badger a glance. "Well, never mind that."

"Where is the Lord Lady?" the shaman asked.

The spirit wrung his hands. "Gone, gone to Heaven to slay the Emperor. The Lord Lady is injured and has gone mad; we will not withstand it here, even if Seijin returns. Everything is starting to crumble."

"Seijin mad is more dangerous, not less," the shaman said in alarm.

"Three beings in one, how can that be sustained?" the old spirit remarked.

Chen said, "There was the ghost of a female demon with Seijin. What happened to her?"

The spirit stared at him. "She went with him. She could do nothing else."

Urgently, the badger said, "You, spirit. Can we reach Heaven from here?"

"You can reach anywhere, from here," the shaman said. "The question is, whether you can get back to where you started."

"I will send you on," the Gatekeeper said.

"You're a member of Seijin's household," Chen said. "Why would you help us? Because the Lord Lady is fragmenting?"

"This household has grown in the years that Seijin has made it a home. It is all these spirits have." The Gatekeeper gestured to the circling ghosts. "Without the Pavilion, they would be out in the wastes of *between,* the prey of ghouls. I have a responsibility to them. If Seijin dies, then we might yet stay on. But if the Lord Lady is mad, then the Pavilion is likely to crumble alongside."

"Who are you, then?" Chen asked.

"I am Seijin's first victim. The Lord Lady killed me when Seijin was eight years old, riding with the horde. They besieged Bukhara. I was a gatekeeper of the city; I was already old. Seijin was just a child on a pony and ran me through. I remember that there was no expression on my murderer's face. I came here: it was smaller then, only a single peak, and stones. The Pavilion came later, along with all the dead."

"You must have desired revenge," the badger said.

The old spirit shrugged. "Terrible things happened in those days. It was the way of it."

"Terrible things are happening now," Chen reminded him. "If you want to save the Shadow Pavilion, I suggest you give us some help."

Within, the badger could barely move for spirits. They thronged the passages and corridors, bumped against the ceilings like moths. Women with their throats cut, eyeless warriors and their mutilated steeds, murdered children. Seijin's legacy was coming home to roost, the Gatekeeper explained. Before, the Lord Lady had worked to keep these spirits invisible, at bay, but ever since the Lord Lady's injury, the Pavilion had become increasingly full of ghosts.

"The perils of a repressed unconscious," Chen murmured.

"What?" the badger asked, but Chen did not reply. They went up a long, winding staircase and out onto a landing. The badger passed through the shade of a slaughtered princess, the long metal tongue of an arrow still protruding from her mouth. Above it, her hair was piled up in an elaborate confection; she moved her head graciously from side to side, as if greeting visitors.

"This is the Lord Lady's own chamber," the Gatekeeper said. "This is where magic is done."

That was immediately apparent to the badger on entering the room. It stank of magic: the old, blood kind that was rarely practiced these days, at least outside of Hell. The walls were stained with it, a red-black substance like mold, and its tarry residue coated the ceiling. On the floor, a smoldering circle stood, similar to the one by which they themselves had come to *between*.

"Can this be used?" Chen turned to the Gatekeeper.

"You can use it, but Seijin will know."

"Is it possible to build another circle?"

The Gatekeeper wrung thin fingers together. "Not two at once, no. The Lord Lady made it this way, so that none should come in through the second circle while Seijin is away."

"We will have to use this one then," the badger said.

"Can you make it ready, Gatekeeper?" To the badger, Chen added, "We'll just have to hope Seijin's got other things on its collective mind."

"Mistress will do her best to provide a distraction," the badger said, stoutly. "I am sure of it. She will know we are close behind."

At a gesture from the Gatekeeper, Chen stepped across the threshold of the circle, grimacing. "I don't like using other people's magic. It's like wearing other people's underwear."

What was wrong with that? the badger wondered. It was probably some human thing, to do with scent and territory. Those, at least, were things he understood. He joined Chen in the middle of the circle. Seijin's presence was strong here, as if the Lord Lady was standing right next to them. In a manner of speaking, perhaps this was so. The badger had only a hazy notion of how all the realms connected; he thought that they were probably like the bulb of an onion, lying closely together and yet separate. He did not like the idea of stepping from air to find himself beneath the assassin's blade, and neither, he could tell, did Chen: he could feel Husband's uneasiness. The thread that connected them back to Earth was visible, but only just and it looked perilously thin where it crossed Seijin's circle.

"When you're ready," Chen said to Bonerattle and the Gatekeeper. The latter spoke a word, the circle flared up, rather as Lao's had done. The badger, half-blinded, closed his eyes; the pattern grew, then faded. He thought he heard Chen say, "We're moving."

A brief flicker of time and the sense of years passing. Worlds glimpsed, all at once, and the badger, opening his eyes again, found it familiar. The cone of the mountain rushed by and this time he was certain he had seen it: its earth core whispered to him, calling his stray spirit home. The badger thought of Mistress and did not listen.

And then—blossom-sweet, sparkling air and the reek of war magic, pungent as decay. Chen and the badger stumbled out into opulence. Seijin's passage was obvious, like stinking footsteps, but so was that of someone else.

"Inari" and "Mistress," spoken at the same time.

"She's here," the badger said, and Chen replied, "I know."

Together they ran through luxury, the badger noting only that this was a place that had been sealed by magic and then blasted open again; the smell of transgression was strong. The opened door hissed and sparked as they went through, but Mistress' scent was very clear and now the badger knew she was not far away.

FIFTY-FOUR

"No trace," Jhai said, putting down the phone. "They've all gone."

"Are you sure?" The demon was peering out of the window of Jhai's topmost office, as if tigers could somehow be seen from this great height, stalking the city in their black and gold.

"According to the security team and the police. There's no sign of them in the market, but they're not reopening the building just yet. Lao and Ma are down there now. Lao says someone's been doing magic: scorch marks all along the floor, apparently. And a fisherman saw a tiger jumping off the dock after a swimmer. Tall young guy, apparently, looked Indian."

"Your friend Go," Zhu Irzh said. "Oh well."

"I told the stupid bastard not to go near them. Conscience is a terrible thing, Zhu Irzh. I'm *so* glad I don't have one."

The demon suppressed a smile. He wasn't sure about that, whatever protestations Jhai might make. It just worked in an unconventional way, that was all.

"I want to go down there, take a look for myself," Jhai said. "Fucking Agni. I might have known he'd be trouble one day."

The demon shrugged. "Families."

"It's not even a question of being dysfunctional," Jhai mused. She slung her bag over her shoulder and made for the door. "It goes beyond that into some other concept."

"Psychosis?"

"You're probably right. Are you coming?"

"Of course. It's my job."

蛇警探

199

In late afternoon, the port area was humid and the rudimentary air-conditioning in the old market building had long since failed. Zhu Irzh straightened up from his examination of two sets of footprints.

"You don't really have to be a detective to see what was going on here," Jhai remarked.

"My dear Watson!" the demon protested. He'd lately got into old, subtitled Basil Rathbone movies; they were having their effect. "The only curious thing here is—"

"Where are they now?" Jhai looked along the line of footprints to where the dock ended and the harbor began. A man, in sneakers, running. A tiger, large. "And I don't think there's much mystery there, either."

"Shit," the demon said. "It's not like I've got a particular attachment to Go. I just don't like to think of *anyone* going through what I did."

"At least he might be keeping them distracted," Jhai said. "But I do wonder about the dynamic. Lara's sisters can't stand her. They keep plotting against Agni. It's a very fragile political balance inside the Hunting Lodge. I'm not sure whether that's to our advantage or not."

"Let's assume not," the demon said with a sigh. "It just makes matters simpler."

He turned at a whistle, to see Exorcist Lao beckoning to him. "Hang on a minute," he said to Jhai, and walked to meet his colleague. "What's happening?"

"I don't know whether they came in this way," Lao said. "They've probably got a number of exit and entry points throughout the city—the meat locker was almost certainly one of them. But they left through here. Come and see." He gestured toward the market and Zhu Irzh followed him in. Paugeng's security teams were milling about, as well as the regular police. Zhu Irzh saw with some satisfaction that the forensic unit was already hard at work.

"Take a look at that," Lao said, and pointed at an empty space between two partially collapsed stalls.

At first, Zhu Irzh thought that there was nothing there. Then, glancing at it from the corners of his eyes, he noticed a faint swirling in the air, as if a congregation of dust motes had gathered.

"Take a deep breath," Lao instructed. The demon did so. Spice, and a rank green odor that was unpleasantly familiar. Black earth and an undernote of water and rot.

"That's the portal," Zhu Irzh said.

"Oh yeah."

"So what are you going to do about it?"

"I've contained it," Lao said. "At least, I think I've contained it."

Zhu Irzh looked at him. "You'd better be sure, Lao. Don't want anything bursting out all of a sudden."

"Well, that's the problem," Lao said. "Now that we've found it, I somehow doubt that they'll want to use it again. They'll know we're waiting on the other side. If Agni's got any sense—"

"But does he, though? I'd say that Agni's gone out through arrogance and into mad."

"These bloody demons," Lao said. "Always getting above themselves. Sorry, Zhu Irzh. You know I don't mean you."

Zhu Irzh was used to being made an exception. "Cool," he said. "If you need extra people, I can probably ask Paugeng Security to do it."

"Good idea," said Lao, apparently keen to make up for his earlier lapse of tact. "They're a lot more gung ho than the police, anyway. You can tell they're just waiting for something to shoot."

Zhu Irzh grinned as he walked out of the market. Probably best not to mention that to Jhai…

She was not where he had left her. Zhu Irzh walked around the side of the building, looking for the Paugeng security team. They were standing in a tight huddle under an awning, one of them speaking into a cellphone.

"Hi," the demon said. "Jhai not with you?"

"No," one of the team replied. "We haven't seen her since we got here."

"I was just talking to her. She probably went into the market." But already, the prickle of unease was starting to make its presence felt. He went quickly back into the market building. There was no sign of Jhai. She had a phone of her own, of course; Zhu Irzh flipped the speed dial and waited. No reply. Eventually he got the answerphone and left a message. Word was already filtering around the teams in the market: within minutes, Ma had ordered a search. Jhai was taken seriously; she would not simply have wandered off.

Half an hour later, there was still no Jhai.

"He's got her," Zhu Irzh said to Lao. "Simple as that."

The exorcist nodded. "I think you're right. Open the portal in the market, create a diversion—he must have been sure that Jhai would come down here when she found out what was happening. And then just—snap."

"I wish Chen were here," Zhu Irzh said. "Any word?"

"Not yet. I left Robin looking after the circle," Lao said, and held out his cellphone. Zhu Irzh looked to see the circle upon it. "Cell cam. If anything happens, Robin will let me know. I ought to get back there, though."

"I'm going to have to go after her," Zhu Irzh said.

Lao gave a frustrated sigh. "Yes, I suppose you are, but you're not going through this portal and you're not going alone, either."

"We're running out of personnel, Lao."

"No, we're not. What about No Ro Shi? Hunting demons is what he does for a living."

"The trouble with No Ro Shi," Zhu Irzh said, "is that I'm never sure whether he'd be happier just hunting *me*."

蛇警探

"It's often a good sign, coming full circle," the demon-hunter said to Zhu Irzh. They were once more standing in Men Ling Street, not far from the place where Zhu Irzh and the badger had been snatched.

"You think so?" the demon said dubiously. Men Ling Street looked different in daylight: even more depressing, were such a thing possible. The area was, however, quieter: a lot of the drug dealers and pimps had moved out of the surrounding tenements, unnerved by such a massive police presence. At least something had improved, No Ro Shi had remarked, although Zhu Irzh, schooled in the rather different agenda of the Vice Division of Hell, had felt vaguely to blame for the loss in people's business. He did not voice this thought, feeling that No Ro Shi might prove unsympathetic.

"So what's been happening with this situation?" the demon-hunter now said to Ma. The crime scene tape was still present, and a forensic scientist was quietly occupied in the area surrounding the underground meat locker, but apart from a single police vehicle, everyone seemed to have packed up and moved on to pastures new, like crime groupies. Most of the original team had departed for the market, Zhu Irzh knew. He said as much to No Ro Shi.

"They've got pretty much all the evidence they needed from this site," Ma explained. "It's all down to the lab now. Marrying up body parts to DNA records, that sort of thing. I gather from the lab that they've already accounted for quite a few missing persons."

"This must have been rich pickings for Agni's crew," No Ro Shi remarked, glancing around the dingy confines of Men Ling Street. "Derelicts, prostitutes, criminals…"

"Having experienced Agni's hospitality, I suspect that's why they wanted to expand," Zhu Irzh said. "The girls seem to like a proper chase—I don't suppose a few terrified humans proved entertaining for long."

No Ro Shi's hand wandered to the hilt of his sword. "I confess, I'm looking forward to getting to grips with your girls."

"I wouldn't be too enthusiastic," Zhu Irzh said. "You haven't met them yet."

Ma's brow creased in worry. "Are you sure you'll be all right, just the two of you?"

"No."

"Certainly!"

"The thing is," Zhu Irzh said, "even if we went in with a whole team of people, they'd probably just get picked off. It's not just the tigresses down there—it's a whole realm of Hell. And we don't, yet, have a team who are experienced magical warriors. It used to be just Chen and this guy—" he gestured in the direction of No Ro Shi "—and that's only recently changed, as you know."

"I used to be afraid," Ma said. "Now I'm just angry."

"I can relate to that. Anyway, No Ro Shi, if we're going, we'd better get on with it."

"I agree," the demon-hunter said. He slapped Ma on the arm. "Look after the portal, Ma. Don't want anything breaking through."

Zhu Irzh followed him cautiously into the empty chamber. In the thin shaft of daylight coming through the door, it was even more out of place: as though the room should properly only exist at night. It was evident, too, how thick the layer of dust was that lay over everything: the forensic team had disturbed some of it, for the room swam with a maze of flying motes, but even so, the tapestries were still gray. It seemed to Zhu Irzh as though this room belonged to some other building entirely, that the rest of the tenement had been constructed around its dusty core.

Lao's wards still held. Zhu Irzh could see them, snaking around the gap in the air that marked the middle of the room. They were a little frayed now, although Ma had told him that Lao had only renewed them a day or so ago. This suggested magical activity on the other side: a depressing, but probably inevitable, occurrence. Lao must have his work cut out, Zhu Irzh thought: what with tiger demons, supernatural assassins, and Chen's personal woes, it had been quite a week for them all. And was continuing to be so. No Ro Shi motioned to the portal. "You want to go first?"

The demon-hunter was actually being polite, Zhu Irzh realized. Keen as he was to get to the action, No Ro Shi was courteously offering Zhu Irzh the chance to do so before him. "You are most welcome," Zhu Irzh said.

"Thank you." The demon-hunter gave him a little bow. Then he drew his sword, whistling down through the motes of dust, cut through Lao's ward as though it was nothing more than cobweb, and stepped through.

Zhu Irzh was close behind. Despite the warmth into which they now came, his skin was icy with apprehension; he had not, he thought, permitted himself to acknowledge just how much the Hunting Lodge had unnerved him. But now, he was in a position to witness the journey through this particular gateway: a journey that he had already made, but being unconscious, had not seen.

It was different to the way that Krishna had shown them. Zhu Irzh and the demon-hunter, unmoving, sped through tunnels as if traveling down through earth. They crossed chasms at speed, looking down to see fires burning and smoldering deep within, occasionally sending up spouts of flame. This was a road of earth and blaze: the walls of caverns illuminated by the flicker of heat. A dryness invaded Zhu Irzh's throat; he heard No Ro Shi give a cough, quickly stifled. They shot through glittering caverns, stalactites of bright gold, encrusted with jewels and crystals. Yet when the demon looked sidelong, all was darkness and shadow. Illusion only, like all riches.

No Ro Shi touched his arm, making him jump. "There's something up ahead."

Zhu Irzh looked to where the demon-hunter was pointing and saw a dim greenness. "Oh great. We're nearly there." And in an instant, the jungle was rushing up, swallowing them into its voracious throat. Zhu Irzh saw the demon-hunter turn, the great sword hissing through the air, and something like a creeper crashed down around them, pumping green blood. Zhu Irzh's own borrowed sword was already whirling, on the principle that even if he wasn't aiming at anything, it would deter anyone who might get in his way. He was distantly aware that No Ro Shi had ducked.

"No sign of incoming, no sign of further hostiles." The demon-hunter spoke urgently, as if into an intercom.

"What was that thing you hit?"

"No idea."

"Oh. Well, never mind." Zhu Irzh looked around him, now that they had slowed to a halt. They were standing in a clearing, not unlike the one in which the deva's little temple had stood, but there was no sign of any structures and the place did not seem familiar, although with all the greenery, it was difficult to tell. Best of all, there was not a tiger in sight.

"They're not here."

"That we can see." No Ro Shi was not so enthusiastic. He circled the clearing, sword drawn. "*Why* are they not here?"

"Business elsewhere?" Zhu Irzh was inclined to an uncomplicated gratitude.

"Let's hope so," No Ro Shi said. He turned to the demon. "Can you find the way to the Hunting Lodge from here?"

"You must be joking," Zhu Irzh said. "I've no idea where we are. Last time I came this way, I was unconscious. But listen, No Ro Shi—the portal in that room was regularly used. There must be some sign of where Agni's girls came from—tigers or women, this is dense growth. There must be some sort of track."

"You're right," the demon-hunter said. "All we have to do is find it."

Swords still drawn, they fanned out, searching the undergrowth around the clearing, and Zhu Irzh was rewarded with a shout from the demon-hunter.

"Over here!"

He had found a narrow path leading through the mass of ferns and vines. It looked long disused: a snaking track no more than the width of a human body and, in places, barely that. But this, Zhu Irzh surmised, was more a result of the speed of growth in this realm of Hell, rather than a proper indication of the last time that the track had been used. He said as much to No Ro Shi.

The demon-hunter gave a grim nod. "I've known places like this. Plant magic. Places where plants grow faster than you can run."

"I've not come across that here," Zhu Irzh said. "Doesn't mean they don't exist."

"Pity there's no way of taking a parallel path." No Ro Shi was studying the terrain. "It's much too dense."

"If we've no option but to go this way," Zhu Irzh said, "then that will have to be it. But I suggest you keep an eye on what's above you." He nodded up to the canopy of interwoven branches, many of them over a foot in width. It crossed his mind to try to climb, but neither he nor the demon-hunter had a cat's dexterity and he'd rather face Agni's harem on the ground.

They started walking, No Ro Shi in front and Zhu Irzh bringing up the rear. He turned often, reacting to sounds imagined or heard. As before, the jungle was full of noises, only some of which were familiar. Zhu Irzh could have sworn that he heard voices, calling to one another in a sibilant, unknown tongue. But whenever he glanced round, there was never anything there.

Ahead, No Ro Shi ducked behind a vine. Zhu Irzh followed; he had full approval of the demon-hunter's instincts. "What is it?"

No Ro Shi pointed. "That's it, isn't it? That's your Hunting Lodge."

FIFTY-FIVE

They were here. Inari sensed the presence of Chen and the badger the moment they set foot in the Celestial Palace, and her spirit grew weak and diffuse with relief. If Seijin noticed, the assassin gave no sign, but strode ahead, still wearing the mask of Mhara.

They had seen no one in their progress through the Palace and Inari could not understand why this should be: Did the Palace have no guards? Heaven was filled with warriors: she had seen that during the war with Hell. She was, for a long moment, tempted to fly back the way she had come, in search of Chen, but when she tried to do so, she found that she was still bound by the assassin's presence.

And then, finally, they encountered the guards.

There were a dozen of them, all running. They wore white and silver armor, ornate and traditional. They looked like Jhai's Celestial bodyguard Miss Qi, with their pale hair, bound into topknots, and their filmy blue eyes. They bowed as soon as they saw Seijin.

"Lord Emperor!"

Seijin waved them up. "No need for that. What is wrong?"

"Don't listen to him!" Inari squeaked. "He isn't the Emperor! He—"

A silvery streak of lightning cut through the air, nearly striking Inari. She heard one of the guards cry, "A demon! See, behind the Emperor!"

"No, wait!" Inari shouted, but her voice was a mouse's voice, here in Heaven's halls, and a moment later the sword struck home. She felt herself split, blasted into a thousand fragments and scattered like ash across the walls and ceiling. The atoms that contained her consciousness heard Seijin say, easily, "Well done, soldier! I commend your swift action. Now, what is amiss?"—and she heard, too, the guard reply, "Someone has broken through the Dowager Empress' apartments, My Lord. Some minutes ago—we set off immediately, but it seems we are too late."

"I must not detain you," Seijin said. "Proceed with your work."

"But Lord Emperor—you are alone, where are your personal bodyguards? I—"

"Do as I tell you!" Seijin snapped.

The guard took a step back and Inari saw the sudden doubt in his eyes. Evidently that was enough for the assassin. Seijin raised a hand, and Inari soundlessly cried out as she felt their bodies ripped apart.

Seijin walked on without looking back, and the atoms of Inari were pulled relentlessly in the assassin's wake. Seijin no longer bothered to speak to her and she wondered, with forlorn hope, whether the assassin had remembered that she was even there.

The beauty of the Celestial Palace continued to be oppressive. Seijin led Inari through rooms lined with diamonds and silk, under ceilings that depicted the night sky in all its wheeling splendor and those that shone like the sun. They passed through a great silent hall lined with war banners: the aristocracies of Heaven, some so ancient that they had become completely translucent, their devices appearing to float in midair, shimmering in the soft light. At first Inari thought this was the throne room, but no: it housed the banners alone, and as she glided past, her spirit beginning to knit back together again, the banners sang their songs of wars fought and wars won, all in the name of rightness. Inari supposed they were entitled, but she found it all a little smug. Yet then again, she was a demon, presumably a wicked thing... What if one of the guards had a sharper sword? Would she be blasted apart, an atomic explosion taking the Celestial Palace with her, or would she simply sigh out on the wind between the worlds, with Chen still so close? The guards' reaction to her had proved Seijin right, and Inari did not like that.

"Nearly there," the Lord Lady said over one shoulder and Inari realized that Seijin was still conscious of her presence. Seijin spoke mockingly, the words coming cruel from Mhara's mouth. And in the assassin's hand, Inari glimpsed the sharpness of a razor.

蛇警探

"They're—well, dead for the moment," Chen murmured, straightening up. The badger peered past him.

"What has happened to them?"

"Seijin has happened."

The guards did not look dead as a human would know it, the badger thought. He could still see the life glowing within them, as if turned down like gas on a stove to a low blue flame. But their eyes were open, staring milkily at nothing; their mouths, too, were ajar, and no breath seeped out of them. Their chests both bore the same wound: a ragged, bloody-edged hole that looked as though someone had thrust out their arms on either side, punched through the ribs and stolen their hearts. He could see their lungs, deflated like balloons.

"Unpleasant," Chen remarked, unnecessarily.

"Indeed. And someone is coming."

Hastily, the badger and Chen took refuge behind a curtain. A Celestial warrior raced around the corner, visible through the thin fabric, took one look at what lay upon the floor, and did not hesitate. The sword hissed upward, but Chen stepped out from behind the draperies and raised a hand. The sword was halted in midswing. The badger could see that the warrior was trying to complete the movement, but could not. His blue eyes bulged, his armor creaked. Chen stood, impassive, one hand gently upraised.

"As you can see," he said, "I have been given a small degree of authority and thus must ask your forgiveness for this impertinence."

He must have seen some change in the warrior's face, for the Celestial stepped back as if released from a string and sheathed the sword. "It is I who must apologize. You hold the Emperor's seal."

Looking up, the badger saw a faint blue glow emanating from Chen's palm.

"I am the Emperor's liaison official, with a small and insignificant part of the human realm. My name is Chen. I and my associate have come here in pursuit of an assassin."

The Celestial puffed himself up like a cat. "One such has already been dissipated."

"Dissipated?"

"The spirit of a demon girl was found in one of the passages. We neutralized it; I have sent instructions to one of our magicians to send it to final dispatch, while we track down any further invaders."

"Ah," was all that Chen said. The badger could barely contain himself: he seized Chen's trouser cuff between his teeth and tugged. Chen ignored him. "Where was this demon seen? Who was she with?"

"She was following the Emperor," the Celestial said. "Such creatures are weak; she was no more than a ghost. No doubt she was spying upon the Emperor in an attempt to supply information to her associates."

"Listen to me," Chen said. "In fact, that ghost—demon though she may have been—is my associate. As is this being, who, as you can see, is a spirit of earth."

The Celestial, radiating mortification, bowed very low. "So sorry."

"You were not to know," Chen told him, with what seemed to the badger to be superhuman charity. "Tell me—what did the Emperor say when you 'neutralized' this entity?"

"He was pleased."

The badger grew still.

"I see," Chen said. "You have been most helpful. I must not interrupt you in your work; you will have matters to redress here." He glanced at the bodies of the fallen guards.

"Do you require assistance?" The warrior was clearly keen to rectify his mistake.

"No, I need to find the Emperor," Chen said. "If you could tell me where he is now…"

"He was heading for the Great Hall."

"Then we will follow," Chen said, and as soon as he and the badger were around the corner and out of sight, they both broke into a run.

蛇警探

The next time they met someone, Inari took care to keep out of sight, hiding high upon the ceiling and riding the heat. The two they met, however, were clearly courtiers and not warriors: both were women, which meant little, given the equalities of Heaven, but they were wearing elaborate costumes that confined their bodies like a hobble. And it looked to Inari as though their feet had been bound: a practice common to certain strata in both Heaven and Hell. Ironic, Inari thought, that even in her current state, she might be more free than they, though presumably they'd had a choice.

They greeted the Emperor with little tinkling laughs, not something that Inari had ever associated with Mhara. No wonder he spent so much time in Singapore Three. They did not appear to notice that the Emperor responded with a degree of condescension that was surely foreign to the original, unless Mhara adopted a very different persona here in Heaven, and given the reactions to his assumption of the role, Inari did not think that this was too likely. They must be very unobservant, these Celestial maidens. Miss Qi would never have been so slow.

But perhaps not as slow as all that. "My Lord," one of them faltered. A puzzled frown crossed her smooth brow. "We have only just left you, in the Great Hall. Were you called away? I hope all is well?"

"Yes, my dear. I was indeed called, upon urgent business. Do not worry yourself."

"If we may in any way assist your august presence—"

"I will of course ask."

The two courtiers tottered away, twittering like little birds. Inari had always regarded herself as a rather feeble creature, taking fright at all manner of things, but then again, maybe she was wrong. She'd stood up to Seijin, after all. But trying to alert the two courtiers would be useless: they'd probably faint. And what was the Lord Lady planning? Surely the assassin would not make an attempt on Mhara's life in the Great Hall, which sounded like the kind of place where the Emperor would be surrounded by courtiers? Perhaps Seijin had gone completely mad, after all. She cried out—*Chen Wei!*—but her voice had been stripped away in her fragmenting, and nothing emerged. She thought his name, all the same.

They came to an enormous doorway, perhaps twenty feet in height or more, covered with thick gilt and red lacquer. How Mhara must hate this! Inari thought. Seijin strode up to the guards on the door, who stood rigidly to attention.

"Lord Emperor!"

"I was called away," Seijin said. "I wish to enter."

"Of course, Lord, of course." The fringes of the guard's helmet brushed the floor as he bowed. *No!* Inari silently screamed, but it was no use, the doors were opening and Seijin walked through.

The next few moments were dreamlike. Inari, hovering futilely near the ceiling, heard the courtiers gasp as the second Emperor appeared, saw Mhara turn upon his throne, saw Seijin raise a blade, watched as that hand expertly flicked out, sending the blade on a spinning trajectory toward the true Emperor, and strike Mhara in the heart.

FIFTY-SIX

They had crept around the back of the Hunting Lodge, to what looked like stables.

"Where are we going?" Go asked the deva, uneasily. He didn't like being so close to this immense, sinister palace, with its over-lavish balconies and verandas, its parody of Simla. The Lodge had weird overtones of the Raj: mock-Tudor beams where they shouldn't be, red brick facades, Victorian crenellations. Go and the deva had even made their way across a croquet lawn, though Go did not like to think what kind of beings played on it, or what they played. He tiptoed after the deva, fearing discovery at any moment, and was glad to reach the shelter of the wall. Then something kicked the door of the stables with a terrible crash and Go leaped.

"Shhh!" the deva said, turning. "It's only one of the horses."

"That doesn't sound like a horse!" An awful shriek split the night.

"Well, it is."

Another kick, and the sound of something scrabbling and scraping around. A head burst over the half-door of the stall nearest to Go and the deva.

It was close to a horse, he supposed. A long, angular head, more bone than anything else, fire-eyed and sharp-toothed. It took a bite out of the stall door and the wood splintered.

"People ride those things?" Go whispered. The deva looked at him as though he were mad.

"Of course."

"I really am going to take you away from all this," Go promised, more to reassure himself than anyone else.

"Don't worry," the deva reassured him. "They can't talk."

Go found himself at a loss for words. He hadn't wanted to approach the Hunting Lodge at all, given what Zhu Irzh had said about it, but the deva

211

had insisted.

"Before, my friends took another route, but Agni closed it off as soon as he found out. I only just escaped—I had to hide for ages."

"Aren't there—well, how many guards are there?"

"I don't know. Agni tends to go through guards rather quickly and it takes time to conjure more. You see, the main guards of the Lodge are Agni's harem, and if they're out doing other things…"

Go was starting to build up a picture of this particular realm of Hell. Not so much a prison for lost souls, as someone's private amusement park. Somehow, he'd expected armies and warriors, but as he had noted earlier, this was more reminiscent of those palaces high in the hills, designed for entertainment.

"Has Agni ever been—invaded?"

Even in the darkness, the deva looked surprised. "Why, no—who would bother? There's nothing here to interest other folk, unless they come as guests for the hunts. Many of them do, of course."

"I guess that's why I'm here," Go mused. "As a party trick."

"They sometimes use human souls as bait for the dogs," the deva explained. Go had visualized himself as forming the central attraction, but now it appeared that he was to be regarded more as a morsel. How degrading.

The horse howled again and the deva seized Go's hand.

"When I squeeze—*run*," she whispered into his ear. She rifled through the pouch that was, apart from her jewelry, her only clothing, and took out a lump of something ragged and oozing. It also smelled strongly of rotting meat. This explained the deva's rather peculiar odor, at least. She tossed it into the horse's stall with one hand and squeezed Go's fingers with the other. They ran past as the stables filled with squeals and the sound of rending.

"Wait a moment—" Go started to say, because they were heading for a blank stone wall, composed of massive blocks. Panicking, he was sure that his companion had gone the wrong way. Then the deva spoke a word and a small, cramped door appeared in the wall before them. She shoved it open and thrust Go inside.

Within, it was hot and the sudden silence was shattering.

"The gate's upstairs," the deva whispered. "I can't remember where, exactly."

"Oh dear."

"But I think I can find it. I'll do my best."

"Please try," Go begged. "What does it look like?"

"It doesn't really look like anything. That's the problem. You'll be able to feel it, though. Probably."

"Probably?" Go echoed. The deva disappeared rapidly into the gloom and he hurried after her, afraid that she might vanish for good. After his experiences with Lara, trusting Sefira seemed like a lunatic option.

But the deva had been correct. He could indeed sense the gate, feel the pull of his own world, surprisingly strong. He hadn't expected it to be so vital and this told him, at a visceral level that Go had rarely experienced before, that he really was alive. Now, he could see it, not glimpsed sidelong as the other one had been, but fully visible at the end of a long corridor. It whirled, a vortex, a galaxy of color, flashing neon blue and then gold and finally green, as sharp and bright as emerald. The deva broke into a run (a remarkably pneumatic girl, Go noted, even given the circumstances) and threw herself at the vortex. Go followed, racing down a corridor that was suddenly clearly lit, torches set in wall sconces flaring into light, the bursts of illumination keeping pace with him as he fled. Go glanced over his shoulder and saw his shadow racing out behind him, thick and black, moving like oil along the floor, and now he was still running, but the galaxy whorl of the gateway ahead was not growing any closer. Go was being pulled back by his shadow, weighed down, and the torches flared brighter and brighter as he struggled to break free. He was trapped in classic nightmare, and it struck him then, horribly, that what he had actually become stuck in was a nest of dreams, an onion-layer of ghastly, never-ending events and that no resolution was possible. Ahead, just before the gateway, the deva turned and he saw her mouth drop into an "O" of dismay. Go's shadow was like lead, it pulled him down to his knees and spread all around him, a dense tarry ooze. He saw the head of the shadow shrink to a pinprick, watched a hand fling up as he tried to grab one of the tapestries that lined the corridor, pull himself back to this one chance of safety—but it was too late. Go fell through the floor, sucked down by his own shadow.

His descent lasted for no more than a few seconds, but it felt much, much longer. He fell through every layer of the Hunting Lodge: past hallways lined with human heads, past a great ballroom shining with candlelight where a ghostly woman waltzed alone. He fell past bedrooms and dining chambers, glimpsing a table where dinner had been served: a white man's head rested on a platter, solar topee perched on top, apple in mouth. A demon with a black, burned face under a crimson turban sat in front of it, knife and fork poised to begin carving. The demon looked up, saw Go falling, and gave a great wide grin. Agni had house guests, it appeared.

It was not lost on Go that he appeared to be falling up. The deva had taken him into the lowest level of the palace: she'd mentioned a cellar, but not this maze of rooms and opulent chambers. Then his rapidly formulated suspicion was confirmed: he fell out through the roof, which opened up like the petals of a lotus to release him. Go was ejected into starlight: constellations that he did not recognize, but which were dizzyingly close. Twisting, he saw the whole of the Hunting Lodge spread out beneath him: the long roofs of the palace, now with no sign that a human soul had just crashed through them;

the balconies, verandas, and terraces, all lit by a streaming, smoking mass of torches; the stables through which he and the deva had so recently—and hopefully—come. Beyond stretched mile upon mile of jungle, with the glint of water showing between the gaps in mangrove and neem. On the far horizon, Go saw a curious, pyramidal structure that he took a moment to recognize as a temple; a fire was blazing at the summit of this, too. Agni's own temple? He was a god, Go knew, albeit a minor one. But even minor gods can be dangerous, as Go also understood, and perhaps more so. Something else he was about to find out.

Go had slowed down now, his fall halted. He spun lazily in midair, wondering what the hell was holding him up. But his father's training, and his own experience, had lent him a little natural ability. He could taste magic on his tongue, cinnamon-scented, as strong and sour as turmeric. Its thread was connecting him to the ground and when Go looked down, between the flickering light of the torches, he saw that the beasts which had occupied the stables had now been released. They had riders, too. He thought he saw a crimson turban. At least one of the riders had twice the usual number of arms. Hounds milled around the prancing hooves, and beyond that, on the edges of the terrace, something much larger was prowling.

A figure stood in the middle of the terrace, dressed in red and gold. To Go, still so high, it looked as though he had simply taken on the fire of the torches, for his clothing rippled like flame, with a glowing orange heart. Agni. The demigod turned and raised a hand, bringing Go down. He hurtled past the front of the Hunting Lodge, skimming past roofs and then over the edge to float down past the balconies onto the terrace. There were people on the balconies, Go noted, an audience for this evening's hunt. If "people" was the right word.

Go had been summoned with such speed that his descent sucked the air out of his lungs. Despite that spice of magic, he thought for a horrible moment that Agni was simply going to bring him crashing down onto the paving stones of the terrace and he tried to cry out, managing only a breathless shriek. But just before the ground could break his fall, Agni's fiery hand flicked up, and brought him to a jerky halt. Go was abruptly turned right way up and his toes touched the ground. As they did so, his shadow—still oily, still black—seeped away between the cracks in the paving stones and was gone.

"Ah," Agni said, and smiled. "I see the evening's entertainment has finally arrived."

蛇警探

Go managed to muster up enough selflessness to hope that the deva had got away, even if his feelings did include the vain hope that, if she had, she might be able to save him. But as he was shackled and dragged down the steps of the terrace by a hulking demon, Go felt hope ebb away: the deva stood at the bottom of the steps, also shackled and quite forlorn.

Go would, at least, have liked to have told her that he was sorry, but was not given the chance to get close enough. He tried to express it with his gaze, anyway, but the deva's head was downcast and she did not see it.

The demon picked up the end of the chain that was attached to Go's ankle, and took it across to the deva, securing it to her own fetter so that she and Go were chained together, over a distance of ten yards or so. It was easy enough to see what the plan was. He and the deva would be given a short head start, stumbling over the lawn with their shared manacles, and then the tigresses would move in. He could see them now: seven women, with another two standing off to the side. One looked very pale, as though she had recently been through some terrible ordeal. Her human skin was not smooth and glowing, like that of the others: instead, she still sported patches of tiger-striped mange, and there was an ugly red line around her throat.

The other woman was Lara, clearly sulking.

Agni now stepped forward to address the eager crowd who thronged the upper parts of the terrace. Go saw a group of beautiful women, dressed in black and silver saris, but when he looked again there was only a flock of carrion crows, sitting on the low terrace wall. A tall, elegant man with long hands transformed fleetingly into a monkey, lips drawn back against yellow teeth in a shriek of fury. And the demon in the crimson turban was there, also, his coal-burned face glowing with greed. These were only a few of the crowd: there were many more, too many for Go's despairing, bewildered brain to take on board.

"The hunt will shortly start," Agni announced. He gestured toward the tigresses. "I present you to these lovely sisters, the scourge of worlds, the hunters of legend! Take your aspects, ladies!"

And one by fearsome one, the women's faces elongated into broad muzzles, eyes glowed gold, tiger stripes slid out to bisect tawny skin, and claws hissed against the stones of the terrace. Only the injured girl and the glowering Lara remained within a semblance of human.

"And for our first hunt—you might view it simply as an appetizer to whet your needs, since it won't last long—we have a spirit of the forest, and a human soul!" Agni clapped his hands and the demon guard gave the unprepared Go a shove between the shoulder-blades. "Enjoy!"

FIFTY-SEVEN

Inari cried out as the weapon sped toward Mhara. She heard other voices from around the hall, shouts of woe and dismay, and underneath it all, a swift, ominous, and familiar muttering. Had Inari still possessed a heart, she might have felt it falter, for the voice she now heard was that of Chen. Then she saw him. He was at the very edge of the hall, half-hidden by a tapestry, with the badger at his heels. Badger looked as though he was about to spring.

"Chen Wei!" Inari mouthed. Her husband did not break his incantation, but he did glance up. She saw recognition, relief, worry, all flow across his face as the incantation went on. Whatever it was intended to achieve was not, however, clear: the blade reached Mhara, striking the Emperor in the middle of his breast-bone. Inari felt a shudder pass through her, as though the entire structure of the Imperial Palace had quivered. Her expectation was so vivid that it was almost as though she had already seen it happen: the Emperor rising, trying to stand, staggering, falling, *lost*—but this did not happen.

Instead, Mhara flew apart, disintegrating into a soundless explosion of dust and ashes. The hall became quite still, a tableau of paralyzed courtiers and Seijin standing frozen, one arm still outflung in the wake of the blade. Inari, looking down, saw the figure of the Lord Lady ripple, as if caught in the shockwave of the blast, and then split. A woman in a gray tunic and leggings stepped to one side, mouth open in a gape of horror. Her sallow skin appeared wrinkled, as if she had been crushed in some kind of press. She was joined by the figure of a man, wearing a helmet and the old armor of the steppes. Male and female self, Inari knew, and the shades screamed as they departed, hurtling out toward opposing walls of the throne room and scattering into shadow.

Seijin turned. The disguise was gone, torn away, perhaps, by the disappearance of the real Emperor. The assassin's gaze slid over Inari, barely registering. The departure of the primary selves, in so short a time, had wrought a great change in the Lord Lady, and not just from the loss of the Mhara-image. Seijin's once calm, once beautiful face had become a pinched mask like a shrunken head. The eyes slanted up, revealing the full extent of the empty socket, the mouth curled back from a demon's teeth. A ragged topknot of greasy hair, more like that of a horse than a human's, spilled across Seijin's hunched shoulders. This is what Seijin truly was, once out of balance, Inari realized. And lack of balance had been occurring over hundreds of years, with every soul the Lord Lady swallowed or took.

Seijin gave a great anguished cry and sprang upward. A moment later, the assassin stood on the balustrade of the gallery that overlooked the throne room. Another spring, and Seijin was gone through the window in a crash and splinter of glass. Courtiers, the bonds of their paralysis cut, fled in all directions as sharp rain showered down. Inari braced herself for the tug that would pull her after Seijin, but it did not come, as though the cords that tied her, too, had been severed by shattered glass. Finally, she was free to soar down to those she loved.

蛇警探

"That seemed to work," Mhara said. Chen, startled, stepped back and trod heavily on the badger's paw. The familiar growled.

"Sorry!"

The Emperor of Heaven had manifested out of thin air, after that unnerving fireworks display during the assassination attempt.

"Shhh," Mhara said. Blue eyes danced; the Emperor appeared to be enjoying himself. "They can't see me, you know."

"What did you *do?*" Chen hissed. There was so much confusion in the throne room that he could, it seemed to the badger, get away with being both a human intruder, and with talking to himself.

"A disguise to fool a disguise," Mhara murmured. "Seijin took on my appearance, in coming here. So I put a simulacrum in my place."

"But—what made Seijin change? Magic?"

"No," Mhara said. "Actually, that was nothing to do with me, although it's certainly helpful. I think the Lord Lady is cracking up."

"Literally," Chen managed to say, before the spirit of his dead wife whisked down from the ceiling and shot straight through him. Demons do not cry, no more do ghosts, but Inari's still-beautiful face was twisted all the same.

"Mistress!" the badger cried.

"Inari." Her name was a breath upon the air.

"He killed me, he stole me, and now I am here, I—"

"We have to find him," Mhara said. "If Seijin dies—" His gaze met Chen's own.

"Then Seijin must not be allowed," Chen said.

Heaven's resources were not as vast as they once had been, with the depletion of warriors by the previous Emperor's war, and then by Mhara's Long March to Earth. But there were still enough people to organize into search parties and squads, and Mhara, restored to visibility, wasted no time.

"My father had an easier task," he said to Chen with a sigh. "If everyone thinks as you do, then they're simpler to predict. Which is the whole point, of course."

"I won't suggest that you reinstate that state of affairs," Chen said.

"I will not." Mhara paused. "And now, I'm not even certain if I could. They've gained a surprising amount of independence in a very short time. Some would hold that to be a good thing."

"I would be one of those," Chen murmured.

"And I," Mistress echoed. The badger said nothing, but he supposed that family spirits tended to have a different view of these matters. Chen was clearly trying to hide his desperate worry over Mistress. On the day of her death, Mhara had explained that he would not be able to bring her back, and now here her ghostly shade was, still with her faculties and personality seemingly intact. But how long would that last, badger wondered. And if anything happened to Seijin, then what would befall the inhabitants of the Shadow Pavilion, Mistress among them? It seemed to him too much to bear, that he and Chen should come so close to losing her once, only to watch her slip from their grasp, a sorrowing shade, slain through mere circumstance. He felt her cold self brush against his fur, and saw the look in her eyes, but that was all she could do. At least she no longer appeared attached to the assassin and that was both curse and blessing, now that they had no idea where Seijin had actually gone.

"I can tell where the smallest beetle creeps beneath the leaves of Heaven," Mhara had told him, mouth downturned. "But I can't find the instrument of my death. Seijin is hidden from me, by the last of my mother's magic."

This was not the time to reflect on how many of the wars of the three worlds had been fought out of familial dysfunctionality, badger thought. Not few, that was for sure. Chen said to Mhara, "I will help as much as I can, obviously. This is your world, your kingdom. You must instruct me."

Mhara smiled. "Just stay by my side. All of you."

蛇警探

Seijin fled through beauty, running down corridors of silk and garnet, across bridges made of silver and pearl. Willows streamed by, their golden fronds trailing across pools that flickered with carp and shone with lilies. The assassin ran down streets lined with marble, under low lacquered roofs, through courtyards where ceremonial braziers quietly smoldered. Seijin passed a lion-dog on a plinth, which shook itself from stone into life, too late, for Seijin was running hard now.

The Lord Lady had failed, and failure was unbearable. Female self had screamed as she vanished, male self had not made a sound. These separate selves, accumulated over Seijin's long lifetime, had not stood the final test and this could not be borne—could not, and had to be. Seijin knew, deep within, that death was close and the memory of female self was there, wailing that it was hubris and madness to think that one could slay a god. Demon and human, Seijin had treated the worlds as a hunting ground and now the hunt had turned.

Seijin had no knowledge of where this flight would lead, running blind in panic, an unaccustomed state. For years, such perfect poise, such balance, had been maintained, but now it did not seem like balance at all, for the seesaw had finally dropped and brought Seijin to ground with a bang. The assassin's only hope lay in returning to *between,* to try to reconstruct more selves in the haunted peace of the Shadow Pavilion, and Seijin did not even know if this would be possible. But the other path led to death, and that was something to fear, the assassin now learned. Up until now, death had been something that was meted out to others.

Intolerable. Unbearable. Seijin ran on, seeing nothing of the wonders of Heaven. To the assassin, it had become a landscape of ashes and dust, a replica of the world that Seijin was seeking, trying to reel in *between* by sheer force of will. And *between* was calling.

蛇警探

"The Lord Lady will try to get home," Inari said. She was drifting around the ceiling of one of Mhara's small chambers, trying and failing to keep closer to the ground. Everyone had to crane their necks to look up at her and Inari was finding it annoying.

"Go to ground," the badger said.

"Exactly, Seijin's tried three times and failed. You saw what happened to those other selves—the assassin's starting to break apart."

"But Seijin is mad," Chen said. "We have to ask ourselves whether there's any rational thought taking place there at all."

"I don't think it's rational," Inari said. "Seijin was cracking up before coming here. Maybe a long time before. But the Lord Lady is bound to the Shadow Pavilion. I know that's where Seijin will go."

"Let it happen," Mhara counseled. "Less harm will be done in *between* than if Seijin's allowed to remain in Heaven. We need to open a door."

"Are you sure?" Chen said, but Inari could see from his expression that he agreed.

"Yes," the Emperor of Heaven said. "Open a door, and enter it. Get to *between* before the assassin."

FIFTY-EIGHT

No Ro Shi's head went up, a hound on the hunt. "Something's happening."

"Shit," the demon said. "It's a hunt."

A long bell-like call sounded out across the valley, an old-fashioned English hunting horn. Where had Agni found *that*, Zhu Irzh wondered: some ill-fated Raj-era fox hunt, no doubt.

"So who are they hunting this time?" No Ro Shi murmured.

"Dunno." But it didn't bode well for Jhai. Zhu Irzh was aware of a compelling, and frankly unfamiliar, anxiety. He wasn't used to worrying about Jhai—at least, not about her safety. He certainly worried about what she might be up to on any given occasion, although it was true that this lent a piquancy to life. But Jhai commanded so much power, so much wealth, was so self-assured even when she was completely wrong, that the demon was simply unaccustomed to concerning himself about her in that way. The idea of offering a chivalrous protection to Jhai was laughable.

At least, on Earth. But they weren't on Earth now; they were not even in Zhu Irzh's own home Hell, and Agni—for all his urbanity and foppery and whimsy—was presenting a real danger. This was his realm, and the encounter with Krishna had shown Zhu Irzh that no one else would interfere: there would be no sudden intervention by a benign deity. Why should there be, after all? If Jhai truly belonged anywhere, it was here among her deranged tiger kin.

He'd fallen in lust with her, like many people of both sexes. He'd agreed to marry her because he'd been maneuvered into it and backing out would have been more hassle than going through with it. Besides, one had to marry someone, just to shut one's mother up, and even demons grew older and more staid. And Jhai was a lot of fun. But suddenly, the thought of something permanent befalling Jhai—of no longer seeing her leaning over the balcony

221

of her Paugeng apartments with a bottle of Tiger beer in one hand, no longer seeing the scheming look that crossed her beautiful face whenever she was plotting something, never again watching Jhai stalking barefoot across the salt-stained boards of Chen's houseboat—the thought of losing this was suddenly intolerable.

He hoped it didn't show on his face. He was reluctant to exhibit any weakness in front of No Ro Shi. Fortunately, it was twilight and the demon-hunter was staring in the opposite direction, toward the Hunting Lodge. Over No Ro Shi's shoulder, Zhu Irzh could see an unpleasantly familiar scene unfolding itself on the terrace.

"Can you see Jhai?" His voice was urgent. So much for concealing weakness.

"No. Who are those two?"

No Ro Shi pointed. Up on the terrace, in the flaring light of the torches, Zhu Irzh saw a couple being locked into manacles.

"Shit," he said again. He'd recognized both of them. One was Go, and the other was the deva, Sefira.

Having the little deva and Jhai in the same realm was disconcerting as well. Under more positive circumstances, women of whatever species were prone to exchange information at a level of intimacy that Zhu Irzh found frankly frightening.

No Ro Shi looked enquiringly.

"One's a spirit. She helped me when I was here—if it wasn't for her, I wouldn't have escaped," Zhu Irzh explained.

"A fine figure of a young lady," was all that the demon-hunter said.

"The other one's Go."

"They're setting up for a hunt," No Ro Shi said. "I still can't see Jhai—" but the next moment turned his words into a lie.

She walked out onto the terrace, flanked by two demons. Zhu Irzh could see her clearly in the torchlight and his heart sank. She was magnificently dressed: a scarlet sari that flared at the bottom, like a hibiscus flower, and a billowing red veil that streamed out behind her as if caught in its own wind. Gold glittered throughout the weave, sparking off the light of the torches. Zhu Irzh wasn't all that familiar with Indian customs, but he did have a marriage coming up, after all.

"That's a bloody wedding dress," he said.

"If Agni marries her," No Ro Shi said, "even if he does so against her will—what effect will that have, magically?"

Zhu Irzh had discussed this with Exorcist Lao shortly before they'd departed. "It ties her here," he said. It had struck him at the time that this was why Jhai had been keen to get hitched, even to someone from Hell: with her own situation in Singapore Three having become somewhat more tenuous than previously (given what Jhai had inadvertently caused to happen to the city on earlier occasions, Zhu Irzh considered it a good thing that the local government was so spectacularly venal), Jhai probably now felt the need for a passport.

Well, it looked like she was going to get one. Along with a permanent residency visa to somewhere she had no desire to live.

蛇警探

A lawn had never looked so long. The world had become very bright, much brighter than it should have been from the flickering torches. Light streamed from the flowers, red columns of illumination shooting up from azalea and rhododendron, showering out across the lawn like a fountain. A bugle sounded, provoking a great roar from the crowd on the terrace, and Go and the deva set off at a stumbling run. Behind, glimpsed over Go's shoulder, the tigresses waited, held back only by the movement of Agni's hand.

It was hard to run in chains. Halfway across the lawn, the deva tripped and fell, nearly pulling Go down with her. Seeing that their only chance of genuine speed lay in dealing with the chain, Go scooped it up and wound it over his arm as he made his way to where the deva was scrambling up.

"You okay?"

"I'll be all right," the deva gasped, but she was limping and from the wince of pain that crossed her face, Go thought she had wrenched her ankle. Great. When Agni finally unleashed his harem, this would be like shooting fish in a barrel. The chain was heavy, slippery, cold. It bit through to the bone, making Go even more uneasy. This wasn't natural, it was some kind of magical fetter, something designed to hold souls, and its presence sipped at what little strength he had left.

"Come on," Go said, all the same. He let the deva lean on him and together they tottered off down the lawn toward the shrubbery, followed by the laughter of the audience. Go thought he heard Agni call out something, a mocking word, and the laughter rose. He and the deva weren't even the proper entertainment of the night; they were the comic turn. But then the bugle rang out again. Go and the deva lurched into rhododendron light, falling into a maze of blossoms, and the tigresses sprang after them.

FIFTY-NINE

Heaven was tearing down all around, shreds and tatters of beauty streaming away in the winds between the worlds, and Seijin could sense it now, the chilly nearness of home. A golden banner whipped by, followed by a young woman. She was dressed in white, her feet tightly bound, and she was smiling beneath her glossily lacquered helmet of hair. Her palms were together, as if praying. She smiled, bowed, and was whirled up into the rising storm.

Seijin now stood on a little bridge, looking down into chaos. The Emperor was behind this: Mhara's presence—calm, implacable, *working*—was very clear: Seijin could taste his spells on the wind and they were strong and sweet. They burst into ashes in the assassin's mouth, like the taste of failure. Once more Seijin howled, any semblance of control gone, as the Emperor dismantled Heaven all around and sent Seijin spinning down.

蛇警探

Chen and the badger were following Inari as quickly as they could, running down their own stretched lifelines back to *between*. The Shadow Pavilion called Inari like the tolling of a great bell: she could hear it ringing across the worlds and pursuing it was easy, she simply let it reel her in. She could not feel Seijin at all and that frightened her, that the assassin had already met an end and it only needed to catch up with her.

"Inari, wait!" Chen shouted once, racing through the ravaged chambers of the Dowager Empress toward the portal.

"I can't!" she cried back, anguished, a fish on the taut and snapping line of *between*. Something old and cold and heavy caught at her flying feet and weighed her down, but only a little; after a moment, she recognized its nature and its source: an earth spell, cast by the badger. It touched her to the core. It also allowed Chen and her familiar to catch up, so that they tumbled through the portal together and left Heaven.

Abyss. The Sea of Night, gleaming dark below. Back across the Three Realms, Heaven on the right, the bright and distant shore, Hell's smoky cliffs looming far away to the left and beneath it all, the endless stars. Inari glimpsed Earth, cried out once more for her home, her body, the smell of salt and tea in the morning, a spray of jasmine, everything she might never know again. *Hold on,* she told herself. *Hold on. Chen and the badger are depending on you.* That thought steadied her, as she had known it would. She turned her face from Earth and flew, hurtling over the Sea of Night and the boat containing the woman who still sat and rocked and schemed and would never, Inari somehow understood, come to terms with changed circumstance. The boat was a single drop of bitterness, in all that bitter ocean, teaching Inari how not to be. And then *between,* glimpsed swiftly under its green and twilight sky, with the impossible edifice of the Shadow Pavilion roaring up to meet her. She shot through into a circle, red heat discharging around them, diving through flame, with Chen and the badger hitting the floor, rather harder, on her spectral heels.

Chen cried out as the flame touched him and the sound tore at Inari, literally dispersing her to the four corners of the dusty ceiling. This frightened her beyond anything that Seijin had done, but again, that touch of chilly earth magic brought her back together again, badger weaving old deep spells, knitting fragments of ghost.

They were not alone in the room. The Gatekeeper was there, wringing ethereal hands.

"The Lord Lady is coming! You must go!"

"No," Chen and Inari said, together. "We're staying."

蛇警探

Between was breaking down. Seijin could tell this easily, flying in. To someone unused to the bleak expanse, it might have appeared unchanged, but Seijin knew the location of each rock, each crag, and it was plain that the landscape was thinning, becoming more diffuse.

Surprising, the extent to which male and female self had held things together, the glue of a personality, and a land. But Seijin was beyond mourning. Matters had been allowed to progress too far; it was time to regroup, redress a balance. But looking down, Seijin noticed a transparency in one hand, the rocks glimpsed through it. *Not too late,* Seijin whispered. *Not too late.*

The Shadow Pavilion was looming ahead, with the red circle of Seijin's own magic burning in the upper chamber. Seijin soared in through gathering twilight, noting the emptiness of the landscape beneath: normally, at this hour, the creeping predators of the shadows would have been prowling around the pagoda. But now, the doors stood firmly shut and the Pavilion appeared closed in upon itself, a shuttered eye.

The circle was waiting, welcoming, drawing in, and Seijin fell, rather than stepped, through it.

And was not alone.

蛇警探

Chen had begun the incantation some minutes before, with Inari hovering in the corner of the ceiling and the badger at his heels. He hoped, Inari knew, to blast Seijin out of the circle, sending the assassin to the limbo between all worlds, including that of the lands of the Shadow Pavilion itself. Seijin would not live, would not die, would hold those who depended so reluctantly upon the Lord Lady in balance. It was tenuous and Inari did not like it, as no more did Chen, but they had little choice.

The incantation tore at Inari, caused the room to rock. She could hear the badger's dark voice beneath Chen's murmured words, weaving earth spells into the conjuring. Power rose, ripping upward through the Shadow Pavilion, drawn by some undreamed-of well in the foundations of *between*. With her ghost's sight, she could see its outline all around Chen, a bright blackness, flecked with gold, growing until Chen had almost disappeared. Soon, all that Inari could see of her husband was a silhouette against a background of power, one hand upraised.

But Seijin was on home ground. The Lord Lady came through the circle and slammed Chen against the wall. The Pavilion shuddered, earthquake on the way. The power that Chen had raised spilled out across the floor, a palpable tide as though a sea wall had been breached and let in the flood. Inari, huddling against the ceiling, saw Seijin give a great raw grin, as primal as an ape. But breaking Chen's power took its own toll. The Shadow Pavilion creaked like a tree in a storm, then groaned with the sound of rending timber, then split in half.

Inari once more found herself outside the Pavilion. The green sky was racing with gathering cloud, and far away on the horizon she saw a lightning bolt bridge cloud and earth. The mists that had so characterized *between* had been blown away: everything was sharp, clear, translucent, breaking. Looking back, the struggling Inari saw that the Pavilion had split in half from summit to foundation. A chasm of some ten feet separated Seijin and Chen.

Chen threw a spell across the gap, but the Lord Lady took a dancing step out of the way and the spell splattered against the wall. He could not win, Inari thought in despair. Seijin, the killer of thousands, had experienced several hundred years of additional practice. The Pavilion creaked again, alarmingly, and the gap widened. Inari was staring straight down the chasm and saw now that it went far beyond the foundations of the actual pagoda. She could see Earth—no, she could see her own body, lying calm and peaceful in Mhara's temple in Singapore Three.

Her lips, blue in a pale face, moved. Her body said to her: *Restore the land.*

"What?" Inari said. It was as though she was at the same moment very close to her body, and very distant from it. Close to it, she could see two faint red threads: the lifelines of Chen and the badger.

"Restore the land!" her body said again, impatient, and when Inari continued to stare blankly at it, her lips moved again with a single name. She could see the words now, a crimson slash of characters. They floated up through the rift between the worlds until the name was hanging in front of her in the storm-driven air.

Inari read it out loud: *Sei Lan.*

At the moment she spoke the name aloud, everything changed. The Shadow Pavilion, the shifting landscape of *between,* Chen and the badger, everything was gone. Inari stood on a slight rise of ground near a river. It was early evening, summer, a light breeze rippling the endless grasslands like a sea. The air smelled sweet, perfumed by a thousand flowers, and a very faint odor of woodsmoke. Looking to her left, Inari saw a distant congregation of round white tents, springing mushroom-like from the surface of the steppe. Tall poles with horsehair banners stood around the yurts, somehow alive and filled with presence. Horses grazed and she heard a voice raised in song.

Then this, too, disappeared, and there was only the grass, and the sky, and Inari.

And Seijin.

The Lord Lady was as Inari had first known the being. Seijin stood in the long grass, wearing a gray robe. The black hair was tied, so that it resembled one of the horsetails.

"Sei Lan" Inari said.

The assassin bowed. "Not yet."

A woman stepped out of Seijin's form to stand beside him: female self, no more than a whisper on the air. Male self soon followed.

"Sei Lan?"

"I am Sei Lan," the child said. Unlike male or female self, the child was quite distinct, solid. Impossible to say whether it was a girl or a boy; it had Seijin's grave face and graver gaze. The child said, "This will not do, O my father/mother."

"Where were you?" Seijin asked, in a whisper, and the child said, "Swallowed in the blood you shed."

"I shed that blood to protect you!" Seijin cried.

"Perhaps at first. But then? I am weighed down beneath the stones of their souls; you must set us free. You must set us all free."

"No," Seijin protested.

Inari felt a curious snap, as though something in the world had broken or, conversely, had been locked together. She looked down at herself. She was no longer a ghost. She had flesh, and it was demon-cool, pulsing with life. But something had joined her, something very basic, that had no voice—a spirit? *I am possessed,* Inari thought in alarm, but the thing did not feel like an alien entity either.

The child—Seijin's oldest self, Sei Lan—turned to her.

"Will you?" the child asked, strangely timid, and all at once Inari knew what it was talking about. She hesitated, remembering the story of the Lord Lady's origins.

Born of a demon father and a Celestial mother.

Born on Earth, the exile of both.

Born to become a killer of gods and demons and men.

Can one really change the destiny of a soul? Make something good, from base clay? Well, Inari thought, *I can try.*

"Yes—" and immediately the child was gone. Across the grassland, the assassin was beginning to collapse, flesh withering, skin sagging.

"Save me!" Seijin whispered, and reached out a hand.

"But I just did," Inari told it, and watched as the Lord Lady sank down into the grass, watched until there was nothing more than a bloody stain on the black soil of the steppe, watched until that, too, was gone.

SIXTY

Inside the shrubbery, it was quiet, but the eerie scarlet-and-white light still played all around Go and the deva, emanating from the myriad blossoms. There was a pungent smell, close to narcotic, and for a moment the panicking Go entertained the possibility of just giving into it, lying down and going to sleep. At least you wouldn't see the jaws closing down. But a heavy body was crashing through the undergrowth behind them and the deva seemed to have forgotten about her injury, or perhaps she was swift to heal. She was sprinting ahead, dodging around the arches of the ornamental plants with a speed presumably born of a life in the forest. Go dropped the chain, which was becoming unfeasibly weighty, swore, gathered it up again before the deva yanked him off his feet, and followed her.

He hoped she knew where she was going—her velocity suggested that she did—but then the deva took a wrong turn. They sped out into a long avenue of rhododendron, densely planted, the glossy, illuminated leaves forming a screen in front of a thickly twisting maze of branches. At both ends rose a high wall of shrubbery, quite impenetrable. The deva and Go looked frantically from right to left, mirroring one another's movements. Behind them, Go once more heard the sound of Agni's guests, cheering, and a very familiar roar. In desperation, they ran up the avenue toward the wall and flung themselves against it. The rhododendrons did not give way. Go beat at them with the chain, whipping it against the branches, but to no avail. The deva cried out. Go turned. A tigress had come out of the gap in the hedge, lazily switching her tail from side to side. She looked pointedly in the wrong direction, as if in mockery, and then saw them. She began to lope rapidly up the avenue.

"Get behind me," Go urged, though he knew he was only delaying the deva's own bloody reckoning.

"No," the deva quavered. She took hold of the other end of the chain and with one accord, they began to swing it. There might be a chance—but the tigress was running now, a streak of black and gold, leaving fire smoldering in her wake. As she leaped, Go and the deva swung the chain, but the tigress saw it and swerved. She snatched at the chain with a massive paw and it caught in the razor claws, dragging Go and the deva off their feet. They hit the short grass like bowling pins, tangled up in the chain and ripe for the catching. The tigress swatted Go with her paw, a cat's playful pounce. The blow hit him in the ribs and it felt as though something snapped. The tigress then lifted him off the ground, hauling the entangled deva with him. Go had once heard that being attacked by a wild animal produced a euphoric sensation of calm, that Zen moment before a bloody, rending death. There was no such sensation here. Go's body let go: he tried to piss himself, but it was as though his system had shut down. He hit the rhododendron hedge full on and slid back to the floor. The tigress was pacing, a gleam of interest in her yellow eyes. Go wondered, frantically, where the others were and then he realized: they hadn't bothered. It wouldn't take more than a minute to finish either himself or the deva off. Agni's harem had sent a single cat, for the fun of the chase and the death for the prince's guests. The tigress leaped. Go threw an arm in front of his face: he didn't want to see what was coming.

Then the tigress disappeared.

蛇警探

"Got her?" Zhu Irzh panted, from the other side of the rhododendron hedge.

"I think so." No Ro Shi was frowning. A short distance away, the tiger revolved, snarling soundlessly, in midair. No Ro Shi's outflung hand betrayed the passage of a recent spell. The demon watched with interest.

"How long do you think you'll be able to hold her?"

"I don't intend to hold her for long." No Ro Shi's voice demonstrated effort. He drew his hand back, bringing the captured tiger with it, and snapped his fingers shut. The tigress dropped to the ground and bounded up with a roar.

No Ro Shi spoke quick cold words. He flung out a spell that brushed Zhu Irzh's face as it passed and left a film of ice across the demon's skin. Zhu Irzh was too intrigued to protest. He watched as a swift ripple of magic passed over the tiger's leaping form. A moment later, all the black and gold was gone and in their place was the statue of a springing tiger. It looked to Zhu Irzh as though it had been there for years; encrusted with lichen and moss, the stone eroded by rain.

"Artistic," he commented. No Ro Shi appeared pleased.

"This realm would seem to be particularly amenable to statue magic."

"Makes sense," Zhu Irzh agreed, thinking of what had befallen the deva. "Let's see how much more trouble we can cause."

"*Help!*"

"That's Go," the demon said. He took out a section of shrubbery with a sweep of his sword. No Ro Shi hacked through as well and a few minutes later, Go and the deva were stumbling through the gap.

"Hang on," Zhu Irzh told them, and brought the sword down onto the chain that connected them. The deva looked as though she was about to burst into tears and threw herself into Zhu Irzh's arms.

Go, very pale, said, "I thought we'd had it."

"Get moving," No Ro Shi told him, and they ran for the forest, Zhu Irzh disentangling himself from the deva en route.

"*Where's Jhai?*" he hissed at Go. "Still on the terrace?"

Go looked nonplussed. "I don't know. I haven't seen her. I've only just— well, arrived here, you might say."

"And will soon be leaving," the demon-hunter told him.

"Hell, suits me. She's coming too."

Zhu Irzh caught No Ro Shi's sleeve. "Get them back home. I'm going after Jhai."

No Ro Shi looked positively disappointed at being denied a further chance to slay things, or enspell them. "Are you sure? Won't you need back-up?"

"Believe me," Zhu Irzh said. "Jhai *is* back-up, all on her own."

蛇警探

Back at the edge of the lawns, the Hunting Lodge was in an uproar. Zhu Irzh crept rapidly back the way he had come, sneaking along the rhododendron hedge until he came to the place where the statue had been created. Then he ducked down behind the undergrowth.

Agni's guests, and the rest of the tiger clan, had streamed down from the terraces and made their way along the lawn to where the new statue stood. Zhu Irzh recognized quite a few faces from his last visit, but was not inclined to stroll forth and be sociable. He could not see Jhai anywhere and this gave him a moment of hope: if they'd left her up on the terrace... Zhu Irzh began to sidle along the hedge, away from the crowd. Agni was there, yes, in his fire-colored clothes. Zhu Irzh caught a glimpse of the tiger prince's eyes and wished he hadn't: Agni's gaze was a feral gold shot with red, like blood over the sun, both angry and mad. *Well,* Zhu Irzh thought to himself, *if I have to take you on, I'll do it. I just hope I don't have to.* It wasn't that he was a coward, just—careful.

But if Jhai was not there, then neither was Lara, and that made Zhu Irzh's skin prickle. He tried to do a rapid inventory of exactly who had come down to see the statue, but it was impossible: there were just too many people milling about. He crept along the hedge until he thought he was reasonably clear, then sprinted up a second long avenue of azalea toward the Hunting Lodge.

There was no sign of Jhai on the terrace, which Zhu Irzh skirted with a great deal of caution. He was beginning to think he'd imagined her, yet he knew she had to be here. Then something caught his eye: a long red and gold thread, snagged on a rough piece of masonry. Zhu Irzh was pleased; it seemed this detective business had something to it after all. He left the thread where it lay and moved along the terrace, keeping to the shadows. Occasionally, he checked the lawn. They were still down there; he could hear the growls of the tiger girls and Agni's voice, raised to a pitch that Zhu Irzh had not previously encountered in the prince, but which betokened an incipient psychotic meltdown. He thought that Agni was probably in the process of discovering that No Ro Shi's spell was irreversible: the demon-hunter tended, necessarily, to be very thorough about these matters.

At the end of the terrace, one of the French doors that lay along the ground floor of the palace was open. Zhu Irzh, with a final glance at the congregation down on the lawns, slipped through. Inside, he found himself in a dining hall. Silver glittered in candlelight, though the candles burned with a steady red flame that was somehow cold to look at. An array of plates and cutlery suggested that whatever meal that was about to be served was not going to take the form of a light snack. Silver platters rested along the table at intervals, their domes rising from spiky flower arrangements like some miniature city. Checking that he was unobserved, Zhu Irzh lifted one of the platters and stared down at a human head. It was white, and male. Its blue boiled eyes bugged out, lending it an expression of puff-cheeked outrage. Half a mango had been stuffed into its mouth. As Zhu Irzh stared, intrigued, the eyes rolled up to meet his own.

"Mgmph!" the head said.

"Sorry," Zhu Irzh told him. "Can't help you right now, old chap. Maybe later." Hastily, he replaced the cover. He didn't want to be grassed up by someone's entrée, but it was too late now, assuming that the head had Agni's best interests at heart, which Zhu Irzh doubted. Cursing under his breath, he left the magnificent banquet table behind and ran through the columns that separated the dining room from a hallway.

Something glinted in the shadows. Zhu Irzh stooped and picked it up: Jhai was unraveling. The thread led him along the hallway and up a flight of stairs. Halfway up, Zhu Irzh heard footsteps coming down and dived behind a tapestry. He peered out, once the footsteps had passed, to see a turbaned servant disappearing down the staircase, carrying a tea service on a tray. Zhu

Irzh followed the thread further and found that it ran under a door. He took a chance, and knocked.

"Yeah?"

Jhai, found!

"Agni, you twat, is that you?" Jhai's voice dripped contempt.

"No," Zhu Irzh hissed, "it's me."

"Zhu Irzh!" At least she sounded pleased to see him. "Get me the fuck out of here. Agni's warded the door."

"All right, stand back. I'll see what I can do."

He'd used opening spells before, in a variety of circumstances, but there was still the issue of how magic worked in this realm. The demon agreed with No Ro Shi: sometimes you just have to take a chance. Zhu Irzh was reluctant to use blood magic—too close to the sorceries of fire, in Agni's lands—so he deployed an incantation instead, one that had been devised for blasting through rock. Not subtle, but he had to work quickly.

The spell worked quite well. Three minutes later, Zhu Irzh was sitting in the middle of the shattered dining table, picking plaster out of his hair. Jhai lay spread-eagled across a dining chair, swearing. The severed heads, freed of their imprisoning platters and domes, bounded around the room like pinballs. Above, a gaping hole in the ceiling gave testimony to the success of Zhu Irzh's conjuration.

"Bloody hell," Jhai said. "Agni won't be pleased."

"I think we'd better go," Zhu Irzh told her, clambering to his feet and brushing forks from his coat. The fallen candles had set fire to the white linen tablecloth and it blazed up in a sudden sheet of flame. Jhai took the demon's hand and they ran out of the French doors. As they did so, the long lace curtains that concealed the diners from view also caught fire, billowing out behind them. As they came out onto the terrace, a shout went up.

"There!"

The assembled crowd was running back up the lawn toward the Hunting Lodge, Agni at their head. Beside the demon, Jhai picked up the trailing skirts of her wedding dress and sprinted for the forest. Zhu Irzh caught a glimpse of Agni's raised hand and then a fireball shot across the lawn and sizzled into the mango trees.

"Shit!" Jhai reeled back against the demon.

"Just run. He's not trying to hit *you*."

Unfortunately, it seemed that Agni was. The next fireball knocked Zhu Irzh off his feet and sent him sprawling into a flower bed. He glanced toward the forest, saw that they were not going to make it, looked back at the Hunting Lodge and also saw—with some satisfaction—that it was well and truly on fire. Then Jhai cried out. Things were swarming out of the trees, blackened shapes that looked as though they had already been consumed in the flames, their eyes as bright as red-hot coals. Some were small, but most of them were the size of a man. They had long, delicate hands and sharp, black teeth. Two of them had seized Jhai by the arms and lifted her off her feet; Jhai was not a heavy girl, but she still had a demon's strength, as Zhu Irzh knew, and these creatures lifted her easily and held her despite her struggles.

"You," said Agni, strolling up behind in dangerous silence, "have set my house on fire."

"An accident." It was ironic, the demon reflected bitterly, that the occasions when he actually spoke the literal truth were those in which he was the least likely to be believed.

"How does a life in the fire sound to you?" Agni still spoke mildly, but only a few minutes ago Zhu Irzh had heard him shrieking down on the lawn.

"A bit Catholic, actually."

Agni smiled. "A lot of them come here. We have a Goanese population on Earth, after all."

"Agni, listen." That was Jhai, speaking quickly. "If you keep me here, this won't be an end to it. You think I'll just knuckle under? Yes, you can control my cousins. They've never known anything else, apart from Lara, and look what a mess she's made of her independence. But I've never known anything *but*. That's why you went after me, isn't it? But can you handle it?"

Zhu Irzh looked from Jhai to Agni, both in their red and gold. Agni's clothes were as impeccable as ever, but Jhai's glossy hair-do had come undone and streamed across her shoulders. The magnificent gown was torn at the hem, fraying into ruffles. She had lost her shoes, or kicked them off, and now stood barefoot on the scorched grass. Her face was flecked with soot.

"Well? Better decide if I'm worth the trouble, cousin."

Zhu Irzh hoped Agni wasn't too far gone to be reasoned with. The prince hadn't even bothered to put out the blaze, but just as this occurred to Zhu Irzh, the tiger prince flicked a finger and the fire went out. There was surprisingly little damage left in its wake, only a little smoke stain on the columns. But then, it was Agni's own element. Would Agni see reason, or would pride hammer him down? Then Agni said, "You've certainly caused a remarkable degree of chaos in the space of your visit. Maybe you're right. I'm not sure I could put up with a lifetime of it." He turned to Zhu Irzh. "As for you, perhaps eternity in a blazing dungeon wouldn't prove as great a punishment as marriage to Jhai."

The demon considered a number of humorous remarks, and wisely kept silent.

"But my guests have come here tonight to expect entertainment," the prince went on. "I can't deny them that. We've already lost one set of quarry. And you're not the only one I'm displeased with, Jhai. I'm not all that delighted with little Lara, either."

"Very well," Jhai said, warily. She could see what was coming, Zhu Irzh thought, and so could he. "What do you suggest?"

"I think a cat fight's in order," the prince said.

SIXTY-ONE

Inari said, "Where do you want to go now?"

"Here," her child replied. "Here, and then home. Will you let me do the working?"

Inari paused. She was not yet accustomed to sharing her self with this *other*. Was this what it had been like for Seijin, living with whispers in the head? Seijin had gone mad, she reminded herself.

"It's only for another eight months," the child reassured.

Inari shivered. "Do the working."

She felt two vastnesses drawn together by the thin red thread that was her body. She became, for a moment, the glowing chasm between continents, then blacked out as they came together and overlapped. When she regained consciousness, she was still standing on the steps of the Shadow Pavilion and the child seemed pleased.

Inari looked around her. "What happened?" But she already knew. A tide of long, sweet grass lapped the pagoda steps. It was still twilight, but the storm clouds had gone, leaving the taste of rain in their wake. A single star hung in the water-colored sky and there, not far away, was the scimitar crescent of the new moon, visible from all worlds except Hell. A flock of birds sailed around the summit of the pagoda, now smaller, yet not diminished. It looked—solid. The crack that had run up its length had disappeared and the pagoda's structure could now be seen, made not from shadows but from oak and stone. It looked like an old family fortress, the sort of place that might one day be a home.

Within, the child radiated assent. "It will do."

The birds wheeled, flying westward, and now Inari could see that they were not birds after all, but spirits: all those whom the Shadow Pavilion had imprisoned, set free for their long journey to Heaven or Hell.

"And you?" the child asked. "What would you do now?"

Inari gave a shaky smile and touched a hand to her stomach. "I think we'd better go and find your father."

SIXTY-TWO

"You know what? I haven't done this enough," Jhai said.

"Tough," Zhu Irzh replied unhappily. He didn't want to sound unsympathetic, but Jhai was right. Deny your own true nature and look what happens: suddenly you're standing on a terrace in someone else's Hell, while a raging, pacing tiger waits impatiently for your blood. "Do your worst."

"I always do." But she was nervous all the same, Zhu Irzh knew. Jhai, still in her tattered bridal finery, stood before Agni and his guests and his harem and closed her eyes. It didn't take long; she must have been really pissed off, Zhu Irzh thought. Stripes barred Jhai's skin. A tail switched her ankles, and that was that: the bridal dress fell to the floor like a pool of blood. Jhai turned, snarled, and leaped at Lara.

She hit her cousin around the waist, bowling the growling Lara across the length of the terrace. Lara was a lot bigger in her tiger shape, Zhu Irzh noticed, though there was little to choose between the two women in their human aspect. Perhaps it was something to do with the number of kills. In which case, oh dear. Lara rose and swatted Jhai with a paw; Jhai went down, bloody grooves along her flank. She struggled up, but Lara was waiting. Lara sprang onto her cousin's back, jaws aiming at Jhai's throat. Jhai rolled over like an angry kitten and raked Lara's gut with her hind claws.

It didn't disembowel her, but it must have hurt. Lara screamed and it sounded more human than cat. She sprang backward, curling into a ball, but one paw lashed out and caught Jhai across the throat. There was a lot of blood. Jhai went down, making gargling sounds. Zhu Irzh started forward and was hauled back by one of Agni's spirits. Lara's tail twitched, she crouched, her head went down, and she sprang, claws fully extended. And Zhu Irzh, a coward after all (or so he would tell himself later) closed his eyes, but only in the second that it took for a spell to go spinning past him, radiating out

238

like the ripples of a stone hurled into a pool and tasting of blood and Jhai and pain.

When the demon opened his eyes again, Jhai was standing on the blood-slick stones of the terrace, naked. One arm dangled uselessly by her side and her ribs were gouged into furrows. A ragged tear ran across her collarbone to the shoulder. But in her good arm, she was holding a small, surprised, striped cat.

"You didn't say I couldn't use magic," Jhai said.

SIXTY-THREE

"Perhaps I should apply for paternity leave," Chen said. "Isn't that the modern thing to do?"

"Don't ask me," the demon shrugged.

"You and Jhai aren't planning to have one?" Chen smiled. "I recommend it. Ensuring one's posterity and all that sort of thing."

"The subject hasn't come up. She seems curiously averse to looking at wedding dresses, too. We might end up having a quiet private ceremony after all."

Chen laughed. "That'll be the day."

"She's already revised the guest list, that's for sure."

Chen raised his eyebrows. "What, won't be inviting that nice cousin Agni?"

Zhu Irzh gave a snort. "She also says there won't be quite so many female guests. Playing havoc with the table settings, apparently. But she's keeping Lara. Bought her a collar and everything."

"And if she turns back?"

"Well, the magic Jhai used won't work outside that particular Hell, so I suppose we'll just have to call the zoo."

They were sitting on the deck of the houseboat, a blue afternoon in early summer. Ma and No Ro Shi were back at the station, piecing things together with the help of Paugeng security. Jhai was recuperating.

"What's that?" Zhu Irzh squinted into the heavens.

"I don't know." Chen followed his gaze. Sparks of light had appeared high amongst the clouds and around them were twists and turns of brightness. They fell rapidly toward the ocean, but halfway down the sky, their trajectory flattened out and began to stream toward the city.

"Oh." Chen said, in realization. Mhara's Long March had finally reached Earth.